the stories (in) between

Edited by
Greg Schauer,
Jeanne B. Benzel, and W. H. Horner

Fantasist
Enterprises

Wilmington, Delaware

Fantasist Enterprises
PO Box 9381
Wilmington, DE 19809
www.FEBooks.net

Cover Designed by Joe del Tufo
Interior Designed by W. H. Horner Editorial & Design

The Stories in Between
Copyright © 2009 by Fantasist Enterprises
ISBN 10: 0-9713608-8-X
ISBN 13: 978-0-9713608-8-4

First printing: November 2009

10 9 8 7 6 5 4 3 2 1

This book is available for wholesale through the publisher and through Ingram Book Group. It can be ordered for retail at most booksellers, both online and off, and is available from the publisher's website.

Fantasist Enterprises grants a discount on the purchase of three or more copies of single titles. For further details, please send an e-mail to payments@fantasistent. com, or write to the publisher at the address above, care of "Bulk Orders."

Please interact with us on the web at the following websites:

The FE Forum:
http://www.fantasistent.com/FORUM/

FaceBook:
http://www.facebook.com/FantasistEnt

MySpace:
http://www.myspace.com/fantasist

Twitter:
http://twitter.com/fantasistent

For my parents.
—G.S.

(foreword)
Joseph Gangemi

I first wandered into Between Books in 1981. Or I should say into "Book Thrift," as the store was known in those days. A scrappier name for scrappier times. A scrappier location, too—the Tri State Mall, a faded shopping center on the Delaware-Pennsylvania border, wedged between an interstate and a dying steel mill.* At the Tri State you could purchase Hagar slacks in "husky" sizes from Wilmington Dry Goods (the anchor store), enjoy a slice of heat-lamp pizza at the Orange Bowl, or pick up a couple of Chinese throwing stars at the Hong Kong shop. You could have your hair cut at Man's World and catch a matinee of *Metalstorm: The Destruction of Jared-Syn* (in 3D) at the Eric cinema.

And if you were a bookish eleven-year-old who had recently made the leap from Hardy Boys to science fiction and fantasy, you could find paradise in the stacks of the very special bookstore whose 30th anniversary this anthology celebrates.

First, an admission: This foreword purports to celebrate an institution, but it's really a celebration of an individual, Between Books' founder Greg Schauer. Is it possible to write about an independent bookstore without talking about the person behind the counter? I don't think so. Bookstores, moreso than other independently owned and operated retail outlets, are a reflection of their owner's sensibilities. Take a stroll through the over-crowded and cheerfully anarchic book stacks, peek at the whimsies within its glass display cases, and you'll get a pretty good sense of Greg: his eclectic and wide-ranging intellect, his playfulness, above all his abiding curiosity. At Between Books, graphic novels co-mingle with classics; Wicca primers are given equal shelf space as works of Christian spirituality. When I worked at the store briefly in the mid-80s I remember being surprised to find *The Joy of Gay Sex* shelved alongside its bestselling hetero (and

---

* Locals will recall that from time to time some fearless vandal would scale the mall's water tower and deface the name so that it read "TRI STATE MALE." Which I'm considering titling my autobiography.

unsettlingly hirsute) predecessor: Greg's characteristically subtle political statement, spoken not shouted, and always restocked.

No self-respecting hagiography—or for that matter, comic book— would be complete without an origin story, preferably apocryphal. The one I've heard begins with Greg's fateful decision in 1978 to abandon plans to study physics at Princeton and try his hand at bookselling. A decision that begs several questions. Was this always intended to be a permanent course-correction, or just a temporary detour—a time out—that got out of hand? And what precipitated it? Some existential crisis? Nervous break- down? A zap to the forehead from the same pink laser that enlightened Philip K. Dick? I could ask Greg, but part of me prefers not to know. Sometimes the uncertain is more telling than the truth.

What I strongly suspect—particularly now that I'm a parent—is that the decision must have come as something of a shock to Greg's mother and father. And yet to their great credit they supported their son, helping him scrape together the $5,000 needed to open his fledgling venture. The first Book Thrift opened on November 12, 1979 on Route 273, next door to a crab restaurant and across from a wheat field. Little more than a glorified newsstand, its inventory in those early days consisted of a few shelves of worn paperbacks and some well-thumbed back issues of "Playboy." A year later, when wheat chaff from the neighboring field began compromising air quality beyond breathable limits, Greg pulled up stakes and relocated to the first of the two storefronts he'd tenant at the Tri State Mall.

Shortly thereafter, I discovered the place. I mention it here not be- cause I claim any special significance in the store's annals, but because my relationship with Between Books—first as a customer, later a clerk, lastly a friend and ardent fan—is emblematic of what makes the place so spe- cial. In 1981, I was eleven, bespectacled, overweight. Greg—barely out of his teens—was clean-shaven, having not yet acquired the beard, beret, and briar pipe that have since become his signatures, calling to mind a long- lost brother of Sherlock Holmes fallen in with *revolucionistas*. I had come in looking for more along the lines of Ursula Le Guin's *Wizard of Earthsea*, a book my father had read to me along with C.S. Lewis's *Magician's Nephew*. (Dad had recently gone back to University of Delaware, where he'd light- ened his accounting course load with an elective called "Literature of the Fantastic.") I remember Greg coming out from behind his register and reaching up to a high shelf to retrieve a copy of Piers Anthony's *A Spell For Chameleon*, first in the pun-heavy and largely forgettable Xanth series. As recommendations went, this was fairly safe. But they wouldn't always be.

Moorcock's *Gloriana*. Frazer's *Golden Bough*. Jaynes' *Origin of Consciousness in the Breakdown of the Bicameral Mind*. Peake's *Gormenghast*.

These were just a few of the titles Greg would pluck from the shelves and press upon me, like the big brother I never had, and thus the corrupting influence I desperately needed. Eventually I returned the favor, introducing him to Clive Barker's short stories and the early novels of Iain Banks, U.K. paperbacks that had to be special-ordered and thus came with the allure of contraband. I can't remember which of us "discovered" the singular works of ex-pat fantasist Jonathan Carroll, but once we did, he was immediately inducted into a pantheon we dubbed the Wicked Author's Club, alongside store favorites Edward Gorey, Lucius Shepard, David J. Skal, and Thomas M. Disch. That this book includes a contribution from Carroll must tickle Greg to no end.

As I've already mentioned, for a brief time I stopped being a customer and became an employee. In fact, Between Books was my first "real" (as far as the IRS was concerned) job. Greg paid me $3.50 an hour, fifteen cents above minimum wage. I was thrilled. Like all writers—and at age sixteen I already considered myself one, even if publication was still some years in my future—books were my life. I coveted them. Collected them. Fetishized them. (Open a brittle mass market paperback from the Sixties—one of Terry Carr's Ace Science Fiction Specials, say—and bury your nose deep in the binding. Smell that whiff of desiccated glue? That musk of decomposing paper? That's my madeleine; the bong-hit of nostalgia that transports me instantly back to adolescence.*) Needless to say, little of my earnings left the premises. My memories of the year or so that I worked at Between Books have blurred into a single endless shift spent making space for mass market paperbacks, a Sisyphean task given the perpetually overstuffed bookshelves and the fecundity of science fiction and fantasy authors. What else do I remember? The customers, of course, some of whom became lifelong friends. You'll find the name of one—John Passarella—listed among the contributors to this anthology. Aspiring authors who enjoyed talking shop, John and I would go on to collaborate on a horror novel that eventually saw print, won a minor award, and sold to the movies—enabling us both to quit our day jobs and become full-time authors. John went on to publish two sequels, and several media tie-ins and standalones; I published a historical novel before drifting into screenwriting. John married a woman I introduced him to. Today they have three kids. (I've been a bit less prolific as both an author and parent—but hey, John's got ten years on me.)

How many friendships were made in the aisles of Between Books? I have no idea, but I'm willing to bet it's more than any one Barnes & Noble

---

* Good luck sniffing your Kindle.

can boast. Despite its lack of a coffee bar, and cushy chairs, and Norah Jones playing incessantly on the in-store sound system, Between Books has managed to create the sort of community of loyal customers and constant readers that the "big box" chain stores so desperately covet. And this in an era of shrinking attention spans, declines in reading rates, fierce on-line competition, and the implosion of the economy. To give you some perspective on the market forces Between Books has weathered: When the store first opened it was one of thirteen independents in the area; today there are two.

The irony is that there's never before been a greater need for indie booksellers like Greg.

Last year in the U.S. alone some three hundred thousand new titles saw print. Winnowing that number to the worthwhile few—and my list will necessarily differ from yours—is an enormous challenge that each year edges closer to the impossible. Especially when you factor in the other print media, TV programming, film, YouTube videos, social networking sites, CNN scrawls, and blogs competing for our attention. What is an overwhelmed consumer to do? Some read reviews, though that's becoming more difficult to do as the newspaper industry implodes. Others join book clubs, ceding the decision about what to read next to the group. Some seek out the imprimatur of Oprah. All are essentially doing the same thing: putting their faith in a "filter" (as media analysts have dubbed them), those trusted gatekeepers whose sensibilities align with their own.

Me, I turn to Greg. For thirty years he's proven time and again to possess an unerring sense of what I like—or will. That he's been doing the same with similar accuracy for thousands of other customers is a testament to his spooky gifts, and, I suspect, the secret of Between Books' longevity. Now Greg is doing it between softcovers, with the 16 stories contained herein, each carefully selected for your reading enjoyment. You'll find no recurring themes in these pages, but that's the point: this anthology's contents are as eclectic and wide-ranging in their concerns as their editor . . .

. . . and his remarkable suburban curiosity shop so many of us have for thirty years called a second home.

(introduction)
Greg Schauer

When I was eighteen, I bought a bookstore. It was 1979, and I was taking a detour on my way to college. I had no idea what I was getting myself into. I loved books and comics and games, and I had the energy and enthusiasm of youth. Those were my only qualifications to run a bookstore, and they turned out to be sufficient.

Thirty years later, I'm a little grayer and a little less spry, but I still love books and comics and games. My education took place behind the counter, as I learned from my customers and colleagues, the friends and family that the store gathered around me. The beautiful thing about an independent bookstore is you can get the answer to any question, on any subject, just by listening to the people who walk through the doors.

Over the years we have had the opportunity to host some amazing events. Several art exhibitions, a couple of lectures by Robert Anton Wilson (we miss you, Bob), other presentations on a myriad of topics both mundane and bizarre, and not one, but two visits from members of GWAR in full costume. (They played their miniatures game.) In other words, we have had a great time bringing the unusual to Claymont, Delaware.

Publishing this anthology is a way to celebrate the wonderful years I've spent as a bookseller, and to thank the talented people I've had a chance to meet. The authors represented here are a few of our favorite people who have visited over the years.

My only direction to them was that they have fun writing a story. I did not set a theme. A few surprised me by jumping out of their accustomed genres; a few sent stories that just hadn't fit anywhere else. This collection of stories—unpredictable, homeless, risky—grew into a perfect reflection of the soul of the store, where the irregular come to rest for a while on the shelves or in the aisles, looking for understanding and inspiration.

Since comics and art are so important to Between Books, we had to include illustrations! Finding artists to illuminate and enhance the stories was one of the most delightful parts of this experience.

This anthology feels both like a grateful look backward and like the potential beginning of a new chapter for Between Books. I approached the publication of a book in very much the same spirit that I took on the bookstore, those many years ago, trusting in my own passion and the kindness and support of the people around me as I learned what I needed to know. I hope you enjoy the result.

I want to thank the authors who trusted me with their words for this collection; the artists, who brought an extra dimension to the stories; Will and Jeanne, for their eyes, knowledge, and patience; Meesh and Paul for their tireless work ethic and invaluable counsel; my family for their support in my follies; my current employees, Chris Foust, Chris Van Trump, and Laura Zieber; my former employees, Paul, Ray Joe, Chris, Chris, Johnnalyn, Alan, Bret, Nate, John, and Maureen.

Charles and Kathy Shattuck for their love and support.

Mort Rosenblatt, mentor and friend, gone lo these many years. You are missed.

Joe del Tufo, who makes the best things happen with a thought.

Jonathan Carroll for his generosity and support.

Emily Ozer for braving mosquitoes above and beyond the call.

Jay Jameson, Rich Pione, Kevin Turner, and everyone else who helped refurbish the place.

And most of all, the people who have supported us over the years and allowed us to reach this pinnacle.

Thank you all.

Shop Independent.

Greg Schauer
Claymont, DE
September 14, 2009

Lawrence M. Schoen, like a surprising number of our contributors, is a triple threat: writer, publisher, editor . . . with a secret weapon: he's fluent in Klingon. Maybe that's why this story, a myth from a warrior culture, rings true.

(the wrestler and the spear fisher)
Lawrence M. Schoen

On the tiny island of Aniwa, the Kefer waged war, one half against the other. It had begun as a question of succession. Fesht, leader of the Kefer, died unexpectedly, the victim of a ceremonial hunt gone horribly wrong. All responsibilities should have passed to his eldest child, except that the eldest offspring was a pair of twin boys. They were identical in all respects, both tall and strong and beloved by the Kefer. Only their father had known which of them first breathed the air of Aniwa. Both claimed right of succession and the war began.

As required by the spirits of the island, the Kefer clashed only on the nights of the full moon, when the healing herbs were their most potent. For the remainder of each month the people set aside their war, lived together, and endured a silent animosity. Such were the ancient ways as set forth by Senjo the Wise, and no previous war had ever lasted to see a third moon. It is a hard thing, to slay a neighbor one day and then return to live peaceably alongside his grieving family the next.

This war was different. Moon after moon it continued. Senjo, Walawa, Colobi, and all the other spirits dwelling upon Aniwa tried to end the war and reunite the tribe as one people. Their efforts failed. This war was not over round-tusked pigs or false claims of virginity or adultery beyond one's station. It split the Kefer in two, as Fesht's sons fought one another.

Years passed without resolution. In desperation, the island spirits imposed their will upon Fate itself and decreed that the war would not end until only one brother lived.

Even spirits can be right and wrong at the same moment. On the night of their forty-first birthday, the brothers killed each other under the glow of the full moon. Fate was not to be so easily controlled.

The war went on with the spirits powerless to stop it, bound by their own pronouncement. They could only wait for the random cycles of rebirth to reflesh the souls of the twins. Years passed. Both were reborn several times, lived, fought, and died, but never both as male and on the same day of the year. Finally, after seven generations the souls of Fesht's sons were reborn, two years apart but on the same day. They were born to different mothers, one on each side of the divided tribe, and named Deyco and Susk. The spirits watched them and waited, their anticipation building. An end was in sight.

Years passed and the boys grew to be exceptional young men, tall and strong, each with his own talents and skills. Deyco possessed greater ability with the fishing spear than any Kefer ever born, and could feed his half of the tribe by himself if need be. Paradoxically he refused to use a spear in the monthly war.

"I will not kill others of the Kefer by the same means with which I feed them," he said, and that was the end of it. There were plenty other weapons of war.

His once-brother, Susk, quickly became the champion of the young men on his side of the war. In friendly competitions, exhibitions, and wagers he had wrestled and defeated every man on the island of Aniwa, many of them taken two at a time.

None of this mattered to the spirits of the island. They bided their time. The young men passed into adulthood, received the tattoos of warriors, took wives, and were accounted full members of the tribe. The spirits allowed another year to pass, conserving their strength. Then it was time.

Senjo, Keeper of Wisdom, sent a dream to every man, woman, and child of the Kefer. In one evening all saw a vision of Susk and Deyco facing one another within a circle of fire. The full moon shone above, though in the waking world the moon was merely a few days past new. Senjo gazed down at the once-brothers, their souls no wiser despite the intervening lives each had led. The time for teaching was past. He painted the mark of the sea turtle on their foreheads so that they might see and speak with him in the dream.

"The spirits of Aniwa have watched and waited. We hoped you would resolve your differences and restore yourselves to one people. Why have you not done so?" said Senjo from the sky, his face made entirely of clouds.

"His people have attacked us again and again without provocation," said the dream flesh of Deyco, pointing at Susk. "They steal our pigs and dishonor our women by moonlight."

"Only in retaliation," said Susk, almost shouting. "His people raid our homes, falsely marked with the paint of a distant island though their deception fools only themselves."

"At the last moon your people set fire to three of our boats and injured two men," said Deyco.

"Do you deny that the month before that, your people blinded our herb woman while she gathered the healing roots shown to the Kefer by

Walawa himself?" said Susk.

"Only after your people cut the tongue out of our herb woman while she roasted those very same roots."

"Which wouldn't have happened if your people hadn't defiled the grave of our greatest artisan."

"Enough," said Senjo. "The Kefer are one tribe, one people."

"That is a story told to children," said Susk.

"Even if true, it is distant history," said Deyco.

Wise Senjo painted the mark of the sea bird upon the brows of both men, and the previous lives of their souls returned to them.

"It is true," said Deyco, flushed with generations of memories, several different childhoods, long dead children of his own, and most curious of all, an image of Fesht teaching him to cast his first fishing spear so very long ago.

"The Kefer are one people," agreed Susk, reeling under the weight of past lives, previous wives, even husbands, and the faces of hundreds of friends.

"I will unite and lead the people . . ." they both said at once, then stopped, and glared at each other.

"The Kefer can be led by but one man," said Senjo. "They must war among themselves no longer. At the next moon you two will decide this, brother against brother until only one is standing within the fire circle. He I will name as victor. The other will be claimed by the tide, swept south to the reef, and ground across the coral by a storm of my making. When life has at last been stripped from him, his blood will feed the coral and his flesh will nourish the fish."

The brothers stared up at the face of Senjo the Wise; they trembled. At last Susk asked, "Mighty Senjo, when I confront Deyco in the fire circle, what rules govern our conflict?"

"We seek to mend history and restore the Kefer," said Senjo. "There are no rules."

Deyco balked. "Great Senjo, for many years we have fought, and always the spirits imposed rules. Walawa required us to spare the youngest of any group captured in battle. Colobi of Blue Water demanded that no new mothers of the past moon, nor any within their houses, be harmed. Each of the spirits has handed down similar restrictions. How can there be no rules now?"

"This is not war," said Senjo. "When brothers battle and know their conflict will end in death, how can the spirits make rules? Your contest will be between you two alone.

"Now go. Leave this dream and awaken. Prepare for the contest at the next moon. All the Kefer have dreamed with us this night, and in the waking day will find the dream's proof upon your foreheads."

Thunder rolled across the sky as flashes of lightning shattered the darkness. Throughout the tiny island of Aniwa, the Kefer awoke from their pallets and recalled the true dream sent by Senjo. Some cried with joy for the coming end of war. Some on both sides sobbed, fearing the loss of the brave warrior who had led them. Some cried out of gratitude to the spirit folk, and some from frustration that the spirits had waited so long. While the thunder echoed and the lightning fell, all the Kefer wept.

In the morning Susk was called before the council of elders representing his half of the sundered tribe. The eldest spat upon his thumb and tried to smear away the mark of the sea turtle and the mark of the sea bird from the young man's brow. They remained.

"We dreamed true," said the eldest.

"Grandfathers," said Susk, "for the sake of all of us, when I confront Deyco at the full moon, I must win."

The elders agreed and discussed among themselves several strategies. In the end they instructed Susk to wrestle Deyco for leadership of the Kefer.

"You are the greatest wrestler Aniwa has ever known," said one of the elders. "Surely you will defeat Deyco," said another.

Susk flushed with pride at the council's praise. Then he grew serious as a question entered his mind. "But what if he will not wrestle me?"

The elders all laughed. "It does not matter what he chooses," said the eldest. "Let him wrestle you or not, but you will wrestle him. The match will end shortly either way."

On the other side of tiny Aniwa, Deyco sat with his young wife, Tamla, and his father, Obji. Like the elders had with Susk, they tried to rub the marks from Deyco's brow; they failed as well.

"I am afraid," said Deyco. "Susk is unparalleled as a wrestler. My greatest ability is in spearing fish. If he defeats me, then the Kefer will be led by a man who excels in victory but cannot provide for his people."

"Can you not spear him like a fish?" asked Tamla.

Deyco laughed, which was the real intent of his wife's question. He lightly stroked her hair and said, "If Susk were a fish and if the circle of fire were a tide pool, the skill of my eye and the swiftness of my hand would have him pierced through the heart before he could speak. But he is not an unsuspecting fish, and there will be no tide pool."

"The circle I saw in my dream was small," said Obji. "Even if you brought a spear you would have only limited time to use it. Before you can take aim and throw, Susk will charge you. Once he manages to close, he will grapple with you and throw you to the ground. I have seen him wrestle. He is unstoppable."

"What am I to do?" said Deyco.

"Senjo has set this in motion. He or one of the other spirits can help you," said Obji. "You have several days before the moon is full. I will give ten round-tusked pigs for you to offer the spirits. Perhaps it will be enough."

Deyco eagerly accepted his father's pigs and the next day took them to his favorite fishing place.

He cried out, his voice carrying over the open sea. "Colobi, Spirit of the Blue Water, will you advise me?"

Deyco's reflection in the water blurred, replaced by the image of Colobi who appeared as a beauteous woman with a mosaic of tiny shells where her eyes should have been.

"You have your nerve, Deyco. Why should I, of all the spirits, share my insights with you? Since you were barely a child you have plundered my waters."

"That is why I have come to you. Who else has more to gain? I ask you to see past our personal differences, Colobi. The spirits of Aniwa are supposed to care about the welfare of the Kefer."

"And we do," said Colobi, her image expanding over the water. "That is why you and Susk will meet at the next moon. We spirits have decided that to end the war, one of you must die."

"But that is too short-sighted," said Deyco. "It makes a difference who lives. It matters for the Kefer."

"How so? Either way the Kefer will be united under one leader again."

"If I live, the Kefer will be led by a man who can provide for them. If Susk wins, they get a leader who is strong enough to defeat any rivals, but little else."

"But if you win, Deyco, you'll continue to fill the bellies of the tribe?"

"Exactly," said Deyco.

"You'll fill them on my fishes. So again I ask, why come to me?"

Deyco bowed his head and made the gesture of oath-taking, his fingers weaving a basket to catch starlight should he ever be forsworn and banished to the sunless realms. "Colobi of Blue Water, if you aid me, I vow that from this day till the day I die, I will ever more cast my fishing spear with my other hand, and should I miss, not cast again at the same fish."

"It is not enough. You are almost as good with the other hand."

Deyco sighed and added, "Further, I will cast my spear only after closing my eyes."

"A powerful oath," said Colobi. "It would surely cause you to miss half the fish you would normally catch."

"Then accept my oath and aid me," said Deyco.

"I don't think so."

"What? Why not? You said yourself, my oath spares half your fish."

Colobi smiled showing her teeth, and her teeth were those of a shark.

"That is true, but your death saves them all. No, I reject your oath. But I will not take your offering and return nothing. I will give you a gift, Deyco, a preview of the death that awaits you."

Instantly, Deyco found himself submerged. The undertow tugged like nothing he had experienced and in seconds it had pulled him from the safe and gentle harbor and dragged him dangerously close to the deadly coral reefs that guarded Aniwa's southern edge. His head broke the surface, and amid great gasps of air he started swimming, eager to put more distance between himself and the coral. The sky had somehow turned dark. A storm broke. Winds that belonged to another season churned the waters and hurled Deyco back toward the reef.

He struck it at an awkward angle, snapping his spine in two places and dying instantly. Then the fury of the storm pulled his body under and pinned him against the countless razors of the coral, scraping him along the length of the reef. Agony flooded his awareness, pain so intense it blotted out everything else and even slowed the passage of time, which only added to the torment. He died a dozen more times before surfacing again, desperately gulping air despite being little more than shredded flesh and shattered bone, despite being dead many times over. Then the storm took hold of him, threw him at the reef, and it all began once more.

Deyco collapsed to his knees, safe upon the shore again. He was soaked with sea water but not shredded or broken or dead. The reflection he saw in the water was his own and whole. Colobi had gone. The ten pigs were gone as well.

Word of Deyco's offering spread across Aniwa. Susk heard and grew worried. His confidence in his own ability did not waver, but ten round-tusked pigs could surely tempt one or more spirits to meddle in the contest, and this concerned him. All his wrestling skill would not help him if Walawa or Fentalo or some other spirit caused the sand to slip beneath his feet.

At his urging, the council of elders brought together twenty round-tusked pigs, though they required two days to do so. Susk took the pigs to the highest point on Aniwa and offered them to Walawa. The spirit appeared as a column of rich soil.

"Why do you call me?"

"Help me, Walawa, Robust One."

"Why should I do such a thing?" asked the spirit. "Your course is clear to you. You need only best Deyco in the circle of fire."

"I can do that," said Susk. "I am more than a match for any man."

"Then why do you waste my time?"

"Because I am only a man. What if Deyco has enlisted the aid of another spirit? It is known he has made offerings. I cannot stand against such powers as your kind possess. Nor would it be a fair contest between us."

"What you say is true," admitted Walawa. "Would you have me grant you some special gift?"

"No. I want nothing for me but my own skill. But if Deyco does receive help, I ask that you counter it."

The column of dirt collapsed to the ground and a giant yam grew from it. The yam opened its many eyes and regarded Susk.

"I have reviewed my sister spirit's realm," said the yam that was robust Walawa. "An offering has indeed been made. I find that Colobi of Blue Water has come into the possession of ten excellent pigs. I cannot tell what boon has been granted, but you are right. The contest is to be between you and Deyco. Colobi has altered that balance. I will visit Deyco in his dreams this evening and ensure he takes no advantage from Colobi or any other spirit."

The yam withered and returned to the earth. The twenty pigs were gone as well. Susk told the council of elders all that had occurred. Then he went home, ate his dinner, and went to sleep.

That night, Walawa snuck up behind Deyco in his dreams, taking care not to be seen. The Robust One could not simply render himself invisible; Deyco still bore the mark of the sea turtle. Instead, he took the form of Deyco's shadow and crept close. He examined Deyco from head to toe, but could find no sign of the boon that Colobi had surely given. All he found was the Coral Death in Deyco's memory.

"Colobi is shrewd," said Walawa too softly for the sound to leave his shadow. "No doubt she showed you the loser's fate to cover any sign of what else she did. But I am shrewder still, and I will foil her plan with her own meddling."

Then Walawa, heartiest of the spirits of Aniwa, created a new mark, the mark of the Coral Death, and he placed it upon Deyco's brow.

Deyco awoke, screaming and flailing. He flung about so violently that he struck his wife, bloodied her nose, and knocked her from the pallet they shared.

"Deyco, what is wrong?" she asked.

Deyco hugged himself and shuddered, his body trembling. "A nightmare," he said. "I dreamed the Coral Death that Colobi showed me two days ago. It was so . . . real."

"It was only a dream, my husband. The Coral Death is not your fate. Susk may be strong, but you are clever and swift. You will find a way to defeat him at the next moon."

Deyco nodded. "I hope you are right. Perhaps I will think of something while I fish today." He drew on his clothing, took up his favorite fishing spear, and kissed his wife. Then he went out into the predawn morning to find a solution in the simple pleasure of what he did best.

He spent the morning uneventfully, catching all the fish he aimed at, but gaining no insight into his coming contest with Susk. As the sun rose high, he found himself a shady spot beneath a tree, laid down his spear, and took a nap. Not long after he closed his eyes, Deyco found himself again caught up in a storm and being torn apart against the coral reef. He screamed in agony and awoke, safely back under his napping tree.

He leapt to his feet, snatched up his spear, and ran to his father's home, calling, "Obji! Obji!"

Deyco found his father digging for yams in the garden. He had described the Coral Death to Obji days earlier. Now he related the day's two nightmares. His father listened calmly and then led him to the home of the mute herb woman.

"You are just nervous, as any man in your place would be," said Obji, though he gazed with silent suspicion at the new mark on his son's brow. "No man wishes to be a force of destiny or a tool of the spirits."

The herb woman gave Deyco a powder to ease his sleep and dreams. Obji escorted his son home and sat with him.

"Worrying will do you no good, my son. It is all but out of your hands. Put it from your mind."

They spent the rest of the day playing games of pebbles and shells, a thing they had not done since Deyco's boyhood. It put him at ease and gradually the horror of the Coral Death left his mind.

Later, after Obji went home, Deyco and Tamla retired to their pallet and fell asleep in each others' arms. No sooner had Deyco slipped into deep slumber than the nightmare returned. He died, and died again and again, and awoke screaming as before.

Tamla soothed him and prepared the sleep powder they had forgotten. Pale and shaking, Deyco swallowed the medicine and lay back down. The powder worked its magic; his mind and body relaxed and soon Deyco slipped back into sleep. Tamla sat up, watching him by the dim light of the nearly quarter moon shining through the high window.

Deyco's breathing deepened. His chest rose and fell rhythmically. He looked peaceful and at rest. In an instant that changed. Every muscle tensed and Deyco's eyes opened wide as he screamed, a hideous cry of the repeatedly dead.

There was no end to it. The nightmare, the experience of the Coral Death, returned every time he fell asleep. The memory, the vivid detail and sensation, only faded while he remained awake.

Deyco spent the day sitting in his house, weary and resting, but not daring to sleep. He stayed awake that night, propping up his elbow and resting his head upon his palm so he would jerk awake if he began to doze. The next day was more of the same. Deyco's color worsened. He could not eat and drank only a few drops of water. Obji and Tamla attended him constantly, taking turns sitting with him and keeping him awake. On the third night Tamla accidentally nodded off; Deyco soon followed and woke both of them with his screams as the coral cut him apart. Panting, his heart pounding, Deyco curled into a ball in the corner of his house. He rocked back and forth, not daring to shut his eyes.

Neither Obji nor Tamla told the rest of the Kefer of Deyco's condition, but neighbors heard the agonized cries night after night, and even at times during the day. Rumors blanketed Aniwa as the Kefer wondered why Deyco no longer ventured forth. All recalled the dream Senjo had sent and looked to the coming moon for answers. Even Susk began to fear again, wondering if perhaps Walawa had taken his pigs, but only to play a trick on him. He could do nothing except wait, like everyone else. Wait, and practice his wrestling holds.

The days passed and Deyco grew weaker. His eyes yellowed and sank in their sockets, the dark bands beneath them became sinister. His hair lay flat and matted and lifeless. The flesh hung from his bones, jaundiced and running with sores. His voice was less than a whisper, and when he did lapse into sleep, which happened more and more often, he jerked back to wakefulness with a faint whimper.

By the day of the full moon he had gone without sleep for nine days. He was no longer truly awake, but existed in a listless waking trance, only vaguely aware of his surroundings. Now Deyco had merely to close his eyes to summon the full force of the Coral Death upon himself. He had long since lost count of how many times he had died.

"This is wrong!" Tamla said as she again tried and failed to get Deyco to drink some broth. "This is not the contest Senjo showed us in the dream. How can Deyco fight in this state?"

"I have spoken to others among our side of the tribe," said Obji. "I have told them very little, only that Deyco is beset by some spirit and is not at his best."

"Not at his best? Look at my husband. He has become an image of death like the nightmare that keeps him from sleep."

"Be calm. I could not tell the others the full truth; they would panic. Instead, I have convinced them to give me many of their pigs."

"Their pigs?"

"They are gathering them now, two thousand of them. I will offer them to Senjo myself and demand justice."

"Do not make demands," said a new voice from beyond the house's threshold. "Speak to me instead. I will be more inclined to listen."

"Who is there?" said Obji, pulling back the curtain but seeing no one outside.

"I came to see who was preparing to offer so many pigs. Invite me in, and I can spare you the offering."

"Senjo," said Tamla, "if you are that spirit, enter and be welcome in mine and my husband's house."

A breeze blew aside the outer curtain and swirled into the house, carrying a spiral of dry grass. The grass transformed into the figure of a small boy, his skin tinted a faint green, the shape Senjo was known to take when he came calling.

"I am the spirit you name Senjo," said the boy. "What justice do you seek?"

"You and the other spirits declared a contest between my son and Susk," said Obji.

Senjo nodded. "To end your war, for the good of all the Kefer. A fair contest, one man against the other. Leadership of the Kefer for the victor, and death for the loser."

"How can it be a fair contest if the men are so mismatched?" asked Tamla.

"Each has his talents," said Senjo. "Susk is stronger, but Deyco is clever and swift. The outcome is in doubt."

"Look at my son, Wise Senjo. Is your contest still in doubt? How can you claim it to be fair?"

Tamla went to her husband's side. She easily lifted him to his feet. Deyco turned dim eyes upon the figure of the boy. His parched and cracked lips parted. The words rushed out too soft for mortal ears, but the spirit heard them.

"Senjo the Wise, all my life I have trusted you. In the memory you gave me of all my lives it has always been so. You tell me that for the good of the Kefer I must fight the brother of my past, and that I might die. I understand and accept this. But tell me, why did I need to die a hundred times and more in the past handful of days?"

Senjo stared at Deyco's gaunt figure and then gazed deeper into the man's mind. He gasped, and reached up to touch the marks upon Deyco's brow.

"You have been wronged, Deyco. This was never to have been. No spirit was to have interfered."

"Then you will call off the contest," said Tamla, "and remove this cursed mark from my husband."

Senjo shook his head. "I can do neither. Once set in motion these things cannot be stopped. Deyco must meet Susk tonight in the circle of fire."

"But he has no chance. He can barely stand. Susk will kill him without effort."

"Perhaps not." Senjo took hold of Deyco's arm and bent it back cruelly. Deyco winced in pain, coming more awake than he had been in days.

"Hear me, Deyco. Close your eyes. The pain of the living world means nothing to a dead man."

Grimacing, Deyco allowed his eyes to close. Immediately he returned to the water and being shredded on the coral. It was agonizing, but a familiar agony for all that. He had endured it so often he was numb to it. As he died again, he was dimly aware of Senjo's grip upon his arm, like a fragment of knowledge rather than sensation. He opened his eyes, banishing the nightmare and awakening to the pain in his arm. He grunted softly and the spirit released him.

"I understand. Thank you," whispered Deyco. He turned to Tamla and beckoned her close so she could hear him. "Broth," he said. "Then you must help me bathe and dress so that I might face Susk when the moon rises."

Obji confronted Senjo once more. "That is all you will do?"

"It is enough. There is balance again. It is up to him how he uses it."

The spirit boy smiled faintly and blew apart, leaving behind only a few bits of dry grass.

Obji and Tamla spent the rest of the day preparing Deyco. He offered no resistance as they bathed him, applied salves to his wounds, fed him, and dressed him. Twice he let his eyelids close for an instant, each time jerking them open, having died again and again.

After sundown and shortly before moonrise, Deyco took his favorite and second favorite fishing spears, one in either hand like a pair of canes. With their help, and with Tamla and Obji supporting him, he struggled down to the beach. Clouds filled the sky. All of the Kefer had gathered. Many had brought torches, which they had thrust into the sand to form a circular clearing.

"The circle of fire," said Tamla, and Deyco barely nodded. His eyes were little more than slits, but they found Susk.

"You look like death itself," said Susk, laughing a bit too hard. "I expected a challenge. I remember you from when we were brothers, seven generations ago. You weren't much fun then; you don't look to be very entertaining now. Out of kindness for your family I will make this as quick as I can."

Deyco said nothing. He shrugged off Tamla and Obji. Leaning heavily upon his spears for support, he pushed his way into the clearing and waited for Susk to join him. The clouds parted, revealing the full moon. The contest had begun.

Susk circled warily, but it was all Deyco could do to cling to his spears and remain standing. Weariness weighed upon him, all the greater because he knew he could have no rest. Susk feinted one way and then darted the other, an elegant and impressive move, wasted on Deyco. Susk closed, swept the fishing spears from Deyco's grasp and tumbled him to the ground. Deyco landed badly, one leg bent awkwardly. A crack sounded, like the snapping of driftwood, and Susk jumped back, surprised.

Deyco grimaced in pain, his eyes squeezing shut for an instant. An instant was all the Coral Death needed. He was again in the ocean being dragged over the coral by the storm. He knew his leg had been broken, knew it with the same certainty with which he knew his wife's name, but he couldn't feel it. He was too busy being dead. The agony of dying and dying yet again blocked it out.

Deyco flailed about in the sand, reaching blindly for one of his spears. His fingers curled around a shaft even as the waves smashed him against the coral. He drew it nearer and then with both hands used it to pull himself upright again. He kept his eyes closed and managed to find his voice over the roaring of the storm.

"How will you provide for the Kefer?" he asked Susk. "Will wrestling matches on the beach keep them fed? Will you simply defeat anyone who opposes you?" Deyco stood upon one foot, his damaged leg dangling uselessly.

Susk's eyes widened but he advanced again. He grappled Deyco about the chest and brought him down hard against the sand. Deyco's spear fell away.

"I will lead the Kefer because I am the stronger of us," said Susk.

"There are many kinds of strength," replied Deyco. His eyes were still shut. Distantly he felt the sand beneath his back and Susk's weight upon his chest. More immediately the coral pierced and tore him.

"I will show you strength," said Susk. He stood, lifting Deyco in his arms like a child's toy. "This is strength," he said and in one swift movement he dropped to one knee, snapping Deyco's spine across the bar of his muscled thigh.

"You are strong enough to break me, but are you strong enough to kill me?" asked Deyco, refusing to open his eyes. All feeling in his legs had fled. Once more his fingers searched the sand and found the other spear. He gripped it tightly.

Susk roared and lifted Deyco again, throwing him to the perimeter of the circle where he smashed into one of the torches before falling forward. Pitch stuck to one shoulder and Deyco began to burn. He thrust his spear firmly into the sand with what strength he could muster and levered himself upward, one hand reaching back, gripping the blazing head of the torch for balance. His flesh sizzled as the flames climbed up his arm, spread across his body and down his other arm until even his spear was afire.

"How will you lead the Kefer?" asked Deyco, his voice softer but still audible. "Will you put their needs above your own? Will you invoke the spirits to aid them before yourself?"

People were shrieking all around the circle. Many turned away, unable to watch. The stench of burning hair and flesh rose into the sky, accompanied by the calm tone of Deyco's words.

"Why won't you die?" Susk screamed at Deyco. "Why won't you die?"

"I've died too many times." The storm thundered again, though only Deyco heard it. The waves crashed against the reef and shredded him once more. "I'm tired of dying."

The flames spread over Deyco's body, burning him to the bone. The stench was terrible and yet he stood. The fire ate away his face, his eyelids still tightly shut, and none of it reached him; he was far away in the water and the storm. Time passed. Susk could only stare as his opponent burned but refused to fall, refused to die. Deyco remained silent. There were sounds of sobbing from some of the gathered Kefer, but no words were spoken.

Eventually fire consumed even Deyco's bones. He fell to the sand as the charred pieces collapsed under their own weight. His spear crumbled into ash. Pale, Susk turned and addressed the people around the circle.

"You all shared the dream," he said. "Only one man shall remain standing, and he shall be the victor."

"I still stand," said a voice behind him. Susk whirled.

Deyco stood amid the pile of smoldering ashes. He stood upon two good legs. He looked healthy and strong though his hand seemed empty without a fishing spear.

"You died!" said Susk.

Deyco shook his head. "Many times." He stared into Susk's eyes. "Remember that in the time ahead."

Clouds moved back across the sky, blocking the moon. They formed a billowy face above the Kefer on the beach. Senjo spoke to them.

"Susk has prevailed. He leads the Kefer now. The war is ended."

"No!" cried Obji. "My son still stands. The contest is not yet won."

"Only one man stands within the fire circle," said Senjo. "The man that was your son lies at the feet of the spirit he has become."

"Spirit?" said Tamla, staring at her husband.

"When the body dies and the mind refuses to feel it, what is left but spirit?" said Senjo. "I name you Deyco of the Coral, newest of the spirits of Aniwa, protectors of the Kefer."

"May I keep this then?" said Susk. He had retrieved Deyco's first and favorite spear from the sand. "Surely a spirit has no need of it."

"What need have you?" asked Deyco.

Susk met Deyco's gaze. The spirit's eyes had changed and were now the pale pink of the coral reef. "I should learn to fish."

An appearance by Lawrence C. Connolly verges closer to performance than a reading. He is a talented composer as well as an accomplished, critically acclaimed author, whose work has appeared in most of the major genre magazines. With his beautiful voice and deft playing, he creates a magical space.

(beneath between)
Lawrence C. Connolly

I was traveling through Delaware when the storm returned, blowing in from the northwest, pelting my windows with rain. I had spent the night at the home of an editor, and was heading toward New Jersey to address a writing group before returning to Pittsburgh. I was tired, road-weary, and in no mood for driving in heavy weather. A dwindling patch of red-sky dawn to the east recalled an old saying. How did it go? *Red sky at morning, sailors take warning.*

I needed to make the state line by 6:00 if I planned to be on time for my talk at the Monmouth Library, but when a fishtailing car nearly ran me off the road, I decided to pull over and wait for the worst to pass.

A McDonald's appeared through the haze. I steered toward it, jumped a curb, and angled into a parking space. Rain assaulted me as I opened the door, soaking me before I reached the restaurant's entrance.

A small crowd had already gathered inside. The air smelled of grease, bacon, and wet shoes. I bought a coffee and made my way to a secluded booth, sliding in to discover that someone had left a paperback book on the seat. It was an old edition. I picked it up, turning it over to find that it was the Harbrace edition of Arthur C. Clarke's *The City and the Stars*. I knew the book, and seeing it brought back childhood memories of reading it for the first time in my uncle's cottage. It had been an old edition then. It was even older now.

I broke it open and pressed the pages to my face. The smell was as I remembered. For a moment, I was twelve again, sitting by a cabin window, listening to waves breaking beyond the forest, reading the story of a young man who left a going-nowhere life to find his destiny among the stars.

Lightning flashed.

The restaurant lights flickered.

A woman spoke in the booth behind me. "Not again!"

"You lost power last night, too?" a man said. "Mine was off for an hour."

I closed the book.

There was something odd about the cover. I pulled it closer, looking again at the illustration of a glowing city beneath a field of stars. Those details matched my memory of the book, but I now realized that the title was not *The City and the Stars*. It was, instead, *Against the Fall of Night*. And the name beneath the title was different, too. Not Arthur C. Clarke, but simply Arthur Clarke.

An earlier edition? A variant?

I opened the book to check the copyright, discovering as I did that both the inside front cover and facing page were covered with a dense cursive script that ran both horizontally and vertically across the panels. The next two pages were much the same, although here the handwriting serpentined around a list of titles by Arthur Clarke on the left and the title-page information on the right. The following pages—the title verso, dedication, half title, and flyleaves—were much the same, covered horizontally and vertically, as if the writer had felt compelled to continue writing after running out of blank or nearly-blank pages.

The first few handwritten sentences inside the cover were easy to read, since the ragged margin of the vertical script did not overwrite the first couple lines. Farther down, the reading became trickier, but by then I was hooked.

I read it through, lost in the story. And when I finished, sitting back to discover that the storm had broken, I felt as if I had awakened from a lucid dream.

I closed the book, looking again at the cover that was at once familiar and strange.

A hoax?

I doubted that. The book looked authentic, as old as the handwriting was fresh.

But it can't be true. It's too fantastic to be true.

I checked my watch. 6:45. My clothes were nearly dry. Beyond the plate-glass windows, my car waited in a pool of sunlight.

Running late. Time to leave.

I slipped the book into my jacket pocket, got a coffee to go, and hit the road.

Five hours later, after a distracted presentation in the Monmouth Library, I asked the librarian to do a database search for a 1956 Harbrace edition of *Against the Fall of Night*.

"I don't see one," she said.

"You're sure?"

"There's a 1953 Gnome Press edition."

"By Arthur Clarke?"

"Arthur C. Clarke." She emphasized the middle initial. "And there's a 1968 Harcourt edition entitled *The Lion of Comarre and Against the Fall of Night*."

"That's not it."

"But it's all I'm seeing."

"How about anything by Arthur Clarke, no middle initial? Any indication that he ever wrote under that name."

She frowned, the screen reflecting in her bifocals. "No. Nothing like that. It's always with a *C*."

I decided to show her the book. "Here." I reached into my jacket. "I have—" The book wasn't there. "Hold on." I checked the other pocket. My wallet was there. No book.

"Something wrong?"

"It was in my pocket."

"A book?"

I looked back toward the parking lot. "Must have fallen out."

"In your car, maybe?"

"Yeah. Maybe. I'll be right back."

But the book wasn't in my car.

I must have dropped it at the restaurant.

I considered driving back to Delaware, but something came over me as I started the engine, a sense that I had already brushed too close to something better left alone. Besides, I was too tired for backtracking. At least, that's what I told myself as I put the car in gear, pulled out of the lot, and steered for home.

But that night, unable to sleep, I set to work transcribing that handwritten story from memory. It is a strange narrative. I cannot vouch for its validity. But I do not doubt its truth.

I must begin . . . write it down while it's fresh. I'll lose it if I don't.

I'm in a McDonald's, off Philadelphia Pike. Soaking wet. It's raining like a bastard outside. But the restaurant has power. The lights are on, though they're flickering. Don't know what I'll do if I find myself in darkness again. A moment ago I leaned back in this booth and saw my reflection in the window. I thought it was someone looking in. Christ! Nearly crapped myself. Not good. Need to calm down, sort things out, write it all down.

It started when I decided to walk home. My former best friend offered to drive me, but I couldn't see spending twenty minutes in the same car with her.

God, I hate her.

It has nothing to do with her selling yet another story to one of those *A* magazines . . . *Asimov's, Analog, Apex,* whatever! That doesn't matter.

What does is how she keeps reminding everyone about her success without ever mentioning it. It's in her every move, in her every gesture, in her every "Well, you know, what the editors really want is . . ." and "Well, the most important thing I've learned about character development is . . ."

I used to enjoy meeting with the writing group. Not any more. And today, after listening to her pontificate for ten minutes straight, I knew I had to split.

I had my manuscripts with me. The same miserable, unfinished, dog-eared, blue-penciled drafts that I have been rewriting and rethinking since college, three stories and the first few chapters of a novel that always seems to self-destruct after about thirty pages. I shoved them all back into their manila envelope and headed for the door. Didn't say anything, just started walking.

Of course, she called after me. "You all right?" she asked.

"Fine."

"Well, you're not acting fine."

"Then I'm sick, OK?"

"Well, then let me drive you."

"No. I'll walk. I need to walk."

And that was it.

Well, *almost* it. She started to get up, but I kept moving, out the door until I reached the street. Then I jogged all the way to Philadelphia Pike. That's when it hit me.

Stupid!

I gripped my envelope and followed the sidewalk, walking against the traffic.

You know what she's doing now, don't you? She's talking about you! Psychoanalyzing!

I could almost see her waving her hand as she spoke, palm up as if cradling some invisible essence of truth: "Well, you know, we're often our own worst critics. . . ."

Funny thing is, she used to be my closest confident, my soul mate. We go way back. In college we talked endlessly about becoming writers. I even let her read one of my stories, which she insisted I finish and submit for publication.

"I'll get around to it," I told her. "One of these days."

"Well, if I were you, I'd do it now."

"But you're not me."

"Right, but if—"

"No time for *ifs*. My life's just too busy right now."

Problem was, my life was always too busy.

After college came work. And soon after that, life really closed in: family life, professional life, the full-but-empty life of raising kids and cultivating careers. Next thing I knew I was pushing forty. That's when I told her (my one-time soul mate . . . my former best friend . . . the one who always told me what she would do if she were me) that we should start a writing group. She liked the idea, so we put out the word: *Calling all wannabe writers!* And the wannabes came. And it was fun for a while, until she began finishing her stories. And then she submitted them. And then they sold. Pretty soon, she was queen of the club. And I was what? The Knave of Procrastination? The Joker?

Don't flatter yourself. You're nothing.

I paused at an intersection, looking back as I waited for the light to change. The sky had darkened. Leaves turned belly up, hissing in the wind. I considered retracing my steps, returning to the meeting, apologizing.

I shivered.

Can't.

I turned again to face the intersection. The light was still red.

I can't go back.

But I didn't want to be alone. I needed to talk to someone, anyone.

The signal changed.

I pushed on, walking faster as lightning flashed behind me. A few seconds later, I heard the boom.

I started jogging again, keeping the pace until a parking lot opened to my left, bordered on two sides by the storefronts of an L-shaped strip mall. There was a bookstore there. I knew the owner, a pleasant guy who seemed to know everything about science fiction, fantasy, and comics. His store, pressed between two nondescript shops at the southeastern end of the mall, always looked much smaller on the outside than it did from within. But even on the inside it seemed far too compact to accommodate the number of books he apparently had in stock.

Years ago, I used to test the size of his collection with impossible requests.

The conversations usually went like this:

"I'm looking for the original *Eerie*," I said.

"Which original *Eerie*?"

"The comic. I think it was published by Warren."

"It was. But do you mean the first *commercial* issue or the *prototype*?"

"What prototype?"

He grinned, stroked his beard, and looked down the aisle to the back of his store. But he wasn't so much looking as thinking, accessing that inexhaustible database behind his eyes. "The first commercial *Eerie* was actually issue two," he said. "The actual first issue, the one listed as issue one, was a prototype that Warren produced for a distribution meeting. Two hundred pamphlet-size copies were printed and bound. That's it, just two hundred. As far as I know, they were never distributed."

"You're joking!"

"You can look it up." He closed his eyes, accessing data. "Archie Goodwin tells the story in *Gore Shriek 5*, 1988. I believe the article is called 'The Warren Empire.'"

"You're serious?"

"Always."

"You have a copy of that one?"

"Which one? *Gore Shriek 5* or *Eerie 1*?"

I called his bluff. "Both."

He thought a moment, then nodded. "Yeah." He looked at me. "Want them?"

"If you have them."

"All right." He stepped out from behind the register. "But it'll take a minute to get them. You'll need to stay here, watch the register." He moved down the center aisle, entered a room in the back of the store, and was gone for maybe five minutes. When he returned, he had the magazines, each wrapped in a plastic sleeve.

Naturally, I bought them. I was too impressed and dumbfounded to do otherwise.

Other challenges followed, all producing similar results: the first issue of Charlton Comic's *Reptilicus*, the January 1963 issue of Forry Ackerman's *Spacemen Magazine*, and an immaculate copy of the Ace Double edition of Theodore S. Drachman's *Cry Plague!* I didn't want any of them. I was just trying to stump him, and eventually I had to stop, since I felt compelled to purchase each obscure gem when he produced it from that mysterious back room. After a while, when life got busy, I stopped going to the store, but now here I was, crossing the parking lot, racing against the darkening sky, trying to keep a few steps ahead of the rain. . . .

The first drops fell, shooting down like bullets, exploding on the sidewalk as I stepped inside.

My friend was there, talking on the phone, looking pensive. He glanced toward me, raised his eyebrows. "Actually," he said, still talking on the phone. "Maybe I can. Hold on." He put the phone on the counter and turned toward me. "Haven't seen you in a while."

"Been busy."

"Writing?"

"I wish."

He glanced at the phone. "Listen," he said. "I'm in a jam. Any chance you'd . . ." He frowned, seemed to reconsider.

"What?" I asked. "You need something?" I was eager for friendship, desperate to feel needed. "Name it!"

"I need to run out for a while."

"Want me to watch the register?"

"Do you mind?"

"Don't mind at all. What are friends for, right?"

He went back to the phone, picked it up, pressed it to his beard. "On my way." Then he hung up and showed me how to lock the door. "Just in case," he said. "In case I'm not back by closing. You're sure you don't mind?"

"Got nothing else to do."

A few minutes later I was behind the register, reading a tattered copy of Theodore Sturgeon's *Voyage to the Bottom of the Sea*, listening to the rain hammer the storefront windows.

At one point the lights winked out, plunging me into a few seconds of darkness. When the power returned, something thumped in the back room, the heavy bang of a restarting compressor. What was back there, anyway?

I checked the clock. Five minutes to kill. I got up from the register, walked down the aisle, and peeked inside the back room.

There was some clutter: empty boxes, trash can, bucket and mop . . . no books. I stepped inside and turned in place. Another door led into a small bathroom, but that was it. No mysterious collection. Not even any shelves. I started to leave, and that's when I noticed the trapdoor.

It was small, barely more than a square hatchway. A piece of knotted rope extended from one end, lying like a coiled centipede on the floor. I picked it up, raising the hatch to uncover a jagged break in the foundation. Beneath the break, a vertical ladder extended down into a flickering space. I leaned closer, listening to the crackling hum of fluorescent lights as the space below came into view.

The lights switched on when I opened the hatch.

I noticed a button inside the trapdoor's frame. I pushed it. The lights winked out. The ladder vanished, all but the top few rungs. Everything below that was now hidden in blackness.

I released the button.

The lights came back on.

I leaned forward, glimpsing the edge of a shelf of books.

So that's where he keeps them!

I remained there a moment, listening to the rain on the roof. Then I got up, hurried back to the front of the store, and locked the door. It was

close enough to closing time. Unless my friend returned in the next few
minutes, he would never know I had closed early.

A moment later, after returning to the back room, I descended the ladder to find myself standing in a long, narrow space that stretched away in
both directions. Floor-to-ceiling shelves lined both walls, magazines and
periodicals on one side, books on the other. To my left, a succession of
hand-lettered signs read 1950, 1951, 1952. . . .

The numbers faded in the distance.

The other direction was much the same, with years descending through
the 40s, 30s, and beyond.

I started walking, moving forward through the 50s, the colorful spines
of *The Magazine of Fantasy & Science Fiction* scrolling by on a shelf a little
below eyelevel. Above them, complete runs of lesser magazines came and
went: *Macabre, Jungle Stories, Infinity Science Fiction, Impulse,* and one that
I had heard about but never seen before—an ill-fated magazine titled *If.*

Everything appeared sequential, no missing dates or numbers. To my
right, each year of books was arranged alphabetically by author: Asimov near
the ceiling, Van Vogt near the floor. The C's ran about eyelevel: de Camp,
Clarke, Clement. . . .

I ran my fingers along the spines, noting the red-and-blue of Ace
Doubles, the yellow of DAW, and the stark black-on-white of the more
traditional, less identifiable imprints. Occasionally a spine bore a sliver of
a wrap-around illustration. One of these caught my eye, not because of its
design or use of color (both were pedestrian), but because the author was
Arthur C. Clarke, one of my childhood favorites. The book was volume
one of the Harbrace Paperbound Library, *The City and the Stars.* I took it
down, studied it through its plastic sleeve, and returned it to the shelf.

This store really does have everything.

I walked on, the books and magazines becoming newer: complete runs
of *Omni* and *Twilight Zone* to my right, works of Stephen King, Marion
Zimmer Bradley, Peter Straub, and Ann Rice to my left. . . .

The lights flickered, threatening to cut out, reminding me of the storm
that still raged above ground. Looking up, I noted fluorescent tubes hanging from a paneled ceiling. I realized that I must now be walking beneath
the alley that ran behind the store, or possibly even the stand of trees that
lay beyond that alley. In any event, I was certainly no longer beneath the
strip mall. Nor was I in any ordinary basement. Indeed, I suspected I was
in some sort of guerrilla interior, a space cut surreptitiously beneath the
property behind the mall, the sort of excavation that would need to be
done carefully to avoid underground pipes and cables.

How did he do it?

The shelf-lined corridor was perhaps 75 feet long, eight feet high, and with three feet between the shelves. Quite an undertaking for one man.

Did he hire a contractor? How long had it taken?

The space ended between a pair of shelves labeled 2000. The back wall was bare, paneled over with the same material that formed the ceiling. And yet, the space did not end there. At my feet, trailing a piece of knotted rope similar to the one I had noticed in the back room above, a square hatch lay in the floor.

Another level!

I raised the door. Once again, lights came on below, illuminating a series of vertical rungs that extended deep into a second shelf-lined space.

Curiosity drove me on, down the rungs and into a deeper corridor that ran at a slight diagonal to the one above. The arrangement made sense, since placing the lower space parallel would undermine the upper corridor's floor.

It's all been carefully planned.

I reached the bottom of the second ladder, feeling and hearing a whoosh of moving air that was even more pronounced in this corridor than it had been in the one above. And I heard other sounds: the steady whirr of dehumidifiers competing with the chug of sump pumps. Even so, the space felt damp, hardly ideal for storing books, yet the spines appeared nicely preserved within their plastic sleeves.

The lower space followed the same layout at the one above, the shelves labeled by year, the ladder occupying a gap between 1950 and 1949.

Once again, the spines of *The Magazine of Fantasy and Science Fiction* greeted me a little below eye level, identical to the ones on the upper level. Or were they? I looked closer, reading through the plastic: *The Magazine of Fantasy*.

I took down one of the issues, January 1953. The title on the cover was the same as the spine: *The Magazine of Fantasy*, no mention of *Science Fiction*.

And yet everything else about the issue appeared as it should. The editors were Anthony Boucher and J. Francis McComas, the imprint was Mercury Publications, the featured writers were Fritz Leiber and John Wyndham. No surprises there. But the title! I was familiar with the magazine, and I knew for certain that only the first issue, published in 1949, had ever been called simply *The Magazine of Fantasy*. After that, *and Science Fiction* had been added to broaden the publication's appeal. But here was a complete run bearing the original title, as if they had been published in some parallel universe, a place where the decision to alter the publication's identity had never been made.

What about the books?

I turned, facing the titles and authors I had encountered on the previous level, but here, too, there were differences: odd color schemes, unfamiliar names, altered titles. One in particular stopped me in my tracks: *Against the Fall of Night*, by Arthur Clarke. I took it down, pulled it from its plastic, opened it. The book seemed to be a retitled edition of *The City and the Stars*, complete with the original artwork and cover design. What was going on here?

I turned back to the magazines and started walking, noting other changes. The ill-fated magazine known as *If*, which had failed in the early 1970s, now seemed to have a run that rivaled the top SF magazines. Each issue had the names of its contributors on the spine: Asimov, Bishop, Bova, and then I saw something that stopped me cold.

It was the July 1989 issue.

My last name was on the spine.

It has been my blessing (or possibly curse) to have a rare surname, one that I seldom encounter in the world at large. But there it was, on the spine between Bova and Davidson.

I pulled the issue from the shelf, unwrapped the plastic, opened to the contents page. My full name was there, as was the title of one of my unfinished stories: "Alternate Paths." I noted the page number, found the story, and read the first page.

It was mine.

That is to say, the concept was mine, but the writing was better than anything I had ever produced, more precise, tighter. . . .

The editor's introduction at the top of the page claimed that "Alternate Paths" was my third story for the magazine. The others were "Parallel Lives" in January 1988 and "The Doppel Gang" in March 1987. More significantly, it announced that my novel *Different Lives* was due out in the spring.

I hurried back along the magazines, found the other stories, and then moved along the other side until I found *Different Lives*, which the subtitle identified as book one of a trilogy. I found the other books, then moved forward, searching for my name and finding that I had become incredibly prolific toward the end of the century. By the time I reached the bare wall at the end of the shelves, I had an armload of books and magazines that did not exist in my world. I did not wonder how such a thing was possible, but already a plan was forming. I could carry these books home, transcribe them, submit the manuscripts, sell them!

I leaned back against the bare wall, intoxicated with the plan. The lights flickered, reminding me yet again of the storm raging two levels above me. The ambient hum of the ventilators changed pitch, straining against the changing current. The lights dimmed once more, then came on full.

I have to get out of here.

Hugging my load of books and magazines, I headed back to the ladder, which now looked incredibly far away.

The lights flickered again.

And this time they went out.

Darkness fell. I paused and waited for the power to kick back on.

It didn't.

The air thickened, becoming stagnant, damp.

I blinked, waiting for my eyes to adjust, but I was in total darkness, completely closed in, cut off from any source of light.

What now?

I pushed on, still carrying the books, wondering how I would know when I came to the ladder.

Have to put the books down . . . feel my way.

The plan made sense. I could always come back for the books when the power returned.

Or I can just stand here and wait for the lights to come back on.

But I didn't like that option. Perhaps it was my imagination, but the air seemed to be growing thicker by the second, closing in until I felt as if I were suffocating in darkness.

I put the books down. They thumped around my feet, settling loudly as I moved away. I took a step, then paused, paralyzed with ambivalence. Did I really want to leave them behind?

The darkness shifted. I felt myself turning about, getting dizzy in the stagnant air.

Get out of here now!

I stumbled forward, steadying myself as I moved along the plastic-wrapped spines, feeling for the gap that held the ladder. But it didn't come. Had I walked too far? I paused, considered backtracking, and then—in the darkness behind me—something moved.

At first it was a dull thump, like the sound the books had made when I dropped them on the floor, only now it sounded as if someone was gathering them back together. I heard a groan, and then a shuffling step . . . then another . . . getting louder . . . coming toward me.

I turned and ran, plastic sleeves crackling beneath my hand as I searched for the ladder. Then, at last, the spines fell away. My hand swept into the gap between the shelves. My fingers closed around the ladder. I climbed as the shuffling sound paused beneath me.

My imagination. There's nothing there.

But I kept climbing, up through the square hole and into the middle passageway. I grabbed the hatch and threw it closed. Then, to make sure it stayed closed, I pulled books and magazines from the shelves and piled them over the door, building a paperback cairn as high as my knees, hoping the weight would be enough to keep whatever was down there from coming after me. Then I hurried on, feeling my way to the next ladder. And then I was climbing again—up into the back room where I again slammed the hatch.

Light seeped through from outside the store, coursing through the windows, lighting my way as I hurried from the back room. The buildings at the far end of the strip mall had electricity.

I stepped outside, set the lock, and dashed into the parking lot. It was still raining, but I kept running, down toward the main road where lights burned inside an Arby's restaurant. I hurried toward it, stopping when I caught sight of someone sitting in a corner booth. It was my friend, the owner of the bookstore, evidently catching a late meal while waiting for the power to return to his store. And he wasn't alone. A woman sat with him. She had her back to me, but I could tell by the tilt of her head and the way she gestured with her hands that it was my nemesis—the Queen of the Writing Group.

I kept walking until I came to a McDonald's. I went inside, and it was only then that I realized that I had left more than an armload of books and magazines in the bookstore. I had left my envelope of unfinished stories, too.

The woman at the register looked at me. "Help you?"

"Coffee." I reached into my pocket, looking for my wallet, coming out instead with the Harbrace edition of *Against the Fall of Night.*

My wallet was in the other pocket.

The woman put the coffee on the counter. "That all?"

I flipped open the book, noticing the empty flyleaves. "Got a pen?"

She took one from her pocket.

"Can I borrow it?"

She set it beside the coffee.

I paid and hurried to a secluded booth, flinching when I glimpsed my reflection in the glass, thinking for a moment that it might be the thing from the bookstore.

But it wasn't a thing.

I looked at the reflection.

It was a possibility ... another self ... the me *who couldn't bear leaving those books behind.*

I was used to such concepts. Indeed, I had once tried writing stories about such things—stories about not-quite parallel worlds where the roads not taken were taken, endless successions of universes populated by not-quite congruent selves:

The *me* who writes nothing. . . .

The *me* who writes everything. . . .

The *me* who gets trapped. . . .

The *me* who escapes. . . .

On and on . . . endless possibilities.

I pondered my reflection in the glass.

What if I had actually finished those stories in college?

I shivered, knowing the answer. The feel of those books and magazines lingered in my hands.

But now another possibility was eating at me.

What if I hadn't put those books down when the lights went out?

My shivers deepened.

I would have moved slower, stumbling in the dark. But I still would have gotten out. It just would have taken longer. Unless—

I glanced again at my reflection.

Unless someone sealed me in!

I leaned toward the window, looking through my reflection to see that the lights were coming back on in the strip mall parking lot.

I have to go back.

I clicked the pen.

Can't. Can't go back. Don't need to go back. I'm here. There's nothing back there. This is the me that I am . . . the one I have become . . . everything moves forward from here.

I stared at the blank pages inside the front cover of my stolen book.

Against the Fall of Night.

I must begin.

(dr. time)
Maria V. Snyder

D r. Clemmer?" Ian Kain called over the rattle of the dehumidifier. "I see you're still toiling away down here in your dungeon."

Gaye Clemmer eyed Dr. Kain's clean white lab coat and slicked-back brown hair with suspicion. Kain never came down to visit her unless he wanted to brag or to harass her.

"I've just finished talking with the head of our department. You remember Dr. Myers?" He paused, giving her a self-satisfied smile. "Since I've proved Young's Generational Theory, I have secured another multimillion dollar grant from Trellanix Corp."

When she failed to respond he said, "Since you don't bother to show up for department meetings, I'm sure you'll read about it in *Time*."

She was right, gloating was on his agenda, yet a hint of malice lurked behind his glib words.

Dr. Kain scanned her basement lab with a proprietary look. Gaye followed his glance. Who would want this dank, under-lit room that reeked of mold? Her ancient desk, tables, and equipment had been wedged in the various open spaces between the water heater, furnace, and her dehumidifier.

"With all that money, I have to expand my operation." He bared his teeth in what he must have thought was a smile. "I need a place to store my files and supplies."

She refused to comment; to give that bastard any satisfaction.

Undaunted, he went on. "Dr. Myers said your funding will expire by month's end. Unless you prove your theories." He smirked. "I'm still amazed that you managed to secure funding for this ridiculous project in the first place."

He walked over to the large, vault-shaped Relocater Device, opening the door. He poked his head inside. "I can use the computer and keyboard in there. Plus, this will be a great place to store my back-up drives. Sealed to keep the humidity out, right?"

"Why don't you step all the way in and see?" Gaye touched a switch at her desk and a bright red glow appeared in the device.

Ian Kain danced back as if threatened with a knife. He shot her a venom-filled glare.

"Funny, Dr. Clemmer, but let's see who's laughing when the janitors are hauling this junk to the dump." He wiped his hands on his coat, and strode from the room without uttering another word.

Relieved, Gaye waited until his footsteps on the gritty cement stairs faded before she accessed her locater program.

As she worked on getting the glitches out of the code, her mind returned to Ian's comments. Department meetings, Gaye thought in disgust, were a waste of time. Why bother to show up when her colleagues used every opportunity to mock her and her research à la Kain?

They had assigned her a lab in the basement of McMullen Hall. Dating back to the nineteenth century, it was one of the oldest buildings on the University's campus. The obvious slight was a mere inconvenience. Gaye had funding and a brilliant idea; all she needed was time.

One month left. The hardest part would be getting the locater program perfected by the deadline. The Global Positioning System had been a boon to her research for coordinates on the ground, but she still needed complex calculations to position the planet Earth in the universe. Determining the Earth's exact position, or locating it at a certain point in time was critical. A miscalculation would be disastrous.

Spending the month working late nights and weekends would be worth the astonished look on Kain's face. To Gaye, that would be better than getting a multi-million dollar grant.

Gaye hunted. She followed the creature's tiny scramblings as she crawled along the cold cement floor, scanning the corners. Catching a slight movement by the waste can, she pounced.

"Got you!" she cried. Grabbing the rat's tail, she yanked it up. The black rodent swung and twisted in the air.

"If you're the critter that's been chewing my papers," Gaye said, "I'll take you over to Runkel Hall where they use poisoned bait."

"Uh, excuse me," said a voice.

Startled, she nearly dropped the rat. A young man with a mess of bright yellow hair and long sideburns stood in the lab's doorway. Piercings glittered in both his ears and hung from his nostrils. He clutched his backpack to his stomach.

"Can I help you?" Gaye asked.

"Um, I was sent to help *you*." He glanced at the steps as if gauging the distance to freedom.

"In my research?" She was the kiss of death to any graduate student who wanted a career, so they avoided her.

"No. Dr. Kain sent me to help you pack."

"You can tell Kain that I still have three weeks. I'm not packing. In fact . . ." Gaye walked toward the student. He shrank back.

"Here." She thrust the rat at the boy.

He pressed against the wall, dodging the creature.

"Take this to Kain. If he's determined to move into my lab, he might as well get to know his roommates. They have a lot in common."

It was too much for the yellow-haired boy. He bolted up the steps, taking them three at a time.

Gaye laughed despite knowing she had just added fuel to the rumors about her. Shrugging, she placed the rat into an old cat-sized crate with the intent of dropping him off at the park on her way home. He'd probably run right back here. She pictured a tiny, well-beaten rat trail from the lake to her lab. They probably had maps, and compared stories of their capture in group therapy.

She placed the crate next to the steps so she would remember to take it with her. When she turned her back to her desk, an icy touch brushed her spine.

She spun. Nobody was there, but something had changed. For a mouth-drying minute, Gaye stood still, unable to pinpoint the difference. Then she spotted a champagne bottle sitting on the portion of her desk that she always kept clear. The section that had a black X taped onto it.

The bright silver ribbon wrapped around the neck held a note. Gaye moved toward her desk while a marching band played in her chest. Was it real?

Her fingers slid along the smooth glass of the bottle and fumbled to untie the note. Familiar handwriting declared: *We did it!*

She dropped to her knees in stunned amazement. Pure stubborn determination had sustained her through years of research, but to have actual proof that her Relocater Device worked overwhelmed her.

Standing on gelatin legs, she stared at the bottle. The champagne was the most expensive brand at the liquor store. She had planned to buy the bubbly and relocate it back in time to celebrate her breakthrough.

A fluted glass waited within her desk drawer. Gaye considered sharing the alcohol with her new rat friend for a toast as she retrieved the glass. But when she reached for the bottle, it had moved to the edge. Impossible.

The room felt excessively quiet. The dehumidifier had shut off, but Gaye couldn't remember when. The water pan must be full. She applied logic to calm her thundering heartbeat.

An unmistakable feeling of being watched hovered in the room. It seemed as if the airborne moisture had condensed into a being, changing the flow and thickness of the air in the lab. She licked her lips, tasting the sudden dryness.

Ridiculous, she chided herself. Paranoid. One minute you're overjoyed and the next worried that someone will steal the technology. And not just a regular someone, but a water-droplet being.

Gaye shook off her apprehension. But when she headed to the dehumidifier, she caught movement at the edge of her vision.

The champagne tipped over the lip of the desk. Unable to catch it, Gaye watched the bottle fall. Glass and champagne exploded as it hit the floor, splashed onto her pants, and soaked her shoes.

When the dehumidifier kicked on with a roar, Gaye moved so fast she left champagne puddles on the ground. Grabbing her briefcase and the rat's cage, she raced up the stairs.

Out in the fresh air, Gaye calmed. She chalked up her overreaction to stress combined with the excitement of success. After purchasing a new bottle of champagne, she headed home to celebrate.

Bypassing the lake, she carried the rat to her apartment. Celebrating alone didn't appeal to her, and, once home, she fed the rat cheese and milk, and went to bed instead of toasting her accomplishment.

When she entered her lab the next morning, the stench of alcohol greeted her. Glass shards and droppings from her other furry roommates peppered the champagne-sticky floor. Gaye set the rat's crate next to her computer, and swept up the mess.

She sighed. When Dr. Myers had seen the grant check for her research project, he had offered her lab space next to Kain's on the sixth floor. That offer had been rescinded as fast as a cockroach evading a foot when that lousy bastard Kain complained that Gaye had stolen his grant money.

Wempor Technology had already awarded her their Futurist Endowment before she finished her Ph.D. She had applied for the endowment along with a thousand other scientists. If Gaye had known Kain would revert to infantile behavior when he failed to win it again, she would have moved to another university.

Opening the one high window, she let the cold March air replace the fermented mildew smell. She kept busy to avoid dwelling on the unsettled feeling in her chest. Gaye worked on her locater program, commenting out loud to her rat.

Little things distracted her from time to time. Like the fact that her storage box had been moved to the right side of her computer, her calculator had been flipped over, and her phone had been turned toward the wall. It was as if her mother had visited and rearranged everything.

Unable to concentrate on her program any longer, Gaye moved everything back into its correct position. Then the dehumidifier kicked off. Gaye fidgeted for a while until the silence drove her to her feet.

Halfway across the room, she paused. Footsteps scraped on the cement steps, warning her of a visitor. Or an intruder? Gaye scanned the room for a weapon until she saw the familiar nest of lemon-yellow hair.

"Hello?" the boy called, starting when he saw her standing in the middle of the lab, staring at him. "I'm here to—"

"I'm not packing."

His Adam's apple bobbed as he swallowed. "Er . . . help . . . help you with your research."

His wide-eyed gaze locked onto the Relocater Device. Perhaps he thought she would relocate *him*. Although, if she sent him back to his barber, she would be doing him a favor.

"Sorry, but my grant money doesn't include a stipend for a grad student," Gaye said. She expected him to sigh with relief and bolt up the stairs.

Instead, with a dread-filled voice, he said, "Dr. Kain is paying my stipend." He swallowed. "I'm on loan. He said it was only fair to help you prove your theories since you have so little time."

She clamped her mouth shut before a sarcastic comment about Kain and fairness could escape. Studying the boy, she considered the offer. Definitely a spy for Kain. But why would he bother? He thought her project was a joke. Maybe he wanted to keep an eye on her so she didn't set any booby traps in the basement before she left.

If she sent the boy back, Kain might be down here more often—rather unappealing. She preferred her rats.

She could agree to the boy's help, but only when she could keep an eye on him. After all, it was free labor. If he proved too meddlesome, she would act out a few of the crazy professor rumors circulating around the department about her, and scare him away. Shouldn't be too hard to do; he looked a little shaky.

"Okay. Can you start now?" she asked.

He nodded, gnawing on his bottom lip.

"First thing." She pointed to the dehumidifier. "Empty the water pan outside. Water that new cherry tree by the front door. Do you know the one? Someone taped an American flag to its trunk."

He stared at her.

"I don't want to waste water; we've had a dry winter." She didn't know what else to say, and the boy still wasn't moving.

"Go ahead." Gaye shooed.

He finally rushed over to the corner. In his haste, he tripped over the power cord, bumped into the dehumidifier, and sloshed water onto his coat.

She suppressed a sigh, and returned to her desk. Her fingers froze over the keyboard. The storage box was once again on the wrong side. Glancing at the crate, she asked the rat, "Did one of your friends move my box?"

"What?" the grad student asked. His foot was on the first step, and he wobbled under the weight of the water pan.

"I'm not talking to you."

"Okay," he said, drawing the word out as if he humored a mental patient. Despite his heavy load, the boy shot up the stairs, splashing water in his haste.

Without him, the air in the lab smothered and pressed on Gaye's face. She noticed additional items that were not in their original place. The overpowering knowledge that someone was in her lab scratched at her skin. The water-droplet being? Gaye tasted the air, seeking answers.

Overworked, she thought. Stressed out. Drawing in a few deep breaths, Gaye rationalized. It could be a rat, scurrying around on her desk when she wasn't looking. And moving the storage box up and over the keyboard? No. Maybe it had to do with the Relocater Device. When the champagne bottle arrived, it had displaced the air. Perhaps the gust of wind blew the items askew. But the storage box hadn't been knocked out of place, it had been moved. Relocated.

Maybe the water-droplet guy was bored, playing poltergeist for a laugh. A feather of fear brushed her stomach. Focus on the science, Gaye chanted in her mind.

When the boy came back, she showed him how to pull coordinates from a Universal Positions Graphic map, a time-consuming but relatively easy task. She set him up at the table.

There were no more "incidents" that day. She only jumped once when the boy stumbled over his metal folding chair. He had class.

He handed her the coordinates and started for the stairs.

"Hey, bo . . ."

"Bradlee, with two e's, Shepherd," he said.

"Are you coming back tomorrow?" The sudden reluctance to work alone pulled at her chest. Ridiculous, she knew, especially since she had been the sole occupant of her basement lab for the last five years. However, the fear remained.

"I can."

Relief puddled. "Same time?"

"Okay."

Getting back to work in the empty lab proved difficult. She stared at the storage box, daring it to move.

An icy hand touched her neck.

She shot to her feet. Her chair slammed into the wall.

Where the champagne bottle had once been, there was now a white envelope. A message from the future. Gaye's fear evaporated as she dove for the letter, and missed. The envelope slid away from her hand. Had her dive blown it? No. The envelope continued to sail across the desk and into the air.

Determined, Gaye chased the message. Defying gravity, the letter headed straight for the water heater. A pilot light burned underneath. The envelope dipped toward the flame.

A suicidal note. She sprinted and snatched the envelope before it could catch fire.

Panting, Gaye held her prize tight. It was too risky to open it in the lab. She picked up the rat's crate and backed out of the basement.

Gaye checked the lock on her apartment door twice. She loaded the dishwasher and tidied her small one-bedroom apartment. She kept glancing at the letter, but couldn't bring herself to read it.

The envelope rested on her scratched kitchen table. All her furniture had been bought at a consignment shop. There were no decorations or pictures hanging on her walls. Her textbooks and old files had been piled in a corner of the dining room to save them from the lab's moisture.

She opened her letter only when her TV was on loud, the rat's crate cleaned out, and Little Devil fed. Yes, she had named the rat. It was yet another lonely, pathetic gesture.

It read: *I thought you might enjoy knowing that Kain's new grant money falls through when his research methods are examined. Seems his science doesn't match his results. This wonderful event happens on March 27. Perhaps you would like to do some gloating of your own before he receives word? Oh, and watch Bradlee with two e's. His klutziness ruined some of Kain's research and Brad's trying to get back into his favor. By the way, Wempor Technology is thrilled with our success and promises tons of money, but asks that we keep it quiet for now.*

The letter was signed in her own handwriting. A queasiness rolled in her stomach. Important events were happening in the future beyond her control, and a strange feeling of wrongness simmered in her chest as if she had committed a crime.

When Gaye arrived at her lab the next morning, Bradlee stood in the middle of the room, looking as pale as drywall dust. In her mad sprint up the stairs the day before, Gaye had forgotten to lock the door.

Scanning the room, she couldn't tell if he had been snooping. Things on her desk had been moved out of place, but that had become the status quo. Her computer was on. She couldn't recall if she had turned it off. A slightly crumpled piece of paper rested on her desk. Another note?

Gaye glanced at Bradlee to see if he had read it. The boy's gaze jumped from corner to corner as if he followed the erratic path of a fly. He turned in a slow circle, yet remained oblivious to her presence despite the fact she stood in full view at the bottom of the steps. The dehumidifier rattled and hummed.

"Bradlee," she said. When he didn't react, she called louder, "Bradlee with two e's."

He spun around, but his feet didn't keep pace and he ended up tripping over them. "Jeez Louise, don't sneak up on me like that," he said.

"What are you doing here?" she asked.

"You told me to come."

"Oh. Okay." Gaye hadn't realized the time. She placed Little Devil's crate next to her desk. Ignoring the wrinkled paper, she rummaged around for the file of calculation sheets. She wanted to give Bradlee something to do before she read the note.

"Do you know this place is haunted?" Bradlee asked. Again he peered into the corners as if searching for something.

Gaye paused. A heavy presence filled the room. "What gave you that idea?"

He shrugged.

"Well, this is a scientific laboratory. Ghosts and goblins don't exist. Science and cold hard facts belong here. Do you understand?"

He nodded and she set him to work on the calculations. It was bad enough being the crazy professor; she didn't need another rumor to start circulating that she worked in a haunted lab.

When she finally picked up the paper, her hand shook. Bradlee had felt a presence, too, so she wasn't imagining it, but she couldn't decide if that was a good thing or not.

To make matters worse, the paper had one word on it. *Stop*. The printed letters looked like a kid had written them. Gaye copied the word below it to compare. Not her handwriting, yet it reminded her of childhood. Maybe a prank sent by Kain via Bradlee.

Instead of working on her locater program, Gaye sat at her desk, trying to figure out why the note evoked images of her youth. At this rate she wouldn't get the Relocater Device working before the university kicked her out.

And that was another problem. She had been so determined to prove to Kain and to the department that she was right, that she hadn't fully thought about all the consequences.

Future Gaye was having fun, sending champagne and notes back to herself, telling Wempor Technology about the discovery. It seemed rash. It seemed dangerous. It seemed irresponsible to mess with her own past and future.

It seemed wrong. And what about the . . . presence? Why would Future Gaye send it? Perhaps it came from the far, far future where humans had turned into condensed water-vapor beings to adapt to extreme greenhouse warming. The being had traveled back to see the great Dr. Clemmer for itself.

Perhaps the department wasn't too far off, calling her the crazy professor.

Like a puppy, logic chased its tail in her mind. She heard a snap. Unfortunately, it wasn't sudden understanding.

"Damn," Bradlee said.

She swiveled her chair.

"Broke my pencil." He sighed. "You know," he said, scratching at a yellow sideburn with the eraser, "I can bring my laptop tomorrow. It would be quicker, and you wouldn't have to input all these numbers into your computer. Just transfer the file."

His comment made her wonder if he had searched through her computer files while waiting for her this morning. "If you want," she said in a neutral tone.

She found another pencil and handed it to him. Bradlee switched the pencil from his right to left hand, and began working.

Must be left-handed, Gaye thought. Then chomp, the puppy caught its tail. She pulled the one-word note closer. Taking a pen in her left hand, she wrote "Stop." The same shaky letters. An exact duplicate. Like when she was a kid, having fun trying to write with her left hand. So much for the prank theory.

Bradlee left for class, and Gaye was alone with her swirling thoughts. The note would make more sense if it had been from Kain. Determined to ignore the strange events, Gaye concentrated on her locater program.

She succeeded in debugging the program, but couldn't get it to link up with the Relocater Device's computer. Gaye planned for a late night until the furnace hissed, disturbing her. The ancient contraption broke every year. The last thing she needed right now was to have the repairmen tramping in here, getting in the way, asking her questions instead of doing their work.

Upon inspection, the furnace seemed fine. Another hiss sounded behind her.

She braced. Reluctant to turn around, she summoned the courage. Just like pulling off a Band-Aid, it was best to do it fast. She spun. A cloud hovered four feet away. It hissed again and transformed into a human shape.

Horrified, yet fascinated, Gaye froze. The cloud woman's face contorted with effort as she tried to speak.

"Kain." A whispery fizz. "Watch."

For a second the woman came into sharp focus. Gaye gasped, recognizing herself sculpted in cloud. The woman pressed her white vapor lips together in frustration as she faded.

Unfortunately, Kain chose this moment to appear at the base of the stairs. Gaye gaped at him, her thoughts as messy as Bradlee's yellow hair. Was Kain made of cloud too? At first, she failed to understand his words.

". . . see how Bradlee was working out," he said.

"Bradlee with two e's?" she asked.

"My grad student," he snapped.

"Oh, fine. Thank you. Did you . . ." She had wanted to ask him about Cloud Gaye, but reconsidered.

"Any results yet?"

Blunt as ever. Gaye was surprised he hadn't brought a measuring tape and interior decorator along.

"Soon."

He laughed. "You still believe you can travel through time in a time machine made of an old bank vault and some junkyard parts?"

"A Relocater Device."

"Relocater, time machine, doesn't matter what you call it, it's still fantasy."

Unchecked, the words burst from Gaye's mouth. "It *does* matter. It makes all the difference between success and failure." She stepped toward him. "I could even relocate your multi-million dollar grant check right into my office. No time travel involved. But I forgot . . ." She smacked her forehead in a mocking gesture. "Your grant money disappears before you even get it. You'll be reading your go-to-hell letter from the government in two days. Fantasy numbers never work in obtaining research money, *Doctor* Kain."

Regret followed Gaye's outburst. When Kain's face emptied of color, she knew she should have kept her mouth shut.

In a tight voice, Kain said, "I should have known better than to try and help a psychopath. Thank God you'll be gone, or should I say *relocated*, from this university in two weeks."

He strode to the stairs. Gaye could have sworn she saw a damp handprint on his back.

With Kain gone, Gaye had to deal with rationalizing the presence of the Cloud Gaye. A message from the future? A warning? Perhaps Future Gaye had tried to relocate herself back in time, and, because she already existed in this time period, she arrived as an intangible being, unable to interact.

Although she had interacted, in a ghost-like way.

Gaye's head throbbed with the complications. She sank to the floor. It had been much simpler before. Prove her theory. Have a party. The end.

As she stood, Gaye spotted an exposed wire lying under her desk. She inspected it and discovered that the wire had been gnawed almost in half. Those rats must feed off the electricity. No wonder they were so bold. Then she realized the broken wire connected the computer to the Relocater Device. She replaced the damaged wire and fixed the communication problem.

Jubilant, she raced back to the computer. It acknowledged the device. Fingers flying over the keyboard, Gaye initiated her first test. She placed a pencil in the device and sealed it tight. Dancing with energy, Gaye started the program.

The Relocater Device hummed, cracked, and pinged. Just when she thought it was either going to explode or melt, she heard a loud pop. The pencil rested directly on the black X on her desk.

Not bad for a bank vault with junkyard parts. Now she had a reason to celebrate. She took the champagne bottle from Little Devil's crate. Should she send it back in time? Done that. Gaye popped the top.

Letting Little Devil free in a surge of happiness, Gaye poured him a bowl of champagne. He sniffed the air, and waddled over to the treat. When he was done, he waddled back into the crate and fell asleep.

Over the next two days, Gaye tested her device on real-time transfers, avoiding the time vector for now. The bigger the object she relocated, the louder the pop. Bradlee never returned, which was fine with her. Busy and excited, Gaye also ignored the hissing efforts of Cloud Gaye. As for the warning, what could she do? She'd been avoiding Kain as always. As long as she kept her mouth shut about the device, she should be all right.

Gaye calculated the coordinates for the night when the champagne bottle arrived. She programmed them into the computer to test if the device would shut down with an error message because of the time vector. Even though Future Gaye had made it work, Present Gaye needed to check.

A bang vibrated through the floor. She glanced up. Ian Kain stood at the base of the stairs, trembling like a revved up engine in neutral. With a paper crushed in his fist, he advanced on Gaye.

"You knew!" He snarled. "You crazy, deluded bitch. How did you know?"

She opened her mouth, but he grabbed her arm and dragged her over to the Relocater Device.

"Are you going to tell me that this piece of junk works?"

"Yes," she said, hoping the answer would defuse his anger.

He stood still for a heart-slamming moment. "Show me."

Gaye heard a hiss. Cloud Gaye gestured madly behind Kain. Too late now. "No. I'm sorry about your grant, Dr. Kain. But I have a lot of work to do." She pried his hand off.

"Show me," he said.

He was not going to bully her. "No."

He pulled a gun from his lab coat. "Show me, now."

The hard metal lines of the gun's barrel pointed toward Gaye. Reason drained from her body, leaving behind a numbing jumble of thoughts. An image of Kain winning awards and accolades flashed through her mind. He was not going to steal her invention. "Go to hell."

A loud roar echoed in the lab as Kain shot her in the chest. She flew back, hitting the Relocater Device's door.

Surprise preceded pain as Gaye stared at Kain. He gaped back in horror as her body slid to the floor.

She couldn't breathe, there was no time left. "Doctor Time," the students had called her. Gaye laughed, but choked on the hot blood pouring from her mouth. Her lab blurred. Kain disappeared. She melted into the blackness.

Later, Gaye's spirit rose from her dead body. The desire to warn herself about Kain was overpowering. The Relocater Device had been programmed for the night the champagne bottle appeared. The computer and keyboard inside the device accessed the controls.

Could she do it? Why not? She had done it before. And this time, she would do it right.

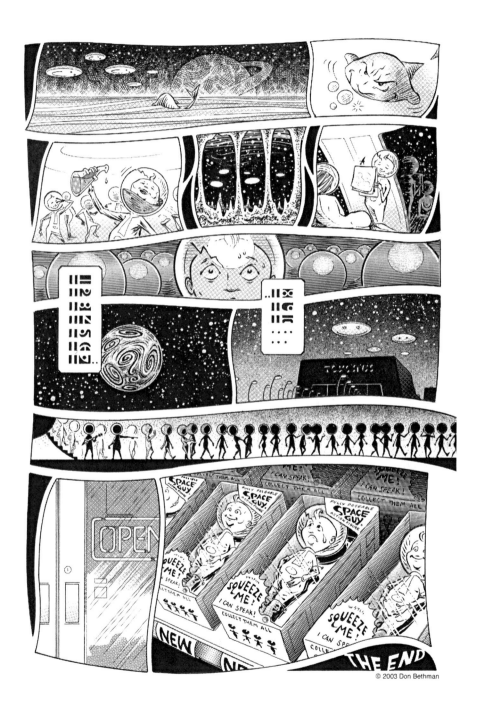

© 2003 Don Bethman

(swift decline)
Gregory Frost

A back asphalt highway off Route 99 led into the town of Dogget. It was one of those state roads with a number assigned to it that nobody bothered to use. The kid in the Texaco outside Eccles had just called it *the Dogget Road*.

I rolled in just as a beautiful splash of sunset spread across the horizon. Smoke in the atmosphere will give you sunsets like that—after Krakatoa, the whole world was treated to them—but I doubted the effects from underground coal fires made it out of the hills.

Even that sunset couldn't do much for the town. Dogget had passed the "Last Chance" sign and run out of gas. At the city limits a rusting sheet of tin on a pole demanded that I reduce my speed. It looked like the last imposition the town would be making on the world. Obediently, I trolled up Main Street as though I were looking for an address instead of Polly Lutts.

The downtown, such as it was, ran for three abandoned blocks. Buildings on both sides of the street stood boarded over and ramshackle. Some had cardboard "For Sale" signs propped in their dusty windows. They looked like they'd been for sale the day Kennedy was shot. I passed two buildings with big old balconies running the length of them. Might have been hotels back in the '30s; they were flophouses for termites now.

I glanced down a side street, Elm. A faded "Drink Double Cola" was painted on the brick wall there, and beyond it lay more buildings, two, maybe three blocks off the main drag. Past them, a plume of smoke hung like a grease stain against the clouds.

I was looking at a rip in the carcass of West Virginia where the cracked and dried–out skin had shrunk back to reveal bones. Back in the middle of the last century, places like this had movie houses, civic pride and fresh paint. More than a dozen mines in a ten mile radius had coughed up coal. The mines had died fast compared to the towns, but they always did. The populace hung on in blind faith, ignorant of the fact that invisible corporate bodies had already bagged the mineral rights and could strip the rest away any time they pleased. It had been the same up in Pennsylvania—people forced to discover how utterly expendable they were. No, that wasn't quite right. "Expendable" implied somebody still had a use for them.

I counted a barber shop, a grocer's, a filling station that might have been operating in the morning, a Church of God, and, across from it at the end of town, The Meteor Bar. A dozen vehicles surrounded the Meteor like piglets feeding off a sow. Everything else looked closed up, giving the impression that the whole of Dogget had moved in there.

Two stone pillars framed the drive of the church. Grass and weeds grew in its yard and boards "x"ed its skinny windows, but lights were burning on both floors of the rectory house adjoining it. God was hanging on by his fingernails, and He still had power.

I rolled past the bar and then pulled off onto the gravel shoulder. The road ahead curved out of sight behind a mileage sign. Lynchburg was closest. I turned the car around and then backed it into the overgrown church driveway. The pillars and weeds would hide it from anyone passing by—not that there appeared to be anyone left to pass by.

After turning off the engine, I pocketed the keys, got out and crossed the road, armed with a small Maglite. The clear air had gone chilly, the way the cold settles into valleys and drags the dust down with it. I hunched in my jacket as I walked along the row of parked cars in search of a blue plate that said, "You've got a friend in—XPN 885—Pennsylvania": Mrs. Polly Lutts's car. If it had been there, I could have gone back to my motel outside Eccles a happy man and gotten a good night's sleep. Curiously, I found cars with tags from Tennessee, Ohio, even North Dakota—a long way to come to be here—but the errant Mrs. Lutts was absent, or at least she hadn't driven to the bar.

Somewhere up in those black, ominous hills something boomed like a freight train shaking loose its cars. That was probably what it was. The noise reminded me of hanging out the window of my bedroom as a kid and watching the headlamps of trains go flickering through the woods way off down the hill.

I wove between a four-by-four and a station wagon, noticing at a touch on the hood that both were cold. "Happy Hour" had been going on a while.

I opened the door to the bar. Everything stood quiet, absolutely still. It was not the sort of stillness where a lot had been going on before I came in, either. There was no music. The TV wasn't on.

I looked around at maybe twenty people—the ceiling lights were so dim that the blinking strings of old Christmas lights around the top of the bar were tossing off most of the illumination. I couldn't be certain how many lurked in the booths against the far wall.

They'd raised their heads at the creak of the door but hadn't paused in their conversations, because there weren't any conversations. These people were sitting still as death without saying one word to each other. I turned and dragged the door shut. What the hell had I walked into?

It was a good-sized place, with an old wood dance floor off to the right between me and the booths. All the bar stools looked taken but there was room to stand at the opposite side, and I headed there, which gave me a closer look at the patrons.

Prominent eyes gave me sidelong glances, a dozen faces that looked deformed by a combination of thyroid imbalance and mongoloidism, half of them under billed caps. People joke about inbreeding in rural populations but this looked like a homologous family reunion. I leaned up to the bar.

The bartender, a wide-eyed chicken ready to be geeked, limped over like it was the last thing on Earth he wanted to do. The leg seemed to pain him a little.

"Beer?" I asked.

"Got Moose on tap," he said, rubbing his thigh.

"That'd be fine."

He nodded and reached without looking for a mug off the shelf. Beside me a tall guy in a short sleeve shirt and dirty trousers got up, saying, "You can have this stool, mister." Looking at him directly I saw that his left cheek seemed corroded, as if by acid. He shuffled behind me to a booth and sat down.

I skooched up on the stool and took out a pack of cigarettes. I didn't know if that was allowed in the Meteor, but even someone telling me I couldn't smoke was the start of a conversation. Not here though. Cigarette in a vacuum here. Nobody said a word or bummed a smoke, but they did watch. They watched me light up as if it were an arcane ritual they'd only heard about.

The bartender set my Moosehead on a coaster, and I paid him. I took a few sips, blew a little smoke, and tried to appear relaxed, which in that atmosphere meant devoid of consciousness. There wasn't a sign of the elusive Polly Lutts.

She'd run away from home, left her teenage son and angry husband. All evidence pointed to this unlikely ghost town as her destination. Their phone bills had revealed that over the past few months she'd placed half a dozen calls to Dogget. Lutts said his wife had a best friend from high school who'd gotten married and moved here, God knew why. He'd given me a snapshot of two high school girls in their blue graduation robes. They were laughing the way you'd expect on so solemn an occasion. "Me 'n Carrie" was scrawled in ballpoint on the back. Big, rounded, childish letters.

The other photo I had of Polly Lutts showed a nice-looking woman with permed sunset-red hair and sad eyes. I had a feeling I knew the source of that sadness, but he'd hired me to find her. I hadn't made any promises to bring her home, though. If I did find her, maybe I could get her to seek counseling, or a restraining order. Lutts claimed she was going through some sort of midlife crisis that he didn't understand, and maybe that's all it was, too. But in that case, had it been me, I'd have fled to South Beach and gotten a tan. I would not have come to Dogget, West Virginia to share the rot with my best friend from high school.

By the time I'd finished half my beer, some of the eyes had stopped watching me, but no one had proffered a conversation, either. They seemed to be waiting for something.

People have a way of assigning a stratification system to themselves. They tend to cluster, to form tightly knit groups within the larger population. They do this in all kinds of situations. Some play pool, others huddle and talk about sports or politics or spouses they'd like to brain. Even in a crowd, if you watch, you can see the individuals connect and divide like cells, spot who thinks he's in charge and who's following. In that bar either nobody connected or they were all of the same grim purpose.

I tabulated the oddities around me. In a booth on my right, one woman had gone bald over the crown of her head in a way that her emplastered, bleached hair couldn't hide, while the man across from her had a goiter a bullfrog would have been proud of. Elsewhere, knots of flesh, all those bulging eyes, and one case of mushrooming lip cancer—I couldn't have found this much deformity in a hospital waiting room. I thought of places like Love Canal and Chernobyl, and towns in Poland and Romania where industrial poisons had soaked into the gene pool. Did toxic wastes permeate Dogget? I'd thought coal mining just promoted black lung.

I drank a little more beer. The guy beside me had on a suit coat, stained and in need of pressing, but probably no dry-cleaning service remained in town. He looked like a fat used-car salesman, or the mayor. He had a mustache over his pushed-out, fishy mouth, and a bulbous nose. In the mirror behind the bar, his large eyes seemed periodically to swivel my way, but when I glanced at him, he was looking dead ahead, his utter disregard of my existence defying my experience. Nobody was this incurious.

"Cold night," I said.

Slowly, as if pulling against enormous magnetism, his head, then his eyes, swung in my direction. Straight on, he looked even more fishlike. The eyes did shift now, as if searching for the memory of speech. "Cold. Nnnh, cold night, sure is." At once he began turning away.

"Is it always like this in Dogget?"

"Always. And forever. World without end." A slow turn to face me. "You passing through?"

"Yup," I said, "on my way up from Lynchburg."

"Long drive. Out of the way, here." Big pearls of sweat had broken out on his brow, as if it strained him to talk. I could feel other customers looking our way.

"Yeah, some business in Eccles," I said.

"I've made that drive. State Patrol like to pick you up on the road. You prolly shouldn't drink too much."

"Thanks for the advice."

"I'd go."

"Right. Thanks." I squashed my cigarette in a tin ashtray and finished off the beer.

The restrooms were at the far end of the bar. I pushed up and headed that way. As I passed each booth, I glanced in but kept my head down as if looking at the floor. Some of them gazed over, big eyes glistening.

In the fourth booth along the wall I thought I saw a familiar face. Her hair was a tangle of thin blonde strands over darker roots. Askance I was sure it was Polly's friend, Carrie. But straight on, I saw that she had the same vaguely amphibian features as the others. While you might put on a lot of pounds over the years, you wouldn't change that much. All the same, I hesitated long enough to look at the other two women in the booth. Neither of them was Polly Lutts. Clearly, I'd made a mistake.

When I opened the restroom door, I found a man inside. Tall and lanky and wearing a billed cap, he balanced on an overturned bucket, looking out the tiny window. Upon my arrival, he became confused, and dropped down off the bucket, then didn't know what to do with himself. His hands twitching, his big eyes contemplated the one stall. Finally he gave up all pretense of having a reason to be there and lit out.

I closed the door after him, then made legitimate use of the urinal. The sink was by the window, and after I washed my hands, I stepped up on his bucket. The lights inside the rectory house shone from across the road. If I looked hard, I could distinguish the glint of metal that was the snout of my car sticking out from between the old pillars of the drive. So much for my cleverness.

Whatever was going on here, I wasn't armed with anything more lethal than a Nikon, a Maglite and two canisters of Mace. This had begun in the category of a simple missing person's case. Most of those, you find out the wife has fled to a boyfriend. You take a few pictures of his trailer and his pickup, of the happy couple on the way to a pancake breakfast, and then you go home, collect your fees and let the husband file for divorce. Later you maybe sit in court and describe what you saw while making eye contact with the adulterers in question. It's no big deal, and no guns, knives, or chainsaws are involved. No idiot car chases through remarkably accommodating traffic. Nobody dies, they just misbehave and get a spanking. Here, I'd thought maybe the runaway had fled an abusive husband—actually, I still thought so. But my inconsiderable case had become entangled in something else, and damned if I could figure out what. Casting call for a Todd Browning film, maybe.

I dried my hands, then eased open the restroom door. The tall guy from the bucket was sitting on my stool. He still had the jitters. I didn't think he would ride that stool for long, but I couldn't stay to find out. Heads were turning my way. I pretended not to see, and strode out through the door.

The cold air stinking of coal fire crossed me like a slap. I lingered a moment to light up another cigarette, then tromped back across the gravel lot to the road, and edged past my car. I strolled up the driveway toward the rectory. If people in the bar were watching it, I might as well find out why.

The man who answered the door showed himself to be confused by my presence, which made sense, given the state of Dogget. His was the first face I'd seen that didn't appear to have a fish in the family tree. Large-jawed and unshaven, he was tall, a little stoop-shouldered, and dressed in a collarless shirt and dungarees held up by old-fashioned braces. It was like encountering a member of the Joad family. His focus flicked past me for an instant, then back again.

"Who you?" he said.

"I'm a fella who's looking for someone." His brows knitted. I took a chance. "Nobody over at the bar could help me, so I thought the town pastor might know the new faces." I handed him the photo of Polly Lutts.

The skin around his eyes tightened as he looked it over. I hoped he wasn't going to lie and tell me he'd never seen her. He swung the door open wider and said, "You'd best come in."

The interior of the house had a grimy antiquity to it—antimacassars on the back of an old worn couch, and lace trimming around the bottom of the rocker. The lamps cast a yellowish low-watt light, and all over the walls hung posters proclaiming "Vita-Z. The Miracle Drink! Become as Reborn!" "Dr. Hiram Fulgit's Amazing Discovery! God's Waters of Life!" and "Life from the Stars. Cures All Bodily Evils! Vita-Z!" A lot of exclaiming. Assorted blue-glass bottles of every shape lined the shelves and mantle over the fireplace, although in the center of it lay what looked like a baseball-sized chunk of dark geode. Some of the old bottles still bore Vita-Z labels.

I stuck a thumb toward one of the posters. "Mailbox out by the road says *Fulgit* on it," I told him as if he didn't know.

"My great-grandad. I was named for him." He closed the door. A shotgun, I noticed, was propped against the wall behind it.

"So, he was in the patent medicine business."

Strands of his greasy hair sliced one of his eyes in two, and he pushed them aside with his palm. "Oh, no, sir, not like you think at all. Show you somethin'."

"Well, okay, but about the woman in the photo—"

"Oh, she's here," he said, as if it were nothing. "I'm keepin' her upstairs and away from *them*." His head dipped toward the front door.

"That's why they're watching your house?"

"Are they? Miserable fools, can they not wait? I say to you, we wrestle not against flesh and blood, but against principalities." As if that clarified anything. "I'll take you up to her, but let me show you this here first."

I followed him through his house. Stacks of newspapers, yellow and dry, stood on the floor and shared some of the chairs along with mail that had never been opened. It was the house of a crazy old man, but at least he'd taken in Polly Lutts.

The kitchen gave onto a mud room full of small crates. An open one revealed more blue bottles amid straw packing. These had new labels affixed to them. He snatched up a big flashlight lying across the corner of the crate and led me outside.

We hiked across a deep yard. On my left the church loomed out of the night, and in the light of the flashlight I could see that it needed a lot of scraping and new paint.

"The whole town's a-cavin' in," he said over his shoulder. "Coal veins run all underneath her. Even here. Some been on fire for decades. Eventually we're all goin' under if we leave things like they are. Can't do that. Here we go."

We walked up a hillock toward what I thought at first was a shrine, like a Catholic grotto. It was a big, open circular structure, and a boulder sat in the middle of it, above a small pool. Hiram stopped in front of the pool and shone the light up at the grotto. I saw that it was made of blackish lumps of rock all cemented together into an arch, a kind of miniature amphitheater.

"'Bout a century ago," he said, "a meteor crashed right here one night. Wasn't no church here at that time, just a piece of land my family farmed and a skinny dirt road out front. Thing came down outen the sky and smacked into the ground here. Old Hiram came running, and stood over it. This one big hunk was bright red and smoking, and the rest had broke into bits spread all over the area. But there was water trickling out from under this one."

"This?" I nodded at the pool. His light sparkled on a thin trickle running from beneath the boulder into it.

"Oh, yeah, hasn't moved." He laughed. "Opened up a natural spring where it hit. Great grandad, he scoured the area and found the other pieces of the thing and built this, like a shrine.

"See, he came with a pail and took some of that water back to the house, and he drank some. He'd been suffering from gout and arthritis something awful. Plagues our whole family, the rheumatism. Anyhows, one sip of the water coming out of the ground here, and he was all but cured of every pain."

"I do see. He built himself this . . . shrine, and started bottling Vita-Z."

"That's right." He swung the light away, and for a moment that trickle of water glowed on its own. I turned to follow him. He waved the light at the church. "Hiram Fulgit had been a man of God, preaching the gospel in tents all around. He saw this as the hand of God touching him, and so he started preachin' here and selling his miracle water, too."

"He didn't give it away?"

He ignored the question. "By the time my daddy was born, they'd erected a church here." By now Hiram was walking along the side of it.

"Well, nostrums and the Bible have mixed before."

"No sir, this here's no confidence game. This is water from the stars. Got properties you can't even begin to imagine."

I thought about the people in the bar across the road. "Maybe I'll have to take a bottle home with me," I said.

"Gotta try it soon. Don't know how long it'll be available. Spring dried up back seventy-five years ago and only just reappeared this year again. Been all I can do to keep up for fear it'll stop. You want to try it. Time's coming, and only the chosen shall be saved."

"God says, 'Drink Vita-Z,' huh?"

"God's not what you think." He held the door for me to go back through the mud room.

"Sorry. You keep your beliefs. I just want to see Polly Lutts, and find out if she wants to go home."

"Her husband beats her, did you know that?"

We were back in the parlor among the bottles and bad lighting.

"She told you that?"

He shook his head. "She told Carrie, and Carrie told me. She doesn't want to go back, mister."

Well, he'd confirmed my own misgivings, hadn't he? I said, "I had my suspicions. I'm not here to make her go back, just to establish this is where she's run to. I'll even help her get assistance if that's what she wants. But I do have to see her for myself, you understand."

"You say so. Well-uh, she's up here, come on." He curled his index finger at me, then led me to the stairs. "You sure you wouldn't want to try some Vita-Z first?"

"Thanks, but the sooner I see Mrs. Lutts, the sooner I'm out of your hair."

Without another word, he led the way up the creaking stairs and into a dim hallway. More yellowish light emerged from beneath one of the doors. He opened that door and stepped back, the light flowing over him like paint.

Tensed against I don't know what, I stepped into the doorway. Polly Lutts lay spread-eagled on a bare mattress on the floor, eyes open, stark naked and chained. A dark lump squatted between her knees—another chunk of that meteorite. Weird symbols covered the floor around her. She was alive, breathing, but she didn't so much as acknowledge our arrival. Like a dope I said, "What?" and then my head lit up. I have vague recollections of pitching forward on top of her, of chains rattling beside my head, of voices, of being kicked, shoved, rolled over.

I came to on my back on the bare mattress. I tried to sit up and my head thundered with outrage. Concussion. I lay still, groaned, waited for an idea.

A door slammed downstairs. I moved again, slowly this time, but my arm wouldn't play. I'd been chained to the leg of the bed beside me. Glancing at the bed, I saw a shape underneath it, and I rolled to the side and reached under with my free hand. It was that damned lump of ugly meteorite. Up close the outer surface of it looked like armor: Small plates side by side forming a thick convex surface, like rhinoceros hide.

I sat up cautiously. Car doors slammed, engines revved. I glanced over my shoulder to see lights moving outside the window. The chain had been strung through a loop on the cuff around my wrist. They must have been in a hurry not to have done me up as they had Polly. I stared awhile at the chains, the chunk of rock. My brain had trouble coming on line, unable to connect any dots. Finally, enough thought percolated, and I picked up the rock and brought it down on the chain. The links, I saw, weren't all that strong. Polly Lutts could have broken it if *all* her limbs hadn't been restrained. What had happened in this room?

I banged down the rock again. My brain pounded to get out of my skull, and the rock, that stupid piece of galaxy debris, began to heat up in my hand. I slammed it down again. Now it hurt to hold onto. Screw the concussion. I yelled, "Jesus Christ!" and slammed it down again, hard. The chain link snapped. I tossed the meteorite and began unthreading the chain. Then out of the corner of my eye I thought I saw the chunk of rock move. I stopped. Turned.

The rock flexed, then wobbled. It was swelling, breathing. I tore the chain out of that cuff as fast as I could, and rolled out of the space between those symbols. My foot kicked the rock and it slid toward the window. The last few cars were pulling out, their lights playing across the ceiling.

Something whiplike snaked out of the underside of the rock and slapped the mattress where I'd been. It was slick, greenish, and the ticking hissed, crackled, and tore where it touched.

I scrambled to the door, flung it back, and ran for the stairs.

Nothing came after me.

The shotgun still leaned against the wall behind the door. I grabbed it, snapped open the breech. Both barrels were loaded. I spent a minute then rooting through various drawers and cupboards, finally opening an under-the-stairs closet where I found boxes of shells. My head throbbed like a boombox.

Out the door, I lurched down the drive and into my car. I gunned the engine, backed out in a cloud of dust onto blacktop. Only one car remained at the bar. I saw it in my rearview mirror as I barreled back through Dogget. Wherever they'd gone, they had all gone together. I passed the center of town before I had the sense to turn off my head-lights and look around. Through the trees to the left I caught a glimpse of taillights in the darkness, like a Christmas tree string, all red, but trav-eling in the direction opposite mine. Next chance I had, I turned left and headed after them.

Navigating by parking lights, I had to go slowly. I didn't want the oth-ers seeing me, but I didn't want to find myself airborne either.

I reached the gravel road I'd seen them on, turned left again. This road ran along the side of a ridge. Far ahead over a small rise I could see a brief bright glow of someone stepping on their brake lights. There was a lot of dust in the air.

The other cars had driven three sides of a square covering a mile or so. Near the top of the rise I shut off my lights and cautiously rolled forward until I could see over it. Down the road a hundred yards or more, flash-lights floated around like fireflies for a few minutes, and then winked out. It was just me and the cloud-covered night.

To be safe, I switched off the dome light before easing out of the car. I stuffed my pockets with shotgun shells, drew the gun out after me, eased the door shut, then started up the road. No silent approach on gravel, but I tried to make as little noise as possible.

Beyond the rise, cars had been parked every which way across a plateau. It was like a junkyard. The plateau pressed up against a sharp hillside. Off past the cars I could make out Fulgit's church tower against what had to be the lights of the Meteor Bar and the highway. We had looped all the way around behind it.

I wove between cars, shotgun at the ready, but no one had stayed behind. They had no cause to expect any trouble: I was chained up back in the house, prey for their little monster.

The hillside, as I approached it, showed a darker patch in the center. At that point, my toe caught on something and I stumbled. I knelt, patted the ground. My hand wrapped around a cold steel rail. It ran toward the dark patch. I realized I was looking at a mine entrance. No wonder the hillside was so steep; it was artificially so.

Inside the mine entrance it was truly pitch black. It smelled like motor oil out of an old Ford pickup.

I listened, but there was nothing, no movement, no one near, so I tucked the shotgun under my arm, took out my Maglite and, with one hand cupped around the lens, twisted it on. My hand abruptly glowed red and slivers of light spilled around my fingers, enough that I could make out the twin rails, wooden ties beneath them, a sheen of creosote or grease. Raising my head, I saw the car.

The cream Toyota had been parked off to the side of the rail, nose-in. The tag, "XPN 885," gleamed dully. Naturally. Who'd ever look for a missing vehicle in a coal mine? Next time I went looking for a chop shop in Pennsylvania coal country, I would have to remember that.

The keys were in it. I supposed there had been no reason to take them. Keep them with the car and then nobody could accidentally leave them lying around for the authorities to find.

Farther down the tunnel, I played my light around for a moment. On a thick beam overhead someone had carved "1924." I swept the light across the ground ahead to make sure the way was clear, then shut it off. I kept one foot alongside the rail.

As my eyes adjusted, I made out a dim glow ahead, which turned out to be from an adjoining tunnel. This one was newer, and strange. The supports were stone, cut like squat obelisks, and though the ground crunched underfoot, the uneven walls and ceiling looked almost polished, or fused, as if intense heat had melted the surfaces.

The light grew brighter and brought with it voices, joined in a kind of chant. All of a sudden came a yell, Hiram Fulgit, shouting something like "Kaykeebah!" The sound bounced around ahead, coming from somewhere beyond where the tunnel sloped.

Reaching the slope, I pressed back behind a pillar and looked down into a broader cavern. Everybody had gathered there. Flashlights and lanterns, set down or stood on end, surrounded a couple dozen figures. It took me a moment to understand what I was seeing.

They'd all devolved further, into something even less human and more froglike: Hump-backed, their arms shortened, hands splayed, webbed; grotesque faces with thickened snouts and bulging eyes. They stood in a circle around a slab of rock. Hiram Fulgit, unchanged, stood upon the slab, declaiming in some language I couldn't identify. At his feet lay poor Polly Lutts. Fulgit held one of his elixir bottles, which he poured over her body as he shouted.

I raised the shotgun, trying to figure out how I could shoot him and not kill her, seeing myself foolishly wading into their midst where I would be torn apart, unable to reload fast enough to kill all of them. As I tried to sort out my options, Polly suddenly arched her back like in an extreme yoga pose. She screamed. The crowd roared—a burbling, inhuman chorus. Fulgit knelt, opened another bottle of his Vita-Z and poured it into her open mouth. He raised his arms to the ceiling and called out, "Come, Nyarlathotep, black wizard! Come Yog-Sothoth! We open your gate!"

I stopped wondering how I would deal with them. I stopped thinking at all.

Polly's body bent up higher. I heard bones snap, joints crack. Her hands slid beneath her and touched her toes—no, joined them. The flesh of her body twisted. Breasts, arms, head, all flowed like some awful putty. A loop of it snagged Fulgit's wrist and he dropped the bottle. He shrieked, "No!" His hand melted into her, and more strands snaked around his throat, his back. The look on his face just before the thing broke his neck said it all: He'd thought he was in charge of this. His mass joined hers and the fleshy ring expanded. The frog people roared, wriggling, wobbling. The ring thinned as it grew. Out of the dark center of it, something began to emerge. Feelers protruded, twitching and alive, seeking purchase. They lashed to the edge of the stone slab and around the fleshy ring, and pulled. A thing like some enormous deformed squid slowly began to appear. Its bulbous, awful head pushed into view, a mouth edged in needle teeth, red eyes on stalks. It moved as if fighting against a relentless current. I turned and ran back up the tunnel.

Skidding into the coal tunnel, I found two more frog things approaching, come late to the party. Waving flashlights at me, they gawped and shook. One of them let loose a wordless bellow. I pulled both triggers on the shotgun, and the things erupted into geysers of blackish goop. The stink was worse than a sewer.

The thunder of the shot echoed everywhere. Now I was in for it. The other frogs would come hunting me while their squid god finished oozing into our world.

I reached Polly's Toyota. I popped the breech of the shotgun and reloaded, then laid it down and opened the trunk. Desperate for something I could use, I was rewarded with two oily rags. I took them, tied them together, then pulled off the gas cap and stuffed them down into the throat of the tank. I slammed the trunk, grabbed the gun, and got into the car.

The engine turned over, caught. I backed up and headed down the tunnel again, felt and heard the tires squish over the corpses just before I swung it into the new tunnel. The passenger side scraped one of the support pillars, snapping off the side mirror.

A few of the frog things had made it up the incline and now shambled toward me. They raised their stubby arms and yowled, goggle-eyed. I stopped the car, climbed out and shot them. I took my lighter out and lit the oily rag behind me. It caught quickly. I dropped the shotgun, got in again, revved the engine and released the brake. The car lurched forward. I floored the pedal, and the car raced for the top of the slope. The instant before it became airborne, I jumped. I hit sharp stones, slammed against the wall, but made myself get to my knees, then upright, as the Toyota sailed into the cavern. Something beyond it squealed.

I started to run back up the tunnel. Behind me, the car exploded, and I fell again, scraping my hands and knees further, got up and reached the shotgun as a second explosion shook the whole place. The end of the tunnel burned brightly with sprayed fuel. A chunk of roof collapsed beside me. I jumped, then watched a fissure split the ceiling all the way from the cavern and past me. I ran for my life then. Everything began falling in around me, and I pressed against one of the uprights, shielding my face, praying the support would hold. Dust drowned me. The gasoline blaze disappeared behind a solid wall of collapsed rock.

When it was over, I stood in a pocket that hadn't caved in. I was coughing so hard that I doubled over, and each cough was like an ice pick to my brain.

Ahead, part of the tunnel remained open, and by flashlight I made my way to where it was blocked. Took me half an hour to clear a passage through for myself. In that time I re-ran what had happened, what must have happened. Something had crashed here a hundred years ago, something that poisoned the population, maybe altering their DNA.

Was it waiting for a signal from somewhere, or just not strong enough till now? Or did the mutation have to work through successive generations? When the call had come, they'd all been drawn back to Dogget. It explained the cars, the license plates. I wondered if Hiram would have served as the goat if Polly Lutts hadn't inadvertently wandered into town. She'd fled one horror only to fall victim to another.

Squeezing through the hole I made, I discovered that the 1924 shaft had withstood the explosion intact. I muttered, wheezing, "Just don't build them like they used to." I stumbled up the tunnel and out into the night air. The stink of coal fires in the night was the smell of heaven.

The rolling landscape back toward the bar was now lit by small fires and half a dozen tendrils of smoke. The church tower had canted to the side. The coal tunnel must have collapsed beneath it, too.

I turned away and dragged my feet towards my car. My pants were ripped, knees bleeding, palms, too. I hawked and spat some crud from my lungs.

I got in. After a minute my head stopped hammering and I started the engine. I would have to take it easy on the way to Eccles, find a hospital there, pray my brain didn't seize up before that. Then, if I lived, I wanted a bath and a smoke and a drink. Only then would I call Albert Lutts and tell him his wife wasn't here anymore, and Dogget . . . Dogget had really gone downhill.

Patrick Thomas seems so normal . . . but his funny urban fantasy series, Murphy's Lore, is as wacky as they come, and some of the answers in his advice column, "Dear Cthulhu" (DearCthulhu@dearcthulhu.com), seem distinctly fishy. Here's Murphy's latest adventure!

(short fuse)
Patrick Thomas

I suppose there must be odder couples, but I hadn't seen one in a while. Jason Cervantes is an NYPD detective who tops out at about six foot four and that's when he's not in high heels. Bubba Sue is a gremlin from the South whose head wouldn't make it past the top of a yardstick in her best work boots.

Despite being on opposite ends of the height spectrum, the pair had been dating a few weeks. I got my updates on the progression of the relationship when they visited Bulfinche's Pub where I tend bar. I didn't expect to see them at the mall, especially sitting on a bench making out, as both are many years removed from teenagedom, but love and lust are a pair of splendid things.

Jas's back was to me and Bubba Sue was positioned on his lap, with her face stuck to his, but pointed in my general direction. I walked toward them, debating if passing by would be ruder than interrupting when Bubba Sue's eyes opened and she spotted me. The gremlin pulled her head back and looked at Jas. In an exaggeratedly childlike voice she said, "Daddy, why do you always kiss me with your tongue like that?"

Jas's ears turned beet red as a mother with a child yanked her son away, beating a quick retreat from the odd couple.

"Young lady, is this cross-dressing man bothering you?" I said in a disguised voice. "Want me to call a cop?"

Without turning back to look, Jas reached in his pocket and flipped his badge at me. "Beat it, buddy. She's a short, but grown woman with a very twisted sense of humor."

"What a fake badge. Like the NYPD would let a cop dress in drag." Actually he got no end of grief for it, but there was a high-stakes bet involved so he toughed it out.

The muscles in Jas's jaw tightened and the color in his ears darkened. He stood up so fast that Bubba Sue practically plopped on the floor. He was in two-inch heels, which put him at an imposing height compared to my five foot eleven.

Jas spun, realized it was me and sighed. "Hello, Murphy."

"Hi, Jas, Bubba Sue," I said.

"Hiya, Murph." Bubba Sue leapt off the floor, wrapped her legs around my rib cage and her hands around my shoulders, and planted a smack of a kiss on my lips.

We'd said hello many times before, so I knew what to do next. I cupped my hands together, she swung her right foot into the support, and back-flipped neatly away to land facing me. A tall man with bushy hair clapped as he passed by, and Bubba Sue took a bow.

"Why do I put up with this?" Jas said, but he had a smile on his face.

"Because I rock your world and women's clothes on a man don't phase me," Bubba Sue said. "So, Murph, what brings you to the mall?"

"The subway and a bus." Jas rolled his eyes but Bubba Sue's lips curled upward. "Terrorbelle's got a birthday coming up next week and I need a gift. What about you two?"

"Lingerie shopping," Bubba Sue said. "For both of us."

Jas gently smacked her shoulder and glared at her, but she only laughed.

"He gets to pick out one outfit for me if I get to pick out one for him. I'm thinking something with handcuffs and a cop hat."

"I have both at home," Jas said, his voice barely a whisper as his eyes darted back and forth as if looking out for anyone else he knew that he might want to hide from.

"Then maybe something with tassels," Bubba Sue said. "I'd like to see you get them going in two directions at once."

"I will if you will," Jas said.

"Deal."

We definitely had passed the point of too much information, so I started to excuse myself, but Bubba Sue spoke before I could.

"So, Murphy, you want to join us? I could help you pick something out for T-Belle's birthday if you like."

"We're friends," I said. "You don't buy lingerie for friends. I'd never buy a corset for Paddy."

"I'd pick something guaranteed to change that," Bubba Sue said with a conspiratorial wiggling of her eyebrows.

"With Paddy or T-belle?"

"Either."

"I'd pay to see you give Paddy a corset," Jas said.

My leprechaun boss is a little uptight in some areas. The suggestion that he wear women's undergarments would undoubtedly be one of them, despite the fact that he's the one with the cross-dressing bet with Jason.

"I'd pay to see him give one to Terrorbelle," Bubba Sue said. She wasn't doing Shakespeare, but Bubba Sue was definitely doing a king-sized leer. "She'd probably break him in two saying thanks."

"She might at that," Jas said. Terrorbelle was equal parts ogre and pixie. Not only was she taller than me, but she was more than a little broader. T-Belle could lift me over her head with one hand without much effort. "But she'd make sure he went out with a smile on his face."

Terrorbelle's said as much herself, minus the breaking me in half part. It wasn't a step I was willing to take just yet.

"I think I'll handle the gift giving on my own. You two have fun now," I said. "And leave me out of it. That means no gifts sent to Paddy with my name on them. I'd like to stay in one piece and employed, thank you."

"If we have to," Bubba Sue said. "By the way, Murph, do you know if they have locks on the dressing room doors?"

"I'm not sure, but they might have cameras." I was never a fan of the fact that dressing rooms monitor people trying on clothes. Most of the mirrors are two-way. Easy way to tell: Hold a pencil point up to the mirror. If it touches its reflection, chances are someone on the other side is watching you. I usually stick my tongue out to say hi.

"Tech I can handle," Bubba Sue said. It was the understatement of the week. Most gremlins can take apart tech, but Bubba Sue can also put it back together and make it do things its designers never imagined. I was peripherally involved once when she disarmed a nuclear missile while it was in flight. Disabling a surveillance camera would be as easy for her as mixing a martini was for me. "A camera would be great. I can get into their security system and make some copies of the footage. I hope you're not shy, Mr. Cervantes."

"I don't consider myself shy, but compared to you I might have to re-evaluate that," Jas said.

"Of course, it won't matter if they don't have my size." Bubba Sue was tiny, but exceptionally curvy, pretty much everywhere a woman should be. "Fortunately, they're supposed to have a little people section that is the best in the tri-state area. Not to mention a big and tall section for my boo here. Now that I've had time to think about it, I may select something in leather, spandex and fishnets for him."

"That's a visual I'm going to have a hard time getting out of my mind," I said with a small shiver.

"Come in with us and I'll have him model for you. That'll cement the image forever."

"Yeah, in my nightmares," I said. "You coming by Bulfinche's later?"

"He's off until 11 AM tomorrow, so I doubt we'll be setting foot outside his apartment before ten."

"Again, that's more than I needed to know." I waved as they went into the lingerie store. Bubba Sue was skipping and Jas was half covering his face, but his pace was brisk.

I trekked up and down the mall searching for a gift, with no luck. As I looped back past the lingerie shop, I was nearly knocked over by people running out. Never one to follow the crowd, even in cases where it is probably the best idea, I crept inside to see what was going on. I was working on the assumption that Bubba Sue had reverted to her trickster nature and was having the animated manikins do bizarre things to each other.

That would have been an improvement over what was happening.

The first thing I noticed was Jas in a cheerleader outfit and Bubba Sue spilling out of a leather corset and matching shorts. The next was the reason for the mass exodus.

Amid the racks of frivolous, mostly transparent clothing stood a brown-haired young woman in a heavy black trench coat. She wouldn't have been out of place at Bulfinche's Pub, as trench coats fit the mindset of some of the patrons and hid the unusual physical features of others. However, at the mall, on this warm a day, she stood out like a sore thumb. Even more unusual was the bomb she had strapped to her chest and the plastic cylinder in the palm of her left hand. And what stood out even more than a sore thumb was her actual thumb, the knuckle of which was white from pressing the top of the cylinder down like she was afraid to let it go. Several people cowered behind the store's counter, afraid that the angry lady with the explosives might let go of the tube and go boom if they made a break for the door.

The exceptions were Jas, Bubba Sue and a man who was on his knees scowling. A second bomb was attached around his chest and neck. His predicament could have been the reason for his unhappy expression, but it looked too natural there for me to say for sure.

I pulled out my cell to call for backup. Jas saw me and shook his head no. I had no idea why. If Paddy could get a hold of Hermes, the god could be in and out with the bombs before anyone could blink. Still, Jas was a good cop, regardless of how ridiculous he currently looked. I knew he had a plan. I wondered if he had his gun hidden in one of his pom-poms. Or if the 'no' was just to discourage me from snapping a picture of him in his current outfit. Even for a man who wore women's clothing on a semi-regular basis, the cheerleader outfit was embarrassing.

The woman was yelling at the man to give back what he stole, and she hadn't noticed me, so I ducked down to hide in a clothes rack. It was already occupied by the gentleman who had applauded Bubba Sue's dismount. I waved. He waved back and offered me his hand.

"I'm Dan Clyne," he whispered.

"John Murphy." I hoped the woman's screaming would drown out our voices. "What's going on?"

"She's upset," Dan said. "He cheated on her and got her deported."

And upset she was. She was figuratively blowing her top. Hopefully we'd figure out a way to stop her from doing it literally.

"The guy in the cheerleader outfit is a cop. The short woman can defuse a bomb." I hoped. It was tech after all. "I'm going to cause a distraction. Are you up for trying to get the people behind the counter out?"

"She'll see us," Dan said.

"I once had a job in this mall." Back when my late wife Elsie had been going through chemo, we had no insurance. Not unusual for a just-barely not-starving artist and her even hungrier husband the writer. I had as many jobs as I could handle to get extra money to try to cover her medical bills. It wasn't enough, but in this instance my experience was coming in handy. "There are corridors behind all the stores. The back storeroom should have a door. Take everyone out that way."

"Are you going to be okay?"

"Sure," I said, not certain if it was a lie.

"Okay," Dan said, with not a squawk about the risk. Who says New Yorkers don't help others?

"Good luck," I whispered.

"You too."

I crawled out of the lingerie rack, staying low until I reached the opposite side of the store so Dan would have a better shot of getting the people out. I grabbed a slinky red teddy on a hanger and stood up.

"Excuse me, miss?" I said. "Do you have this in a 42 long?"

Bomb lady turned toward me, her expression making it clear she thought I was an idiot. I got that a lot. "I don't work here."

"That's good, because I would have to question your taste for letting that woman wear that cheerleader outfit. It's not flattering." I put my hand alongside my face and stage-whispered, "Makes her look like a man."

"It is a man!"

"Well, it takes all types I suppose," I said. Dan had commando crawled his way over to the folks behind the counter. "No idea where I could find this in another size, then? Maybe in a nice plaid? It's my favorite color."

The woman turned toward me so I couldn't miss the explosives. As an added benefit, she couldn't see Dan ushering the people toward the storeroom.

"Miss, do you realize you have what looks like a bomb strapped to your chest?"

"Of course, you idiot," she said. "I put it there."

I'm an expert at annoying people. The majority of folks feel the need to correct me at length. I just had to keep her from noticing the hostage exodus, although she hardly seemed to be a professional or to have even thought this out very well. And maybe the correcting would also take her mind off any thoughts of detonation.

"Why?" I asked. "Is it the latest style? If you don't mind my saying, it's not a flattering look and simply not your color. A woman as pretty as yourself in a place like this could find dozens of much better outfits. I'd say you're an autumn. Maybe something in yellow?"

"You think I'm pretty?" The bomber brushed her hair behind her ear and actually smiled.

"Yes," I said. "Although the anger on your face and that bomb distract from it a bit."

"See, he thinks I'm pretty." She kicked the kneeling man in the thigh. He fell forward but oddly reached out to hold his hair. And not terribly good hair at that. "But that wasn't enough for you, was it?"

The man smirked. "Did I say you were pretty? Was I drunk at the time?"

She smacked him. "No, you said I was the sexiest, most beautiful woman you had ever met. But that didn't stop you from sleeping around, did it, Kev? I caught you and what did you do? First you fired me. Then you used your factory security to take my purse, my money, credit cards and driver's license. You ripped my engagement ring off my finger. When I started to cry, you wanted to get me to shut up so the rest of the workers didn't see the scene I was making, so you gave me a drink. Next thing I know I'm waking up on a deportation flight out of Kennedy on the way to Mexico City."

"You didn't have a job. No job means you couldn't stay in the country."

"I was born in this country, you idiot." Her face was turning crimson and two veins had popped out on her forehead. "I'm a citizen. I can't be deported."

"Obviously, you could." Kev smirked again.

"You drugged me then called your brother to get rid of me." She jabbed her index finger in front of his face like a dagger.

"Tilly," Kev said, "there's no way Mike would jeopardize his position at ICE to do something like that."

Tilly threw her head back and yelled that his statement was an oversized load of bovine excrement. Then she stomped away. Kev crossed his arms over his chest, looking very pleased with himself. Meanwhile, Dan was helping an older lady get out the back door.

"ICE?" I asked.

"U.S. Immigration and Customs Enforcement," Jas said. "Part of Homeland Security."

"Well, someone put me on that plane and faked the paperwork. I woke up on the flight and federal agents refused to believe I was an American citizen. They cuffed me and put me through Mexican customs with only the clothes on my back. I don't even speak Spanish! You have no idea what I had to do to get back into the US!"

"No," Kev said. "And neither do you. You're insane. That could never happen."

"Actually, it happens," Jas said. "The Vera Institute of Justice released a report that alleged there were at least 125 people in immigration detention centers who had valid U.S. citizenship claims. And several have turned out to be correct, so maybe she's telling the truth."

Kev's face wrinkled up and he stared at us in disbelief. "You are going to believe a stalker with a bomb over me?"

Bubba Sue and I looked at each other.

"Yep," she said.

"Pretty much," I said.

"See? You're going to get what's coming to you," Tilly said.

Kev tilted back his head and let rip some very impressive mocking laughter. I half expected him to bend forward and start rubbing his hands together like some bad villain. "You think the word of a domestic terrorist is going to hold up in court? Think again."

Tilly slapped him across the face.

Kev spat at her. "You whine a lot. You threatened me. I was just protecting myself. I'm not going to apologize for it. I had an affair? So what? All guys do it. I didn't owe you anything. As for the ring, I paid a lot of money for that rock. I wasn't going to let it go to waste on your dumpy hand. And I had put a lot of things in your name for tax purposes. I couldn't have you getting to the bank before I did. But I have no idea about this deportation thing." The smirk on his face said otherwise.

"Wow, you're such a great guy," I said.

Dan waved to me and quietly closed the storeroom door behind him.

"Mind your own business," Kev said.

"Nope. I think I'll mind yours for a while," I said. "I'll only charge you ten bucks an hour plus snacks." I put the teddy back on the rack. "Tilly, I understand your anger and the impulse to hurt Kev, but why hurt yourself?"

"I loved him and he broke my heart. Have you ever had your heart broken?"

"Yes," I said.

"I doubt it was anything like mine," she said.

"No, his was worse," Bubba Sue said.

"You heard what he did to me," the woman snapped. "How could it be worse?"

"His wife, the woman he loved more than life itself, died."

Tilly looked at me. "Is that true?"

I nodded.

"How?"

"Leukemia. Elsie was my world. When she died, the most important parts of me felt like they died with her."

"You got over her?" she asked.

"Nope, but it got easier to be without her. I learned to live again. I found people and a job I love. These days I spend my time helping people, even if it's just by making them laugh. I'd like to help you too, if you'll let me."

"Fine." Tilly put her free hand on her hip. "Go ahead. Make me laugh."

"Okay, but remember you asked for it." Being funny comes naturally to me, but being put on the spot does tend to make me a little nervous. Better not to think about it, so I took a deep breath and plunged forward. "Is that a bomb in your pocket or are you just happy to see me? After what Kev did to you, blowing him off makes sense, but blowing him up seems a little extreme. I mean look at him. If brains were dynamite, he couldn't blow his nose. I'm sure he's a real treasure. I'll help you bury him. I'm not sure what you ever saw in him. Is that a toupee or did a cat vomit a hairball on his head? He's so ugly—"

"Do you mind?" Kev self-consciously touched his hair and started to get up from his knees. Tilly kicked his legs out from under him and held up the dead man switch threateningly. Kev lay still.

"Do I mind that you not only screwed around on this nice woman but screwed her over so royally that she feels this is her only option? Yes, actually I do mind. And then deporting her on top of it?" I turned to Tilly. "Hell, this isn't the best way to get even. It's over too quick. Forget the bomb. If you really want him to suffer, get a lawyer."

"Nobody will believe her cock-and-bull story about my brother somehow having her magically deported to another country. Where's the proof? I'll sue her for slander. My lawyers will bury her."

"My, you are dumb. Gravediggers bury people, not lawyers. I mean unless maybe they had a night job, but in my experience there's not a lot of crossover between the two professions. Keep it up if you want to see who'll bury what's left of you." I pointed to the bomb he wore. "Not that it sounds like it would be that much of a tragedy for the world at large. I'm just thinking of the poor gravedigger. With no body to bury, how will he feed his family?"

"Tilly is a stupid tramp with a wild imagination," he said, "and got what she deserved. She can't even satisfy a man."

"How would you know who she can satisfy? Have you ever seen her with a real man? Not only are you the worst fiancé and boss ever, but you're a peeping tom as well. I bet you kick puppies, rip the wings off of flies and have a flashy sports car to make up for personal deficiencies."

"Hey!" Kev grabbed his belt buckle. "I'll drop 'em right here."

"Please don't. I just ate," I said. "Just tell us what you drive."

Under his breath he muttered, "A 'vette."

"Bingo," I said.

Tilly smiled and gave the tiniest snort of a laugh.

"This is all a joke," he said. "She doesn't have the brains to make a bomb."

"I know how to use the internet," Tilly said.

"Maybe, but you don't have the guts to blow me up."

"Actually if she blows you up," I said, "she'll have all the guts she'll need. Of course, they'll be yours."

"This is all a desperate cry for attention, a ploy for me to take you back. Take the bomb off me and you can come home."

Tilly stood there, lowering her left hand and the switch. She was really thinking about it.

"Oh no, girlfriend, you aren't going back to that," Bubba Sue said. "He's something that doesn't deserve to be on the bottom of your shoe. You got off lucky."

Jas and I both looked at her. Sure, he was a nasty piece of work, but if this got the bombs off both of them, it was worth the deception. We could sort the rest out later.

"Lucky? What part of this is lucky?" Tilly tilted her head to accentuate her point.

"You could have married him first," Bubba Sue said.

"True," Tilly said.

"May I talk to these gentlemen alone for a second, dear?" Bubba Sue asked. Tilly looked at her nervously. "Don't worry. We aren't going yet. I personally wouldn't leave you alone with him."

Tilly seemed to be judging if Bubba Sue was on the level. "All right."

Bubba Sue motioned for us to join her by a rack of corsets.

"Nice outfit, Jas," I said. "NYPD have a cheer squad now?"

"No, but I'm working on it," Jas shot back. He turned to Bubba Sue. "Why didn't you let him convince her to kiss and make up so we could get the explosives?"

"Because the bombs are fakes," she said.

"You sure?" Jas asked.

Bubba Sue nodded. "Her dead man switch is the nunchuk handle from a Wii with the wire cut off. The tubes are junk with some dollar-store electronics. There's no power source or explosives. It won't blow up. It can't. But there is a digital recorder in there. She's just trying to get a confession in a real bad way. I don't think she planned to hurt anybody. We need to get her some self respect and make him pay at the same time."

"So I can call for help?" I said.

Bubba Sue nodded. "Jas was going with the NYPD playbook. With an unknown bomb, there should be no radio or cell signals because they could trigger the explosives. But hold off on the call. We can handle this ourselves."

"Then we need to do it fast," Jas said. "Someone has to have called 911. SWAT will probably be here soon, and I'd prefer to end this fast so nobody gets shot." He paused to look down at his cheer ensemble. "And I'd like to be out of this outfit before that happens."

"I'd like you to be out of it too." Bubba Sue gave him the once over and pinched his butt.

"Me too," I said, "but for a different reason. That short skirt really doesn't do anything for you."

"It does for me." Bubba Sue wiggled her eyebrows lasciviously then got serious. "We're all in agreement that Kev's the one deserving of punishment, not her?" We were. "I have a plan on how to do that. Jas, hang back. Murphy, you're with me."

"You're picking Murphy over me to deal with a hostage situation?" His voice went up half an octave. "I'm a trained and decorated detective."

"Yep, those pom-poms sure make great decorations," I said. "Have you considered a Christmas wreath as a necklace?"

Jas's hand shot out to point at me. "Murphy, this is serious—"

"Which is why Murphy will be more helpful for what I have planned. He has more of a trickster mentality than you do. And he's survived multiple Fools' Days."

Every April 1st many tricksters of legend meet at Bulfinche's Pub to see who has pulled off the best prank of the day. It tends to get messy. I always make it out intact and even helped save the world once. Gives me trickster street cred.

"Here's my plan," Bubba Sue said.

It was a doozy.

"I like it, but can you pull it off?"

Bubba Sue grinned mischievously. "Can you?"

"I'll give it my best shot," I said. Bubba Sue told Jas to get dressed in his man clothes that he kept in his man bag, aka his purse, while she and I returned to the unhappy ex-couple.

"Tilly, can we speak for a moment, girl to girl?" Bubba Sue asked in a sweet Southern drawl. "I think you'll like what I have to say."

"Okay," Tilly said as the pair disappeared behind a rack.

I stepped toward the scumbag. "Quick, while she's not looking, let's get you out of here."

Kev was taken aback. "You've been insulting me since you got here and now you want to help me?"

"She has a bomb," I said. "You think I'm going to side with you?" Kev seemed to buy it. I helped him to his feet and slid off his jacket. Playing my hunch, I grabbed his hair and pulled. "And your toupee."

"Hey!" he yelled, making a grab for his stolen hair substitute.

I put the rug on my head and donned the coat. "Shh. I'll take your place and let you get away."

"But the bomb . . ."

"If you get far enough away, she won't be able to trigger it," I said, grabbing a brown wig with a style similar to Tilly's hairdo off a manikin, and a black silk robe from the rack. "Put these on so she won't recognize you if she spots you leaving. I'll stay here." I got on my knees next to him, put the man wig on my head and pulled the jacket on.

"Why would you do this for me?" he said.

"She can't blow me up unless she gets close enough, and I'll run before I let that happen. I just want to make sure you get what you deserve, and who deserves to be blown up?"

He bought it, and without a word of thanks, put on the wig and robe and broke for the door. He had no clue that he looked a lot like the description of the female mall bomber with the brown hair and black trench coat.

Bubba Sue cut him off at the pass. She grabbed his robe and pulled him down, making him hold onto a metal rack to keep from falling. "Get down! You don't want her to see you."

"Let me go," Kev said, crawling as if he were competing in a horse race. When he was out in the mall proper, at which point he stood and ran.

"Glad to." Bubba Sue grinned, sprinkling talcum powder on the rack's metal bars. Then she placed pieces of scotch tape over the sweaty residue his hands left behind. She pulled each off and held them up to the light. "Beautiful."

Now came the tricky part. The mall had been evacuated and police had cordoned off the building and were waiting on SWAT and the bomb squad. We wanted Kev to pay for his misdeeds, but we didn't want him to go down in a hail of bullets.

Bubba Sue hacked into the mall's security cameras so we could watch everything. Jas, now in guy clothes, hustled Tilly out the back corridor in a new outfit and ponytail, using his badge to get her past his fellow cops.

He then went in the front door of the mall and met Kev coming out. Out of earshot, but in plain sight, he removed the so-called bomb, placed it on the floor and walked Kev out where he was promptly set upon and arrested by the waiting officers.

Kev protested his innocence, but couldn't produce any identification.

After years of being pick-pocketed by the god Hermes, I developed my own wallet lifting skills in self-defense. While not as good as the god of thieves, I could make a disrespectable living if I ever decided on a life of petty crime. Kev had been too concerned with the loss of his hair to notice my lifting his billfold.

When Kev got to the station, they ran his prints and, lo and behold, he came up as a suspected terrorist. Considering Bubba Sue only got to the station a few minutes ahead of him, her planting the information with the lifted prints was impressive. Fortunately, gremlins have a gift for blending in, so none of New York's finest noticed her or what she was doing.

When his brother came to bail him out, they took him into custody and ran his prints also, because of the warning to look out for the brother of the terrorist. His prints came up a suspected terrorist match as well, but only because Bubba Sue had rigged the reader to have that response to the next inquiry.

Tilly lawyered up and got her life back. And ownership of the factory. Once they were in court, Kev and his brother had the questionable pleasure of learning that sometimes, the truth does not set you free. Posting an incriminating hacked video on YouTube that showed the brothers handing an unconscious Tilly over to ICE agents at Kennedy Airport didn't hurt either.

And best of all, I never had to see Jason in Bubba Sue's final choice of lingerie.

John Passarella and I have known each other for longer than either cares to remember. I have a soft spot for his character Wendy Ward, as her story in some ways began in Between Books. I am very proud to present a new tale from the bedeviled town of Windale, MA.

(blood alone)
John Passarella

After an exhausting three days, the New England Fantasy Worlds Convention withdrew from Windale—taking with it the crowds of tourists dressed as medieval wenches, witches, wizards and elves—much to Kayla's relief. Wendy appreciated all the extra business that had flowed through the Crystal Path over the long weekend, but Kayla had never before welcomed a Monday with such intense gratitude. Simply tolerating Mondays was her usual limit, and never with any grace or good cheer. But this Monday was different. Her bruised ribs were safe from the army of elbows, her throbbing toes from the procession of boots. She could talk without yelling to be heard. And she could breathe again—which was why she volunteered to pick up supplies for the Crystal Path's break room. The new Stop-N-Go mini mart was three blocks from the store and Kayla thought the crisp February air would be refreshing.

She walked up and down the aisles, a red plastic shopping basket dangling from her left arm. She grabbed snack-sized bags of chips and pretzels, candy bars, along with coffee and tea supplies and individual bottles of water and soda until the basket overflowed. With her attention on the shelves, she almost didn't notice the middle-aged woman in a red wool coat walking toward her, a vacant look on her pale face.

"Oh, hi, Mrs. Shanley!" Kayla said. "We got in that foil-embossed tarot deck you asked us to order. Stop by and pick it up on your way . . ."

Millicent Shanley walked by without pausing.

"Whoa! Mrs. Shanley, are you okay?" Kayla hurried after her, caught her shoulder and moved in front of her again. "Is something wrong?"

The woman fussed with the collar of her coat, as if the button had recently fallen off. Her vacant gaze drifted toward Kayla's face, but Kayla saw no hint of recognition in her eyes. She spoke softly, in a monotone. "Forgotten why I came here."

"Happens to me all the time," Kayla said. "Usually when—"

"Excuse me."

Again the woman walked past her.

"Don't forget the tarot deck!" Kayla called.

Shaking her head, Kayla dumped her brimming basket onto the counter. The bored sales clerk—a guy with more facial piercings than Kayla and an Egyptian hieroglyphic tattoo on the side of his neck—waved a bar code scanner over the items, eliciting a series of beeps, and dropped them in a succession of flimsy plastic bags.

"What's up with her?" Kayla asked the guy.

"Drugs. Dementia." He shrugged. "Could give a fuck."

"Great attitude," Kayla said as she pulled two crumpled twenties out of her jeans to pay the bill. "You'll go far."

"Minimum wage shithole," he said, repeating his shrug. "Can't get out of here soon enough." He counted out her change methodically and slid the singles and coins across the counter, dropping her receipt on top. "Thanks," he muttered. "Come again."

"Right," Kayla said and rolled her eyes. As she pocketed her change and the receipt, she glanced toward the back of the store. Millicent Shanley was staring at a wire rack stuffed with maps. She appeared to be talking to herself. The clerk lounged on a stool, flipping through a skin magazine, oblivious to his surroundings. *Must be new in town,* Kayla thought. Apathy was unsustainable in Windale. When you live where monsters roam, you learn to be vigilant. Or else—

"A zombie?" Wendy Ward asked skeptically. She swept the fingers of her right hand through her auburn hair, tucking a loose strand behind her ear.

Kayla shook her head. "Not a literal zombie. She had that thousand-yard stare. Lights on but nobody home."

"So she was distracted?"

"Worse than that," Kayla said. "She didn't recognize me."

"You can't be serious," Abby MacNeil Nottingham said, chuckling. She had turned eighteen a month ago, and had been working with them at the Crystal Path for almost a year. But Wendy had known her much longer than that, long enough to watch her transform from lonely girl to attractive young woman. Looking at the lithe, tow-headed blonde with sparkling blue eyes, an outsider would never guess Abby could also transform at will into a white wolf or a red-tailed hawk. "Kayla, how is that even possible?"

Abby was right. Nobody ever forgot Kayla's face. The facial piercings were secondary to the shock of cobalt blue hair with the white streak—Wendy called it her racing stripe—arching over her right ear.

"Exactly," Kayla said. She took a deep breath and said what they were all thinking. "I think she's one of them."

"No," Wendy said, pressing her palms against her ears in her best impression of the hear-no-evil monkey. "Maybe she's absentminded."

"She's staring at Kayla," Abby said.

"What?" Kayla followed the direction of Abby's gaze to the front of the shop. Through the Plexiglas door, she saw a familiar red wool coat. Millicent Shanley stood immobile, staring at Kayla.

"Okay," Kayla said. "She's officially creeping me out."

"Join the club," Abby said.

Wendy looked at the woman expectantly. Not a visible threat. But something wasn't right. The fingers of her right hand drifted to the multi-bead bracelet she wore on her left. Over the past few years, she had broken her dependency on the bracelet to perform magic, but she still took comfort in its presence against her skin. "Let her in."

"Door's unlocked," Kayla said. "Sign says, 'We're Open.'"

"Let's force her hand."

Kayla shrugged. "She's probably just here for her tarot cards."

She strode to the door and opened it wide. "C'mon in," she said cheerfully. "Here for your tarot cards?"

"You're Kayla Zanella," Mrs. Shanley said. "You work here."

"And you shop here," Kayla said, her sarcasm lost on the woman. But Wendy could tell Kayla was nervous. She might not know what to expect, but she'd been conditioned to expect the worst. "Follow me. I'll ring you up."

Millicent Shanley trailed Kayla to the cash register island.

Abby crouched behind the display case facing the front window. From among the shelves featuring crystal balls and figurines, Celtic and Wiccan jewelry, and various stones and gems used in magic rituals, she removed a deck of the foil-embossed tarot cards the woman had ordered when she stopped in the Crystal Path two weeks ago. "Here you go," Abby said, handing the deck to Kayla as she stepped behind the counter.

While Kayla rang up the purchase, Wendy observed the woman's behavior. Millicent pressed her left hand against the collar of her coat while she reached into the right hip pocket with her free hand and removed a change purse. She ducked her head as she withdrew a twenty and two ones. "Is that enough?" she asked absently, even though Kayla had stated the total a moment before. Kayla nodded and gave the woman her change.

"Have a good day, Mrs. Shanley," Wendy said.

Millicent's head rose slowly in Wendy's direction. As her eyes fixed on Wendy's face, they opened so wide that Wendy saw the whites were rimmed with inflamed capillaries. She had the impression the woman hadn't slept in days.

An insomniac? Wendy wondered. *No more than that?*

"You're Wendy Ward," the woman said, as if it were a revelation.

"You've been coming here for two years, Mrs. Shanley."

"Yes," she said. "Yes, I have."

Without saying another word, she turned and walked out of the store with long, purposeful strides.

A moment after she was gone, Kayla exhaled forcefully. "Tell me that wasn't odd."

"You're right," Wendy said. "She fits the pattern. Something weird is happening to the people of Windale."

"Wait here!" Abby ran past the half-empty racks of exotic and fantasy-inspired clothing that had enchanted the convention goers, and ducked into the break room. She returned moments later carrying a three-by-two corkboard over which she had taped a map of Windale. "I made this last night." She placed the bulletin board on the glass countertop and turned it toward Wendy. "See that?" she said, indicating a rough grouping of a dozen red pushpins.

"Looks like the letter C," Wendy said.

"For creepy?" Kayla shrugged. "Crazy? Crackpots?"

"Not a letter," Abby said. "More like a semicircle. The pins mark the addresses of the people we've witnessed acting bizarrely. Plus a few we've heard about second-hand. There could be more—probably are more—but these are the ones we know about."

Wendy's index finger hovered over the opening in the C. "The effect radiates outward from here." She looked up, grinning. "Abby, you've found the focal point."

"Let's not jump to conclusions," Kayla said. "There could be a simple explanation. Tainted ground water. Toxic waste dumping. Psychotropic mushrooms. This doesn't have to be part of Wither's curse."

Wendy shook her head. "I wish I could believe that."

"This has been going on for a couple weeks," Kayla said. "And no one— no *thing*—has attacked you. Right?"

"She's got a point," Abby said. "Supernaturally speaking, it's been uneventful here for quite a while."

Fifteen months, Wendy thought, *since the last attack triggered by Wither's dying curse.* The longest gap in several years. It had seemed too good to be true. And perhaps it was.

Wendy had studied the intervals between attacks, thinking the lengths of the gaps might provide some clue about how the curse worked and how she might break it. After she defeated Yuki-Onna in January 2005, nine months passed before Black Annis, the one-eyed, blue-faced hag arrived in Windale. "Black Annis was October 2005."

Kayla nodded. "The one we trapped in that old barn with the handbells my mom, um, *liberated* from church."

"Yes," Wendy said. "And ten months later, in August 2006, it was the Ho'ok demon."

Abby snapped her fingers. "Alex, in the parking lot, with a Molotov cocktail."

"You guys missed out on that fun," Wendy said. "Alex was so nervous, I was afraid he'd accidentally torch *me* with one of those things."

Kayla quirked a smile. "Not the way he tells it." In a deep voice, she said, "'A lone warrior with ice in his veins and fire in his hands.'"

Wendy laughed. "Yeah, well, he watches too much Sports Center. Anyway, we had a whole eleven months of sanity until May 2007 and the lamia."

"Eww," Abby squealed and shuddered. "Don't remind me! You smashed those eyeballs like soft-boiled eggs. And the head chopping—and the body ooze . . ."

"Yuck!" Kayla grimaced. "Glad I wasn't around for that one."

"We only had six months after that," Wendy said.

"November 2007," Kayla said. "The shape-shifting ghoul."

"Bzzzt! Wrong answer," Abby said. "Not a shape-shifting ghoul. A *glamourous* ghoul. I should know, being a shape-shifter myself."

"She got you on a technicality," Wendy said to Kayla. The ghoul had never actually changed its shape. It had projected a series of innocuous human glamours to disguise its true appearance. All of Wendy's warriors—as Alex would probably call them—had a hand in defeating it. "That was the last one. Fifteen months ago."

"What about Alethea?" Abby asked. "June 2008."

Wendy shook her head sadly, remembering the gentle grace of Alethea Brynn Cavendish. The old woman had stepped briefly into Wendy's life—had saved her life—and left a huge impression on her. If not for Wither's curse, Wendy would have met Alethea under much different circumstances. The woman might have been Wendy's mentor in magic. "Alethea isn't part of the Wither curse timeline," Wendy said. "She came on her own, to help."

"Right," Abby said softly. "So, fifteen months, curse-free. Maybe it's finally lost its mojo."

Fifteen months since I watched the ghoul burn, Wendy thought. She had never consciously assumed the curse was over. But somewhere inside her, hope had begun to grow, a belief that the curse had . . . failed. Right. Who was she kidding? She couldn't afford false optimism. "Let's face it," Wendy said. "It's much more likely that the creature summoned after the ghoul died is simply taking longer than usual to reach Windale."

"It's insane that you have to live your life this way," Kayla said.

"That's what Alex always says."

"You two okay?" Abby asked.

"Same old argument," Wendy said. Alex was back in Minneapolis, his home town, interviewing with a biotech firm. Said if he got an offer, he wanted them to relocate—as if that would solve anything. Wendy could sell the Crystal Path and leave Windale, but she'd still have a magical bull's-eye on her back. Why bring living nightmares to another unsuspecting city? "He wants the big commitment, the ceremony and the happily ever after. I want to end the curse first."

"No luck with Wither's journal?"

Wendy shook her head. Wither's recovered journal, what was left of it after the wendigo attack, had been magically encrypted, indecipherable to the human eye. Border vision, the magical ability that allowed Wendy to see through a demonic glamour, allowed her to read Wither's recorded thoughts. If there had been pages devoted to the application or revocation of the curse, they were not among the sections that remained. Nor was the mechanism or cure for Hannah's rapid aging. Temporally, Hannah was a few months past nine years of age but physically, emotionally and mentally she was three times that, close to Wendy's twenty-seven years, at least in the present—Wendy's present.

As if thinking of Hannah were a means of summoning her future-self, Wendy saw the kindly apparition of the Crone resolve before the cash register, her translucency somewhere between mist and smoke. Wendy could tell by the others' reactions that they could see the manifestation of the old woman as well. "Hannah," Wendy said, delighted. "I was just thinking about you."

The Crone's voice was haunting and filled with remorse. *"My thoughts are with you as well,"* she said. *"All of you."*

"Hi," Abby said, executing a tentative wave.

"Hey," Kayla said, feigning composure.

Knowing the Crone's visits were often brief, Wendy addressed the current problem. "We've noticed something strange happening to the people here."

Hannah's future-self nodded. *"Something is happening at your point in time. But the events are obscured. Unnaturally so."*

The Crone's revelations about past events—Wendy's present—had a tendency to alter the timeline, which cast the Crone's perception of those past events in doubt as soon as she revealed them. Time was fluid and there were few certainties. The timeline they shared accommodated small changes, but not major shifts. As a result, key events tied to major shifts were blurred in the Crone's memory. To the Crone's perception, this was normal. So what constituted *unnatural?*

"Not sure what you mean."

"Whoever is affecting these people is also . . . clouding my perception."

"Intentionally?" Kayla asked nervously.

"In the future?" Abby wondered.

The Crone shook her head. *"No. There. Then. A natural—that is,* super-natural *defense. Probably instinctive, but possibly premeditated."*

"What else can you tell us?" Wendy asked.

"That your foe is compelled by Wither's curse."

Wendy glanced at Kayla. "That settles that."

Kayla stuck out her tongue.

"Unfortunately, I do not know the nature of the foe or how you should prepare yourself."

"Not good," Wendy said. Over the years, she'd come to depend upon the Crone's early warning system. Maybe too much. Would she be able to adapt without any foreknowledge? "Okay, we'll deal with it. We've had lots of practice. Thanks for telling us what you could. I know it takes great effort for you to make these trips to my time."

"There's more."

"More would be good," Kayla said.

"You must act soon. Whatever your foe is, it can influence and overpower the minds of others. It is cunning."

The Crone's misty blue eyes closed. Wendy thought she was about to fade away, giving into exhaustion, but her eyes opened again and she looked at Wendy with growing concern. *"One of you is in grave danger."*

Kayla quirked an eyebrow. "No surprise there."

Wendy held up her hand, palm outward to silence Kayla. She turned back to the Crone, sensing that the old woman was holding something back. "Go on."

"I sense two timelines, fighting for control, one much worse than the other," the Crone said. *"Wendy, as always, you are at the center of it, but you are not alone. Your friends, these two, are intertwined in these two timelines."*

"I can send them away," Wendy said. "Right now. Take them out of the equation."

But the Crone was shaking her head before Wendy completed the thought. *"Their absence, as easily as their presence, could cause the more troubling timeline. They are instrumental in the events to come."* The apparition sighed and lost some consistency. *"My words have become as nebulous as my form. I wish I could tell you more. Be safe . . ."*

She was gone before Wendy uttered, "Goodbye!"

Something about her sudden disappearance was more ominous than the message she had delivered. Abby and Kayla exchanged looks of concern.

They sensed it too.

"Don't worry," Wendy said. "I have a plan."

"Spill it!" Kayla said.

Wendy nodded toward the map on the cork board. "Abby and I will conduct some stealth reconnaissance. We need to figure out what we're up against."

In the back room of the Crystal Path, Wendy caught Abby's shoulder while she disrobed. "Remember: observe. Don't engage."

"How could I forget? You've told me three times."

"And this is air recon—"

"—only. No wolf patrol. Got it."

"Your hawk form will be less noticeable, less threatening if anyone spots you."

"Wendy, I won't set foot on the ground. Promise!" As she undressed, Abby stuffed her winter clothes into a gym bag and shook her head, no doubt contemplating the mid-February temperatures and wind chill. After a moment, she unhooked her bra and slipped it down her arms, then skimmed off her panties and shoved both undergarments in the duffel bag. "Okay. Here goes."

"Wait!" Wendy said. She grabbed a small pouch with a slender elastic strap off the desk and handed it to Abby. "Just in case."

Inside the tan pouch, Abby kept a light and basic change of clothes: short white linen dress, flimsy canvas shoes, and a pair of white cotton underpants. If she had to revert to human form outdoors, she would be nude. Abby dangled the pouch by its strap with her index finger and frowned. "Lot of good this will do," she said. "I'll still freeze my ass off. Doesn't matter, right? I don't intend to change out there."

"Right."

Abby slipped the strap over her head and under her right arm, uncomfortably snug in her human form but that wouldn't matter after her change. She stepped away from Wendy and focused her thoughts. After nearly ten years of practice, Abby had honed her shape changing skills. She twisted and convulsed, as if a hot current raced through her bones and nerve endings. With every sinuous movement, her body contracted and condensed, her toned flesh rippled and puckered and sprouted feathers. Her head pressed inward and her nose and mouth merged and extruded, hardening into the predatory beak of a red-tailed hawk.

Wendy opened the back door, checked the alley and gave Abby the all-clear signal. A few hops across the tile floor and Abby was in the alley, her avian head appraising her surroundings before she launched herself up into the late afternoon sky.

As the hawk's distinctive shape receded, Wendy whispered, "Be careful, Abby."

Wendy closed and locked the door, crossed the back room to the paneled wall Alex had installed for her protection. Her palm pressed against the spring release and one floor-to-ceiling panel popped open. Wendy slipped inside the narrow room-within-a-room, and slid the three evenly spaced bolts into place, effectively locking herself inside. Not a panic room by any means, the secret space was designed to fool casual inspection while Wendy was hidden inside and vulnerable. She called it her meditation room though it was barely wide enough for her to assume the lotus position without her elbows bumping either wall. Mainly she used it for astral projection. And for that, the narrow cot was sufficient. Where she lay, she could see the amber bulb of a nightlight plugged into the wall outlet. In such a confined space, and while she would be in an altered state of consciousness, she never burned incense or candles.

Right arm at her side, left hand holding the crystal pendant she always wore, Wendy used the wan light as her focus and slipped into the self-hypnotic state conducive to astral projection. Just as Abby had years of shape-changing practice, Wendy had long ago mastered this particular magical skill. In moments, she felt her consciousness slip free of her physical form and rise above her body. Her pinpoint of consciousness expanded until she had formed a complete ghostly replica of herself. For this trip, she wouldn't need to manifest her image to others. To the rest of the world, she would be ethereal and invisible. *Stealth doesn't get much stealthier than that,* she thought as she left her "sleeping" form behind. She ascended through the ceiling and rose above the roof of the Crystal Path with less substance than smoke. After a momentary pause to get her bearings, she embarked on the same trajectory as Abby's hawk form.

Now that Kayla had the Crystal Path to herself, she almost missed the convention crowds that had jammed the aisles of the store for three days running. Almost. She was determined to enjoy her quiet time, even if it left her feeling a bit useless. Besides, she wasn't truly alone. Wendy was hidden in her meditation cubbyhole. Okay, her body was there. Her mind had taken flight. Even Hannah, three thousand miles away, had already done more than Kayla. "I get to sell incense."

She drummed her fingers on the glass countertop.

"I must be crazy," she whispered, shaking her head in disbelief. "Or have a death wish." What was that cautionary expression? *Be careful what you wish for, you just might get it.* Bobby was convinced she enjoyed pain, to some degree, the rush of adrenaline, the throbbing ache and the relief afterwards. Said her body piercings were exhibits A through F. But she wasn't seeking pain or punishment or oblivion. What bothered her was watching her friends take action, placing themselves in jeopardy while she bided her time in a safe and charming little shop in downtown Windale. Knowing that Wendy left her to mind the store only made it worse. "She thinks I'm helpless. She's protecting me. Ugh!"

There must be something I can do!

Kayla examined Abby's corkboard map. It showed roads, but not individual houses. Abby had estimated where the addresses were. Kayla had never visited that part of town, but she could find it easily enough if—

She noticed folded paper underneath the map, its corner slightly exposed. Lifting the taped bottom left edge of the map, she slid out the single sheet of lined paper. Written on the page were the dozen names and addresses Abby had compiled to locate her pushpins. Kayla knew most of them. The others she might recognize if she saw their faces.

The front door bells sounded a few startling but pleasant notes to announce the arrival of a businessman in an overcoat with disheveled hair. Not a regular. He nodded toward her and proceeded to the back of the store. Kayla took a few steps after him and said, "Can I help you find something?"

"Browsing," the man muttered. "Gift for my wife."

Kayla stood still, holding the paper absently at her side as he paused between racks of clothing and shelves of books on magic and metaphysics. She watched him discreetly for a moment, unable to shake the eerie feeling that he intended to sneak into the back room and look for Wendy. She'd never seen him before, in the store or anywhere in Windale. *So why is he giving me the creeps?*

The bells rang again.

Kayla spun on her heels and saw two teenage boys enter the Crystal Path. Hooded sweatshirts, wispy facial hair, baggy jeans, and unlaced sneakers. Not typical Crystal Path customers by any means. *This is odd,* she thought. *Maybe they're looking for drug paraphernalia.* She wanted to say, *"Sorry, boys, no bongs or rolling papers here. Move along."* Instead, she asked, "Can I help you. . . ?"

As the boys separated, walking around either side of the cash register island, Kayla realized she knew the one closest to her. Ricky Devlin, one year out of high school and—

Her fingers twitched convulsively around the paper in her hand. She skimmed the list and . . . there he was. Number eight: Richard Devlin. "Oh, shit." She shoved the paper into her hip pocket, out of sight. Clearing her throat, she took a side step, closer to the cash register island—and the store phone. "Hi, Ricky. Didn't know you shopped here."

"Don't," he said, watching her impassively. "Never been here before."

"Well, there's always a first . . ." Her voice trailed off as she noticed a middle-aged man with silver sideburns staring at her through the front store window. Gerald Cutter. Owned the local hardware store. She didn't have to examine the paper again to know he was on the list. A week ago, she'd witnessed him pushing an empty shopping cart down the street, half a mile from the Windale Grocery King market, on some kind of weird mental autopilot.

Without glancing away from her, he walked to the door and entered the shop.

Behind him, entering from the opposite direction was Brenda Swinton, divorced cougar with a predilection for fur coats and construction workers half her age. She'd been the manager of a chain jewelry store in the Harrison Mall—until she walked out of the shop in a haze, carrying a black velvet tray of diamond engagement rings to the food court. After mall security returned the rings, the jewelry store owner agreed not to press charges contingent upon Brenda entering a drug treatment program. Kayla doubted drugs were involved. Brenda was number ten on the list.

Millicent Shanley came through the door a moment later. She flipped the store hours sign over so it showed "Closed" to the outside world and stood with her back to the Plexiglas. They were all connected somehow. Mrs. Shanley had brought them here—and they had come for Wendy.

The stranger in the overcoat had meandered to the back of the store. He opened the door and slipped into the back room.

"Hey!" Kayla yelled. "You can't go back there."

Abandoning subtlety, she rushed to the raised cash register island and swept her Betty Boop backpack off the floor, taking only a moment to fish her cell phone out of the front pocket.

"She's not here," the stranger called to the others.

"Where is Wendy Ward?" Gerald Cutter asked.

"We need to speak to her," Brenda Swinton said.

"Personal errands." Kayla fumbled with her cell. "Left for the day."

Her hand shook as she flipped open the phone. She pressed her index finger to the speed-dial key for Bobby's personal phone.

Ricky Devlin charged, chopping the edge of his hand across her palm. The cell phone flew from her grasp. Ricky's friend vaulted over the display case behind her. His sweeping feet scattered a row of incense holders and a basket of muslin pouches. Kayla shrieked and backed into the far corner, hands held up in a defensive posture. The boys had cut off her escape. If only Wendy kept a baseball bat behind the counter. Better yet, a shotgun. She cast about for anything remotely dangerous—a letter opener, staple gun, anything—but saw only the broken pencil Abby used with her book of Sudoku puzzles.

The businessman strode forward, reached into the pocket of his overcoat and withdrew a serrated knife, something he had probably swiped from a place setting at a steak house after a late lunch.

Kayla could scream, but Wendy wouldn't hear her. The Wiccan might as well be comatose while astral projecting. That's why Alex had built the secret room for her. He knew how insensate and vulnerable she was during her ghostly jaunts.

"I—I told you, Wendy's gone for the day. You missed her. And I called the cops."

Kayla snatched the computer keyboard off the countertop and swung it two-handed at Ricky's face. A dozen plastic keycaps scattered with the impact. She'd split his lip open but he smiled back at her as if he were immune to pain.

Instead of retaliating, Ricky crouched and picked up her phone. Kayla could hear the tinny sound of distant shouting coming through the small speaker. Bobby would see the call came from her and assume she was at the store. "Bobby! Help!"

The other boy slapped her across the mouth with an open hand.

She winced in pain. A warm trickle of blood oozed from her split lip. She had to stall for a few minutes. Long enough for Bobby to arrive. That's all. Ricky snapped the clamshell phone shut, disconnecting the call, and tossed it into the plastic trashcan behind the counter.

Kayla stood her ground. "Cops'll be here any minute."

The man with the serrated knife joined them in the island. "Then you have two choices," he said. "Come with us now or die."

"W—what?"

Ricky and his friend took positions on either side of her, each taking an arm and clamping down. They would hold her motionless while the businessman gutted her like a fish.

"Dead you aren't a witness," the man said, leveling the tip of the knife at her abdomen. "Alive . . . well, my master is intrigued. Decide!"

Hostage or corpse? "Fine!"

"I'll bring the van around back," Gerald Cutter said. To Millicent, he added, "Lock the door behind me."

Brenda Swinton gazed at Kayla appraisingly and said, "Better tie and gag this one."

Kayla heard the plaintive sound of a distant police siren—Bobby's cruiser? But too far away to give her much hope.

"No time," said the businessman. He pressed the point of the steak knife under her chin. "Scream or struggle and I cut your throat. Ear to ear. Understood?"

With a timid nod, Kayla whispered, "Yes."

"Let's go!"

They hurried to the back room. The two teens clutching Kayla's arms almost lifted her off her feet in their haste. If she screamed or struggled, they'd kill her. Either action might trigger Wendy's awakening, exposing her to this gang and their master while she was too groggy and befuddled to protect herself. If they had Wendy, Kayla was dispensable. Without Wendy, Kayla might have some value as a hostage. A chance to escape.

As the knife-wielding businessman opened the back door of the Crystal Path, Kayla saw the white Cutter Hardware van waiting for them. Brenda Swinton rushed to the back of the van and opened the double doors. In a moment of inspiration, Kayla dropped the crumpled list of names on the floor. Ricky and his pal hustled her into the back of the van. They piled in after her. And as they pulled the doors shut, a grim thought occurred to her.

What if I'm not a hostage?

Gerald Cutter backed out of the alley and turned away from the approaching siren. Within a minute, the wailing sound faded and was gone—and with it, her hope.

Kayla wrapped her arms around her knees and shivered.

What if their "master" turns me into one of them?

Abby winged her way to the row of homes along Canton Creek.

From studying her map the previous night, she knew the general location of the focal point, but not the exact address—or if the focal point even had an address. It could be an obstruction in Canton Creek, a dumping ground, a field of wildflowers, a grove of trees or a clearing in the woods. But she doubted it. Whatever hunted Wendy this time, it wasn't a wild beast. It was cunning, and patient. It could insinuate itself into human minds, bend people to its will and use them like tools. Abby suspected it was hiding among these humans. And that meant inside a house.

Her flight had taken her almost five miles from downtown Windale. She swooped down toward Canton Creek Drive. On one side of the meandering two lane road, she saw a barren phalanx of deciduous trees; on the other, a staggered and eclectic mix of homes, each with backyards overlooking the frozen creek.

Dusk had already begun to leech color and light from the sky. The world beneath her seemed to have been sapped of vitality. An eerie stillness greeted her and she experienced an oppressive sense of foreboding. She chalked it up to nerves.

She alit on one of the top branches of an old oak tree, her weight causing it to dip and creak under her. Her talons bit into the dry bark, securing her grip as she examined the line of houses. Various ages and architectural styles: A-frame, Tudor, split-level, brick, even a modern log cabin. A random, rather than a planned, community of homes.

Her head tilted as she focused on the oldest house, a century-old, three-story Victorian. Her sharp eyes catalogued the wraparound porch and gothic touches—a turret on the right side, widow's walk to the left.

A buzzing sound invaded her skull, like an angry advance of wasps. And then she heard a voice.

"Come closer."

Abby's head darted nervously. She'd heard a voice, but not with her ears. . . .

"Are you her familiar?"

Abby's heart raced. In this form, as in her wolf form, she was a predator. And yet, somehow, that voice relegated her to the role of prey.

"No. More than a familiar. Much more."

Abby couldn't speak in hawk form and she repressed the urge to emit a challenging shriek. With no actual sound for her to locate, she nevertheless *sensed* that the voice was coming from the hundred-year-old house. She scanned the yard and porch, steps and doorway, and each of the many windows—if a face peered back at her through a gap in the curtains she would spot it as easily as she could detect a field mouse scampering along the forest floor. Motion caught her avian eyes—

The flourish of an arm, a beckoning hand.

A pale man in dark clothes standing on the widow's walk.

Why hadn't she seen him?

Before his arm gesture he'd been as still—and lifeless—as a statue!

"Come to me."

Without a moment's hesitation, Abby launched herself from the branch and swooped down toward the widow's walk. Her clothing pouch thumped against her side, jarring her flight trajectory and breaking her concentration. *What the hell am I do—?*

"To me!"

Less than ten feet from the widow's walk, Abby caught a glimpse of the man's hypnotic, smoldering eyes. They seemed to radiate an inner glow, like the embers in a banked fire ready to roar back to life. Desperately, Abby veered away from his reaching hand. Her wings pounded the air as she sought distance between herself and the pale man.

As she wheeled around, the man leapt to the metal railing of the widow's walk and launched himself off the roof, arms extended, fingers reaching for her. Two powerful wing flaps elevated her inches beyond his grasp—

—and he plummeted three stories to the ground.

She expected a gruesome impact. Instead, he landed with the grace of a cat, as casually as if he'd stepped off a curb. He stared into the sky, following her flight with his eerie eyes. If Abby had been in her human form, she would have shuddered.

What could she tell Wendy about him? That he appeared human—but the similarity ended there. Maybe he disguised his true appearance with a glamour. With the exception of Wendy using border vision, the ghoul had fooled them all with its magical projections. And yet this one hadn't fooled her for a moment. Superficially human, his true nature—his malevolence—was right there, behind those burning eyes, and it had scared the crap out of her. Those eyes—

She soared over the first line of trees, well out of reach. Or so she thought.

"Come back to me, little bird. Last warning."

No! Her protest came out as a defiant shriek: *KEE-Arr!*

"So be it."

The beat of Abby's wings faltered. *What's happening—*

Pressure wrapped around her mind, a throbbing pain that pressed inward, filling her consciousness with a mental fog, drowning out thought, crushing her will to escape, vacating her instinct for self-preservation. She wanted to collapse into a huddled ball, wrap herself in the numbing darkness and forget everything.

Her wings stopped beating. She fluttered downward, a dead weight, the cold air rushing across her feathers and down. She welcomed the darkness, the quick end.

Perhaps sensing her surrender, the pressure abated.

Abby stirred, awake but confused, in a rush of wind. Only instinct saved her, with a frantic flapping of wings. Branches lashed at her one after another as she plummeted toward the cold hard ground. A low-hanging branch snagged her pouch, jerking her upward for a fleeting moment, enough to slow her fall. She performed an impromptu barrel roll through a mass of rotting leaves and twigs and tumbled across the ground, completely exhausted.

Battered and trembling, she tested her wings and felt an ache in the one above her clothing pouch. *Probably wrenched something when that last branch caught me. Can't risk flight.* She glanced around, saw that she was alone. And no sign of wildlife. That stillness she'd sensed earlier. Had everything living fled this area?

Since she couldn't trust her wing for flight, she transformed back to human form and immediately felt the ache in her shoulder. Sprained maybe, but not dislocated as she had feared. Her legs were fine. She could flee on foot.

As she tried to stand, the ground seemed to sway beneath her and she collapsed to hands and knees, panting with the failed effort.

The metamorphosis had exhausted her. The final straw. The mental mojo attack had sapped more than her will: she had no energy. She yawned so wide she felt her jaw crack. And for a moment, she considered curling up on her side, on the frozen ground, naked as a newborn, to sleep. *Yeah,* she thought, *ten hours ought to do it.*

"Abby!" a familiar, ghostly voice called. *"Wake up!"*

Her eyes snapped open. She'd actually done it. She'd fallen asleep!

Still groggy, she sat up, drawing her knees close and wrapping her arms around them. She shivered from the cold. Wendy's astral image hovered before her, not quite touching the forest floor. "What happened?"

"Was hoping you could tell me," Wendy said. *"I was about a mile away when I saw you drop out of the sky."*

"Pale man," Abby said, her teeth beginning to chatter. "Very still. Burning eyes. He . . . got inside my mind. He commanded me and I wanted to . . . but I got away." Chagrined, she looked down. "Not for long, though. So tired . . ."

"Fight it! You need to get dressed and get out of here."

Abby nodded, pulled open her pouch and hastily donned her emergency clothing. As she had surmised, they offered little protection against the cold. "What about you?"

"I need to find out what he is."

"Old Victorian house. Can't miss it." Abby said. "He's unnaturally strong. Jumped off the widow's walk without a scratch. Don't let him see you!"

"I won't," Wendy said. *"Only manifested for your benefit."*

Wendy rose into the air and faded from sight. "Good luck," Abby called. With her arms wrapped across her chest, she navigated along what appeared to be a deer trail running parallel to Canton Creek Drive. Once she put enough distance between her and the pale man's house, she'd emerge onto the road and jog back to town from there.

Is that it, Abby? One embarrassing flyby and you head for the hills, tail between your legs? But what else *could* she do? Her cover had been blown. And—

Tail. *Hmm. . . .*

Whatever the pale man was, he was expecting a red-tailed hawk.

Wendy relaxed her concentration and her physical appearance faded away before she cleared the trees. She doubted the "pale man" could exert mental control or influence over her astral projection, but she saw no reason to alert him to her presence. When she came after him in the flesh, she wanted surprise on her side.

She rushed toward the old Victorian home, made one swooping circuit around the perimeter, darting around a wooden utility shed in back, but found nobody guarding the grounds. Drifting past the cone-shaped turret, toward the wrought iron railing of the widow's walk, she had the sensation of being watched. But the widow's walk was empty. *Abby said the pale man jumped off the widow's walk. So he—*

The sound of mingled voices floated up from below.

Two men—one carrying a canvas sack—descended the porch steps, crossed Canton Creek Drive and slipped through the tree line. With a sinking feeling, Wendy realized they'd been sent to find Abby. But they would be looking for a downed, wounded bird, not a young woman walking briskly north along a deer trail.

Wendy drifted down to the porch level, hoping to catch a glimpse of the pale man.

For a moment, her gaze slipped right past him. Then, as his head turned slightly, he jumped into focus. Dark tailored suit, jacket unbuttoned over a white shirt opened at the collar. Dark, shoulder-length hair framed a handsome face, sharp-featured and pale with a Greco-Roman nose and full, sensuous lips. Some part of her warned against looking into his eyes, something beyond Abby's experience, something instinctual, an atavistic alarm. But here and now, unseen, unheard, un-*sensed* at all, she had her best chance to fathom what type of threat the man presented, including his eyes. And with that rationalization, she forced her attention up from his strong jaw, across his gaunt, sculpted cheeks to—

His eyes were so luminous she imagined they would shine in the dark. They were flat and bottomless at the same time, inviting and repelling. Ardent heat and complete oblivion churned within their depths. But above all, they were utterly compelling. And as she stared, a strange and hypnotic fascination crept over her.

The man smiled, as if at a private joke.

"Ahh," he said. "What is *this* now?" His voice was deep and soothing . . . and almost as compelling as his eyes.

"You wish to dance close to the flame, my little moth."

He laughed, a thoroughly masculine and enchanting sound. His head tilted back, revealing a flash of white teeth and, at either side of his mouth—fangs.

Oh, shit! Wendy thought. *A vampire.*

Startled, she drifted backward several feet, but couldn't look away from his eyes. Somehow, he sensed her presence, enough to know he wasn't alone, that someone was studying him.

The vampire extended his arm, palm up, as if expecting someone to take his hand. "It is time we met, little moth," he said. "We must discuss this difficulty between us."

The heavy wooden door behind him opened and an attractive woman in her mid-thirties stepped onto the porch, barefoot, wearing only a sheer peach peignoir against the February cold. Her face was slack, her movements languid, and if the frigid temperatures bothered her she showed no signs of physical discomfort. "Nicola?" she said, her voice lethargic. "You called?"

"Yes, my love," the vampire said, turning to her.

If not for the woman's gaunt appearance—she looked at least fifteen pounds lighter—Wendy might have recognized her right away. Tricia Howell managed the Fireside Tavern, one of the more upscale restaurants in Windale. Wendy seemed to recall that she had inherited her house from a grandparent, who died while Tricia was renting an apartment in Chicago. She had returned to her Windale roots and lived alone—or had until the vampire took up residence with her. Though Tricia wasn't on Abby's "odd behavior" list, Wendy couldn't recall seeing her in town in the past few weeks. *She must be patient*—victim—*zero*.

The vampire placed his hands on her shoulders. "I require a small favor."

Voice quavering, Tricia said, "Of course. Anything for you."

For a brief moment, the vampire touched his lips tenderly against Tricia's. Then he kissed a line down the side of her slender throat before pausing near the base. Tricia's head tilted back suddenly and she let out a low, pleasurable moan.

He's feeding, Wendy realized, *and I'm helpless to stop him.*

After five long seconds, the vampire straightened.

Wendy shifted her line of sight and glimpsed the twin telltale punctures in the woman's throat. Tricia's trembling fingers caressed the paired wounds, and her face flushed with joy and something akin to wonderment as both red-rimmed holes healed with magical speed. All that remained was a single smeared drop of blood.

Could his saliva contain a healing agent? she wondered. *Or maybe the intimate contact temporarily conveys some of the vampire's supernatural healing ability to his victim.*

"Return inside and rest, my love," the vampire said to the scantily clad woman. "We have company."

Tricia smiled, nodded and slipped back through the doorway.

Wendy shifted her perspective again at the sound of an approaching vehicle: a white commercial van. *More minions,* Wendy assumed. *But why refer to henchmen as* company?

The van sped toward the house and swung into the asphalt driveway, screeching to a stop. 'Cutter Hardware' was painted on the side panels and Wendy recalled that Gerald Cutter *was* on the list. The back doors swung open and a pair of teens jumped out, Ricky Devlin and some other boy Wendy didn't recognize. Ricky was on the list too.

"C'mon," Ricky yelled to someone inside the van. "Get out!"

Wendy saw the black boots and jeans first. *No! It's not possible—it can't—*

Kayla hopped down from the back of the van, her teeth worrying the ring that pierced her lower lip, which was flecked with blood.

Kayla! But of course Kayla couldn't hear or see Wendy in the most basic stage of astral projection—without any sort of aural or visual manisfestation.

The two teens caught hold of Kayla's arms and forced her toward the front of the house and the waiting vampire. Gerald Cutter, Brenda Swinton, Millicent Shanley and a man wearing an overcoat exited the van and followed the others.

"Greetings, Kayla Zanella," the vampire said, executing a slight bow. "My name is Nicola Varrato. I am pleased you have decided to join us."

"Not like I had a choice."

Varrato laughed heartily and Wendy wondered bitterly if his amusement was affected, the better to reveal his fangs to his next victim.

Kayla flinched. "Fuck this!"

She thrashed wildly, nearly freeing herself from the grip of the teens. But Varrato darted forward, a blur of motion, as if he'd skipped part of the distance between the porch steps and Kayla. His thumb and forefinger gripped Kayla's chin—and yet Wendy hadn't seen him move his hand.

Don't look into his—

Too late. Kayla's initial defiance betrayed her. She couldn't stare him down because once she focused on those eyes, she was lost. Varrato spoke soothingly, "You will end this unpleasantness." Her body relaxed, Kayla nodded once. "Good! Then we may proceed. Something about you intrigues me, Kayla, and I would know why."

Varrato and his minions—Kayla now included among them—walked toward the house. With one last backward glance, uncomfortably close to Wendy's current position, the vampire said, "It is time we met, little moth. In the flesh."

Horrified, Wendy simply stared as the enthralled group followed the vampire into Tricia Howell's home. The door shut with a sense of finality. Wendy wondered if she'd ever see Kayla again. Or if Kayla's mind, and soon her body, would be forever lost to Wither's curse.

I need to get—

"*—back!*"

Wendy gasped and almost fell off the cot, struck by a disorienting moment of vertigo. She felt as if someone had tossed a bucket of cold water in her face. "What happened?"

Normally, during astral projection, Wendy traveled the distance to and fro, at varying speeds, but with a sense of the passage of time and distance. But this time, the simple *thought* of returning had triggered something like astral teleportation.

"*I summoned you,*" the Crone said. "*Couldn't be helped.*"

"Crone, you came back and . . . oh!"

Belatedly, Wendy realized her secret room door was dangling crookedly from its hinges and that Bobby McKay, Windale's chief of police, was glaring at her with unconcealed impatience, a sheet of crumpled paper clutched in his white-knuckled hand.

He waved the paper at her. "These people—do they have Kayla!"

"Yes," Wendy said, still trying to get her bearings. "I saw them."

"What the hell's going on?"

"The curse." Shorthand. Bobby knew all about it. Ever since his close encounter with the wendigo. "Vampire this time."

"Vampire!"

"*A master vampire,*" the Crone said. "*Centuries old. Very powerful.*"

"Wait—you came back!" Wendy said excitedly. "You know more, don't you?"

"*Once you encountered him here in astral form, new details surfaced.*"

"Before, you said one of us was in grave danger. It's Kayla, isn't it?"

"*Yes. If the vampire gains control of her mind. . . . You must not delay.*"

"No, of course not," Wendy said. "But what do we do?" She turned to Bobby. "Has Abby called? I left her in the woods along Canton Creek Drive. Two of the vampire's mind-slaves are looking for her."

"Nothing," Bobby said. "Try her cell phone."

"She doesn't carry it in her pouch." Wendy looked at the Crone. "How do I fight a master vampire? Crosses, holy water, stake through the heart?"

"*Silver burns his kind, but will not kill him,*" the Crone said. "*Shove a wooden stake into his heart to paralyze him—aspen, ash and whitethorn are best. The organic material interferes with the vampire's supernatural healing.*"

"Staking only paralyzes him? Then what?"

"*Chop off his head. Burn the remains and scatter the ashes.*"

"Wow," Wendy said, overcome with the enormity of the task before her. "It's getting dark. Don't vampire hunters usually wait until morning to stake the vamp?"

"*If you wait until morning,*" the Crone said grimly, "*Kayla will be lost.*"

Bobby shook his head. "We're not waiting."

"No," Wendy said. "We're not."

"You know where he has her?"

Her mind racing, Wendy stood, nodded and clasped her hands together, trying to squeeze the tremors out of them. "The old Howell house. On Canton Creek Drive."

"Makes sense," Bobby said, jabbing the crumpled page with his forefinger. "Most of these people live nearby. I can have a couple patrol cars there in five minutes." He reached for the radio mic clipped to his left epaulet, but Wendy caught his hand and shook her head. "What?"

"We can't rush in unprepared," Wendy said. "A full SWAT team would be no match for a master vampire. You know that, Bobby. You've been through this weirdness before."

"You're right," he said quickly. "It's just—Kayla. I'm not thinking clearly. What's your plan? You do have a plan, right?"

"I have a few daggers for sale in the front display case. Mostly decorative, not really weapons, but they're silver and pointy. What about you? Any silver rounds left over from the *wendigo?*"

Bobby nodded. "A few. Locked in a file cabinet in my office."

"That's a start."

"What about wooden stakes? Guessing you don't have those for sale."

Wendy smiled. "Believe it or not, that won't be a problem." For her birthday one year, Alex carved her a set of three wooden stakes. "*In case you ever run into a vampire.*" Wendy laughed at the time, but a part of her wondered, *What if I do?* So she had kept them, safely tucked away in her cedar chest, along with other magical paraphernalia.

"I have a fire axe at the office, and a meat cleaver at home," Bobby said. "Either should take care of the beheading. I can stop for a can of lighter fluid or fill a container with gasoline for the bonfire."

"Let's see if I have this right," Wendy said. "We wound him with silver bullets or a silver dagger, I stake him, you behead him, and then we burn him. No sweat."

Bobby sighed. "Not that easy, huh?"

"We'll need to get past his minions."

Bobby patted his sidearm. "I have plenty of regular bullets for them."

"*No!*" the Crone protested, the same moment Wendy said, "You can't!"

"Am I missing something?"

"*Those people are under the vampire's spell, forced to obey his mental commands,*" the Crone said. *"When you kill the vampire, they will return to themselves."*

"They're innocent victims," Wendy said. "Same as Kayla." Wendy chose not to mention that Kayla had already fallen under the vampire's spell.

"I'll bring backup then," Bobby said. "Non-lethal force. Keep my men outside to take care of the . . . minions, as you call them."

"I need to enter first," Wendy said. "I think he's expecting me. And he'll let me get close, close enough to stake him. But I won't be able to overpower him. That's where you come in. When I have his attention, you need to make those silver bullets count."

"Okay," Bobby said, rubbing his hands together. "Let's get moving."

"Wait," the Crone said. *"Wendy, you must also prepare yourself mentally."*

"How? Put on my game face? Gird my loins? Eye of the tiger?"

"You conjure a protective sphere to guard yourself physically," the Crone said. *"But that protection is insufficient against a master vampire."*

"You're worried he'll get inside my head?" Wendy asked. "And minion-ize me?"

"Or worse," the Crone said. *"Remember, he has touched your mind once. You felt his pull. The next time will be easier for him. His strongest hold will be over anyone whose blood he has tasted."*

"So how do I prepare—or *prevent* him from getting inside my head?" Wendy asked. "Avoid eye contact?"

"His eyes trigger a near-instant hypnotic state in his victims," the Crone said. For the first time, her image began to waver. Two visits in one day. She was tiring fast. *"But his eyes are a mere shortcut to what he can do naturally—well, supernaturally. Anyone in his vicinity with an open mind—an unprotected mind—can fall prey to his mental voice and succumb to his commands."*

"Telepathy," Wendy said, nodding. "I've witnessed it. That's how he called Tricia Howell to him on the porch. How he gives orders to his minions."

"He also has the power to take over their bodies, to manipulate their actions, like a remote puppeteer."

"How do we shield our minds?" Bobby asked. "Tinfoil hats?"

"First, be prepared for the mental . . . invasion. Expect an attack on your mind and you will be prepared to fight it."

Wendy frowned. "If it's all in our heads, how exactly do we fight it?"

"It's a mental battle, your will against his," the Crone said. *"Envision your mind as a steel vault or an impenetrable stone fortress. When he attacks your mind, that's what he will encounter."* The Crone's translucent face looked forlorn. Wendy knew her well enough to sense she was holding something back, and she knew herself well enough not to bother asking. If it was that bad, she was probably better off not knowing. *"Be strong, Wendy. This vampire has had*

hundreds of years to harden his will. Most humans are helpless against such power."

Kayla should have been terrified.

Instead, she felt calm. Once inside the old Victorian house, the vampire Nicola Varrato commanded Ricky and his fellow teenaged miscreant to release her. After he assigned them to guard duty, he told Kayla to follow him upstairs. The entire house was shrouded in deep shadows. A single freestanding lamp provided the only illumination on the first floor. The men and women who had brought Kayla to the vampire stood or sat alone in the shadows, eerily quiet and motionless . . . awaiting orders.

When the vampire turned his back on her, Kayla could have run—*should* have run—but had trouble remembering why she needed to flee. Instead, she followed him to the second floor. Surrounded by the vampire's minions, she had little hope of escaping. At least that's what she told herself while she tried to understand the real reason. Logically, she realized the vampire had taken control of her motor reflexes if not her mind, and yet she felt at peace. She couldn't think of another place she'd rather be at that moment.

When they came to a stop, she stood before the vampire in the master bedroom, which was dominated by a mahogany four-poster bed with white sheets and a quilted white comforter. The room also featured a mahogany highboy opposite a long dresser, and two night stands adorned with Tiffany lamps. Other than the glow cast by two flickering tea candles on either side of the room, the only illumination was celestial in origin, the scattered and diffuse spill of starlight and moonbeams.

Tricia Howell had followed them and waited languidly in the doorway, her hip leaning against the doorjamb. *Unwilling to leave, or waiting for an invitation?* She appeared ghostly and forlorn in her long peach nightgown.

On the far side of the room, mounted above the dresser was a three-paneled mirror, in which Kayla saw her reflection—and that of her supernatural captor.

"Yes, I have a reflection," the vampire said, as if—

Can he read my mind?

He smiled slightly, not enough to reveal his fangs. Then his gaze, with his eyes luminous in the dark, shifted to the doorway. "I told you to rest."

Tricia lowered her head demurely and took a hesitant step into the bedroom. "I was hoping I might stay . . . with you."

"As you wish," he said, but his attention returned to Kayla. "You are a riddle for me to solve."

"No, I'm fairly straightforward. No mystery here. Is that all? Because, I should—"

"Interesting," he said. "You resist me."

"I do? Because I think I should run away . . . but I can't remember how or why."

"That's natural."

"No," she said. "It's not! You're already inside my mind, aren't you?"

"*That* is as natural for me as breathing is for you," he said. "I find it more difficult to try to stay *out* of human minds. It is why Tricia's neighbors have drifted into my service. Proximity."

"Like your mind is . . . radioactive."

"I prefer to think of it as encompassing," he said, and flashed a wry grin. "That is why you fascinate me. Parts of your mind are unusual and . . . sealed."

Kayla grinned. "So I have some kind of human firewall?"

"Ah, but no," he said, shaking his head. "You see, it's just the opposite."

"Opposite of what? Human? You mean . . ."

"Yes, Kayla," he said. "There are recesses in your mind that are inhuman."

"No," Kayla said vehemently. "You're wrong! She's gone! I'm fine. I've been fine."

"She?"

"W—Wither," Kayla said. A nightmare almost forgotten now raced along the pathways of her subconscious and threatened to overwhelm her. "She tried to infect me, but she failed."

"This . . . Wither. This thing you still fear. She is the reason I am here."

Kayla nodded. "Her curse summoned you."

"A voice, a compulsion outside of time," the vampire said, nodding. "We have much in common then, you and I."

"No," Kayla said. "You're lying. Trying to scare me. I'm free."

"Free?" He shrugged. "Then go."

Kayla couldn't move. "Touché."

"I could rid you of this . . . taint. If you wish."

"Why would you help me?"

He glowered and she fought the urge to fall to her knees and beg forgiveness. "I have roamed the world for nearly five hundred years, and I refuse to bow to the whim or will of a foul, hibernating creature that wasted countless centuries of life gorging on human flesh!"

"Well, when you put it like that."

"Say it. Admit you desire your freedom from this creature."

"Yes," Kayla said. "I want to be free." *Free of her —but enslaved by you.*

The vampire took a step closer to her and her breath caught in her throat. *Proximity? Yes!* Sexual heat rose inside her, a sudden wave of longing. She trembled in anticipation of his touch. His right hand reached out, poised beside her cheek for a moment, and then the tip of his index finger touched the silver post in her left eyebrow.

He winced and pulled his hand away. "Silver."

"Here too," Kayla said, indicating the post in her right eyebrow. "Do . . . do you want me to take them out for you?" *What the fuck am I saying?*

He smiled again, broader this time, exposing the tips of his fangs. "No," he said after a moment. "You are my new rose and a rose should have thorns." His index finger approached the ring piercing her right nostril, then dipped toward the one looping through the middle of her split bottom lip, but touched neither. "Many thorns." His gaze met hers again. "Any others?"

No! "Three."

Shit! She couldn't lie to him.

"Show me."

Without hesitation, Kayla pulled off her black wool sweater and tossed it on the bed. Then she removed her white Betty Boop tank top. Since she wasn't wearing a bra, the vampire could see the silver ring piercing her left nipple. The right one, however, was unadorned. Without noticing any movement on his part, she was suddenly aware of his cool palm cupping her right breast and then his thumb brushed her already erect nipple. She shivered under his touch and fought the urge to press herself against his body.

He noticed the ring in her navel and nodded. "Continue."

With fumbling hands, Kayla unfastened the top buckle on her boots, exposing the zipper. Before she could continue, the vampire beckoned Tricia from the doorway. "Help her undress, my love."

The gaunt woman nodded and came forward, assisting Kayla as she tugged off her boots and striped socks. Once they were tossed aside, Kayla unbuttoned her jeans and skimmed them off her hips. Tricia steadied Kayla as she freed her legs. Finally, Kayla slipped her thumbs under the waistband of her black thong, pulled it down and stepped out of it.

"Ah, my beautiful rose."

She stood naked before him, breathless with excitement she had trouble controlling. *Supernaturally induced lust,* she thought. But her physiological responses were achingly real even if their cause was unnatural in origin. *Turned me into his horny little love slave.* Her hands were trembling. The thong slipped from between her fingers and fell silently to the carpeted floor. Swallowing hard, she looked into his lambent eyes and never wanted to look away. "Please," she whispered. *I'm so fucking wet. . . .* She looked to Tricia for support and received a sympathetic smile and a slight nod of confirmation. Tricia had already shared the vampire's bed. "Oh, God. Nicola, please . . ."

The vampire was well aware of the libidinous effect he was having on her. He was inside her mind, after all. She could no longer separate what she desired from what he wanted her to desire. He glanced down at the final glint of silver. "Naturally," he said. "One last thorn."

"I'll take it out," she said breathlessly. "All of them. Please . . ."

"We must postpone that particular indulgence," he said. "First, I need to unlock your mind, expose its secrets and strip away that foreign presence. And for that, I need something else from you." Placing his hands on her hips, he pulled her willingly into his embrace.

She molded her body against his and whispered, "Anything!"

"Just a little favor."

Kayla gasped when his cool lips made contact with her throat, and again when his fangs penetrated her flesh.

Wendy steered her Pathfinder onto the gravel shoulder of the winding Canton Creek Drive, rolled to a stop and extinguished her headlights. The streetlights along this stretch of road were far apart. Too dark for her liking. But the next bend in the road would reveal her to the occupants of the Howell house. She shivered, imagining some horrific creature dropping out of the night sky onto the roof of her SUV, clawing through metal and cloth to snatch her out of the driver's seat. Something right out of Wither's bag of nasty tricks.

A Windale patrol car swung into position behind her, its headlights blinding in her rearview mirror for a moment before winking off. Bobby climbed out of the front passenger's seat and approached her car.

Wendy lowered her window and waited.

Bobby leaned his forearms on the window frame and looked in at her expectantly. Hoping to relieve the tension, she said, "Was I speeding officer?"

"I wish," he scoffed. "Listen, I brought three patrol officers with me, Mike Magano, Irina Vasquez, and Leroy White. They've all been in Windale less than a year, so they're—"

"In the dark."

Bobby nodded. "So we'll go over this and I'll filter it for them." Wendy started to protest, but Bobby held up his hand. "We don't have time for me to explain. Master vampires aren't in their law enforcement paradigm. Besides, I plan to keep them back, crowd-control mode."

"How?"

"Tasers, Cap-Stun—er, pepper spray—and batons. Nothing lethal. Enough force to incapacitate and cuff any minions."

Wendy nodded. "Leaving me to go solo with the vampire."

"About that," Bobby said, frowning. "If I had the luxury of time and materials, I'd wire you. Barring that, I want you to carry this two-way radio."

He handed her a compact radio with two plastic ties cinched around the middle. "It's already on. I've locked down the transmit button so I'll hear everything. I need to be within striking distance the second you distract him. I show too soon, he might . . . neutralize me."

Again, Wendy nodded. Their plan was desperate, and far from fool-proof. The police might not immobilize all the vamp's minions. They weren't even sure how many mind-slaves were holed up in the house. Might be a dozen or more. Wendy slipped the radio into the left pocket of her green Danfield College hoodie. She'd keep two of the wooden stakes in the right pocket, the silver dagger inside her right boot.

"I have the last four silver rounds in my Glock," Bobby said. "I stun him, you stake him. Right?"

"Better idea," Wendy said. "Give me the gun. I'll be face to face with Varrato. I'll shoot him and stake him. You rescue Kayla."

Bobby was shaking his head before she finished. "Can't risk you juggling a gun and a stake. We only get one shot at this. Stick to the plan."

"Then consider this a contingency to the plan," Wendy said, reaching across to the passenger seat where three wooden stakes rested next to the cloth-wrapped decorative silver dagger. She picked up a stake and handed it to him. "In case I miss."

"And the third one?"

"Hoping I can slip it to Kayla," Wendy said. *Assuming she's still on our side.*

"Of course," Bobby said and swallowed. She suspected he had the same thought.

Wendy placed her hand over his and squeezed. "We'll get her back, Bobby."

"Right," he said confidently. "Kill the vamp and everyone resets."

At first, the blood flowed out of Kayla with the shuddering sensation of sexual release. Soon she became lightheaded and dizzy. Although her eyes were closed, she sensed a deeper darkness swirling up to claim her, something separate from herself—and powerful. Nicola Varrato was there in her mind, light and nimble, a bold consciousness assessing all that he had claimed as his own. Kayla became passive and eventually dormant, a contented and sleeping passenger on the back seat of the bus of her own mind.

She stumbled, abruptly awake but exhausted, falling.

Tricia caught her from behind and eased her to the floor.

Kayla's fingers found the twin punctures in her neck and marveled as they healed in the span of seconds under her blood-damp fingertips. She looked up at the startled vampire, her blood a dark smudge across his lips. "What—what happened?"

"Distractions," he said. "I drank more from you than I intended. And lost my focus."

"What distractions?"

"Intruders. Approaching," he said. "And you. What I found . . ."

"In my mind?" she said. "Tell me."

"A . . . seed," he said. "A dormant seed."

"Dormant? That's good. Right?"

"I should have allowed more time to remove the taint," he said. "Instead, I seem to have . . . awakened it."

"Seeds grow!"

"My rose, do not worry," he said. "I will remedy everything later." He addressed Tricia. "Find her something comfortable to wear." Taking Kayla's hands, he helped her to her feet. The room seemed to tilt before righting itself. "When this Wendy Ward business is concluded, come to my bed and we will spend a most enjoyable night together. Would you like that?"

Cursing her utter lack of resolve, Kayla said, "Very much, Nicola." She clenched her jaw and thought, *I am so fucking lame!*

The other homes along the winding stretch of Canton Creek Drive were unnaturally dark for that time of the evening, every one of them abandoned. Alone now, Wendy slowed as she approached the Howell house, the only one with any signs of activity.

Bobby assured her he'd be watching her progress with night vision goggles and listening over the two-way radio, but that was small comfort. He would approach the house on foot from the cover of the trees. The three police officers would drive the lone patrol car to the house and proceed to clear a path for their chief.

Wendy swung the Pathfinder into the driveway, blocking the Cutter Hardware van. Anything that denied the mind-slaves a quick exit would keep the battle contained. Taking a deep breath, Wendy switched off the ignition. She placed her left hand over the crystal pendant that dangled from her neck to center herself. Then she erected a magnificent stone fortress around her mind. After years of meditation and magic rituals, this was a simple and natural exercise for her. She hoped Bobby—with the benefit of her five-minute meditation primer—could shield his thoughts long enough to facilitate his attack. Otherwise, this might be a suicide mission for all of them.

With the two wooden stakes tucked in her right sweatshirt pocket, Wendy leaned forward and slipped the silver dagger inside her boot up to the hilt. She climbed out of the Pathfinder and took a moment to examine her surroundings. Though most of the Howell house was dark, a low-wattage downstairs light bulb cast an amber smear across pulled blinds. Across the road, she glimpsed a flash of yellow directed at her and then a low, fluid movement—*wolf-Abby!*

Until that moment, Wendy hadn't realized how much she'd been worried about Abby, ever since leaving her alone in the woods with two mind-slaves searching for her. She must have circled back after the men gave up, waiting for Wendy's eventual return. *Good thing I already visualized my fortress,* Wendy thought. Her surprised excitement might have given away her position and Abby's presence.

Of course, it was possible Abby was now in the vampire's control, a glorified watchdog prowling her master's grounds. *No!* Wendy chided herself. *Can't let myself think that way.*

"What have we here, Kyle?"

Wendy spun around. Two silhouettes rose from the porch steps. Kayla's teen captors: Ricky and his pal, Kyle. "Wendy Ward," she said. "Varrato's expecting me."

Ricky smiled, appraising her head to toe and back again. "So he is."

Look all you want, Wendy thought as she stood casually before them. *As long as that's all you do.* Ready to raise her protective sphere at a moment's notice, she said, "Well?"

"Second floor, turn left, last room on the right."

Wendy walked up the porch steps and placed her hand on the doorknob.

A buzzing filled her ears. She whirled toward Ricky and Kyle but they seemed oblivious to the noise. Then she realized the annoyance came from within her own mind, a series of buzzing, scratching, skittering sounds . . . or at least that's how she interpreted the sensations. Something—*someone!*—was testing the walls of her mental fortress.

Stay out, Varrato! For Bobby's benefit, she repeated the thought aloud, hoping the two-way radio was sensitive enough to pick up her voice. Since the radio was locked in transmit mode, she couldn't confirm that he'd heard.

She reached for the doorknob again, but it spun before she could touch it and the door opened. Stepping to the side, she watched in stunned silence as Varrato's mind-slaves marched single file out of the house and spread out on the front lawn. Those on the edges circled back around the house. "Forming a defensive perimeter," Wendy said, continuing her running commentary. "Guess Varrato doesn't want any interruptions during our alone time."

After a deep breath to calm her nerves, she said, "Here goes."

She slipped through the doorway into the darkened house.

A figure blocked her way.

Wendy paused, her eyes adjusting. "Brenda Swinton?"

"You're not good enough for him."

"Good thing I'm not applying for the job."

"You don't be—" Brenda winced and cowered slightly. "Yes, Master! Sorry, Master." She edged past Wendy, delivering a little bump of indignation before darting out into the night with the others.

Wendy tried to recall the faces of those who had filed past her. Guy in an overcoat, and the two men who had stalked Abby in the woods, Millicent Shanley, Gerald Cutter, and a few others. But cataloging them seemed pointless. She had no way of knowing how many humans were enslaved by the vampire. He could have two or twenty more hiding in the deep shadows of the house.

Buzzing! More insistent this time. *Loud, hollow banging.* Surround sound roaring inside her skull. "Enough!" she shouted in exasperation. If she gained better control of her mental defenses, she could probably silence the attacks.

She approached the stairs on the balls of her feet and took them slowly, her ears straining for any *real* sound that might prove helpful. Of course, the vampire probably had acute hearing and perfect night vision. She struggled to find any advantage against this latest threat.

"Kayla?" she whispered. "Can you hear me?"

Wendy heard a squeal of tires outside followed by shouting voices. Brenda had left the door ajar and it sounded as if the cavalry had arrived. Bobby had feared Wendy would have a brief window of opportunity and he planned to strike shortly after her arrival. With Kayla's life in danger, he refused to compromise. But Wendy feared that once Bobby entered the house, he might have a minute or two before the vampire penetrated his mental defenses. She faced the frightening possibility that the vampire could turn everyone within sight of the house against her. With a renewed sense of urgency, she hurried up the stairs, turned left and crept toward the last door on the right.

She pulled the silver dagger out of her boot and reversed her grip so the tip of the blade pointed toward her elbow, concealed until she was ready to strike. With another steadying breath, she stepped through the doorway and scanned the master bedroom.

Scattered candles cast flickering shadows across the walls. Tricia Howell lounged in her peach peignoir near the headboard of a four-poster bed, half-reclined, cheek resting in one palm, her eyes languid.

The vampire stood facing Wendy, eyes aglow with their preternatural gleam, hands clasped together in delight, a wide smile lighting his pale, handsome face. "My little moth returns," he said warmly. "In the flesh."

Wendy's gaze was drawn downward, to his left—and she wondered if this moment had been staged for her benefit, to demoralize her with the grim futility of resistance. Kneeling at the vampire's side, one arm curled possessively around his leg, a look of sleepy contentment on her face, and wearing nothing but a sheer, frilly nightgown that fell to mid-thigh—

"Kayla!" Wendy gasped. "Oh, Kayla, I'm so sorry."

Nerves got the better of Mike Magano, Bobby's junior patrolman. Instead of a casual approach to the Howell house, he raced down the street and had to pump the brakes loud enough to elicit a squeal. Varrato's mind-slaves reacted with alacrity, massing toward the cruiser.

Senior patrol officer Irina Vasquez and junior Leroy White launched themselves out of the cruiser as if they were on a drug raid. In a weird psychological way, Bobby supposed they were. Vampire as pusher and his minions as users, out of their mind. Vasquez and White were quick and efficient. Their tasers took down Ricky Devlin and Kyle McIntyre; both boys flopping like fish on the ground. Coming around the front of the patrol car, Magano nailed Cutter with his taser. As instructed, Vasquez and White switched to Cap-Stun on the women, catching Brenda Swinton and Millicent Shanley full in the face. Both women screamed and fell to their knees. Magano slapped cuffs on the incapacitated minions before any could recover their senses. Each of his officers had been instructed to bring extra cuffs. If what Wendy said was true, and these people were innocent victims who would return to normal after the death of the vampire, his officers needed to take them out of the battle fast, with minimal injuries.

His two-way radio squawked: *"Kayla—Oh, Kayla, I'm so sorry."*

No! Bobby flinched at Wendy's relayed words, imagining the worst. Casting aside any lingering caution, he leapt to his feet, plunged out of the tree line and sprinted across the two lane road to the Howell house. From the back and sides of the house, more mind-slaves converged on his outnumbered officers. *This could get dicey!*

A white wolf flashed past him, leaping into the air and bowling over a barrel-chested, middle-aged man in a black leather jacket. Growling, wolf-Abby clamped down on his arm with her powerful jaws and prevented him from joining the others.

Vasquez, White and Magano formed a defensive triangle, backs to one another, their ASP extendable batons out, snapped open, awaiting the next assault. Bobby raced through the gap in their formation, saw White sweep the businessman's legs out from under him, and whip the baton across the back of the man's head. At the moment, Bobby had no sympathy for the man's probable concussion. Kayla was foremost in his mind.

An instant before throwing his shoulder against the open door, he remembered his approach was supposed to be stealthy and pulled up. Because Wendy's transmission could now give away his position, he switched off the two-way radio. Then he popped the snap on his holster and tugged the Glock into his palm, entered the house and crept up the stairs. With his night vision goggles in place, he had no trouble navigating the dark interior of the house. Back against the wall, he stalked down the second floor hallway toward the last doorway on the right.

With his left hand, he waved impatiently at the buzzing sound around his head. Despite his efforts, the insectile sound became more persistent.

"What have you done to her?"

"Kayla is fine," Nicola Varrato said. "Other than granting me a small favor."

"Son of a bitch!" Wendy said. "I know about your damned favors!" Her grip tightened against the hilt of the dagger. She couldn't be sure Bobby was ready with the silver bullets. *Stall for another minute or so,* she thought. *Can't risk more than that.*

"I am not here to debate the morality of my dietary needs."

"I know why you're here," Wendy said. "For me. So let Kayla go. You don't need another mind-slave." Shielding her mind seemed to have the added benefit of dulling the hypnotic effect of his lambent eyes. He still oozed sexuality in supernatural spades, but her thoughts remained clear, her mind unsullied by his influence.

"True, I tasted her blood," the vampire said. "But she is alive and unharmed. Her body will replenish what she has given."

"That's not the point," Wendy said. "You've tainted her. Turned her against her own kind."

"My influence over her will end with my departure."

"I'm counting on it."

"I have not *turned* her," Varrato said. "She is no more a vampire than you are. She was tainted long before I arrived in your charming little town."

"What are you talking about?" Wendy asked, but her indignation had grown hollow. She had a good idea what the vampire meant. Wither, in the human form of Gina Thorne, had forced Kayla to drink her blood. Kayla had purged the blood from her system, but she could never be sure what lingered behind.

"Let's not get mired in the past," he said. "I have a proposition for you."

Wendy glanced at Tricia and Kayla, lounging decadently in their Victoria's Secret finest for the delight of Prince Bloodsucker. "No, thanks. I'll pass on the whole harem scene."

"Ah, you mistake my intent."

"Your intent is kinda obvious."

The vampire scoffed. "Superficial pleasures of the flesh. And blood, yes.

Most certainly blood. But I have something else in mind for you."

"I'm honored," Wendy said, heavy on the sarcasm. "Really."

Bobby should be inside the house. A few moments more.

"I am here because of Wither's curse," the vampire said. "As are you!"

"What?"

"You have come to kill me before I kill you. But I am not so easily killed."

"That's what they all say. What's your point?" Wendy's hand slipped into her pocket, swapping the dagger for a wooden stake. *Let Bobby take his shots, I'll give the vamp* my *point!*

"Simply this," he said. "Wither's unguided curse finally made a mistake."

"What, you're not one of the bad guys?"

"After I was turned, I lacked guidance and discipline. Over the years, I have learned to control my—as you might call them—undesirable impulses."

"You already admitted to drinking human blood."

"Yes, I drink human blood—to survive. But never enough to kill. My victims experience ecstasy in the moment, after which I *help* them forget my nocturnal visits. Physically, they may feel faint for a while, but they move on with their lives. Though I have been tempted many times, I have never turned anyone into what I am."

"What do you want? A gold star?"

"An understanding, an accord, if you will," he said. "Suppose by some miracle you manage to slay me. What happens then?"

"Something else crawls out of the sewer."

"Exactly," the vampire said. "Eight months ago, I was struck with a compulsion to find and kill you. But I was powerful enough to ignore that planted urge."

"And yet here you are." *Eight months? Is that why the reprieve lasted so long?*

"Out of curiosity," Varrato said. "Nothing more. The compulsion is an itch that I refuse to scratch."

"So you're not here to kill me?"

Varrato waved a hand in dismissal. "Why should I succumb to the posthumous raving of that grotesque creature? Why should I deign to complete what she could not? I refuse on principle. Assuming . . ."

"What?"

"That we have an accord," he said. "Live and let live. I leave your town, and these people resume their everyday lives. In return, you forget about me. And so, the curse stays and ends with me."

"Because you're undead." Wendy saw the logic of it. The curse *had* made a mistake, attaching itself to an immortal powerful enough to ignore it. "As long as you're alive—er, undead—the curse can't seek someone else to do its dirty work."

The vampire gave her a little bow.

"What's in it for you? If you hadn't come, I never would have known you existed. There would be no need for an accord between us."

"Curiosity brought me here," he said. "To meet you, Wendy Ward. A mortal who had inspired pathological anger so powerful it survived the death of the affronted party. Priceless!"

"Not a word I would have used. Ever."

"You are the most formidable mortal I have ever encountered," he said. "You shield your mind from my persistent prodding, you are undeniably fearless, and you . . . glow with magical ability."

"Would you like an autograph?"

He laughed heartily. "And there is that, your wonderful sense of humor."

"I'm not sure I like where this is going."

"When I said before that over the course of centuries I have been tempted to turn others but never have, I was paying you an inadvertent compliment." He spread his arms. "In you, I believe I have found the perfect companion for eternity."

He doesn't want me dead, Wendy thought nervously, *he wants me* undead*!*

"Think that's all of them," Senior Patrolwoman Vasquez said to her fellow officers. She was breathing heavily, the adrenaline rush subsiding now that the crowd had been subdued. A few were unconscious, several moaned in pain, and a couple glared at them. "Now what?"

"This is wrong," Magano said. "What have we done?"

"Mike? You okay, man?" White asked.

"No," Vasquez said, comprehension dawning. "Magano's right. We need to stop the chief. Before he hurts . . . Nicola."

White looked up at the second floor windows, his face slack. "I'm down with that."

"Get these handcuffs off us," Ricky Devlin said. "Hurry!"

Vasquez fumbled with her keys and nodded, hoping she wasn't too late.

Standing on all fours in the shadows, haunches trembling, the white wolf shook her head and whimpered.

"Not interested."

"Allow me the chance to persuade you."

Was it her imagination, or had the buzzing in her head suddenly become more insistent?

"Bobby!" Wendy shouted. *"Now!"*

She dropped to her right knee, clearing the line of fire, praying that Bobby had her back and was still of sound mind. To her relief, she heard the loud crack of a gunshot. A lampshade shattered. A second shot rang out and Varrato's left shoulder flinched backward. The vampire grunted in pain and flashed his fangs with a reflexive hiss.

The third shot missed high. A fourth never came.

Wendy pushed herself up, driving from her bent leg, and shoved the wooden stake on an unerring line toward the vampire's heart. But Varrato was too fast for her. His left hand caught her right in an iron grip and she felt bones snap in her wrist. A white-hot flash of pain brought a strangled cry to her lips. The wooden stake dropped from her numb fingers.

Wendy heard the muffled sound of the Glock striking the carpeted floor.

Bobby was lost. His mental block failed before he could fire the last silver bullet.

"I apologize," Varrato said. "Hurting you was never my intention."

"Forgive me if I don't believe that."

He cradled Wendy's arm and gently lowered her to the ground.

A woman shrieked, banged into Wendy and knocked her sideways. *Kayla!*

She scooped up the wooden stake and lunged upward with it, ramming it between the vampire's ribs and deep into his heart.

Varrato's eyes flared. "Kayla! *Stop this!*"

Her momentum drove him back and, paralyzed by the wood piercing his heart, he collapsed, lying spread-eagle. Grimacing, her own eyes wild with rage, Kayla's ferocity was a stark contrast to her earlier submissiveness as she literally pinned the vampire to the floor. Through clenched teeth, she screamed, "Why isn't he dead!"

Wendy knew. She turned toward Bobby. With his night vision goggles flipped up, she could see his eyes—vacant. He had his extendable baton out, directed at her. "Sorry, Bobby!" She raised her protective shield and warped its dimensions so that it slammed Windale's chief of police into the wall with enough force to stun him. As he crumpled to his knees, baton slack in his hand, Wendy dropped her shield, unzipped the canvas satchel on his back and removed the meat cleaver.

With her right wrist broken, she'd have to swing it with her left hand to behead Varrato. Maybe not the most gruesome deed she'd performed because of Wither. But right up there.

Seeing Wendy's intention, Kayla yelled, "Hurry!"

"Don't worry, he's paralyzed."

"I want him dead! Now!"

Varrato's lambent eyes glared at Kayla. Though paralyzed, he sought to regain control of her mind. "It's the taint," he whispered fiercely to her. "The seed has become a seedling!"

"No!" Kayla shrieked, shaking her head back and forth. She released the stake and scrambled away from him, trying to escape his words.

"It is *she* who wants me dead, Kayla," Varrato said. *"Not you!"*

A thunder of footfalls rumbled toward them. Varrato's minions racing up the stairs to his aid. Time was running out.

Wendy moved into position to chop his exposed throat.

Two bullets whizzed over her head and thwacked into the wall beyond her.

Bobby's patrol officers were leading the charge through the hallway— Varrato had control of them!

A flash of peach caught Wendy's eyes.

"No!" she shouted.

Too late. Tricia Howell yanked the stake from Varrato's heart.

At that moment, everyone under Varrato's mental control collapsed.

Wendy looked down at the vampire—

Varrato was glaring at her with the full force of his hypnotic gaze. A hammer slammed into her forehead. Her head whipped back from the force of the mental attack. The meat cleaver fell from her senseless hand with a heavy thud. A moment later, she dropped to her knees. He'd released them all to unleash a concerted attack against her mind.

Her stone fortress had taken a direct, undiluted strike from the master vampire's will. The walls were riddled with fissures and cracks. *Too many distractions,* she thought ruefully, *and the throbbing pain in my broken wrist. I lost focus. He's won.*

"I've won nothing."

He's reading my mind.

"A bit of despair leaked out, that is all."

Kayla, who had remained conscious when the others collapsed, had retrieved the stake from Tricia's limp hands, but she'd lost the element of surprise. Varrato caught her hand and pried the stake loose, crushing it to splinters, then flung her across the bed. "I should have attended to you earlier, my rose," he said. Kayla winced and pressed her hands to her forehead, writhing on the bed for long moments, before sagging into unconsciousness. "It is done."

While his attention was on Kayla, Wendy transferred her remaining stake to her left pocket and gripped it there, out of sight. She could strike him with her protective shield then attack with the stake—

Varrato blurred toward her. Before she could act, he was pressed against her, his hand wrapped around her pocket, pinning her hand and the stake. "You still leak thoughts, little moth."

Her injured right arm stretched to the side, her palm forming a cup, pulling heat from the air, concentrating the energy.

And Varrato's left hand caught her broken wrist in a gentle but firm grip. He chuckled in disbelief. "You never give up."

She shrugged. "Bad habit."

"You can conjure fire," he said. "Impressive."

"Want a free sample?"

They stood face to face, arms locked together, like dancers frozen in the middle of a complicated routine. "Seems we are at an impasse," Varrato said, looking into her eyes with unconcealed desire.

With her mental defenses crumbling, the heat and power of his gaze became hard to ignore—or resist. Her body trembled with desire, her heart raced and her breathing had become shallow. She was almost panting, and it had nothing to do with the pain in—

That's it, she thought. *I need a distraction. Focus on the pain.*

She concentrated on her aching wrist, the painful grinding of fractured bones, until the rolling waves of agony filled her mind . . . and the overwhelming desire began to subside.

"The more you fight," Varrato said, "the more I am drawn to you. And yet, if I stay, one of us will surely die."

"That's how it usually works."

He sighed. "I meant what I said. Unfortunately, the truth of my words is lost to you as long as I remain here. It is cruel irony that to prove myself worthy of you, I must leave you."

"Keep deluding yourself, blood boy."

She was pinned against the highboy, one arm extended, the other pinned down, and his body was pressed so close to her that she had no hope of kicking or kneeing him. Not that either option would prove effective against a master vampire. She imagined he could pull her arms from their sockets without working up a sweat. And that's when the finality of the situation hit her. She had run out of options and allies, unable to fight or resist anymore. It was over. End of the road. But she would go out on her terms, not as a mindless slave or a lingerie-clad love doll. She tried to speak, but her voice caught in her throat. She took a deep breath to regain her composure and whispered, "I'm ready. Make it quick."

"Foolish girl." He leaned forward and touched his lips to hers. She turned her head aside, but his lips sought hers and found them again for a long, gentle kiss that sought no more advantage than that. She had a fleeting urge to bite his lip, but worried that blood might trigger some sort of vampire feeding frenzy. Better if he simply snapped her neck. His full lips caressed her ear as he said, "Our accord is now sealed with a kiss." He then released her arms and stepped back.

"Wait," Wendy said. "You're really not going to kill me."

"If I had wanted to kill you," he said, "you would already be dead."

Wendy heard the rhythmic flow of soft footfalls a second before the vicious growl.

A blur of white flashed by as wolf-Abby leapt into the air. Her dark lips curled back from her fearsome lupine teeth, as she attempted to rip out the vampire's throat.

Varrato spun toward her and caught her forepaws in his hands to hold her snapping jaws at bay. "Ah, three forms for this one!" A moment later, wolf-Abby whimpered and transformed in his arms from ferocious predator to naked eighteen-year-old woman. As soon as she was comparatively harmless, he released her and turned back to Wendy.

"Oh, crap!" Abby said, face flushed as she backed away and covered up her bare skin with flailing arms. Crouched behind the foot of the bed she yelled, "Perv!"

Varrato winked at Wendy. "Remember what I said, Wendy Ward."

"Wait—!" she called.

A breeze ruffled her hair.

The downstairs door slammed shut.

Before sunrise, the vampire Nicola Varrato had left Windale.

With her forearm in a cast, Wendy had to take care writing the check for the workman who replaced the glass in the front door of the Crystal Path. Otherwise the bank would assume it had been written by a precocious first-grader. The workman thanked her and walked out, passing Chief Bobby McKay on his way in.

Bobby joined Kayla at the counter, gave her a quick hug and a peck on the cheek. She smiled in return and bumped her hip against his. "Door looks good," he said. He'd had to bust the glass after Kayla's cell phone call for help.

Wendy smiled. "Good as new."

"Maybe you should give me a spare key," Bobby said. "Or bill the city."

Wendy shook her head. "Small price to pay for normalcy. Well, that and six weeks in a cast."

"Someday you'll figure out how to heal yourself," Abby said.

After Varrato's abrupt departure, and ignoring her own painful injury, Wendy had made a quick circuit of the fallen and unconscious former-minions. Focusing on her rose quartz bead, she had magically healed their bumps, bruises and lacerations. But she couldn't be the agent of her own healing. Not yet, anyway. Meditation helped numb the pain—but not the itching, which was probably all in her head. She kept a thin plastic ruler handy to slide under the cast for itch relief.

"Your healing trick probably saved the city a few civil lawsuits," Bobby said. "Although none of Varrato's mind-slaves seem to recall much about the last few weeks. Some of them are chalking it up to a virus and fever dreams."

"Sounds like a good 'official story' to me," Wendy said.

"Agreed," Bobby said. "I should go. See you for lunch, Kayla."

After he left, Kayla's smile faltered. Wendy noticed her staring at her hands a lot in the last few days. She almost expected Kayla to say, à la Lady Macbeth, *"Out, damned spot! Out, I say!"*

"Kayla, stop beating yourself up," Wendy said. "You were ferocious. You fought off his mind control and nearly took him out single-handedly."

"So I should forget about waking up as a vampire's lingerie model?"

Abby chuckled. "Like I should forget he transformed me into a *nude* model!"

"Definitely," Wendy said, smiling. "On both counts. But what about Bobby?"

Kayla nodded. "He vaguely remembers coming at you with his baton, so he's cool with the whole mind control get-out-of-jail-free card. Just wish I knew what really happened to me."

Wendy had the advantage over all of them. She'd never lost control of her mind, although she'd come frighteningly close at the end. She remembered what Varrato had said about Kayla's attack. *"It is she who wants me dead, Kayla. Not you!"* And he wasn't talking about Wendy. Because he'd mentioned a *taint* and something about a seed becoming a seedling. The implication had been clear: he'd sensed something of Wither lurking inside Kayla's mind and his meddling had somehow agitated it. But if she could believe him, he'd fixed the problem. *"It is done."* But had he? How could he—or Wendy—know for sure?

"Even though he's a five-hundred-year-old perv," Abby said, "I believe him."

Distracted by her own concerns, Kayla reacted to the comment with surprise. "About what?"

"That he's strong enough to ignore the compulsion of the curse," Abby said. "That he won't kill Wendy. And since the curse is locked into him until he dies—which he can't, being undead and immortal—it's basically over."

"You trust a vampire?" Kayla asked, eyebrows raised.

"Look at the evidence," Abby said. "He overpowered all of us and had the advantage over Wendy. He could have killed her but didn't. Plus, he didn't kill anyone. He drank the blood of his minions but he didn't drain anyone dry or turn any of us into the undead." She shrugged. "For a vampire, he wasn't that bad of a houseguest."

Kayla burst into laughter. For the first time in days, the tension seemed to ease out of her. "Look out, Windale, there's a new Pollyanna in town!"

"After the last ten years, I take good news wherever I find it," Abby said, her face aglow with a carefree smile. "What do you think, Wendy?"

"I'm hopeful," Wendy said. "The curse might not be officially over, but it could be nullified for a long, long time." Alethea Brynn Cavendish had left Wendy with parting advice, *"Only you can end the curse. Find a way."* Maybe this was the way—*a* way. To accept that the vampire could keep it contained within himself as a dark impulse ignored. "So this is definitely good news." *But . . . I have this feeling Varrato will come calling again to repeat his undead proposition. With the curse inside him, he can always locate me. How long will he take* no *for an answer?*

"It's time, Wendy," Abby said. "Time to live your life free of the curse."

"That sounds wonderful."

(beyond imagine)
Mike McPhail

"As soldiers, we may all fight together, but we die alone."
— William Kriegherren

There was the sound of breathing—very close and confined. Ingram sensed the rise and fall of his chest, and realized that it was in unison with the sounds. Hot air flowed back against his face with each breath. It was as if he were just an observer in all this; there, but not a part of it.

Muffled voices filtered in to the enclosed space. He couldn't understand them, but subconsciously they represented a comfortable connection. The world around him was black, still, and without meaningful form. Then something shifted nearby. He could feel it. His eyes snapped open and consciousness rushed over him; he was back. *But back from where?* he thought.

His body suddenly spasmed, trying to move in any way it could, but to no avail. He was trapped.

Panic welled up from the hardwired part of his brain; hormones surged and his breathing quickened.

There's no air. He wanted to scream.

If you panic, you're as good as dead, yelled a voice in his head.

"Stonebridge," he panted, finding reassurance in the memory of his combat instructor; a man who could have been punched from the same mold as every British drill instructor throughout history.

Assess your situation, the voice said, *and then work with what you've got. Don't panic, Death will just have to wait its turn.*

Calmer now, he slowed his breathing and tried to concentrate. He still couldn't move. "Hello," he called. His voice sounded muffled to his ears, like he was. . . . "Damnit," he said, cursing his own stupidity.

"Suit-mode, power up." In a flurry of lights and sounds—and an accompanying rush of cool air—his helmet displays came to life; the world outside remained black except for the familiar green triangular identification icons; one topped with MGN floated just before him.

His comm crackled, and her voice sounded by his ear. "Ingram, can you hear me?"

"Yeah, I'm with you, Morgan."

"Stay calm and engage your active light-amp; we'll have you out of there in just a moment."

"Acknowledged," he said. "Suit-mode, active night-vision." The suit's on-board computer—Pacscomp—turned the scene into a daytime-bright, false-color image, lit by a cluster of infrared diodes mounted on either side of his helmet. Although distorted and washed out due to bounce back from some sort of transparent covering, he could easily make out the smooth, body-armor carapace of his fellow troopers. To an outsider, they could have easily been mistaken for faceless creatures of war; they would have been half right. These were soldiers of the Allied Defense Force, his comrades in arms; more importantly, they were his friends.

Morgan stared straight back at him and waved while the other troop-er—his icon read MKC—seemed preoccupied with something just off to the right.

"Morgan, what's going on?" Ingram asked.

"Got it, give me a hand," MacKencey, the other trooper, called to Morgan as he secured his fighting knife. Together they pulled aside the thick transparency entombing him, but Ingram still couldn't move.

"Almost done," Morgan said as she put her hand firmly on his chest, holding him still.

There was a snipping sound, and suddenly he could move his legs, then his arms. He reached up and grabbed Morgan's forearm.

"Easy, sir," MacKencey said as he came into view, now holding a pair of wire cutters. With his other hand he tipped Ingram's head back, and moved in toward his throat.

Snip. Ingram immediately found himself slumping forward. If not for Morgan's hand bracing him, he would have fallen. He felt like he still might. He tried to shift his weight to compensate, but it was no good; he was too stiff and had a hard time just moving.

"We have you," Morgan said as she and MacKencey helped him shift position.

Ingram grabbed hold of MacKencey's shoulder and worked himself loose. "Thanks."

MacKencey tapped him on the shoulder in response, and then stepped around him. Morgan moved back and un-slung her gauss rifle.

Ingram stood there for a moment and took in the scene; they were in an enclosed compound, a massive storage area of some kind. He couldn't see much detail across the distance, and no color through the night-amp setting, but the place reminded him of the supply depot on base, only on a gigantic scale. He couldn't even hazard a guess at the items he was seeing, but if it was anything like Supply, there was everything imaginable between these walls. The architecture itself was comprised of many flat surfaces which met at 90 degree angles to form what appeared to be free-standing buildings inside of the main structure extending well beyond the edge of his scope's range. All of those he could see were crammed full of whatever this place supplied. The ground level was covered in some type of composite or laminate; it was dirty white, with a slight sheen to the surface.

Off in the distance, two more troopers slowly moved about—icons BUR and KTV—while icon MRU floated near the bottom of his screen. A Parr scout sat upright just a few feet away, his head slightly cocked to one side as if he contemplated Ingram in that all too familiar way that only a cat can. Ingram resisted the urge to bend down and pet him. Kind of senseless as the cat, too, was clad in lightweight-polymer armor. But nevertheless, the sight of the Parr and his fellow troopers was comforting.

"Okay, Morgan, fill me in." It was more of a command than a request.

Morgan paused for a moment before answering. "I woke up over there, lying on the ground out in the open." She pointed toward the remains of a container; its transparent facing had been torn off. "Beyond that, I'm a blank. Not sure how I got free."

MacKencey reappeared holding a gauss rifle and several magazines. "Here you go, sir."

With a nod, Ingram took the ammo and secured it to his carrying gear, then ran a quick check on the weapon.

"There was no one in sight," Morgan said. "Then I saw the other capsules all lined up." She gestured behind Ingram, who turned in response. The container he had just been liberated from stood at the end of the line between two parallel rails. There were markings on every surface, interspersed with graphic images, his face disturbingly among them, but he couldn't decipher the meaning of it all. The container was still secure between opposing sets of notches; there were spaces for five other containers. "Mac was in the second capsule. . . ."

"Sarcophagus might be a better description," MacKencey said. "After all, they did pack us off in full armor with hardware."

Ingram held up his hand. "Please continue, corporal."

She shifted her weight from one leg to another, as if the thought made her uneasy. "I could see there was an ADF trooper inside, but there was no Pacscomp activity." She looked away for a moment. "Nor any bio-signs; no movement, venting, or even residual heat. I thought he was dead." She looked over at MacKencey.

"Sorry, maybe next time," he said.

Ingram slung his weapon across his chest, and then made a quick head-count. Six slots, six troopers present, and six containers lay open. "Is there anyone else?"

"No, sir, you're the last one we know of," Morgan said. "Also there's no comm traffic beyond the squad-band. Sergeant Bauer has a signal booster, but that's also a negative. Sir, we're not even picking up the local Comm or Navsats."

"Right." Ingram ran through the possible ramifications.

"Ah, sir . . ." MacKencey said, almost apologetically.

Ingram paused for a moment before answering. "Yes?"

MacKencey took a deep breath before continuing. "What's the last thing you remember?" It almost sounded as if he already knew the answer.

"I . . ." Ingram drew a blank. "I've got nothing."

"Do you remember home?" Morgan asked.

Ingram just stood there, a sense of despair pushing at him deep and hard. He looked over at Morgan and just shook his head.

"But you do remember us?" she asked.

"Yes, that much is clear," he said with a feeling of some certainty against the unknown. Anything related to his military career was solidly in place, like it was hardwired. Everything else. . . . *Damnit*, he thought, *you're the one in charge, so be in charge, take control of the situation, not the other way around.*

"Right, everyone form-up," he said over the squad-band.

"Acknowledged," voices chorused from his comhood's speakers, as the other troopers jogged over to join them.

Now together, Ingram took stock. Everyone was outfitted with what the ADF called AS-Is (Allied Standard-Issue) as far as individual weapons, ammunition loads, and munitions. The heaviest weapon belonged to Sergeant Kotov, the team's gunner: the medium gauss rifle—the ADF's base-of-fire machinegun. The massive piece of hardware was typically hung from a shoulder sling and rested at the user's hip. The sergeant, not being typical, used it like a rifle.

Your men are counting on you to have the answers, Stonebridge said from the recesses of Ingram's mind. *Never be indecisive; make a decision, even if you have no way of knowing whether it's right or wrong. YOU have to make a decision.*

"Listen up . . ." Ingram said, forced to rely on his common sense until something better came along. "We need to check the area for anyone else. Have any of you had a chance to look around?"

"Da, Centurion," Kotov said, pointing off into the darkness. His other hand rested gently against the side of his weapon to keep it from swinging, as it now hung loosely from its straps. "At about twelve meters there is a sheer drop-off which runs in both directions out beyond my scopes."

"We also have a bit of high ground back that way," Bauer said, gesturing behind the group. "Like everything else so far, it seems to be made up of multilevel platforms packed with storage containers of some sort; it goes well up over twenty meters higher than any point in this place."

Ingram turned; he could just make out the structure.

"This place reminds me of the cargo-staging area at Churchill Spaceport," MacKencey said. "You know, that place where they off-load the box containers from the trains, then stack them up for later use?"

"So are you saying someone packed us off for shipment?" Bauer tightened his grip on his weapon.

"I don't know. I'm just saying this looks like a storage hangar," MacKencey said.

"Are we inside a building?" Morgan asked.

"Most likely," Kotov said. "Look up, no stars, not even overcast glow."

MacKencey stared up. "If we are inside, then this space must be at least as big as a Terran sports stadium."

Stay on top of things, Squad Leader.

"Okay, just put that on the growing list of things we need to find out. Until we do I want everyone to maintain light-discipline; I.R. only." Ingram waited a moment. "Understood?"

"Acknowledged," the team replied.

"Sergeant," Ingram said, looking at Bauer. "Deploy a beacon; we'll use this as our rally point."

Bauer pulled what looked like a small, rounded can from his side pouch. Unscrewing the top, he depressed the activation button. Throughout the team, a yellow icon appeared on their displays, bearing the label RP01. The sergeant then placed the can down among the remains of a container.

"Good. Has anyone scouted beyond this point?" Ingram asked, gesturing toward a wall of boxes opposite of the drop off. The reply was "negative."

"All right then; MacKencey, you and Ma'Rou do what you do best." He motioned them off in that direction then turned back to the others. "Morgan, you head for that high ground Bauer scoped out; we could do with a little bird's eye view of this place."

"Sergeants," he said, pointing at Bauer and Kotov. "Check out the other side of that wall, while I go with Morgan. Any questions?" There were none. "Move out."

"I still think it's some type of test," Ma'Rou SIcommed over the squad-band; he was currently riding on top of MacKencey's pack, facing back.

Nature hadn't equipped the Parr with the ability to speak any known human language, and in fact they didn't even try. Since the early testing phase of Doctor McPherren's Synaptic Interface—a system that allows direct mind-machine communication—a Parr's thoughts could be interpreted and synthesized into speech by the suit's Pacscomp.

MacKencey only half listened, his weapon at the ready as he moved across the maze-like terrain. "So, Mr. Sterling, who do you think managed to pull this off?" he asked, as he approached a tall, narrow gap in the structure.

"My first guess would be the Ka'nigits," Ma'Rou said.

"The Ka'nigits?" MacKencey laughed. "Right. You've been hanging out with our expatriate friends again."

Ma'Rou's tail twitched with uncertainty. *"Yeah, they let us watch those old movies."*

MacKencey smiled at the thought of a dozen sentient house cats sitting around a theater display, trying to interpret what humans thought was funny almost a century ago. "The colonel is the only person in the known universe who refers to the Teutonic Knights as Ka'nigits. True, they're an elitist techno-terrorist group, with more money than common sense, but that's still no reason to be rude."

"Is that a bad thing?" Ma'Rou asked, as he nervously started kneading the pack.

MacKencey stopped and peered around the edge of the gap; it was black beyond the opening. Looking up, he judged the height to the top of the next platform.

"Can you make that jump?" he asked.

Ma'Rou sat up on the pack without answering. MacKencey felt the Parr revving up for the leap; he barely had time to brace before the fifteen pounds of armored cat pushed off his pack like a spring. Ma'Rou caught the edge of the landing with his back legs—his armor's claws dug into the side—he then pushed off to land with a thump somewhere on top.

"Okay, give me an—"

Ma'Rou's scream of terror flooded the comm.

It was like climbing on some over-sized child's playground. The box containers came in several sizes, and many could easily be stacked to act as steps. Morgan had just climbed up onto one of the bigger boxes when she suddenly doubled over as if to instinctively protect herself from some unseen horror. The impulse was external and not unfamiliar. Her superiors were not aware of it, but she sensed highly charged emotions. She turned and looked off in the direction her squad mates had gone. Something was wrong.

"Morgan?" Ingram said.

"Sir . . ." She pointed off into the distance, just as MacKencey's voice came over the comm.

"—under attack! Ma'Rou's mis—" The message ended in a burst of static.

Ingram turned, looking for his trooper's icon. MRU was nowhere to be seen, while the MKC switched from the familiar green to a bright red with a time stamp, recording the moment the suit's Pacscomp self-destructed upon the perceived death of its user.

"MacKencey!" Bauer yelled over the comm. "Mac! Damnit, trooper, what is your status?"

Ingram forced his voice to remain calm. "MacKencey, Ma'Rou, report." Despite what the technology said, there was always a chance.

"It's no good, sir," Morgan said, her voice now steeled against the reality; she then turned and continued her climb. "Nothing can sneak up on me here, sir. I recommend that you join up with the others."

Ingram thought it over as he watched the two sergeants' icons heading for MacKencey's death marker; "Acknowledged, Corporal, keep me informed," he said as he slung his weapon and started down.

The troopers' jog slowed to a walk as they approached their target, cautiously moving beyond the stack of massive storage boxes. Kotov carried his weapon at the hip, moving it slowly from side to side to keep its momentum up; on his display, its targeting reticle and pip floated ethereally out in front of him. Bauer flanked him to his left; his own weapon was up and at the ready. They stopped. Bauer turned so he was standing almost back to back with Kotov.

The death marker was somewhere on the other side of a low wall of a stone-like substance jutting out across their path. To their left, a massive one-story structure extended off into the distance; it appeared to be a glass-enclosed holding area. On their right was the drop off.

"I'm moving up to the wall," Kotov said, already on the move.

"Acknowledged." Bauer swung around and aimed past his comrade.

Kotov stood facing the wall. "Suit-mode, gun view." An inset screen opened at the bottom of his display, showing a live feed from the targeting scopes mounted on the nose of his weapon. He slowly moved it out and away from cover.

The image was surreal; Kotov wasn't a religious man *per se*, but he was brought up within the teachings of the Church. At this moment, he truly did believe in the existence of hell. After all, that's where demons came from.

At first it was hard to make out what was going on without a point of reference. Then Kotov spotted what he assumed was Mac's body face down on the ground, his standard-issue backpack clearly visible. In comparison, the man-like beings were short and compact, only about four feet tall. They were clad in some type of sloped body-armor, made up of rows of small, overlapping plates.

Three of the things were searching MacKencey, while two more stood across from each other. One was gesturing, using what looked like some form of sign language; the other held Mac's helmet at arm's length, slowly looking it over.

The helmet's neck band was torn and hanging down, as if it had been crudely cut away from the armor's chest section. The beast then rolled it over to look at the top, shaking it sharply.

"*Chyort!*" Kotov shouted as MacKencey's head dropped from the open end, dangling in place from the wires of his comhood.

A stream of steel darts suddenly lanced out at the creatures. He opened fire and rushed the enemy before he realized he did so.

Bauer, not knowing what was happening, ran to catch up.

Morgan had just set up her gauss rifle with several smaller boxes acting as a platform, when the firing alert came up on her display; Kotov's, and now Bauer's, icons flashed. She knelt behind her weapon and activated its stabilizers, while bringing its electro-optical targeting scopes on line. The weapon's view of the world now dominated her display; quickly she swung it onto Kotov's icon.

"Twenty power, maximum light-amp." As the scene came into view, Kotov was partially blocked by a wall, while Bauer seemed to be moving in among several bodies. Morgan had felt MacKencey die, so she didn't need any confirmation; but now at the sight of his mangled armor, she had to fight to keep her emotions down. "Your friends need you," she reminded herself. "Stay sharp."

"Get Mac," Kotov said, panting from the adrenalin rush; he leveled his weapon at the gap in the wall as he watched for other possible threats.

Bauer tried to get a handle on what just happened, as he slung his weapon and started clearing the bodies away. The bad guys were heavy, making them difficult to lift, so he just dragged them clear from MacKencey by whatever body part was handy.

"Sergeant, status," Ingram said over the comm.

"Sir, we found Mac. Negative." Kotov answered the unasked question. "We have engaged and terminated five unknowns."

"And Ma'Rou?"

"Nothing yet."

"I'll be there shortly," Ingram said.

After dragging the last one off by its arm, Bauer now saw the carnage that had been wreaked on his friend. In the back of his mind something didn't make sense. Looking around, he found his answer. "Sergei," he called out.

"*Da?*"

"These things didn't use small arms." Bauer stepped over one of the bodies to reach down to draw up its arm. Held in a death grip by its four-fingered hand was a stylized axe. The blade was broad, and narrowed down to form a buckler over the grip; opposing the blade was a long, thick spike.

The snap of a passing bullet startled the men. Nearby something fell, and fell hard.

"They're coming over the top!" Morgan yelled over the comm, as she rained down gauss darts on the enemy still out of sight atop the one-story structure to their left. Some rounds struck the glass, but it must have been tempered as it dimpled but did not shatter.

Kotov back-stepped away and quickly opened up his field of fire. Standing next to MacKencey's body, Bauer retrieved his weapon.

Now at the ready, all Kotov heard were the sounds of metal smashing into armor, and the thuds of bodies. *No screams of pain, not even the yells of an infantry charge*, he thought. "But I know you can die, you *sukinsyn!*" he said, as his fear turned into the need for bloody vengeance.

As the first of them boiled over the top, Kotov opened up at full cyclic; the magnetic rails of his gauss rifle hummed with surging power as multiple darts entered and exited the tracks simultaneously at supersonic velocity.

Kotov swung the weapon using the stream of fire like the teeth of a chainsaw. The darts punched through the attacker's armor, tumbling away as they tore through flesh and smashed bone. Spinning at odd angles, many rounds emerged from one victim only to rip into another. Most of the creatures died before they reached the ground, while Bauer—firing more selectively—picked off those remaining.

An alert tone sounded in Kotov's helmet as his ammunition counter tracked rapidly down toward zero. "I'm out!" he yelled as his weapon went dry; with a practiced hand he released the spent drum and reached for a new one.

"Acknowledged." Bauer picked up his rate of fire.

Then, as if on cue, like a cresting wave, the enemy poured over the top and pressed through the gap. It was like standing in front of an oncoming truck: every fiber of your being screams for you to run, as you just stand there and yell back *No!* Bauer concentrated on dealing with the most immediate threats, but for each one he dropped, another one pushed past and continued to press forward. Both time and distance were running out.

With his weapon pointing downward, Kotov had just slotted the ammunition drum into its top feedway when the creatures reached him. With a slap, he locked the drum home, as an accompanying tone signaled that the weapon was loading. Acting on instinct, Kotov swung his weapon up as he reached for its trigger group.

Before he could fire, an armored hand reached up and grabbed hold of the barrel's frame, attempting to wrench it free. Kotov grunted as the sudden jerk caused burning pains across his shoulders and chest.

"Sergei?" Bauer called as he stole a quick glance; Kotov was being over run. Bauer turned and fired; both darts hit home, dropping the attacker. As he swung back, the first blow struck him in the abdomen, somehow managing to punch deep through his body armor. In that instant, the ancient part of Bauer's brain kicked in, shifting reality into slow motion as survival hormones surged through him.

He wanted—he *needed*—to react, but couldn't. He heard the medium gauss rifle buzzing off in the distance, as darts poured out of the weapon so quickly, the individual sounds blended together. He then knew the truth of his situation: although men fought together, they died alone.

Kotov struggled for control of his weapon as the creatures swarmed him. Screaming with the effort, he forced the weapon's muzzle down toward the ground; the impacting darts threw out a wave of splinters, causing several of the creatures to jump away. Pivoting, he brought the weapon up, still firing. At point-blank range, the force of impact shattered the darts into blazing bits of glowing metal as they danced over the creature's armor.

"Bauer, fall back!" Kotov shouted.

No response.

"Bauer!" As he looked to his right, a new red death marker appeared among a group of creatures. "*Chyort!*" he yelled as he brought his weapon around hard and cut them down.

Something smashed into his helmet, making the left side of his face go numb. Turning in the direction of the blow, he hosed down the creatures rushing him. The demons danced as they were torn apart by his murderous fire.

"Now . . ." he started to say to his fallen comrade, as something hit him hard in the lower back. It burned like a red-hot piece of metal. It was like someone had thrown a switch; his legs would not bear him, and he fell over, dragged down by the weight of his weapon.

He lost contact with himself as shock set in. Beyond his rapidly fading world, he faintly heard his suit's Pacscomp. He could not understand what it was saying—then its neutral voice boomed directly into his mind.

"Your situation is critical; Engaging *Combat*," the automatic system SIcommed.

Kotov reared up, pulling in a deep lungful of air as cardiac stimulates and synthetic hormones ignited the cells throughout his body; his mind cleared and his vision sharpened to a high contrast. He tried to get up, but could only manage to bring himself up on his elbows. He looked back over his shoulder; the enemy soldier stood there, one hand still holding whatever it used to kill him. The creature put one foot on Kotov's back, driving him down; with a yank, it pulled the weapon free. It stood there, hefting in both hands what appeared to be a larger version of the hand axe; the six-inch spiked end wet with blood.

"Not like this!" Kotov cursed. "Suit-mode—"

Morgan continued to pick off targets as Kotov fell out of view behind the wall, leaving only his superimposed icon; Ingram now came into view as he approached Kotov's position.

"Morgan, what's . . ." Ingram said as there was a brief warning flash around Kotov's icon. The explosion was fierce. Its pressure wave wrenched bone and metal and glass alike into lethal fragments that flew out to find other victims. Face down against the container, Morgan felt the shockwave passing through the tower, followed by the boom. She opened her eyes; her scopes showed that where two of her friends had recently stood there lay only carnage.

In the foreground, Ingram stood up; Morgan shifted her weapon to cover him. "Sir, are you all right?"

"I'm in one piece. Are there any more of them?" he asked.

Morgan panned across the scene. "Sir, nothing's moving over there. In fact, I'm not even getting their death markers," she said, wondering why she felt nothing at the words.

"Kotov command-detonated his grenades. That would have fried what was left of their comm-gear," he said. "I'm falling back to your position."

"Acknowledged." Morgan zoomed out the scopes to take in a larger area.

Ingram bounced along at a fast jog some five meters from the edge of the drop off. As he passed a cluster of containers, something ran out.

"Sir!" Morgan yelled as she zoomed in; several of those things—axes held high—were heading for him. There was no time for an aimed shot. As her targeting reticle's pip crossed the attacker, Morgan fired. In an explosion of armor, the first one went down; she shifted to the next and fired. Her rounds slammed into the creature, but off center. It kept moving, one arm smoking but not out of action.

Ingram turned and opened up as the last two closed to within just a few meters of him; one ran right behind the other. He caught the closest one in a hailstorm of gauss fire, but the other used the body as a shield to gain that last meter. The thing came in low and drove its shoulder up and into Ingram's gut like a linebacker, forcing him back, off balance, half-carrying him toward the edge.

Morgan hesitated as the two forms collided, but it was obvious what the thing intended—*Shoot!* someone screamed. Her index and middle finger depressed the weapon's electronic trigger; with a crack, the dart cut through the air, leaving a distorted wake behind it.

It struck; the thing toppled forward still holding Ingram. Both went over the edge, disappearing into the black.

The targeting reticle hovered over the spot. Morgan stared in disbelief as her emotions threatened to overwhelm her.

Then the lights came on overhead.

Automatically, the Pacscomp disengaged her light-amp and switched to day-view. The brilliantly lit world around her was at once familiar, but yet somehow beyond her ability to imagine.

The sun was barely up when Greg pulled in to the shopping center that housed Between Books. At this hour the place was care-worn and deserted, but later he would be lucky to grab time for a breath, let alone a pipe. He glanced toward the store; Laura waited for him beneath the overhang. They had some inventory to take care of before things got busy. With a sigh, he slipped out of the car. On his way across the parking lot, he placed the stem of his pipe between his lips and lit up, watching the black cherry-scented smoke swirl in contrast against the fog. He only had time for a couple of puffs before putting it out again, but it was enough.

"Hey." A sleepy-eyed Laura nodded vaguely in his direction as he came up.

"Morning," Greg said, moving past her to unlock the door and flick on the lights. "Thanks for coming in early." He left her up front as he hurried in to disable the alarm. As he was moving down the aisle, his foot came down on something hard. It nearly sent him to the floor, but he caught himself on the counter.

"Ah, crap!" Greg limped toward the keypad, getting there in time to punch in his code just before the alarm sounded.

"You okay?"

"Yeah ... yeah, I'm fine." He made his way back to where he'd stumbled and bent down to find a mangled Hellion figurine beside an ADF Special Forces action figure.

"What the hell?" His tongue ran along the back of his bottom lip as he considered them. "Hey, Laura," he called out. "Last night, did you see anyone fooling around over here?"

She peeked her head around the bookshelf and her eyebrow quirked as she spied him still crouched on the floor. "No, why?"

"Someone's been into the action figures." He straightened up, holding the Alliance Archives figure. "They're from Mike's new role-playing game. We'd better keep an eye out for the vandal. In the meantime, put this one and the others in the locked case." He handed her the Ingram character and tossed the mangled Hellion into the trash can before heading to the back and the new stock waiting to be shelved.

It moved at a slow pace down the valley that ran between the cliff-like structures making up this place; the top of its head rode past some twenty meters below the edge of the drop-off. She felt each of its steps as a dull thump beneath her.

Confusion and a growing feeling of helplessness replaced her grief. Frustration at her inability to help her friends screamed through her. "Well, Stonebridge, what sage advice do you have for me now?" she said to the ghost of her past, her only solid memory outside of the squad. Again, memory failed her.

She felt the vibration of several thumps as something landed at her back. Her heart felt like it would blow out of her chest; she knew there was no room to fight, let alone a place to hide. She spun, reaching for her sidearm.

With the weapon halfway out of its holster, she stopped. Standing there without his helmet was Ma'Rou; his left eye wept and part of his ear was torn; blood caked the side of his furry face and ran down his shoulder armor.

Morgan pressed her sidearm back into the holster. She dropped to her knees and reached out for the Parr. Ma'Rou limped to Morgan, who gathered him into her arms.

"Suit-mode, external." She activated the suit's exterior speakers. "You look like shit," she said in a laughing tone; tears welled up in her eyes. "Can you travel?"

Without his Pacscomp, Ma'Rou was reduced to what the Parr called the "monkey nods." As he signaled yes, Morgan gently lifted him up toward her shoulder, where he worked his way back onto her pack.

She stood up carefully and retrieved her gauss rifle, which she then slung across her chest. Turning, she looked in the direction the giant—for lack of a better term—had gone. A city-sized field of colorful containers, punctuated by a multitude of bizarre objects, stretched before her.

She had to rescue Ingram. "You set?" She heard two taps on the back of her helmet; with that, she started the climb down.

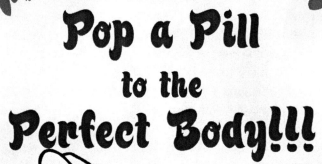

Pop a Pill
to the
Perfect Body!!!

EXERCISE

DIETING

Pop a NAPETIENE®

and go from
THIS

to **THIS**

Pop a NAPETIENE®
TODAY!!!

(appetite)
Jonathan McGoran

Frederick had been gone since eleven and he still wasn't back. Not good news for either of us. It was a quarter past three now, and the idea of lunch had grown on me.

At some point, I knew, I would have to start taking care of these sorts of things myself, but I was not looking forward to it.

Gazing out my penthouse window at the city below, it was easy to imagine life going on as it had in the past. I didn't often ask Frederick what it was like out there, but I picked things up. I knew the world had changed.

The thought of it didn't bother me, as long as I didn't have to deal with it. Nothing bothered me much anymore, but change never had. Some people are afraid of change. Once I used to seek it out, but eventually I just didn't care.

Maybe I was content. I might have smiled at the thought, but then my belly growled loudly.

It wasn't content. It was hungry.

I draped my hand across it, letting my fingers rest between the hard ridges of muscle that ran across my abdomen. Even after all this time, I was still pleased by the feel of it. Reflected in the walnut-framed mirror on the other side of the room, I was pleased by the look of it, as well. I wasn't blind to the shortcomings of my appearance, but after growing up awkward and pudgy, I still got a thrill at the sight of my lean, hard musculature, even after what, three years? Four? I couldn't say for sure how long.

It was probably five years since the idea first struck me.

I'd been toiling away as a lab rat for a company called Taylor and Rice, a transnational behemoth that sold everything from baby shampoo and pharmaceuticals to floor wax and industrial solvents. I was actually working in the solvent division when I had the idea, a bolt from the blue.

I quit the next day, but I had signed a non-compete, so I had to wait two years before I could even start working on it. Two years without the paycheck or the meager satisfaction of the job I had worked so hard to get.

That was the hardest part, two years working at a convenience store. But that was also how I met Frederick. Our coworkers teased us both mercilessly: him for being a lumbering oaf, me for being soft and weak and uniquely unqualified for the work at hand.

As it turned out, I had a problem completing meaningless tasks. Not Frederick, though. The barbs of his coworkers notwithstanding, he had a considerable aptitude for mindless endeavors. He even seemed oblivious to their cruelty—at least until I pointed it out to him.

I confided in Frederick what I was working on, and unfortunately, he told the others. They teased me even more after that. Those last few months were the hardest.

I didn't need a magic pill, they all said—I needed to hit the gym. "Try a salad," they said, at least a few times a week, and each time they'd all laugh like it was the first time anyone had ever said it.

The worst of them was a guy named Gerry. He called me a few years later. I was doing well by then, and I guess he had heard. He needed money for an operation or something.

"Oh, that's terrible," I had said, as if I cared.

I let him tell me his whole tale of woe, and he piled it on. He seemed to think that if he laid it on thick enough, I'd not only pay for the operation, but I'd throw in a new car, as well.

When he was done, I wished him the best of luck and thanked him for calling. Then I hung up.

The last thing I heard him say was, "But . . ."

I still smile at that memory. Occasionally, I wondered what happened to my former coworkers, but I knew it was either one thing or the other. Same as everybody else.

When my non-compete expired and I could do whatever I wanted, I quit my job and took Frederick with me. He was a little uneasy about leaving the security of the only job he had ever known, but I convinced him it was for the best. I had told him it might take two years, but as it turned out it was less than six months. In that regard, he got off easy.

Certification was surprisingly simple. Each component had been previously tested. It wasn't hard to convince the FDA that together they were safe, too. Venture capital rolled in by the truckload. I could have sold out then and I would have been rich beyond my wildest dreams, but I kept it under my control and I brought it to market. I made billions.

You didn't need to go to a stupid gym. And you didn't need to watch what you ate. But every morning you had to take one little pill called Napetiene. And you had to buy that pill from me.

Napeteine basically turned off your digestive tract, so you could eat whatever you wanted, as much as you wanted, and the fat would disappear. Maybe the best part was, it didn't matter what you ate. If you had high cholesterol, you could eat steak and butter and pizza—it didn't matter, because it didn't get absorbed.

Is it any wonder I got rich?

Sure, there were critics. Nutritionists said you lost valuable nutrients, but all you had to do was stop taking the Napetiene and eat healthy once in a while. Or just take some vitamins. And it wasn't like morbid obesity was all that good for you, either.

To prove it was safe and effective, I used it on myself first. I went on it for three months before letting anybody else even try it. Napeteine worked like a dream. It even enhanced the muscle that was hiding under all that fat.

Within months, I was thin and I was ripped. I became the spokesperson, the poster boy. Billboards, magazines, television commercials—I was a star.

Some people said I became arrogant, but with a product like this, why wouldn't I? When sales leveled off, I brought down the price, and obesity became a thing of the past. It wasn't just fat people taking it, either. Once they saw these formerly fat people binging on chocolate cake and losing weight, thin people started taking it, too. And eating like pigs.

Of course, not everyone went on it. The health freaks and Luddites said it wasn't natural, it was too good to be true. They refused to even try it. I wasn't crazy about them at the time, but I grew to love them. Some, including Frederick, were just happy the way they were.

For the first year I used Napeteine, I was careful to come off it periodically. After a while, though, I noticed some long-term changes.

Skin tone was one—a kind of grayish pallor—but that was a small price to pay for those rock-hard abs. I went back into the lab and created a tanning cream that struck gold again. It didn't sell like Napetiene, but it sold quite a lot. After that I looked even better; tanned and fit.

The Napeteine also started to affect my thoughts, though. I couldn't say exactly how, but I had a sense that it did. I became more impulsive.

On a hunch, I sold the Napeteine at the height of its popularity. And I made sure it was to my old employer, Taylor and Rice. I could have gotten a few hundred million more from some other suitors, but I wanted it to be Taylor and Rice. I almost felt guilty about the sum I got from them, but that was another change: I had all but stopped experiencing feelings like guilt.

The biggest change, and the most disturbing one by far, was that food just didn't taste good anymore. I no longer enjoyed it. And what good is a pill that lets you eat whatever you want if it also makes you not want to eat anything? For a diet pill, it was ideal in a way, but I liked food and I wanted to continue to enjoy it.

That was when I came off Napeteine for good. And that was when I realized the changes were permanent. My taste for food never did come back, or at least not like before. Instead, I felt a sort of deep, constant craving that was never sated.

Sales of Napeteine leveled off and even started dropping, but I didn't care—it was Taylor and Rice's problem, not mine. I suspected that those who started taking it earliest were beginning to feel these other effects, as well. I knew for sure I wasn't the only gray when sales of my skin coloring went through the roof.

I grew even richer, but I did miss my food. I took supplements and protein, but there was no joy in that. For the first time, I wondered: Was I getting too thin? Others wondered, too. I remember seeing the question on the front page of the Weekly World News, as if I were some kind of celebrity freak, like Michael Jackson or something. It irritated me to no end.

It became a hot topic: Had I lost too much weight? Ironically, they wondered if I was addicted to Napetiene. I didn't tell a soul that I had stopped taking it months earlier. Between the hunger I couldn't satisfy and the constant badgering, I'll admit it, I was becoming a little testy. I was one of the richest men in the world, and I was miserable.

I withdrew quite a bit after that, just me and Frederick. We moved into the penthouse quietly, anonymously, my name kept entirely out of it. Frederick signed everything for me. Nobody had any idea who he was. I paid him well and trusted him completely. He was useless in many ways, but he came in handy then, and even handier later on.

Maybe I had known what was coming. Like so many rich geniuses, I became a recluse. After buying the penthouse, I bought the rest of the building. I moved my lab there and everything, all of it in secret. And even for a genius, I was smart: I fortified it and stocked it with food and water and guns and fuel and books and movies—everything I could ever want. Well, almost everything.

I stopped going out in public and cut way back on my personal appearances, but I still had obligations I could not deny. The last of those was a one-on-one interview with Jerry Prince, the host of a popular cable news show. I tried to cancel it, but the network said that wouldn't do. I had signed a contract a year earlier: They aired a flattering segment on Napeteine, and in exchange, I had agreed to a sit-down. I had already postponed it several times, and they would allow me to put it off no longer.

Prince was one of those pushy, annoying types who prided himself on his tough questions and soft features. I was determined to have none of it, and I went in there ready to give as good as I got.

I'd seen his show, and never particularly liked him, but when I met the man, I felt differently. I'd never been a particularly sexual being, and not the least bit homosexual. But meeting him in person, there was something about his soft, doughy features that I found absolutely captivating.

As we exchanged pleasantries before the interview, I couldn't take my eyes off his face.

Once the cameras came on, he started in on me immediately: Would I admit I was addicted to my own product? Had I concealed any detrimental side effects? He even asked me if I was wearing make-up, as if my skin coloring was any of his business.

And he didn't ask just once. He hammered away, again and again and again, asking the same questions over and over, as if he wasn't going to stop until he got an answer.

He finally did stop, but I don't think the answer he got was the one he was looking for.

In the middle of one of his sarcastic diatribes, calling me selfish and careless and negligent, I found myself staring uncontrollably at his smooth skin and his supple, fleshy features. He was so full of himself, he didn't stop talking even as I leaned over across the table. At least, not until I clenched my teeth on his nose and bit down as hard as I could.

I wouldn't have thought my jaws were strong enough, but they were. I bit it off easily.

Perhaps the world could have forgiven me for that, but when I chewed it up and swallowed it, I knew I had crossed a line.

I couldn't help myself. It was astonishingly delicious—everything I had been missing in food and in life, and more.

The studio was silent for a moment. Jerry Prince was in shock. Everybody else was staring at me like I was some kind of monster.

I realized then that I absolutely did not care. Not one bit. After a few seconds, Prince started wailing and the rest of them started screaming bloody murder. I guess they were right about that, because I went back for seconds.

In the pandemonium, Frederick somehow hustled me out the back door and into our car. Luckily, people seemed more interested in getting out of my way than stopping me.

Frederick looked at me differently after that, but not completely so. I think he already understood, the way a dog understands his master. I think he had known it was coming.

The interview played nonstop, on every television channel and every news website. It was the biggest story in the history of garbage media, and I totally understood why. I watched it myself, over and over, for hours on end.

Prince looked ridiculous, even before I bit off his nose. Clearly, he was asking for it. But in the moments before I finished him off, with his nose gone and his mouth wordlessly quivering beneath it, he looked absolutely preposterous.

The commentators said I was obviously evil or insane, but for the life of me, I couldn't see it. Even with the blood running down my chin, I thought I looked quite dashing.

We hunkered down after that, Frederick and I. The entire world was looking for me. When I grew weary of watching the search on TV, I went down into the lab and started working on understanding what was happening to me.

It very quickly made perfect sense. The same mechanism that prevented the nutrients from being absorbed allowed certain other compounds to enter the bloodstream, and then the brain. That caused some of the changes. And it was only logical that when a body was no longer able to absorb the materials necessary for human life, it would begin to crave the finished product instead.

After a couple of months, the furor died down. A sex scandal mercifully knocked me out of the headlines. But things were never the same. I slowly wasted away, wondering if I was suffering from depression. But I didn't feel sad, I felt resentful. Having a mysterious void in your life is bad enough, but knowing what's missing and being unable to do anything about it is far, far worse.

I continued to work in the lab, out of boredom more than anything else. I came quite close to reversing the process, but by that point I had decided I didn't really care. Then I was back in the headlines.

"He's turned up in Chicago!" the television said, after a young woman was found with her face chewed off. Two days later, they said I had eaten someone in Cincinnati, and then the next day, Detroit. The day after that I turned up in San Antonio, Texas and a small town outside Buffalo, New York. On the same day.

They scratched their heads at that point, but I didn't. I had known for some time it would be coming. And if the other grays were going to be out there satisfying their appetites, I would be damned if I was going to sit there in my high-rise fortress being denied.

"Frederick!" I called.

He came running, but there was a wariness in his face that I had never seen before.

I sat him down in the chair across from me and I looked him in the eye. "Frederick," I said. "I'm hungry."

His eyes darted to the door, but then they came back and he swallowed hard. "What do you want me to do?"

I let him decide who. I thought maybe he'd come back with someone who had wronged him, maybe one of our former coworkers, or a bullying old classmate. But Frederick was never vindictive. He returned with a fifteen-year-old prostitute who said her name was Rhianna.

The streets might not have been kind to her, but she smelled like heaven and under her tattooed skin she was fresh and delicious and the loveliest shade of pink.

Frederick went downstairs and turned the music up as loud as it would go. I tried to keep the noise down, but there's only so much one can do.

I felt magnificent after that. I saved what was left, not wanting to waste it, but even in the refrigerator it just doesn't keep. It's not the same when it isn't fresh.

Frederick kept his distance from me for a while after that, but he came when I called and he did as he was told. Soon, he got over it.

A week later, I called him to me and said, "I'm hungry again."

He nodded and disappeared.

I watched the television while waiting for him, but by then, it was a blaring cacophony of hand-wringing and panic. You would have thought it was the end of the world. Luckily, I had stocked up on DVDs.

Frederick was shaken when he came back, this time with a girl named Stephanie. She seemed relieved to be off the streets, as well. I guess it was getting pretty intense out there.

In deference to Frederick's sensibilities, I did Stephanie throat-first. She still managed to make some noise, but I don't think Frederick heard much of it. He still looked at me funny, but not as much, and only for a day or so.

The next time, I went out myself, figuring nobody would be bothering to look for me anymore. Besides, my appearance had continued to change. For the first time in several years, I was able to walk around unrecognized. That was a pleasant change. The rest of it, though, I didn't care for at all.

It was loud and dirty and violent. I had my first encounter with another gray. I think it was a woman; I'm not sure. She jumped out at me from behind a bush, of all things, snarling like she thought she was going to eat me.

She sniffed me and stopped. I don't know how I smelled to her, but she smelled awful. Definitely not something you would put in your mouth. She nodded politely to me, and we went our separate ways.

Half a block away, I found a twelve-year-old boy pulling a television through the smashed back window of an electronics store. Having smelled another gray for the first time, I appreciated that much more the irresistible scent of pink meat.

I dined al fresco in the back alley. There wasn't much to the boy, but perfect for one sitting.

As nice as it was to be outside, though, it was not worth the aggravation. I stayed inside after that. Frederick and I settled into a routine. I didn't need much, maybe one a week or so. Things continued to deteriorate on the outside, I knew. But Frederick never once complained. I think he realized how lucky he was, living with me in our well-stocked fortress while the rest of the world went wherever it was headed.

Occasionally, there was tension. Once, he even asked me, "You would never eat me, would you, boss?"

"Good lord, no," I had told him. "We're friends, you and I. I'd be lost without you."

"You mean it?"

"Have I ever lied to you?"

He accepted that at first, but a few seconds later, he looked back up at me. "If you did, though, you'd kill me first, right?"

I realized then that he was smarter than he let on. "Enough of that nonsense," I snapped.

Then I sent him out for a snack.

Six o'clock now, and Frederick still wasn't back. Out the window, the city was sinking into a sea of darkness. Only the tips of the skyscrapers reflected the dull glow from the darkening sky. Frederick had been having more and more difficulty keeping me fed. Too many hunters and not enough prey.

It occurred to me, as it did with increasing frequency, that this might be the time he doesn't come back. My belly growled at the thought.

It wasn't as though I sent him out there unprotected. I gave him a gun from the arsenal—along with strict rules not to bring it into the living quarters. And that wasn't his only defense. Once, he brought back a gray by accident. The thing was quite agitated by the time he got it home, and I ended up having to kill it. I almost killed Frederick, too, in my anger; as impressive as it was that he was able to subdue the thing, I was astounded that he couldn't smell the difference.

It occurred to me, though, that if other grays could smell the difference the way I could, my dear Frederick wasn't going to last long out there.

I dragged the dead gray into my lab and distilled its essence. I made Frederick a scent he could wear to mask his own, so he wasn't out there smelling like everyone's favorite meat pie. He smelled the difference then, and he wasn't too fond of it, but he had to admit, it made his job easier.

The moon was just starting to come up over the river when I finally heard the faint metallic clank of the elevator doors from twenty floors below. The hum of the generator was loud, but the grumbling of my stomach was louder.

I tapped my fingers against the glass, listening to the grinding music of the elevator bringing me my late lunch. The heavy metal door to the living quarters rang like a bell, a lunch bell. But when it closed, I heard only a single set of footsteps: no parallel steps, no scuffling struggle, not even the soft sibilance of dead weight dragged across the floor.

The smell of fake gray and poorly concealed pink filled the room.

When I turned away from the window, I saw Frederick standing there. Alone. Just him, lurking in the shadows, his eyes hooded and haunted. He had a deep cut across one cheek.

I held out my hands, palms up, and gave him a questioning look. "Where's lunch?"

He shook his head.

"Well, that's not good," I said. "Is it?"

"It's . . . it's bad out there." He shuddered and shook his head again. "There's not much left."

I nodded and took a deep breath. There was plenty of food for him here, a lifetime supply. I had taken care of that. What about me?

"Well, there's always tomorrow," I said, but that's not what I was thinking.

He smiled nervously, but he didn't come any closer. "You're not angry?"

I smiled back and crossed the room toward him. "You did your best, right?"

"I did, boss, I tried. I went—"

"Sh, sh, sh," I said, soothingly. I could feel him tense up when I placed my hands on his shoulders.

"I'm not angry," I told him, and for a moment, his shoulders relaxed under my hands. "I'm just hungry," I said as I slid my hands up under his jaw. "And you know when I'm hungry I've got to eat."

His eyes widened as my hands clamped either side of his face. He reached up to grab my wrists, trying to pull my hands off him.

Frederick was a strapping boy, and quite strong for a pink, but my hands were unmovable. They didn't even wiggle. I loved that about myself, the strength I had in my rock-hard muscles.

"You said you wouldn't," Frederick said in a sad, strained voice. "You said you'd never lie to me."

The cut on his cheek had opened up, a single, fat droplet of blood welling up along it.

"I said I never had lied to you, Frederick, not that I never would. I figure I'm due."

I held him like that for a second, savoring the moment.

Then I went in.

The nose was right there, but I went for that cheek. It was obviously meant to be. But as my teeth closed and tore and came away, I heard a thunderous explosion and felt an unimaginably solid punch to the chest.

Frederick screamed as I released him. He staggered back away from me, stumbling and falling, cupping his cheek. Blood seeped between his fingers.

Despite the scent of gray on him, his taste was as exquisite as Jerry Prince, all that time ago. I closed my eyes as I chewed, and when I swallowed, he was still whimpering on the floor.

I wasn't done by any means, but when I tried to get more, I realized I couldn't. Somehow, I found myself sitting on the floor, crumpled against the wall. My legs wouldn't work, no matter how hard I pushed them to.

That's when I saw the hole right in the middle of my perfectly sculpted chest. Purplish blood was pouring out. That couldn't be good.

I felt a flash of anger; we had a rule against guns in the living quarters and that deceitful punk knew it. But my anger was quickly replaced by frustration; he was right there on the floor, just a few feet away, and I couldn't reach him.

When I tried again, I found that my arms were no longer working right, either. A rushing sound grew in my ears. I found another morsel between my teeth. It still amazed me how delicious it was.

With great effort, I took a breath, and a bubble formed in the blood at the hole in my chest. As I watched, it grew and then popped.

Frederick had stopped whimpering now, and had gotten to his feet. He had a bloody crater where his one cheek used to be. I moved my eyes to look up at him, but even that was difficult. When he stepped to the side, I could no longer follow him.

"Boss?" he said quietly.

I couldn't reply. I couldn't even blink. I felt my eyes glassing over, drying out, even though I could still see.

When Frederick stepped back into view, the gun was out in plain sight. I wanted to scold him, but I couldn't speak.

He pointed the gun at me, but then he lowered it. "Boss?" he said again, panic creeping into his voice.

He crouched down to peer in my face, tears showing up in his eyes. His other cheek was right there, less than a foot away. If my neck were working I could have reached it, but there was nothing I could do.

"Oh, no," he said, crying now. The tears mixed with the blood on one side. The other side was pristine, glistening. I hoped he wasn't going to shake me, but that's exactly what he did, the dolt. My head lolled to one side.

I could feel myself dying from the outside in.

"No, no, no, no," Frederick said, over and over again, frantically pacing back and forth, then crouching down again, staring at my face.

"What am I going to do?" he asked. He knew I was just about gone, but he was asking me anyway.

He leaned in even closer and he looked into my eyes. What he saw must have scared him, because he yelped and jumped away from me.

For a moment, he froze, his eyes closed in concentration, his forehead wrinkled with effort. Then he put the gun under his chin and he pulled the trigger.

The explosion echoed through the cavernous penthouse, followed by the brief sound of gentle rain as the contents of his head sprinkled down onto the floor.

He stood there for a moment, as if struck by second thoughts a moment too late, then his body toppled over and hit the floor next to me with a thud.

As my vision faded, Frederick let out a long sigh.

I thought, what a waste. I wasn't done eating.

BVR
09

(doctor nine)
Jonathan Maberry

They blew into town on a Halloween wind.

The Mulatto drove the big roadster, and the Sage sat beside him, snickering into his yellow beard. Telephone poles whipped by, one after the other, and Zasha made a joke about their looking like crosses waiting for saviors. They all laughed and laughed, except for Doctor Nine who always smiled but never, ever laughed.

The car tore through the veils of shadow that draped like sackcloth between the distant lampposts. The night was in no way larger than the car, though it tried—and failed—to loom around the vehicle. The car was really the darkness of that night; it was far more a part of the night than the shadows. You couldn't imagine what that car would look like in daylight. It wasn't that kind of car.

Flocks of shapeless nightbirds flew on before the car, and whenever the roadster would stop the birds would wheel and circle beneath the hungry stars. Against the fierce glow of the sneering moon the birds were tatters of feather and bone. Their call was more mocking than plaintive. The birds were always there; as long as Doctor Nine was there, they were there. It was in the manner of things and both the birds and Doctor Nine accepted the arrangement. It suited them both.

The Mulatto never spoke when he drove. He never spoke at all. He could, but he chose not to, and his throat had gone dry and dusty over the years. When he laughed, it was the whisper of rat feet over old floorboards. Knuckly hands clutched the wheel and his bare feet pressed gas and brakes and sometimes clawed the carpeted floor. Around his neck he wore a medicine pouch, a medicine pouch he'd taken from a Navajo crystal gazer, and some parts of the crystal gazer were in there, too. He wore jeans and a faded Dead Kennedys t-shirt, a stolen wristwatch and seven wedding rings, one on almost every finger. He was working on a complete set. Little sparks of light flickered from his hands as he wheeled hand-over-hand around bends in the highway.

Beside him, the Sage ate chicken from a metal bucket. The bucket was smeared with chicken blood, and feathers drifted lazily to the floor. He offered a wing to Zasha, who declined with a wicked smile, but Spike bent forward from the back seat and plucked the wing out of the Sage's fingers. In the brief exchange, their hands were contrasted in a display-counter spill of light from a passing streetlamp: the faintly yellow, faintly reptilian mottling on the Sage's fingers, the thin webbing which had begun to grow between his thumb and index finger; and the overly-long, startlingly delicate fingers of Spike, dusted now with a haze of brown hairs, nails as long as a fashion model's though much sharper. The wing vanished into the back and Spike bent forward to eat it. He shot a quick, inquiring glance at Doctor Nine, who nodded permission and looked away out into the night. Spike ate with as little noise as he could manage, the bones crunching softly between his serrated teeth.

Doctor Nine looked dreamily at the passing cars, imagining lives and hearts and souls contained within those fragile metal shells like tins of caviar. In the hum of the car's engine he could hear the hum of life itself, the palpable field of human energy. As subtle as *chi*, as definite as arterial pumping. In the whisk of cars passing one another he heard gasps and soft cries, the stuff of nighttime encounters, expected and unexpected.

"Take the next exit," he said to the Mulatto, and the big roadster followed a line of cars angling toward a big city that glowed like embers under a cloud of carbon smutch.

Doctor Nine smiled and smiled, knowing that something wonderful was about to happen.

Bethy sat awake nearly all night watching Millie die. She thought it was quite beautiful. In the way spiders are beautiful. The way a mantis is beautiful when it mates, and feeds. If her sister thought it was something else . . . well, so what? Bethy and Millie had never seen eye-to-eye, not once unless Bethy was lying about it. Bethy was a very good liar. All it took was practice. It was a game they had started playing just a couple of hours after they all got home from camping. Mom and Dad were already asleep in their room, and Bethy had convinced Millie that it would be fun to stay up and pretend that they were still camping, still lost in the big, dark woods.

Millie thought that would be fun, too. Millie was easy to lead, though she truly had a completely different sense of what was fun.

Millie thought Pokémon was fun. Millie liked her Barbies unscarred and her Ken dolls unmelted. Millie liked *live* puppies. Millie was blind to the sound of blood, the song of blood.

Bethy said that they could pretend that Doctor Nine was going to come and tell them spooky campfire stories. Dad's big flashlight was their campfire.

Millie, sweet and pretty in her flannel robe with the cornflower pattern, her fuzzy slippers, agreed to the game even though she thought that Doctor Nine was a dumb name for an imaginary friend. Well, to be fair, she truly did think that Doctor Nine *was* imaginary, and that Bethy had no actual friends.

The clock on the wall was a big black cartoon cat with eyes that moved back and forth and a tail that swished in time. Millie loved that, too. She called it Mr. Whiskers and would tell time according to what the cat said. "Mr. Whiskers says it's half-past six!"

Mr. Whiskers was counting out the remaining minutes of Millie's life, and wasn't that fun, too.

Bethy looked at the clock and saw that nearly an hour had gone by since Millie had drunk her warm milk. Plenty of time for the Vicodin to enter her bloodstream through the lining of her stomach wall. If Millie was going to get sick and throw them up it would have happened already, but . . . nothing, and that was good. It kept this tidy. Getting her to take the pills had been so easy. Once mashed with a hammer from the cellar the powder was easy to dissolve. It was no matter if it made the milk a little lumpy, as Bethy had brought big cookies upstairs as well. Cookies to dunk in the warm milk. Just perfect. Millie had swallowed all of it. Bethy only pretended to drink hers.

Now it was time to watch and learn. Bethy took out her diary and her pen and sat cross-legged on the floor, and watched.

Doctor Nine smiled as the car whisked down the ramp and entered the city. He stretched out with his senses, with perceptions grown old and precise and indefatigable with long, good use. Hearts pumped for him alone, of all the creatures on the window-black streets; minds thought for him, stomachs ached and rumbled with hunger for him, hands groped with lust for him. Eyes searched the shadows for delicious glimpses of him. Tongues tasted waiting lips and flesh ached to be touched. All by him, for him, with him. He knew that; just as he knew that these hearts and minds were few—fewer than in years before, but still there. Still strong and waiting and wanting.

Doctor Nine knew all of this, knew it without the dizzying rush of ego that might taint another creature of less cultured understanding. He licked his lips with a pink tongue-tip.

An SUV came abreast of their car and Doctor Nine turned in his seat to examine it. The Mulatto sensed his desire and shifted lanes occasionally so that Doctor Nine could see each passenger in turn. It was a family car burdened with a roof rack heavy with suitcases and camping tents. Each window of the car was like a picture frame that contained a separate portrait. One showed a wife, a pale creature defined by that label. Just wife. If there had ever been a more definite and individual personality, it had either been leeched out of her along with the color of her skin, or she had put it away in some forgotten closet, perhaps with some thought that a life spent in sacrifice and servitude was a life well spent. Doctor Nine fought the urge to yawn.

The driver's window framed the father. Haggard, bored, distracted, and bitter. A jock-type with a soft jaw and receding hairline. Of no interest at all to Doctor Nine. This one wouldn't even have fantasies dark enough to be interesting.

The window behind the driver showed the profile of a pretty little girl with pigtails and pink cheeks who was bent over the piss-colored glow of a Game Boy screen, her face screwed up in concentration and her mind distressingly empty.

But then, as the Mulatto slowed the car just a little, Doctor Nine came abreast with the rear window, back where the luggage was usually stored, and there, with her face and hands pressed against the smoked glass, was a pale figure that stirred something old and deep in the Doctor's heart. She was the same age as the other girl, perhaps nine; but as unlike her twin as two creatures can be, born in the same spill of shared blood. Dark unkempt hair and luminous brown eyes, large in the small, pale mask of her face.

Doctor Nine looked at her, totally aware of her. He could feel the intensity of her mind, the sharpness of it, the need of it. Just as he could feel the ache and the pain as she rode through the night surrounded by these meat sacks that pretended to love her and pretended to care for her when in reality they probably feared her.

As they should. He smiled at the thought and tested his senses against the razor sharpness of her need, knowing that she could and would cut, given the chance, given some direction.

Doctor Nine moved his consciousness deeper into the young mind and found that, though young in years, the hunger he encountered was every bit as old as that which coiled and waited within his own soul. Her darkness was too lovely, too profound to be trapped in the cage of meaningless flesh which contained it. Her soul was a screaming thing, locked by circumstance in the fragile shell of the human form. It shrieked for release.

Doctor Nine felt her fear and her need, and measured them against each other. He would not come to her to relieve her fears; nor would he come to satisfy her needs. He might come, however, if her need was strongest of all, stronger than all of the other splintered and badly formed emotions, because to him, need was the only true emotion.

He exerted a fraction more of his will and the little girl lifted her sad eyes toward his window. He made her see him through the dark glass, and as she turned toward him, she saw him and she knew him.

From dreams she knew him. From dreams that her parents and her sister would have called nightmares; dreams that, had they been unlucky enough to share them, would have sent them shuddering and screeching into the nearest patch of light. As if light could protect them. He knew— could feel and sense and taste—that this little girl had dreamed of him, that she knew his name as well as she knew her own pain. As well as she knew her own need. Doctor Nine looked into her mind and knew that there were no gods in her dreaming world, just as there were none in her waking hell. When she looked into darkness, whether behind closed eyes or under the bed or into the moonless sky she saw only him. He was always there for her kind. Always.

Doctor Nine smiled at her.

The little girl looked at him for a long time with her owl-brown eyes. When she finally smiled, it was a real smile. A smile as hot as blood and as sweet as pain. Her small mouth opened and she spoke a single, silent word, shaping it with her need and her love for him.

"Please."

The SUV veered suddenly and turned onto a boulevard and headed south toward the smutch and gloom that was clamped down around the heart of this city. It vanished from sight in a moment and the Mulatto rolled to a slow stop at the next corner. Everyone in the car stopped and quietly turned toward Doctor Nine.

Above them the nightbirds wheeled in the sky. Then one by one they peeled off and followed the SUV down the boulevard. Soon only the big roadster was left, alone and waiting.

Without haste Doctor Nine reached forward and touched the Mulatto's shoulder.

"Follow," he murmured.

The Mulatto nodded and turned the car around and then turned again to enter the boulevard. Spike and Zasha exchanged a glance.

"Something. . . ?" Zasha asked casually, hiding the interest that brightened her eyes.

Doctor Nine nodded.

"What?" Spike asked. "That car we just passed?"

Another nod.

"Too late, Boss," muttered the Sage. "We'll never find it again."

Zasha jabbed his shoulder with a long fingernail. "Of course we will," she said, looking to Doctor Nine for approval.

They all looked at Doctor Nine, and he endured their stares mildly. After a long while he said, "We've been invited to a coming-out party."

He smiled at them.

Soon, all of the others laughed.

The night followed them like a pack of dogs.

Bethy wondered how it felt for Millie to die. It was something she tended to think about, even when she was killing a cat, or a dog. Poison sometimes hurt and so she stopped using it. Not because she wanted to spare pain— that was just a silly thought—no, it was because pain was such a distraction. Medicine was so much easier. No pain, just a fuzziness and a sleepy feeling that was warm and a little fluttery, like moth wings in the head. Bethy knew because she had tried the pills herself. First one of them, then two. The most she'd ever taken at once was six.

According to the Internet, four was supposed to be fatal. She tried six just to confirm a theory . . . a suspicion, or a hope. The moths had fluttered around in her head for a deliciously long time, during which Bethy had so many strange thoughts. Almost feelings, but not quite. Close enough so that she guessed that anyone else taking the drug would have had true feelings. It gave her perspective on what Millie's reaction might be.

Millie was probably having such feelings now. And thoughts, too— Millie wasn't completely incapable, Bethy had to remind herself of that and to be fair to her sister. Millie's expression kept changing as if she'd had a sudden idea, but when she spoke, which was less and less often now, her words were a junk-drawer jumble of nonsense, half-sentences and wrong word choices. Bethy found it interesting and she wished she could read minds. She bet that a mind-reader could make sense of what Millie was trying to say. Mind-readers didn't need actual language, she was sure of that. Then she wondered if a mind-reader could read an animal's mind, and if so, could they translate the thoughts into human words? Would an animal's thoughts change as they died, especially if they realized that they were dying? She hoped she would find out one day.

Maybe she could ask Doctor Nine. She was sure that he was coming tonight. She was sure that she had seen him out there, driving in a big car that was the color of night. When she looked at the window she could see that there were dark birds lined up on the sill and on the power lines across the street. The birds belonged to *him*, she had no doubts.

"B . . . Bethy. . . ?"

Hearing Millie speak now—very clearly except for a purely

understandable hitch—broke Bethy's reverie.

"Yes?" Bethy asked, utterly fascinated by anything Millie would say at this point. She pulled her diary onto her lap and picked up her pen.

"I don't feel . . ." Millie lapsed back into silence, her eyelids flittered closed.

Hm. What did that mean? *I don't feel.* Feel what? Bethy wondered. Was Millie losing her emotions? Did they die first before the rest of the body?

No, she didn't think so. She'd read about dying confessions, which was guilt; and about dying people saying nice things to comfort the people sitting around a death bed, which was compassion. Weird, but there it was.

Then she got it. Millie was trying to say that she didn't feel good. Or maybe that she didn't feel quite right. How . . . ordinary.

"It's okay, Mils," Bethy said. "It's just the medicine."

Millie's eyelids trembled, opened. There was a spark of something there. Confusion? Bethy could recognize emotions even if she didn't have any. Or, at least she could recognize emotions that she didn't share. She saw fear there, and though she didn't understand, it she enjoyed seeing it.

"I'm . . . not sick." With a furrow of her brows, Millie whispered, "Am I?"

"Sick?" Bethy replied with a comforting laugh. "Oh no, honey! You're not sick." She patted her hand the way Aunt Annie sometimes did. "No need to worry."

She saw relief in Millie's eyes and Bethy took a taste of it.

"Not . . . sick. . . ?"

"No, sweetie . . . you're just dying," Bethy said, and wondered if teasing this way was being greedy, and . . . was that okay?

Millie's eyes snapped wide and she tried to move. Bethy estimated that it took every ounce of her strength to move as much as she did, but all she could manage was a flap of one hand and a slight arch of her body. Then she collapsed back onto the pillows they'd brought down from the bed.

Bethy wrote a quick description of it in her diary.

The clock ticked, Mr. Whisker's eyes flicking one way, his tail swishing the other. Bethy counted seconds. She got to one-hundred and sixteen before Millie's eyes opened again.

"Why?"

Just the one word, and it was clear that it cost her to get it out. Bethy wondered how many words Millie had left to spend.

"Because, Mils. It's for me. And for him."

Millie looked confused. Her lips formed the word 'who,' but she could not afford the breath to say it aloud.

"For *him.* For Doctor Nine."

There was another flare of expression—mingled confusion *and* fear.

Nice. Again Bethy wished she could read minds, though she was pretty sure she knew what Millie was thinking, how she would be sorting it out. Doctor Nine was the boogeyman. Bethy's imaginary friend. Something she and everyone else laughed about behind her back. A dream, a nothing.

Even before Bethy had started experimenting with Aunt Annie's pills she had wanted to kill Millie for that—though strangely, and appropriately, that's not why she was killing her now. It wasn't revenge because revenge was soft. Revenge would disappoint Doctor Nine the same way rage would. There was no beauty in a lack of control.

Besides, this was not about punishment . . . it was about rewards.

Bethy thought about that as Millie's eyes focused and unfocused over and over again. 'Rewards' wasn't exactly the right word either. She chewed her lip and thought about it as her sister died, bit by bit.

There was a sound and then blades of light cut into the room between the half-closed blinds, and Bethy got up, excited, knowing who was outside. She started to run to the window and then in the space of two steps slowed to a walk and then stopped, still yards away. Running was silly. Running to check if he was out there was bad. It wouldn't show faith, like that Bible story about Moses tapping the rock and then not being allowed into the Promised Land. After everything he did right, he was reminded that *everything* had to be done right, and so Bethy turned around and sat back down, picked up her diary and pen, and continued making notes until Millie stopped breathing. It took nearly forty minutes, and she would have been lying if she didn't feel the tug of that window and the image she would see through the blinds. But feeling a thing and becoming its slave were different. Doctor Nine had told her that in her dreams.

When Mr. Whiskers said that it was two-thirty in the morning, Bethy put down her diary, set her pen neatly on top of it, and took a couple of slow breaths just to make sure she was calm. She reached over and touched Millie's cheek. The skin was still soft, but it was already cooling. Bethy sat back, leaning on both palms, and watched for a little while longer. There had been no more words from her sister. No additional emotions had crossed Millie's face. After that last outburst she had simply gone to sleep, and in sleeping had settled down into a deeper rest. Her body had not visibly changed except that her chest no longer rose and fell. While she watched now, though, Millie seemed to shrink in on herself, to become less solid, and it took Bethy a while before she realized that it was just the blood draining from Millie's flesh and veins to the lowest possible point in her body. She'd read about that on the Internet, too.

When she had surfed the Net, Millie had read a lot about killing. About the laws of it, the history of it. The art of it. There were so many killers that she felt happy that she would always have new brothers and sisters. Some of them even killed in the name of God, which was a funny thing. She'd have to ask Doctor Nine about that, but she already knew what he would probably say—the essence of it, at least. If God is All then God is killing, too. And really, God kills everything, from microscopic life forms to whole worlds. Maybe that was why so many have worked so hard to make killing a ritual and an art: it was their only way to try and connect with God. Even at nine Bethy understood that. If God made man in His image then man reflects the killing nature of God. To kill is to be Godlike. That should be obvious to everyone.

And yet they didn't call killers 'gods' or even 'godlike.' They called them monsters.

Bethy got up and walked away from Millie and stood in front of the mirror that was hung on the door of their shared wardrobe. She still wasn't letting herself look out of the window. Instead she looked at the monster in the mirror.

It still looked like her. The *her* she had always seen.

"Monster . . ." she murmured. Not for the first time she wondered if every one of the godlike monsters she'd read about on the Net had stood in their rooms, just as she now stood, and looked at themselves and announced who and what they were.

She hoped so. It felt like a family thing to do.

Finally Bethy turned away from the mirror and walked past the cooling meat. Millie was gone now; the body was nothing to her. She paused for just a moment, bending to pick up her diary and trying not to feel disappointed. Millie had been her first, but she hadn't learned as much from her as Bethy had hoped. Maybe next time she would use less of the Vicodin. Or maybe she'd re-visit pain. Perhaps she'd been too hasty in deciding that it had no place in the process.

Doctor Nine would be able to advise. Bethy was sure he would have something interesting to say about that.

Bethy changed into jeans and a t-shirt, put on her sneakers and brushed her hair. She put her diary and a change of clothes into her backpack.

When she was ready she took her pen and tested its point against the ball of her thumb. It seemed sharp enough. She held out her left arm and held the pen tightly in her right fist. She wasn't afraid of pain and so there was no hesitation at all as she abruptly jammed the point into the soft flesh of her inner forearm. The pen bit deep as she knew it would and blood—so rich that it looked more black than red—welled out of the puncture. Bethy licked the pen clean and put it in her bag and then she walked around the room and dribbled blood here and there. Then she put a Band-Aid over the puncture and put the wrapper in her pocket. Then she picked up a pair of bedroom slippers and used the sole of one to scuff some of the blood, drawing the line in the direction of the window. She left the slipper lying on the floor by the wall, just where the hem of the long sheers would brush against it. She put the other slipper in her backpack. The effect was pretty good.

Satisfied, Bethy finally stood in front of the window. She grasped the cord and pulled the blinds all the way up. The line of nightbirds scattered from the sill, their caws sounding old and rusty as they flew to join their brothers on the power line. The window was already raised a few inches and she raised it the rest of the way and for a moment she looked out and down at the street.

The big black roadster was there, idling quietly, parked across the street in the glow of the sodium vapor lamp. Just as she always knew it would be. There was almost no traffic, not this late. No pedestrians. And just for a moment—for a single, jagged second—Bethy stared at the roadster and saw that it cast no reflection, that the fall of lamplight did not paint its shadow on the street. Doubt flickered like a candle in her heart.

What if it wasn't real?

That voice—sounding more like Millie than Bethy—whispered in her ear. What if Doctor Nine wasn't down there at all? What if Doctor Nine was never down there?

Millie's voice seemed to chuckle in her mind.

What if. . . .

What if Doctor Nine was not real?

"But I'm a monster," Bethy said aloud. Millie's voice laughed, mocking her.

Then the roadster pulled away from the curb . . . very slowly . . . and moved into the center of the boulevard on which they lived. Bethy watched, suddenly terrified. Was Doctor Nine a ghost of her mind? Was he leaving now that she had started to believe that he was only part of whatever made her a monster?

Bethy's stomach started to churn.

"No!" she said firmly. "No . . . he's here for me."

Another car came down the street and Bethy realized that it would have to either veer around the roadster or pass through it. If it was real, the car would veer. If Doctor Nine lived only in her head, the oncoming car would just pass through it, reality passing through fantasy.

"No," she said again. She felt that her feet were riveted to the floor, held fast by nails of doubt driven through her flesh and bone. All she had to do was wait there, to see the car and how it reacted, or didn't react. Just five more seconds and then she would know whether she was a godlike monster or a mad little girl.

"Doctor Nine . . ." she breathed.

The car was almost there. Moses doubted, he tapped the rock.

The cartoon cat on the wall mocked her with its swishing tail.

"No," she said once more.

And Bethy turned away from the window before the car reached the roadster. Her decision was made. Without proof either way. She picked up her backpack, slung it over one shoulder, and left the bedroom. Left Millie and the blood and the fiction that she had constructed. She left her room and her parents and her Aunt Annie. She left her life.

She never looked back.

In the end she did not need to look to see if the car veered or drove straight through. She walked quietly down the stairs, placing her feet where she knew there were no squeaks and headed to the front door, flitting out into the night.

To the roadster. And to Doctor Nine, and to the other monsters he had collected along the way.

She knew they would be there.

She had no doubts at all.

Henry Long expresses himself through poetry, prose, and painting. Henry first came to us as part of Damon Betz's performance series The Adventures of Mercy. *Since then he's gone on to garner international attention for his mythic paintings. Here he combines mythic archetypes and conspiracy theory into a complex intergenerational saga.*

(my grandfather was adolf hitler's roommate)
Henry Long

Chapter One: Karl

Like all family histories, this story is based on actual experience, memory, speculation, hearsay, and in some instances, lies. Where the truth swerves into a lie is not really for me to decide, but rather the reader, in his or her own way, and on their own time.

With that said, let it now be known that my grandfather was Adolf Hitler's roommate.

This was Vienna, long before those world famous Munich thousand-seater, biergarten lecture hall days. The date: 1908. Hitler's around nineteen, and trying to make a living selling his simple little oil paintings and pleasant postcard watercolor art to *der Mittelstand* tourists in the cafés and Austrian K-martz.

Karl Lang of Southwest Germany's Oberammagau was my grandfather. Woodcarver. Gilder. Bartender. Painter. Worked in hotel kitchens shoulder to shoulder with Italians, Russians, Poles, Czechs and Jews. Moved to Vienna to continue his painting and got a job as a dishwasher and assistant bartender at der Schenkwirt Bottling Works and Prater Tavern.

Hitler, new in town, was a frequent customer at the very same Prater Tavern and had quickly run up a substantial beer tab. My grandfather poured many of those beers himself, and felt strangely sorry for the shabby, compact man. One day he asked to see what was in the greasy, over-stuffed black sketchbook Adolf always carried under his arm. Adolf showed him and Karl bartered the beer tab for a couple postcard-size academic nude sketches, some architectural renderings and a few lazy watercolors of the Danube. The twenty-year-old Karl said something like, "I'm an artist too," eager to share his own amateur oil paintings with Adolf.

Karl's work was dramatic. Stage-lit scenes of Christian martyrdom and curious fantastic landscapes of blazing cadmium-orange forest fires. Hitler took an unusually enthusiastic liking to my grandfather's art, and they became quick friends. Both were living in less than ideal flop house arrangements on opposite ends of town. Young Adolf suggested to Karl that they move in together. They split the rent in an unassuming but relatively clean flat above das Restaurant der Gastwirt, only a few blocks walking distance from the Prater Tavern. There, they painted and sketched daily, read voraciously, attended Catholic Mass together and tried to outdo one another's jokes about the anti-beauty of Modern art.

"Cubism is ugly negative art for ugly negative people!" Hitler would say.

"Expressionism is another word for 'I don't know how to paint!' Ha! Ha!" Karl would respond.

Adolf didn't have a job, so he usually slept well into the afternoon and did most of his creating after dark. On Karl's days off they'd wake early and go for long walks with bruised fruit and cheese rinds tucked in the pockets of their overcoats. They would have long conversations over just about everything, ranging from the weather to the local architecture.

In hindsight, Hitler comes off not too far removed from our own contemporary politically correct times. Anti-smoking, he would not sit anywhere near someone who'd just lit up, and would frequently advise smokers that they were "polluting their bodies and minds." He would not allow sexist jokes or derogatory slang remarks to be made about women in his presence. Bi-polar. Germaphobic. Celibate. Committed animal rights activist and a fanatical vegetarian. A firm believer in the Law of Attraction.

His personal style at the time consisted of a black, thread-bare full-length coat, long, greasy Rasputin hair and patchy beard, and a pair of beat up black army boots. A bohemian art student stereotype if there ever was one. The future Fuhrer possessed a profound fondness for the neoclassical. Grandiose bridges. Colossal structures and monuments. Demanding Egyptian scale perspectives. The whole landscape redone operatic. Majestic. Romanesque. Germanic. Extensive living spaces for all Deutchlanders!

Over Adolf's little bed, in a carved wooden frame, hung a slogan in black Deutsch Gothic calligraphy:

"We look free and open!
We look steadfastly.
We look joyously across
To the German Fatherland! Heil!"

Above Karl's bed was small, cheap print of Rubens' seventeenth-century masterpiece, *The Crucifixion*. Below that, a long horizontal landscape of an imaginary forest fire, signed *Karl Lang* in bright red. The juxtaposition of the two paintings together gave Adolf an aesthetic, if not ironic, delight.

"Our Hebrew Savior is burning in Hell," Hitler joked.

"I love Rubens," Karl said, lying in his bed looking upside-down at the picture. "Such luminosity. So fervent. What a painter!"

"They have *Treasures of the House of Hapsburg* on permanent display at the Hofburg Museum," Adolf replied. "They will have many Rubens."

Karl agreed wholeheartedly.

They went the following day. The Monarchy had accumulated a substantial, even overwhelming collection over the 630 years of the Hapsburg Global Empire. Karl and Adolf walked together side by side the whole afternoon, excitedly weaving in and out through countless displays of imperial regalia. At some point my grandfather lost track of Adolf. He was nowhere to be seen. After almost two hours, Karl considered leaving, but while navigating the various exits and entrances, he caught sight of his frumpy friend standing alone in a dimly lit room in front of an ornate display case.

Karl approached Adolf, a little annoyed. "I was looking everywhere for you! What the hell happened?"

Adolf said nothing at first, but stood still, looking straight ahead at the object in the case, and slowly, dreamily, uttered, "This."

"This?"

This was the Spear of Longinus. The purported actual weapon used by Gaius Cassius Longinus, the Roman Centurion. Christian folklore suggests he was at the crucifixion. *Jesus of Nazareth's* crucifixion. Gaius used the spear to pierce the rabbi's side to make sure he was really dead. He was.

"The Spear of Destiny," Hitler said.

According to the legend, Longinus was nearly blind, a condition which could be somewhat difficult for a Roman soldier. When he thrust the spear into the ribs of the crucified Jew, blood and bodily fluids came pouring out, splashing his eyes. His near-blindness was instantly cured, and the pagan son of Roman nobility converted to Christianity on the spot, even though Christianity wouldn't be invented for quite some time. The spear, it was believed, because it had been drenched in the sacred blood of the sacrificed God-King, was infused with supernatural powers.

"I had no idea it was real," said my grandfather.

"It protected Constantine," Hitler read from the case description. "Charlemagne. Barbarossa. All who possess this lance are victorious. Atilla the Hun." They studied the artifact in silence. An elongated piece of time-blackened iron, with a hammer-headed nail centering the long, tapering point to the wooden shaft, wound with threads of gold, copper and silver wire. It looked old, but still functional. Eventually, a museum guard came and informed the pair that the museum was closing for the day. They left. Hitler brooded silently as they walked back to the Gastwirt.

"What is it? What's wrong?" asked my grandfather.

"Nothing. I . . . I do not wish to talk about it," said Adolf.

"Is it the spear? Did seeing it upset you?"

"I should be in there, Karl. My work. My art belongs in a museum."

"Well, sure it does, Adolf. But museums are for dead things. They are the cemeteries of culture. You, my friend, are alive! "

"I would rather not talk about this."

"Okay. Fine. So we won't talk about it," my grandfather said, and they continued walking home without speaking.

Back at their flat, Hitler remained quiet and gloomy. Attempting to coax his roommate out of his funk, Karl made a positive suggestion. "Adolf, why don't you apply to the academy?"

"The Vienna Academy of Fine Arts?"

"Yes."

"Bah! Why should I?" He paused. "Do you really think I am good enough?"

"Of course! Why not? You're just as talented as the other artists making a living around here, if not better."

"Social parasites!"

"That's what I'm saying! Schedule an appointment, get your portfolio together, and see what happens! You get in, great! If not, nothing changes and you can still try again next year."

"What about you? Why not apply, yourself? You are a good painter too, in your own way."

"I'm a house painter, not an artist. I don't have those kinds of ambitions. My talent is a slight one. But you, Adolf, you've got something big to say to the world."

"Hmmm. I do. Yes."

"You could become really great."

"Yes. Yes."

"You could change the world!"

"That is not a bad idea."

"The world is full of far worse ideas."

"I am going to do it! I am going to attend the Vienna Academy of Fine Arts! I will show the world what Adolf Hitler is capable of!"

"That's the spirit!"

They celebrated this new venture by drawing each other's caricatures. Adolf drew Karl lighting the edge of a forest with a candle and smiling devilishly at the viewer. Karl drew Adolf wearing a long artist's smock and holding an oversized painter's palette and brushes. Behind him, a "Vienna Academy" banner was held aloft by grinning, impish cherubs. They laughed and patted each other on the back. The future was looking bright.

A few months later, at the Prater Tavern, Karl served sausages and beer to Werner Weizman. Weizman was a local celebrity of the Jewish bourgeoisie and Professor at the Vienna Academy of Fine Arts. Karl recognized him and asked the Professor how Adolf had been doing in his art classes. Weizman protested that he'd never heard of the student, and as he was Headmaster of the Painting Department, would know who was attending and who indeed was not.

"There is no Mr. Hitler in attendance at my academy," said Weizman.

"You must be mistaken, sir. He goes to classes there every day!" said Karl.

"You are wrong, young man," the Headmaster said, "and my beer is empty."

Adolf, in fact, had been turned down by the Academy of Fine Arts. His overstuffed portfolio was renounced. The painstakingly copied photographs of Vienna city streets and buildings were degraded. The small gouaches of large-breasted, nude nordic women were laughed at. The postcard watercolors of the Danube ridiculed as "technical and dry." The interview critique was so harsh, it actually made Adolf Hitler shed tears.

"You are, at best, a limited technician," said one teacher. "A moderately skilled factory worker. Your work is schmutz! Ihre kunst ist schlecht! Kunstwerken schrott!"

Emboldened by my grandfather's supportive urging and lacking any other real direction, he simply hadn't anticipated or considered what he would do if his application was declined. He kept the Academy's rejection to himself for over two months. Most mornings he'd sleep in late. If Karl was still around the apartment, Adolf would fabricate a deceitful scenario. "I am late! I must hurry or I will miss Dr. Kruger's Roman Architecture lecture!" He continued the ruse, pretending to be attending day classes when actually he was reading newspapers in the Austrian National Library, or wandering around the Textile Quarter in his tattered, disinfectant-streaked suit. He became depressed. His personal hygiene worsened and a growling, loathsome sneer took residence upon his face. On occasion he would attempt to engage in chess games in the public square, but typically lost badly, firing a barrage of anti-slavic or anti-semitic obscenities at his prevailing opponents. Frequently, the pieces went flying.

Having already pawned all of his humble belongings, he eventually ran out of money and could no longer make rent. Desperate, he took his entire portfolio of drawings and paintings to Y. Menschenmann and Sons Pawn, Resale and Auction House in the Mazzesinsel. Yosef Menschenmann at one time had purchased a small pencil sketch Hitler had done of the facade of the shop. The drawing hung behind the cash register with a small price tag tied with string to the corner of the Dutch metal-gilded frame.

"I am offering you five signed original works of my art for less than the price of one!" said Hitler.

"I wouldn't give you five Kronen for the whole damn lot!" said Yosef.

"I thought Yosef Menschenmann was a patron of the arts!"

"The Arts? Yes! You? No! I am a patron of what will profit Yosef Menschenmann. Your silly drawings I couldn't give away, unless they were to line my customer's onion bins!"

"I do not understand. You bought my sketch of your shop when—"

"When you pestered like a yapping mongrel, nipping at my heels for a soup bone! I gave that awful dog a bone. I have no more bones. No more bones for Adolf Hitler from Yosef Menschenmann"

"You Zionist son of a bitch!" Hitler spat.

"Get the hell out of my shop and never come back, you nasty, dirty man!"

Following his meeting with Professor Weizman, my grandfather confronted Adolf with the truth. Rent was past due. Karl's hours were cut at the Prater Tavern and promises of a part-time job in the soup kitchen fell through. Adolf was defensive. Words were said. Accusations made. It got personal. Insults flew. Karl accused Adolf of being a homosexual. Hitler questioned Karl's ethnic heritage, then threw a knife at Karl's head. My grandfather ducked and *The Crucifixion* by Rubens was accidentally stabbed. Hitler sliced the print vertically in two while removing the blade. He turned and stuck his tongue out at Karl.

Karl approached Adolf slowly and got very close to his face. The two men glared at each other in silence. Finally, Karl spoke calmly and clearly, "I am leaving now and going for a walk. When I return, I want you gone. I don't want to find a trace of you left behind. Do you understand?"

Adolf silently looked away.

And so, Adolf Hitler and Karl Lang parted ways.

Hitler eventually showed up at the Mannerheim, a kind of Victorian YMCA which, for half-a-crown a day, offered a dry place to sleep, a small wooden cot and a woolen blanket. Group showers and bathroom facilities were included. It could accommodate 500 men at one time. There, among the lowest of the low, Hitler stayed, shoulder to shoulder with Italians, Russians, Poles, Czechs and Jews. No plans, no Deutchmarks, not a friend in the world. He had burned all his bridges and was now a lost man.

After only two weeks, he was kicked out of the Mannerheim for his dysfunctional hygiene and for provoking the other men to fight him. It was a cold and rainy autumn. Hitler shifted for many days around the ghettos of Vienna, homeless, filthy and starving. One night, while getting drunk around Matzoh Island, he was severely beaten by a street gang for lecturing too loudly on the spiritual attributes of Richard Wagner's musical dramas. They dragged him to the outskirts of town where they stuffed him like a rag doll into a hole in a stone wall outside an abandoned furniture warehouse and left him for dead. And there he would have died, and the twentieth century would have followed a very different course. However, the Fates are curious sisters.

This abandoned furniture warehouse was more than it appeared. In the floor of its basement, inside a coal bin, lay a secret door. This door led down into an underground tunnel and eventually to a network of ancient passageways and Baroque burial crypts. These mysterious caverns and labyrinths deep beneath Vienna had been built around the twelfth century, forgotten, and then re-discovered by a clandestine order of Kabbalah masters six centuries later. They spent decades connecting all the chambers into the shape of a gigantic, subterranean *sefirot* of sorts, and it eventually became their headquarters, treasury and library.

On his way to this kabbalistic warehouse, a Jewish mystic named Yitzchak Sholem discovered Adolf's twisted, dying body in the stone wall just hours after he was placed there. Under the cover of darkness, he carried the broken man into the abandoned building, through the coal bin, down into the basement and into the order's secret underground lair. There, in a sort of holding chamber called the Malkuth, the mystic treated Adolf's various wounds and fractures, and waited for him to regain consciousness. When Hitler awoke three days later, he was disappointed to find himself still alive.

"Where am I? Why am I still alive? Who saved me?" he asked his cloaked comrade in a barely audible and raspy voice.

"I found you. You are safe. When you are feeling better, we can talk. For now, drink." Yitzchak offered Adolf a cup of a warm, herbal concoction and adjusted his blankets.

Hitler began sob. "I did not want to wake up. I did not want to live. I wanted to die. You should have left me to die!"

"To live is the greatest gift the Universe has given you!" said the mystic. "To refuse this gift is a sin against the Universe. For me to have done nothing would have my sin of indifference added to your sin of wishing to die. Two sins against the Universe? This is not a good thing for our souls."

"I would not have saved you," said Hitler.

"That doesn't change anything," the mystic replied, his face mostly hidden beneath the deep red hood. He put one arm of support around Adolf's boney shoulders and held the herbal brew up to his battered face with the other hand. "Now drink."

Adolf took a sip and coughed blood. Tears rolled down his face and onto the man's slender but strong hand. "Thank you," Hitler said, and reclined into a deep sleep.

Yitzchak visited Adolf daily, feeding and nursing him and tending to his wounds. Adolf slowly recovered. He stayed in the labyrinth for nearly two months, exploring its complex web of pathways and catacombs by lantern light whenever he was alone. He occasionally saw other hooded Kabbalists wandering about the underground chambers, but they mostly kept to themselves and said nothing to him. He pretended to barely be able to walk, even though except for a slight limp, his injuries had mostly healed. One day upon his regular visit to the Malkuth, Yitzchak noticed Adolf was missing from his cot, his clothing left in a dirty pile beside it.

He followed the scent of the lantern's burning oil down into the Cave of Scrolls. This was the order's hidden library. Coptic papyruses and codices were stored here, away from the torches of ignorance and fear. Centuries of Hebrew scholarship. Other Torahs. Sufi treatises on mathematics and philosophy. Persian astronomy and alchemy. Translations from Sumerian and Babylonian cuneiform clay tablets. Alternative Christian gospels. Magic spells. Histories lost to the rest of the world. It even contained items rescued from the devastating fires of the great Library of Alexandria, preserved and passed down through bloodlines and generations of Jewish lineage.

Yitzchak discovered Hitler butt-naked, masturbating like a naughty schoolboy amid the racks of antique scrolls and writings. "I am extremely disappointed in you," the Jewish man said.

"I felt better. I wanted to stretch my legs and try to walk. I got lost," said Hitler.

"Your convalescence has come to an end. Now you must leave here."

Hitler was gagged and blindfolded by the Kabbalists and taken by carriage during the night back to Matzoh Island.

Adolf Hitler emerged from the labyrinth a changed man. Determined. Confident. Driven. He made a personal oath to turn his back on alcohol. Never again would he foul his brain chemistry with intoxicating drink. His near-death experience (or something else he had discovered while healing in the subterranean bowels of Vienna), triggered within him a new fervency. He had an invigorated zeal for life's high perfection, and there would be no going back. He quickly got out of Matzoh Island and began his reclamation.

Hitler left Vienna to avoid the draft of the Austrian military service. He wound up in Munich, Germany, hiding from the authorities by staying with sympathetic Catholic pacifists and members of the Christian Socialist Party. Less than a year later, Germany proclaimed war, and World War I was underway. Hitler immediately and eagerly volunteered with a Bavarian Regiment, and his draft dodging was forgiven. The year was 1914. He was twenty-five years old.

On the battlefield, Hitler seemed blessed. Though thousands died or were injured beside him, he remained magically untouched by danger. He would frequently sit on a rock or tree trunk, mid-combat, take out his watercolors and paper, and create a portrait of a fallen soldier or battlefield landscape. Upon completion of his art, he would pack up his paints and walk away, leaving his makeshift seat to explode under the impact of a round of mortar shells. He rose from the trenches without a scratch, and felt he was personally protected by the Gods.

Perhaps it was the *Aurea Catena Homeri* which gave him this confidence and seeming invisibility. The Golden Chain of Homer. A small scroll Adolf had stolen from the underground Kabbalah Cave of Scrolls and kept with him at all times. Inscribed on it was a diagram of ten connected circles in a column, with various horizontal and vertical lines rendered inside the circles. It was an ancient alchemical symbol of *the great chain of being*, metaphorically connecting the "Divine Realm" with the "Lower Astronomies" of human experience. When viewed correctly, it could be a complex and sophisticated machine. A code to the cosmos. Rolled tightly, the animal skin vellum was about the size of a fat cigarette, and could be easily hidden anywhere. And hide it well he did. He wrapped it in in a rubber condom and kept it inside his anus, changing it every new moon. He continued this magical practice up to his very end.

In 1923, Hitler was arrested for treason for his leadership role in the Beer Hall Putsch, and faced life in prison without parole. He served four months and two weeks, during which time he dictated his book, *Mein Kampf*, to his cellmate and personal secretary Rudolf Hess. It was published in two volumes in 1925 and 1926. He was now an author.

Hitler continued to paint and draw, but his focus shifted to a different kind of creativity. Looking back to the Teutonic Gods for inspiration, he employed their ideals of sacred geometry and magical proportion. He used symbolism and psychology to create powerful political images and statements. Most famously, he appropriated the Sanskrit Swastika 'Sun God' emblem into an Aryan icon of Germanic destiny. Politics replaced the canvas. Propaganda was the new medium. Adolf Hitler had finally discovered his artistic style.

He went on to be elected Party Chairman of the right-wing extremist National Socialist German Workers' Party. Following his rise to power as Chancellor of Germany, he annexed Austria in March of 1938. On October 12th of that year, he ordered that the entire Habsburg Museum collection be sent to Nazi central in Nuremberg. There, he had the Church of Saint Katherine converted and rededicated into a Nazi shrine of the glorious Third Reich. A special bomb-proof chamber was built in the church basement, and there Hitler stored his plundered collection of empowered occult objects, not the least of which was the artifact which had captured his attention that day in the museum with my grandfather: The Spear of Longinus. He assigned armed guards to keep watch over it twenty-four hours a day, seven days a week.

Then, World War II.

Germany was losing. On April 30, 1945, as *die scheiße* was hitting the fan, Adolf Hitler and Eva Braun, married only five days earlier, did themselves in. They chose cyanide capsules, and to top it off, Hitler used an ordinary pistol. Their eternal honeymoon was on the cinderblock floor of the Fuhrerbunker beneath a burned down and occupied Berlin. That same day, just an hour before their mutual suicide, Lieutenant Walter William Horn of the United States Army entered the basement of the renovated Church of Saint Katherine and took possession of the Holy Spear in the name of the US Government. There were no armed guards to stop him. Munich was captured, and Germany, out of fuel due to Allied oil embargoes and other sanctions, surrendered. This brought an end to Hitler's Thousand Year Reign, about 994 years earlier than he anticipated. Eventually, General Eisenhower, on behalf of the United States Government, returned the Spear of Longinus to the Hofburg Museum's *Schatzkammer*. Most of what remained of the Nazi-confiscated Hapsburg Imperial tchotchkie also found its way back home to Vienna, more or less.

After his split with Adolf, Karl Lang also continued to paint and draw. He worked as an illustrator for a while at Leon Trotsky's *Pravda*, but it was not the "Truth" he had been looking for. Violence and rumors of war fueled a hateful zeitgeist. He got the hell out of Europe, avoided World War I, moved to the German-friendly Heights section of Wilkes-Barre, Pennsylvania and had his last name changed to Long. He met a Welsh seamstress named Lizzie Byrd who had a theatrical flair. She posed for him in the role of various Catholic saints and martyrs, making the simplified toga costumes herself. It was during the creation of his *Joan of Arc* painting, capturing the rapture of the rising flames and the ecstasy of her last mortal breath, that they fell in love. They married and had ten children.

Karl stayed out of the anthracite coal mines of Wilkes-Barre by finding employment through his painting and architectural designs. He painted religious scenes inside churches and created decorative gold leaf embellishments. Gold leaf: The mysterious membrane of the gods. Neither solid, liquid or gas. Insubstantial substance of divine wealth. A delicate, other-worldly sheet of 24-karat ghost, used to give ornamental flourish to signs, windows, picture frames and architectural moldings. Whatever needed the regal look of gilt.

Karl Lang mastered the medium. The preparing of the surface. The careful applying of red sizing. The patient wait to hear the perfect, subtle "teck" of a knuckle lifting from the drying adhesive. Raising the golden gossamer delicately with the static electricity of a horse-hair brush, his steady hands moving like a surgeon. The laying, like a gentle angelic breath. The burnishing and polishing. The wiping clean and transcendental gleam of the finished gold surface. "The man with the golden hands," his fellow craftsmen called him.

He designed wallpaper patterns. Got factory work painting roses and butterflies on watering cans and lampshades. Did freelance sign, billboard and house painting. Anything involving a brush and turpentine he was able to turn into a paycheck. For his own aesthetic needs, he continued with depictions of forest fires, burning buildings and other fanciful depictions of flaming destruction. It was a personal obsession.

Being somewhat of a kitchen alchemist, and out of necessity from thirteen years of prohibition, he developed an alcohol-based spirit. It was suitable as a solvent for cleaning or thinning oil paints but could also be used as a heavy duty cocktail. Lizzie kept the keys to his art supply cabinet on a chain around her bosom, and the mason jars of brush-cleaner martinis were marked with daily allowance lines. Karl's bathtub paint thinner was a popular beverage among the Depression-era neighborhood house painters, whether they had brushes to clean or not. It helped supplement his income and cope with the hard times. And these were hard times.

One day, while Karl was out painting a four-story high Mister Peanut advertisement on the side of the Planter's Peanut factory, the Long family was visited by three German men. "Relatives of Karl from the Old Country," they said. They were dressed impeccably in suits and hats and spoke very highly of my grandfather's old roommate in Vienna all those years ago.

They had pamphlets with swastikas and little storybooks for the children, and talked at length to Lizzie about how much newly elected Chancellor Adolf Hitler was doing for their Deutchland. They said they had, in fact, been sent by Hitler personally to offer Karl a job with the German Propaganda Ministry. Adolf wanted him to work on creating graphic posters celebrating his new, mythic Germany. "Look Towards the Future by Looking Back!" That kind of thing. Karl came home to see his young sons and daughters parading the "Goose Step" on the front porch and into the street. He knew well what that dance was all about, and where it came from. He told his children to stop, and they did.

"Karl, these are your cousins from Berlin," Lizzie said.

"I do not have cousins in Berlin," Karl said.

"We are *distant* cousins," said one of the three well-dressed men.

Lizzie and Karl and their guests all sat down around the kitchen table on wooden benches. The three men talked about the new Germany that Adolf Hitler was creating. The Chancellor wanted only the best individuals working on his campaign. They also said Mr. Hitler was aware of Karl's artistic progress since they both left Vienna to pursue other interests, and that his old roommate would indeed be an excellent choice for his personal graphic designer.

Karl, who had remained silent up until now, placed his hands on the kitchen table and said, "Lizzie, gather up the children."

Within minutes all ten children were crowding each other around the table. There was hardly room to raise a hand, but Karl did, pointing a finger at the visitors.

"These men are not our family. They are not Germans. They are not even human. Look at their faces and remember them. Look into their cold snake eyes. You cannot see their hearts. If you ever see them around here again, or anybody who looks and walks and speaks the way they do, I want you to kill them. Do you understand?"

"Yes, Father," Henry, my grandfather's third child said.

"Yes, Father," said his younger brothers George and Carl.

"Yes, Father," said Regina, Elizabeth, Grace, Gertrude and Walburga.

"Okay, Daddy," said Joseph, the youngest boy, my father.

"Be-tay, Baba," said Irene, the baby.

Lizzie, standing behind her husband's chair, wiped her hands against her apron, motioned towards the front door and said, "You lied to me. Now you must leave here."

The well-dressed Germans left, clicking their tongues. Lizzie gathered the pamphlets and little storybooks and threw them into the coal stove. They made green flames and popping sounds.

Five years later, on a brisk October morning in 1941, my grandfather's lifeless body was placed in a wheelbarrow and left in front of his house for his wife and family to find. He went out the night before to paint a forest fire, which had apparently started in one of the nearby coal mines. That last canvas was never recovered, and nobody ever came forward with information concerning what exactly had happened. There had been rumors Karl's death involved union coal mine workers who had recently gone on strike. One local drunk joked he had seen Karl "wrestling an alligator" down by the river, but of course there were no alligators in the Susquehanna. The official death certificate read "accident from fall." When he was buried, the local paper's obituary read "Man with the Golden Hands Dies."

The boys grew up and each joined a different branch of the military to fight my grandfather's old roommate in Europe. My father was a sergeant in the army, the famous 88th "Blue Devil" Division, and was stationed in Italy towards the end of the war. He watched along with a handful of servicemen as crowds tore apart Benito Mussolini's corpse. The locals hung Il Duche's body upside-down along with fifteen other fascists in front of a gas station in Milan, and took turns beating their former Dictator and ally of Hitler until chunks of flesh fell from his dead body. A bank now stands on the street corner where the gas station used to be.

Everyone in my family—everyone in my country—came home from that war, drank a lot of beer and tried to forget it ever happened. My father regretted not grabbing the rope which had bound Mussolini's neck and hands. "I could have had the rope that hung Mussolini," he'd say, and that was pretty much all he had to say about it. Days before he died from congestive heart failure at 74, he gave me a German army helmet and two rusty German bayonets he brought back with him from the war. I later sold them for $120.

"Don't ever call them Nazis," he said. "They were German soldiers. They were just young, frightened boys. We all were."

Chapter Two: Henry

My uncle Henry, oldest of the four brothers, was a different story. He had much to say about that war, and many other things as well. I was named after him on a dare.

"What are you going to name the baby?" asked my Aunt Irene to my Father, before I was born.

"Henry," said my Father, jokingly.

"You wouldn't dare!" Aunt Irene said, and that became my name.

I didn't know Uncle Henry until he was an old man. He looked like a cross between Willie Nelson, Charles Bukowski and Pablo Picasso. Demeanor, long hair and beard of Willie Nelson. Posture, dress and drinking habits of Bukowski. Intensity and dark, piercing, crazy eyes of Picasso. He came back from the war and ended up working in Washington D.C. with President Harry Truman and later Eisenhower, Kennedy and Johnson. I only saw him a couple times, when I was younger, but had heard that he turned his back on the family, "forgot where he came from," and was now considered a black sheep. Whenever Uncle Henry's name came up, people in my family generally changed the subject. Of course, they changed the subject every time anything really interesting came up.

It was August 2nd, 1990. I was in my studio apartment off Public Square in Wilkes-Barre, working on a painting of Icarus. 6 feet high, 12 feet wide. Acrylics. About 7:30 p.m. my phone rang. It was Uncle Henry. He was in town and wanted to see me. He said because I was named after him, it was his duty to tell me about our family. Out of all the other relatives, it seemed I was the one he felt least judged by. Perhaps this was because I was the youngest of the nephews. Or maybe it was due to my own propensity towards the drink which I maintained at the time. Either way, he seemed urgent and sincere, he was nearby, and I needed a break from the Icarus painting.

He suggested Stachu's, a small beer garden on a dead-end street just a few blocks from his childhood home in the Heights section of Wilkes-Barre. About a mile walk from my studio, but I could use the fresh air. They had two beers on tap: Stegmaier and Genesee. He drank Genesee, as did every man, woman and child in my family, like it was grape Kool-Aid. When I got there, he was already seated in the corner facing the door, at a small round lacquered table, his back to the TV. It was a dimly lit room, where nothing had been changed since the 1940s, except perhaps the pickled eggs in a huge glass jar behind the bar, but even that was iffy. Two other men sat hunched over their drinks, murmuring with Stanley, the owner and bartender.

Uncle Henry rose when I walked in and bear hugged me. He looked tired, red faced and leathery. He had to be in his mid to late sixties, but he looked older by a full decade or more. He was also shorter than I remembered. And skinnier. But he had a devilish twinkle in his eye and shoulder-length white hair. We sat. He was half way through a pitcher of Genesee. He poured me a glass, we exchanged the typical social niceties, and he said how good I looked a number of times, to which I responded in kind, if not in exaggeration.

"Listen," he said. "I'm an old man, and getting older by the minute. I feel like I'm out of time. I want you to know my story, Henry. I want you to know the *Truth*."

I took a breath and said, "I'm all ears, Uncle Henry."

He took a drink of beer, leaned into the table, and proceeded to tell me his story. He said he had worked for the United States government for thirty years. Then he corrected himself. He said he had actually worked for an underground agency called the "Obsidian Authority," a sort of shadow government which operated behind the scenes, outside the boundaries of the U.S. Constitution. It worked through various heads of state, as opposed to working for them.

There was a long pause. I drank some of my beer. He traced his finger around the condensation along the outside of the glass pitcher. I smiled. He cleared his throat. Then he told me he knew all about the so-called flying saucer that crashed on a ranch outside of Roswell, New Mexico back in early July of 1947.

He also told me he was one of the instrumental players in assisting

President Truman with writing up the National Security Act. This act re-organized the government's foreign policy and realigned the armed forces and other intelligence agencies. It went into effect three days following the Roswell crash. This, in part, led to the creation of the C.I.A., which also formed a few days after the crash. "But that crash wasn't no damn flying saucer!" he said.

He explained that in the late 1940s, a covert arm of the United States government, working with the Obsidian Authority, had been doing classified, top-secret, high altitude aircraft tests near the southeastern deserts of Nevada. "These aircrafts were disc-shaped spy planes," he explained, "and used an advanced experimental propulsion system. Hypersonic Nuclear Frisbees. Made U-2's look like the *Spruce Goose*. We had one craft operational, code named the 'Aether-7.' Only they weren't using it to spy on the Russians. They were spying on Americans." He held his beer glass with both hands, piercing my soul with those crazy black Picasso eyes.

"Why would they want to spy on us?" I asked.

"The American government's biggest fear is loss of control. It always has been, and it drives every single action they take and every decision they make. 'The citizen is the enemy.' That's their motto," he said. "Don't believe that 'this land is your land, this land is my land' sentimental bullshit. It's *their* land, and they'll never let you forget it, one way or another." He said the Roswell incident changed American politics forever. World politics, even. He also said William 'Mac' Brazel, the ranch foreman who discovered the actual spy plane debris, truly believed what he had found were five alien bodies and a crashed U.F.O.

"It was chimps that were in that wreckage, Henry. Five chimpanzees in oversized, silver space suits."

"How could someone mistake a monkey for an alien?" I asked.

"Ever see a burned-hairless chimpanzee in a space suit?" Uncle Henry asked.

"Nope!"

"It looks just like an alien." He remained expressionless. Then he laughed once, and I laughed politely back, and that was that.

He got quiet and looked down at his hands on the table. He picked up a stack of beer coasters from behind an ashtray and began playing with them. I noticed he wasn't smoking cigarettes, which surprised me. Everyone in my family, except myself, smoked cigarettes. My mom and dad were both three-pack-a-day addicts. All my uncles and aunts as well. I assumed Uncle Henry would be no different. I tried smoking a cigarette once when I was a kid and broke blood vessels in my eyes from coughing. Same thing with weed. I decided I would lean towards other, perhaps more gentler vices.

"Did you quit smoking?" I asked, disturbing his quiet coaster contemplation.

"Yep. After my wife, Mary, died in 1972 from lung cancer. A cruel, agonizing way to die. After that, I decided to stop paying R.J. Reynolds and Philip Morris to kill me. They put all kinds of crap in cigarettes, Henry. Arsenic. Ammonia. Saltpeter. Rat shit. Stuff to make you impotent. I quit cold turkey and haven't lit up since."

"Good for you. That's great! I wish my folks would quit. It's going to be the death of them."

"It's all about control," he said. "Everything is. Self control, chemical control, religious control, corporate control. What you control versus what controls you." He downed the last swallow of Genny in his glass, lifted the empty pitcher towards Stanley, and cleared his throat. I thought it was a rather rude way to order another, but decided it must be an old beer garden custom.

"About Roswell," I said, returning to his story. "I thought the government's official version was that the debris from the crash was an experimental weather balloon or something,"

"It was in everybody's best interest, at that time and to this day, that the alien story be believed," he said. "So that's what was circulated. The Pentagon diverted the public's attention with the weather balloon yarn. That didn't cut it, and they knew it. Then it was 'Aliens from outer space crashed in the desert!' And now that's become gospel. Over 200 people at the time, civilians and military personnel, either saw the Aether-7 wreckage or had some kind of contact with those five poor passengers. Remember, the project was classified. Top-secret Q-36 security level. 'Shoot first' shit, y'know? Today, everybody knows about Roswell. Most believe there was a government cover-up, but no one knows about the chimps. Smoke and mirrors. Business as usual."

"So we were lied to!"

Uncle Henry laughed a dark little chuckle. "World War II didn't end Fascism. The Fascists just changed uniforms."

I tried to follow his line of reasoning. I must have look perplexed.

"I'm going to let you in on a secret," Uncle Henry said. "A big secret. And I'm telling you because I don't want to leave this world without you knowing the *Truth*. There's a lot you don't know. Don't get me wrong, it's not an insult. There's a lot of shit nobody knows, because it's been set up that way for a long, long time. The Great Deception is so built into the works, so much a part of the system, woven into the fabric of our reality, that everybody expects the same things and nobody ever really questions the Big Picture, because everybody's standing so close, so caught up in their nine-to-fives, so nose to the surface, that nobody can see what the hell they're looking at anymore. Follow what I'm saying?"

"Like a tapestry? We're standing so close, too busy looking at the weave, that we don't see the whole picture," I said. "We can only see our little section."

"Yes. Very good. I need you to step back and take a look at what I'm saying, okay? I know this is going to sound crazy, but it is the truth." He blew into the air and began rubbing his hands together. "Okay. There are these highly evolved reptiles. We call them 'Reptilians.' They call themselves Diapsidians, or Diapsins. Sometimes they call themselves a word which nobody can pronounce without having two large temporal openings in the back of their skull."

"Reptilians," I said. "Diapsins."

"Yes. Reptiles from the future. But they're also in the past and in the present too. They've been working behind the scenes here since Thomas Jefferson dipped his turkey quill in the ink. Shit, since the damn dinosaurs I suppose, but that's a whole other can of worms. They're from our future. Way, way in the future. And Venus is involved as well. The planet, I mean. It . . . it gets complicated. They are the inheritors of the Earth, Henry."

I guess I was still looking at him funny.

"I know this must sound loopy," he said.

Loopy? Hell yeah. I admit, it was a challenge to not crack up. Maybe this was a joke. A long set up for a great punch line. But I didn't think that was his style. He seemed so earnest.

"They're the ones who were teaching us about harnessing the power of the atom, nuclear weapons, time travel, all that stuff."

"Time travel."

"They developed time travel, in the future, post-humanity. Time tourists. Some of them decided to stay in the times they traveled to. So they show up in our pre-history, in our biblical era, the Middle Ages, decades from now, centuries. Shit, they're all over the time charts! They figured out a way to communicate with one another through the various epochs, using symbolic codes under everyone's noses. They formed an alliance across time, and we've been in on it and caught up in their mess and taking their crap for quite a while now."

"Jesus!" I said. My inner voices were saying much more. On one shoulder was a loving, non-judgmental nephew who smiled and said, "Really? Wow! How interesting." On the other shoulder, a reasonably intelligent young man shouted in my ear, "Your uncle Henry is madder than a box of frogs! Get out! Now!"

My uncle continued. "We took the information the Reptilians sold us and utilized it for our own short-sighted interests. The Aether-7. They used atomic energy and nuclear propulsion for time travel. We took that technology and made bombs. Sure, we set up some nuclear power plants here and there to keep everything progressing towards 'The Future,' which is what everyone was expecting, you know, the nose to the surface, the tapestry thing. But that was not the point. The future ain't what it used to be, Henry."

Stanley brought another pitcher of Genny to our dark corner table. Uncle Henry nodded and winked. I studied our bartender. My educated guess; he was of Polish decent. A definite pork eater. His belly was a pregnant basketball. It got to our table long before the rest of him did. He was in his sixties, short, stocky, and balding with a dyed black, shiny comb-over. Black-rimmed Buddy Holly glasses. Moist, fleshy, pink lips. A mouth breather. A low talker. He mumbled something that sounded like "Turkestan pie?"

Uncle Henry said, "I'm good, Stanley," and filled my glass with the beer, poured his, and Stanley returned to his station behind the bar. "So that's what really happened out in Roswell."

"The Reptilians?"

"Exactly."

"But you said it was chimps. In the Roswell crash. Do you mean it was actually reptiles from the future, flying that secret Aether-7 spy plane thing?"

"I said it was chimps in the wreckage, boy. Chimps and debris. Let's see. How do I explain this? Okay. We sent men up there, Henry. Five grown men history would never record, personally groomed by the Obsidian Authority. They had families for Christ's sake. We used Diapsin engine specs to make a spy plane for reconnaissance missions, observing American citizens. But those designs were specifically intended for time travel, not merely stealth, high altitude aerophysics. We followed their directions, and ended up with . . ." He looked away briefly.

"Something happened to the ship."

"Yes. The A-7's engine operated on Superstring Mechanics, a dynamic frequency nearly an exact match to the frequency required for organic time travel. It did what it was intended to do, but the physical craft itself wasn't built for it. We didn't have the same materials the Diapsins used, so we compromised. There was a Chronological Entanglement. A time dilation and contraction, in the same micro-moment. The craft skipped around, millions of years, back and forth, in a matter of seconds. We got the signal to terminate the mission, that something had gone terribly wrong. The ship's control was over-ridden, and the power cut from Central Command. The A-7 was supposed to auto-destruct, but instead, she crashed in the desert near Roswell.

"No one will ever know what those five men experienced, Henry. Eons were concentrated into seconds. Did they change instantly upon time propulsion? Did they know they were devolving? Did they know that when their ship crashed, they were closer to a primate, a chimpanzee, than to a human being? One of the men survived the crash long enough for us to have to kill him. Human or not, his eyes pleaded for death. It was the only humane thing we could do, given the circumstances. I've seen a lot, you know, but never anything quite like this. Of course, their families were told a different story. Jeep accident. Injuries from a fall. A fire or something."

"Wait. I'm stuck here. Why don't the Reptilians have the same problem? Why did the men devolve? Why didn't those five men change back when the spy plane crashed?"

"Reptilian ships are built for time travel. Machines created with technologies a million years in the future. They have Relativity Buffers, Quantum Stabilizers, Temporal Conditioners. All kinds of things to protect the occupants and the craft itself through time travel. We bit off more than we could chew. We were arrogant and impatient. We got the engineering notes on the motor and thought we knew everything! We weren't prepared for a Chronological Entanglement! We didn't know it would skip through time. We just wanted to make sure it couldn't be detected by radar. That, and it had to move incredibly fast without warming up or cooling down. We didn't even have a vocabulary for what eventually happened to those men, until the Reptilians explained it to us.

"We signed an agreement. The Obsidian Authority, the U.S. government and the Reptilians. The engine specs were classified 'Theoretical Purposes Only.' The Aether Program scrapped. There'd be no more messing around with time travel. Of course, I'm sure somewhere there's a reverse-engineered prototype sitting in someone's secret laboratory or garage, but it's not one of ours. Money and science went into a different methodology. So ten years after Aether-7, you have NASA."

"Those poor men," I said, imagining what the pilots of the Aether-7 must have gone through.

I excused myself to use the bathroom, and left Uncle Henry alone with his thoughts. I looked at myself in the bathroom mirror for a long time. I searched my face for his features and found them. The nose. Crooked smile. The tired eyelids. The lines around the corners of my mouth. Why was he telling me all this? Was he dying? Was someone after him?

I washed my face and had the feeling I was about to cry. I swallowed back a sob. Genny, I thought. That beer had brought out the tears in my mom on a number of occasions. Must be something in our genetics that reacts to the hops.

"Don't judge him," I said to myself. "Maybe he *is* crazy. Let him tell you everything he has to say. There's a reason. And if it is true, nobody is gonna believe it anyway. Just listen and give him love."

I walked back to the table, and Uncle Henry was drawing some symbols in red marker on the cardboard Stegmaier and Genny beer coasters which he had been shuffling earlier.

"What took you so long? I thought you drowned in there!" Uncle Henry laughed.

"What are those?" I asked, truly curious.

He looked at me and said, "You tell me."

I took them in my hand. A shell form, a pair of connected X's, a pentacle, Pegasus, a flame, a pyramid seen from the top, a diamond and a few other occult looking symbols. "Tarot?"

He laughed once, and said, "That's a very good guess, but not quite. Keep looking. Step back from the tapestry."

I laid them out on the table like playing cards, but that only reinforced the tarot connection. Then I stood up to see them from a distance. I tried to spell them out, like a picture word game.

"Star Wing Horse? Pyramid Flame? Diamond Shell? Double-X Shell? Shell? They're logos! Famous brand name corporation logos!" I said, proud to have caught a glimpse of the tapestry.

"What kind of brands? What corporations? What's the product?"

"Um, Gas."

"Oil," he said. "Petroleum. These are the symbols of oil companies. Flags of the Power Nations. You see them everywhere, every day. On gas stations, television commercials, movies, magazines, race cars, t-shirts. They're sigils. They have magical properties. These represent a subliminal codex, continuously working on our psychic cortex and central nervous systems. The Reptilians developed a representational language system and embedded it in our culture to communicate with one another across time, like points on a map. And it's right out in the open, under everyone's nose."

"So what are they saying to each other?"

"Well, they're saying plenty! But essentially they're saying, 'Eat Here!' It's about their food."

"Whose food?"

"The Reptilians. They need oil to survive. It gives them a buzz. It's what brought them back in time to begin with. They need it to live like we need water. They drink it. Absorb it through their skin. Mate in it. We sold it to them in exchange for teaching us what to do with it once we pump it out. Only we got just as addicted as they did. We got greedy, made some bad deals, went back on our word. Now we're locked into a commitment, supplying them with oil without having enough for ourselves. Look at the world! Look at a damn map! Where's all the oil?"

"In the Middle East, for the most part."

"That's where they are, too. Hundreds of thousands of them. They're in bed with the Saudis. The Reptilians get the oil almost as soon as it comes up out of the sand. That's the deal."

"I don't understand. What about the Oil Crisis? What about OPEC? Plastics? Everything is made from petroleum! It controls the world's economy. Why would we, why would the government . . ."

"Why would the government *what*? The government is based on hypocrisy. The 'Corporation' is the State! The United States government cannot be trusted to tell the truth about anything, Henry! Pearl Harbor? Vietnam? Three Mile Island? Legionnaires' Disease? Chernobyl? What you've been told has been carefully orchestrated to further their agenda. If it's splashed across the front pages of the newspapers over and over, eventually it becomes fact. That fact then gets put into the schoolbooks and becomes truth. Wars are fought over these so-called truths. People murdered. Families destroyed. Countries. Nothing could be more corrupt and downright dangerous to democracy than this sick cult of deception called 'the Media.'"

I needed to reel Uncle Henry back in. "Wouldn't someone have seen these Reptilians by now? Got them on video, out in the open? Taken a picture?"

He took a deep breath followed by a drink. "Some have, only they didn't live long enough to tell their story or print the photos. The Diapsins knew it was in their best interests to not be seen. Some developed surgical and cloaking technologies so they could walk in the times they found themselves in. Most went underground. A nice-sized chunk of the eastern Mediterranean just happens to be directly over their underworld. They live where the source of their food is. The creation of Israel was part of the arrangement we made with the Reptilians, following World War II. They live miles under the earth, in catacombs and labyrinths that they constructed by going into the past 10,000 years and using slaves from what is now Jordan, Syria, Lebanon. Even Egypt. Time travel allows for all kinds of advantages, but it has its share of risks as well. RIP's, for instance. That's the biggest problem."

"Rips?"

"Reticulated Induction Phenomenon. R-I-P. Rips in space/time. A quantum byproduct of nuclear-generated time travel. If too much energy is spent too quickly, if something goes wrong, like what happened in the Roswell Chronological Entanglement, the recoil creates a RIP somewhere else in time. It's like a shock wave of a split second being turned inside-out on itself, on a world-wide scale. So you get these terrible events happening throughout space/time, manifesting on the physical Earth in real time, and the puppet masters, the deal makers behind the governments, have to come up with something for the official story behind the disaster. Tsunami, earthquakes, forest fires, floods. Most of these natural disaster events are actually RIP's. The Tunguska Explosion of 1908 is a perfect example."

"Tung-what-sa?"

"Tunguska. The Tunguska Event, 1908. Dead center of the northern forests in Siberia along the Tunguska River. That one was 1,000 times more devastating than the nuclear bomb we dropped on the island of Hiroshima in 1945. The Tunguska RIP vaporized 900 square miles. Manhattan is about twenty-three square miles. Can you imagine? Windows were shattered 200 miles away from the RIP's ground zero. It felled 80 million trees. That was the RIP felt around the world."

"How come I never heard of it?"

"Ever hear of the Cold War? It happened in Russia. Siberia. We don't get much Russian news here, do we? The American and Soviet governments blamed the event on everything from a meteorite to a black hole to contact with antimatter. Eye witnesses were interviewed. Survivors. We later brought in our own translators. Now it's called the Russian Roswell! Only it wasn't a UFO, it was a tear in space/time. The impact of that event is still emerging to this day. I wouldn't go anywhere near there if I were you."

"Don't worry, I wasn't planning to."

"And another big RIP is coming in 22 years. 2012."

"How do you know?"

"You can chart it from the Reptilian's vantage point of the future. They have a way to see chunks of time all at once. It's there, already. We caused it, once again. Our little spy craft incident made a real mess of things. Area 51 is a spot in southern Nevada that's not on any map. Try to find it. Groom's Lake. It ain't there, but it is. That's where the Aether-7 was created, among other classified projects. Now it's full of physicists and Reptilians trying to mend the 2012 RIP. They're working to prevent it, but it hasn't happened yet, so it's difficult. It all makes sense when you step back from the tapestry. 'Oh, look here: there's the big RIP of 2012.' Remember that date, Henry. 2012. Head north. Take guns and granola bars. Trust me on this one."

"So all UFO sightings are really time-traveling reptiles?"

"Most of the flying saucers you hear about are the Reptilians', yes. Or the Obsidian Authority's. Or just regular U.S. government covert operations. They wouldn't own up to it, of course, so it's labeled "Unidentified" to cover their ass. NASA is looking through the wrong end of the telescope.

It's not about space. It's about time. There are no Martians or little green men from outer space, Henry. That's comic book stuff. Believe it or not, it's easier to travel through centuries than it is to go billions of light years in space.

"Be right back. I gotta piss like a race horse." He finished his beer and went to take a leak. TV droned in the background, punctuated by the occasional muffled cough from the barflies. Sometime in the last hour, the two men had been joined by three other old-timers, and they were now all huddled at the bar's far end in a right angle, leaning over their beers like raptors guarding their eggs. Suddenly, all their heads rose together and looked at me.

The inner voices on my shoulders were having a wrestling match. Time traveling Reptilians! Men turning into primates! Oil Company restaurants? RIP's causing earthquakes and future calamities? What the hell? All this shit was starting to make me extremely self-conscious. My uncle had a resonant speaking voice, even when he was whispering. The barflies must be hearing all this! They probably think we're a couple of Looney Tunes.

Then again, this is Wilkes-Barre.

Uncle Henry came back to the table and sat down. Stanley looked up and pointed at something above our heads. I followed the direction of his finger, and turned. I then realized he and the others hadn't been staring at us at all. They were watching the TV, which was above and behind my uncle, back and to the left. Our little bar table just happened to be directly beneath the object of their attention. I felt foolish, but I also felt a calm wave of relief wash over me. Stanley took the stool he was sitting on, came out from behind the bar and carried it over to the ancient RCA above my uncle. He mumbled something that sounded like "mayonnaise ballroom," and stood on the old wobbly stool to adjust the rabbit ears and dial controls. He slammed the side of the set a few times. The TV got louder.

". . . and the President has sent the USS Dwight D. Eisenhower to the Mediterranean, bringing the total number of ships to eight, including the six US Navy war ships already in the Persian Gulf," said some glassy eyed news anchor. "Again, repeating tonight's breaking news headlines, Iraq has invaded Kuwait. President Bush has ordered immediate economic sanctions, and has called an emergency meeting of the Joint Chiefs of Staff to . . ."

Uncle Henry gave me his Picasso eyes. "You know, you look a lot like your grandfather," he said. "You're also the only one in the family to pick up where he left off. With the paint brushes, I mean."

"I wish I knew him," I said. "I would have loved to have seen him paint."

"He made it look like magic, Henry. Never used guides or preliminary drawings. Could start out the morning hand painting a name in reverse

on a butcher shop window. Gold leaf and all. Then he'd go down to the
Immaculate Heart of Mary Church on Hazel Street and work on the
Stations of the Cross, painting all those little blood drops and bruises
on Jesus. Finish at the Comerford Theater on Public Square, painting a
wallpaper pattern on the walls because the theater ran out of the wallpaper. Wallpaper he designed! It was all the same to him. Karl Long was a
painter's painter. He knew how to make oil paint sing. He never got the
attention he truly deserved. He liked to paint forest fires. Did you know
that? Other artists did flowers, landscapes, red barns, street scenes. We
had dozens of orange and red forest fire paintings around the house."

"How come nobody else in the family got into art?"

"Well, I think they all associated his art with his drinking. He had some
pretty bad moments with the drink. Listen. I'm glad you could come out
tonight, Henry. Life is short, you know? You probably think I'm a crazy
old man who's had a few too many himself, but I'm telling you, every word
I'm saying is true."

"I know. I believe you," I said. "I can totally see everything you're saying. It's just so different than what I've been told, you know?" Studying his
face, reading his expressions, I knew he believed everything he was saying.
Of course, that did not necessarily mean it was the truth, it just meant he
believed it was. I decided that was enough for me. I chose to believe him,
scary as it was.

"Don't believe any of what you're told, and even less of what you read.
Look, in a way, none of it really matters. Truly. You can live your life, have a
job, get married, have kids, have grandchildren and die without ever knowing the truth, and be none the worse for it. All I'm saying is that for some
people, people like us, that simply ain't good enough. We're strongly at-
tracted to certain things, all our lives, for no apparent reason. These things
are clues. Hints from the universe which make up our destinies: people,
places, jobs, ideas, books, objects . . . and if we just had a clearer picture of
the truth, it would all come together, and we'd see our place in all of this,
and what it is the universe wants us to do." He looked away and forced a
cough. "Another over here, Stanley."

"I believe the universe believes in me," I said. "I believe one has to find
their own truths, make their own gods. Create their own religion."

"Henry, you've been lied to all your life. I want you to know that. At
church, at school, and at home." Uncle Henry pushed his hair back from
his brow with both hands. "Especially the Church. The fuckers. There is
no separation between church and state! All lies. And the government has
made a business out of it! Lies, lies, lies."

"Give me an example."

"Give me a topic!" Uncle Henry laughed. "Anything you could possibly think you know has a back story that you don't, from Hershey Bars to Fort Knox."

"Fort Knox?" I could have said, "Hershey Bars?" but Fort Knox came out of my mouth first.

He smiled. "You ever hear of Fort Knox?"

"Sure. I guess. Who hasn't?"

"What is it?"

"Where the government keeps the gold?"

"Whose gold?"

"I don't know. Theirs?"

"Nah. What was left of *our* gold is buried in twenty feet of concrete beneath London. No. They got bricks of freeze-dried concentrated heroin. Gold spray-painted bars of pure pharmaceuticals. Empowered ancient occult objects. Holy relics. Sumerian artifacts depicting the Reptilians. Frozen Diapsin eggs. Enough Mastodon DNA to make an army. All kinds of weird shit."

It was like a game. Pick something everybody knows about and get the Uncle Henry version. "Okay, what about the moon landing? The astronauts and all those Apollo missions I watched on TV. What's the back story on that one?"

"Oh Jesus, you had to pick the Apollo Program, didn't you?" he said, shaking his head and looking down at the oil-logo Stegmaier and Genesee coasters he was fumbling with in his hands. "Let's just say we got very close to an all-out war with the Reptilians over those theatrics, and it's still not resolved. We're still up there."

"I thought we stopped going to the moon in 1972."

Picasso eyes. "Short version: RIP damage control. Mare Desiderii, the Sea of Dreams, on the far side. Never faces the Earth. Taken off the lunar maps over a decade ago. This one's the Reptilian's fault. The long version would take us into tomorrow morning, and I don't think Stanley would keep the place open that late. Most people think only twelve men, Americans, have set foot on the moon. There's been hundreds, from all over the world. Someday, go to a library and look up Vedic philosophy and Nikola Tesla. Now there was one smart Serb. You can connect the dots yourself."

"Tesla. Um, okay."

"Something else."

I was going to go back to the Hershey Bars, but instead I said, "How about the Kennedy assassination?" I figured that one was chock-full of conspiracy theory possibilities. The Granddaddy of them all! What was Kennedy *really* into that he shouldn't have been? What about Marilyn

Monroe? What about the grassy knoll? How many gunmen where there? Who was behind it? Communists? The Mob? Frank Sinatra? My Uncle Henry certainly must have had some crazy Obsidian Authority back story for this one.

"What about it?"

"Who killed JFK?"

"Lee Harvey Oswald shot John F. Kennedy in Dallas Texas on November 22, 1963," my uncle said, without expression.

"Right. That's what we've all been told. So what's the *real* story?"

"It's 100 percent true. He acted alone. Lee Harvey Oswald assassinated the President."

"You've gotta be kidding me! The biggest source of conspiracy theories of the century, and you're telling me there's nothing more behind the story?"

"I never said that. I said Oswald did it. He acted alone. He pulled the trigger."

I looked down, actually disappointed.

"Do you want to know who Oswald *intended* to kill?"

"Hold on," I said. Stanley was pouring our next pitcher behind the bar. I went over to save him the trip. Stanley nodded and I said, "Could I have two bourbons, also, please?" He murmured something that sounded like "chrysanthemum," and reached for a bottle under the bar. He then poured two large shots of Bellows Club. I thanked him and brought the drinks back to our table.

Uncle Henry smiled at me. "You're a good boy, Henry," he said. "I mean *man*. You're a good *man*."

"Thank you, Uncle Henry," I said. "So are you."

"Let's talk about Lee Harvey Oswald." Uncle Henry downed the Bellows. I followed. It burned, but after the initial sting it mellowed into a slow warm feeling in my belly and frontal lobes. "While in the Marines, he got into a little trouble. Shooting off his mouth, shooting off his rifle, that sort of thing. Got into a row with his sergeant. Shot himself in the elbow. Nothing super serious, but enough to piss off a lot of people. Military Personnel. Commanders. To balance out his record, or as punishment, depending on how you wanna see it, he 'volunteered' for a number of tests. LSD tests. The United States military were using enlisted men for all kinds of chemical and psychological testing. Top secret clinical study. This was the fifties. Brain control. Memory rehabilitation and modification. All kinds of nasty shit. Between 1956 and 1959, Oswald had been given hundreds of LSD injections. He was examined like a bug under a microscope. Every hole which could have something shoved up it was explored. Finally, he'd had enough. He began to complain, refused any more injections and was dishonorably discharged. What was the first thing he did when he left the Marines? He emigrated to the Soviet Union! The Commies. Our sworn enemy, at the time. Think maybe he was a little resentful?"

"Did the Military tell Oswald what they were giving him? The LSD?"

"Hell no. Top secret! He didn't know what in the name of God was happening to him, the poor son-of-a-bitch! While in Russia, it started to become clearer. Distance does that to perception. He realized just how badly his trust and personal dignity had been violated. He wrote letter after letter to a number of congressmen and even President Eisenhower, going on about the 'Crocodile Men' and 'Lizard People' he had seen in various labs and underground testing facilities while involved in the secret Military LSD tests."

"I'm sure they took him seriously," I said sarcastically.

"Well, they actually took him very seriously. But they also knew they had an 'out' in case he went public. The LSD had fried his brain. Hallucinations, y'know? He was just another druggie nut case. So they didn't kill him. Yet. Oswald was no dummy. Ended up working undercover for think tanks in Cuba, Mexico, Haiti, South America. Then Fort Worth, Texas. You know who his best friend was? In Fort Worth, I mean."

I shook my head that, no, in fact, I hadn't any idea who his best friend was in Fort Worth, or any place else, for that matter.

"George de Mohrenschildt. A genius Russian Petroleum Geologist who worked for a number of American oil companies based in and around Dallas. Had deep ties with the intelligence communities of several countries. Befriended a Rolodex of rich and influential political families. High society. Blue Bloods. The Ruling Elite. He was also a Nazi agent during the war. Now, what family was Mohrenschildt tight with, do you imagine? I'm talking tight like blood, for decades, years before he met Oswald. Sustained, intimate, hand-in-hand kinfolk get togethers. Backyard barbecues. Pool parties. From the late thirties on. No guess?"

I had no guess.

"The Bouviers," my uncle said, expecting me to have an instant name epiphany, like "Oh! The Bouviers! Of course!" I shook my head. No idea.

"Jacqueline Lee Bouvier's family," he said, watching for some sense of recognition to sweep across my face. "Went to her birthday parties. Bought her a pony. They corresponded for years. She stayed with him while she finished her junior year of college in Paris. He watched her grow up from a little girl to—"

"Watched who grow up?"

"Jacqueline. Jacqueline Lee Bouvier, later to be known to the world as

Jacqueline Lee Bouvier *Kennedy Onassis*."

"Oh my God!" I said, having the epiphany my uncle expected. "Jackie O!"

"Jackie O. Treated Mohrenschildt like a favorite uncle. Uncle Georgie. In fact, he introduced Jacqueline to her future husband, when John F. Kennedy was still a green senator from Massachusetts. After JFK's assassination, she married Aristotle Onassis, another friend of Mohrenschildt. Onassis was the richest drug dealer ever. One of the top ten wealthiest men in the world, in fact. Made his first couple million selling heroin to the U.S. Mafia under Franklin Roosevelt's guard. Palled around with Howard Hughes, the Rockefellers, Saudi Royalty. Presidents. And how did Onassis become a billionaire? Crude oil transportation!"

"It's all connected," I said.

"It gets better. Mohrenschildt ended up being committed to a mental institution, seeing visions, ranting about upright reptiles in thousand-dollar suits who controlled everything. Lizard Men, Croc People. Telling anyone who'd listen that the FBI, CIA and the Jewish Mafia were trying to kill him. They were. While institutionalized, he wrote and mailed several letters to various congressmen, newspapers, the news departments of the three television networks. He wrote to Johnny Carson, Walter Cronkite, President Gerald Ford. Of course, they never saw the letters."

"Johnny Carson?"

"Everybody watched Johnny Carson. I guess he figured if Carson got his letter and read it, he could go on the *Tonight Show* with the Reptilian story. That never happened, of course. Would have made a great show if it did."

"So no one believed Mohrenschildt?"

"Those who knew about the Reptilians believed! But Mohrenschildt was locked away in the looney bin. No one had access to him. Finally, he escaped from the institution in March of 1977, stole a rifle, put it in his mouth and pulled the trigger."

"And this guy was Oswald's best friend?"

"He was in 1962. They both lived in Fort Worth, Texas. Ate lunch together at least twice a week at the Ol' South Pancake House."

"Did he tell Oswald to kill President Kennedy?"

"No! Jesus. Nothing like that. Shhh . . . listen." He leaned into the table, got quiet. "Those guys at the bar have been watching us all night. Let's finish our beers and get the hell out of here."

"It's the TV, Uncle Henry," I said. "They're watching the TV. Not us."

Uncle Henry turned around and looked up at the television. "Imminent war," one of the television heads was saying. "The line in the sand has been crossed," another reporter said. There was bombastic music in the background. Trumpets. Lots of spinning graphics of the American flag. Stars. Red stripes. The Statue of Liberty. Children with their right hands over their hearts. God bless America.

My uncle nodded, sat back in his seat, and poured the rest of the Genesee. "Messengers of the Great Deception! Don't watch television, Henry. Coca-Cola. Caffeine and sugar. Candy bars. McDonald's. It's all about selling something. You're giving away your power every time you turn that box on. It's a propaganda machine that uses your pain for fuel. Put it on its side and use it as a night light, but don't watch it. Get a mouse and a wheel and watch that instead. Now *that's* entertainment.

"TV is pure evil. There's always an enemy they want you to be afraid of. The Enemy is Cancer. The Enemy is the Sun. The Enemy is these people over here. It's those people over there. This skin color. That country. The Enemy is who or whatever they're told to say it is. Terror. Terror. Fear. Fear. 'Watch out! Look over your shoulder! Who's in your back yard?' Madness. The bottom line is, they don't want you to think, and that's what *they* call entertainment. *Panem et circenses*. Bread and circuses. And you know what? They're so damn good at it, they got it down to such an exact psychological science, that we end up begging for it. 'I want my MTV!' We choose it, God damn it! We're asking for it! We have it wired right into our bedrooms for Christ's sake!"

He shuffled the oil-logo tarot deck. He was digging his upper teeth into his lower lip, and his hands were shaking. "Oswald and Mohrenschildt knew about the Diapsins. Not everything, but some firsthand stuff. They'd both seen them with their own eyes, at different times, and knew that a few of them, a split-off group who called themselves the 'Hive Diapsins' were dangerous."

He picked up the Texaco Oil pentacle coaster and showed it to me, as if to make the visual connection clearer. Behind the pentacle I could see the original Genesee coaster art. It was a cartoon chipmunk or squirrel drinking a beer and winking. Below the little furry critter it said, in quotes: "The Great Outdoors in a Glass!" I laughed a short "heh" through my nostrils.

Uncle Henry noticed my distraction. "The Hive acted like the Mob, and somehow Oswald and Mohrenschildt nosed around in their shit. These particular Reptilians hated their own future world. Desperate, sociopathic and hungry, the Hive Diapsins were less interested in time travel and more interested in world control. A 'One World Government,' with them in charge! They stayed here, in our time, and dug in."

He showed me the Shell Oil logo. The Double X's of Exxon. "They perfected surgical camouflage techniques and DNA manipulation. They are quickly adaptive, long-living, super intelligent, incredibly strong, upright-walking, time-traveling chameleons! Consummate mimics. They are able to manipulate and control their coloration and form. This isn't science fiction, Henry. It's the *Truth*. They infiltrated world governments from the inside.

"Both Lee Harvey Oswald and George de Mohrenschildt loved John F. Kennedy! Morenschildt knew Kennedy's old man for Christ's sake. Oswald and Mohrenschildt compared notes in Fort Worth. Both had the exact same sketches in their diaries. Sketches of the Lizard People. The Reptilians. They had notes about the Hive's 'New World Order.' Mohrenschildt had proof that Jacqueline Kennedy, a woman who had been like a loving niece to him, was now a Reptilian! He had known her since she was born! Now she was a Hive Diapsin! A perfectly successful transformation. He had no idea what was done to the 'real' Jacqueline Lee Bouvier, but he knew this creature was *not* her. He made his case. Oswald believed him. They both feared with a Hive Diapsin in the White House, in the President's bed, the world would end up in chaos. Human beings would become slaves, like the underground labyrinth diggers in Persia, 10,000 years ago. It would be the beginning of our end. The start of Reptilian world domination. Something drastic had to be done. Something for the good of our country. For the whole world. Oswald volunteered."

My uncle stood up, held a pretend rifle in his hands, and looked down its invisible barrel. "November 22nd, 1963," he said, slowly aiming his unseen weapon.

I watched, transfixed.

"Bang!" he shouted, cracking the air. "Shit! Bang! Bang! SHIT!" The room echoed his expletives. "Lee Harvey Oswald wasn't aiming at JFK! He was trying to kill a Hive Diapsin! The Reptilian Jacqueline! And he blew it!"

Now the men *were* looking at us, not the TV. Uncle Henry was really shaking. He sat back down and wiped his sweaty brow with a handkerchief. Stanley folded his arms across his chest and glared at us, mumbling. The five barflies were rustling over their beers, making weird clicking sounds.

"We'd better pay up and leave, Uncle Henry," I said.

He licked his lips and looked down at coasters. Then he slowly brought out a beat up, black leather wallet from his back pocket. He opened it just a crack and glanced inside. "I don't carry credit cards," he said. "They can be traced. Plastic money. Bad idea. Do you have change for a hundred?"

"No. I got this, Uncle Henry," I said. He made a slight protest. "They don't take plastic here anyway. Besides, I sold a painting last week. I'm rich!" Actually, I hadn't, and I wasn't, but I had enough cash on me to pay for the drinks. I walked over to Stanley, pulled two twenties and a ten out of my pocket and politely laid them on the bar in front of him. "Sorry about all that," I said. "He likes to tell stories."

Stanley looked at the money for a long time, as if he didn't know what to do with it. He said something that sounded like "tuberculosis salami," picked up the bills and shuffled over to the cash register. It was an antique metal machine with an embellished pressed-tin surface. The dollars and cents popped up on tabs in a window on top. The whole thing looked like it weighed 300 pounds. He strained to reach the round register keys. His medicine ball belly pushed against the cash drawer as he rung up the sale, and he had to back away as the drawer opened, or quite honestly it simply would not have.

One thing about small dark corner bars on dead end streets in Wilkes-Barre: You can drink all night and still wake up with money in your pocket. I'm sure the tab would have been less than thirty bucks. The extra twenty I gave him was in case we ever came back.

I didn't know it then, but we would, in fact, never come back. The place would be burnt to the ground within a week. The newspaper police reports would say the fire was caused by bad wiring. Only the cash register survived. Nothing else. Not a shot glass to be found. Damn well-made cash register. Pretty crappy wiring job.

We left Stachu's and did not look back. "Uncle Henry, you should get a cab," I said.

He was staggering a bit, still daubing his brow. "I'm okay, I'm okay. I'm going to go for a little walk, get some air. Go past the old neighborhood, maybe look up an ex-girlfriend." He winked and flashed me a quick smile. "Thanks for the drinks. You didn't have to do that."

"Don't worry about it. They can be on you next time."

"Henry, every word is true. I swear it. You've got to believe me."

"I believe you, Uncle Henry," I said, and I did. I put my arms around my Willie Bukowski Picasso and hugged him. "Everything is gonna be okay. I love you."

"Wait," he said, suddenly excited. "I got something for you in my car."

I walked him to his car. It was a huge blue 1964 Buick Electra Sedan. It was packed full of garbage. Piled up past the windows with clothes and boxes, garbage bags, newspapers, notebooks, magazines and fast food containers. The dashboard was equally adorned. Only a little space in front, as wide as Uncle Henry, was carved out in the driver's seat. But even that contained stray plastic straws, pencils, maps and gum wrappers. He fumbled with the keys and opened the trunk. That too was jammed, stuffed with all kinds of shit. Filled black garbage bags, clothes, beer bottles, cans, papers, books, fishing poles, and what looked like a small satellite dish.

With some difficulty, he extracted a duct-taped cardboard box about the size of 2 large pizzas from between what looked like radio hardware and a bag of mannequin heads and slammed the trunk shut. It wouldn't stay closed. He lifted it again and brought it down hard with the full force of his body. It opened again. He repeated this a few times, and finally, I helped him out, laughing. We brought the trunk lid up as high as it would go, and crunched it down with all of our strength. It closed tight with a bang and stayed that way.

He was out of breath. "Here. This is for you. I want you to have it." He handed me the somewhat mangled, cumbersome box. "It's all yours now."

It was heavy as hell. I looked at him.

"It's just some stuff. Your grandfather's. Nobody else deserves it. You should have it. You don't need to tell anybody I gave it to you. The rest of the family, they don't like me very much." He seemed to study my face. "God, you look just like him. Your grandfather."

"Thank you, Uncle Henry. You sure you're gonna be okay? You want me to. . . ?"

He started up the street, away from the car. "I'm fine, Henry. I'm fine. You're a good man."

I watched him walk away for a few seconds, he turned and waved once. "Remember 2012. Head north!" he shouted. "North!"

I nodded back. "Got it!" I walked downhill and headed back to my studio, carrying the package like a Buster Keaton pizza delivery man, delivering the Rosetta Stone.

By the time I returned home, I was exhausted. How many pitchers of beer did we have? Four? Five? Six? Shit. I was drenched with sweat. The evening had grown hotter. My biceps and shoulders were shaking from the strain of carrying Uncle Henry's gift. I let it drop onto my bed.

I pissed, rinsed my face in the bathroom sink, and looked at my reflection in the mirror. I could plainly see Uncle Henry now, as well as images of my grandfather I'd seen in family photographs. My dad was in there, too, and my mom. Everybody. I was an amalgamation of everyone who had come before. Naturally. That's how we human beings are. "Life is strange," I said to myself.

The room was spinning. I had so many questions. What happened to the Hive Diapsins? Was Jack Ruby a Reptilian? Was Aristotle Onassis? What did the Warren Commission have to say about Mohrenschildt? What happens on Venus? What's wrong with Hershey Bars? I would have to go to the Osterhout Library tomorrow and do some digging. I flopped onto the bed and passed out, cradling my duct-taped package.

The phone rang. In my dream, it was an alarm, like a fire alarm. I was getting a small cylindrical tube, about the size of the plastic end of a shoe-string, surgically implanted in the back of my neck. It burned. I grabbed the arm of whatever was putting it in there, and an alarm went off in the tiny tube. It was ringing in my brain! I woke up grasping the back of my neck like a bee had stung me, and stumbled to the phone. It was daylight outside. Probably noon.

"Hello?" I said, all foggy, freaked out and hung-over.

"Henry, it's Dad. Sorry to wake you. I have some sad news."

I looked at the digital clock radio. 9:11 a.m. "What? What is it?"

"Your uncle Henry was in a car accident last night. He's dead."

"Oh no!"

"The police said something must have gone wrong with the oil line. A rupture. It was all over the inside passenger seat of his Buick. He lost control and flipped the guardrail going over the Market Street Bridge. Some people saw it, including the guy he almost ran into. They told the cops he was doing over a hundred miles an hour. Paramedics pulled him out of the Susquehanna River, but there was nothing anyone could do."

"Oh God."

"The oil must have sprayed into the car and choked him. They said his lungs were full of it. He was dead before he even hit the water."

"When did this happen? I was with him last night."

"You were with him?"

"Yeah. Well, he called me around 7:30 or so and wanted to go out. He said he needed to talk. We went to Stachu's up on Coal Street in the Heights and had a few beers." I rubbed the back of my neck.

"A few beers. What time did you get home?"

"I don't know, 11, maybe 11:30. 12." I said.

"Did your Uncle Henry have a lot to drink?" my father asked.

"Yeah. I guess. He—"

"The accident happened around 1."

My stomach turned. I began to feel terrible, guilty for buying him so many drinks, not making him take a cab. Oil line rupture? His lungs were full of oil? I wasn't really comprehending what was being said or what I was saying. My father's words turned fuzzy, out of context, floating.

River. Drinks. Cops. Body. Car. Family. Church. Funeral.

"So what was so important that he had to tell *you?*" There was anger in his voice. An anger I had heard and internalized all my life.

I think I vaguely said something along the lines of "His government job."

"Your uncle Henry never worked for the government!" my father said. "He hasn't held down a decent job in his entire life! He's a bullshitter, Henry. He's an alcoholic! He lived like a bum with the Indians outside

Lubbock Texas in a shack. A deadbeat drunk. Look where it got him! You know how many times he's called your mother and me looking for a hand-out? You ended up giving him money, or paying for his drinks, didn't you? He probably told you some sob story about how sick he was, or that some-body was after him . . ." He went on and on and on.

I hung up the phone and threw up.

When I came back into the room, I looked at the box that was still ly-ing on the bed, then grabbed a kitchen knife and cut through the layers of duct tape. As I opened it, a bunch of photographs slid out. Pictures of my grandfather, Karl. Pictures from when he was young and married. Pictures of their children. There were a dozen or so colored rolls of old coins, all banded together like toy bombs. I peeled back a little of the dried green paper from one of the larger rolls. Gold. Shiny gold coins. Jesus Christ! No wonder this box was so heavy. I removed the coin bundles and set them aside. *I'm rich!* I thought.

There were some letters, some old newspapers, some old pamphlets, a small black leather book and a large black leather book. There was a dry-rotted rubber band stuck around an inch-thick stack of postcards. I peeled the rubber band away and looked through the stack. They weren't post-cards. They were art. Small sketches of buildings on paper. Some female nude studies. A few unimpressive faded watercolor landscapes. My grand-father's work, I figured. I looked for the signature, but they had the letters A.H. on them in the lower corners, not K.L. I put them aside. Maybe there was a letter of explanation in with the other papers, or in the leather books.

There would be a funeral, of course. The whole damn family. They'd tell their stories. The same stupid stories they always tell. Talk about tele-vision shows. Talk about their jobs. Their surgeries. Their pills and medi-cations. Operations. Talk about so-and-so leaving her husband. So-and-so getting a new car. Talk about the War!

They'd talk about Uncle Henry, the black sheep of the family. Hypocrites. Liars. Chugging back beers while going on about how he was an alcoholic. They'd all offer their expert opinions about how an oil line could leak into the car. Give lectures on drunk driving. Say he had a death wish. They'd stand around his closed coffin box laughing loudly in their filthy, cheap shoes, stinking of cigarettes and pork, and ask me all serious and shit why I was so upset. Then they'd put their pudgy, clammy hands on my shoulder and ask me how I was doing, if I was okay, as if they gave a rat's ass. As if they knew me. As if they knew anything about me.

They'd blame me, the artist. I bought him the drinks! I let him drive home! They'd ask me what we talked about. What was so important? *I think I'll tell them! Tell them all of it!* "What did we talk about that was so important? He told me all about the time-traveling Reptilians, you stupid fucks!" Yeah.

The phone rang again. I walked over to the jack behind my desk and yanked the line from the wall. I wanted to scream. I sat back down on the edge of the bed. The contents of Uncle Henry's box lay before me. The two black leather books lay side by side, one small, pocket sized, the other larger, about the size of a phone book. They reminded me of childhood images of family. Like a mama bear and a baby bear, hanging out together; similar proportions, colors, but not the same thing. I picked up the larger one first. Nothing fancy, no title or embossing, just an old book that had taken some abuse in its lifetime. Three wide leather belts held it closed. A folded piece of paper bearing my name—or my uncle's—was duct-taped to one side. I removed the tape, opened the paper, and read the following hand-written note:

Dear Henry,

This book was left to me by my father. Around 1939 it was sent to him in the mail by its author, an old acquaintance from Germany. I am now giving it to you. It is a diary. But this is not just any diary. It's a *secret* diary, unrecorded by history. The author's name: Adolf Hitler. (Here he underlined Adolf Hitler three times and drew a smiley face with a little Hitler mustache and slanted hair.) He and your grandfather were once friends, a long time ago. Think of this as a sort of unknown shadow-self to *Mein Kampf.* There is a story here. A real story which needs to be told, and you, Henry, are the man to tell it.

Love,

Uncle Henry

PS: The spear we returned was fake! Ha Ha!

I felt like I was being set up for one last laugh, as if paper snakes were about to come exploding out of the book once I opened it, or a thousand chirping crickets.

I removed the belts and opened the book carefully. Inside, page after page was filled with crowded lines of tiny writing in what looked at first like a child's handwriting or a crazy person's obsessive scribbling. It was in German, written in a variety of inks and pencils, but always sloppy, small and slanting awkwardly to the right. I could make out some dates and a few names, sometimes an English word or two, but that was it. Leafing through, there were no drawings or any other markings, until it got closer to the end, where it seemed the penmanship became even looser, more careless, heavy-handed, growing bigger and fiercer, until the last few pages where filled with only a few scrawled sentences. The last page of the book had one single word etched across its smooth, slightly yellow-green surface, breaking up into meaningless curves, loops, and jarring slashes of black ink. It looked less like writing and more like a drawing of a battle scene.

"I'm going to have to learn German," I said out loud, feeling a lead weight sink deep in my gut. I laughed a quick desperate laugh. I think my brain was flooded, like I simply could not take it all in. Like I was absolutely filled to emotional capacity. But I was also curious and needed to examine everything. I needed to know it was all real.

I rubbed my face and took a long, slow breath. I closed Adolf Hitler's secret diary and touched the smaller book. It had a tight, black elastic band holding it closed vertically. Beneath the elastic band was another smiley face in red marker on a torn piece of a Wendy's bag, signed "Good Luck! Uncle Henry." The smiley face had little lines coming out from it, like sunshine rays in a child's drawing. I loosened the elastic band and opened the book. It had "Henry Long" written in red pen on the first page. Right. Uncle Henry, not me. So this was Uncle Henry's diary or journal.

Flipping back to front, I saw pages and pages of more chicken scratch writing, only in English, not German. Sketches of the Reptilians. Pencil drawings of various countries with little red dots and stars. A dollar bill from 1925 with the words "in gold coin payable to the bearer on demand" circled in red across the bottom. Drawings of symbols, some familiar, some not, with detailed notes corresponding on the opposite pages and little red arrows going every-which-where. Newspaper clippings with words underlined in red. A whole bunch of corporation logos cut out from magazines and paper-clipped together. Shopping lists. Receipts. Beer labels.

In the front of the book, between the cover and the first page, was a scarred black and white photograph of my grandfather from when he was young, maybe in his early twenties, standing next to a shabby little man with greasy long hair and a beard. Their arms were around each other's waists. Some art hung on a wall behind them, but I couldn't make out what they were. Maybe charcoal drawings. The men were both smiling. You don't usually see that in old photographs: smiles. They looked very pleased with themselves. It made me smile, too. I wiped my runny nose into my wrist. On the back of the photograph was written "Karl and Adolf. 1908."

I envied those two men. They were young. They were artists. They were happy. They had the whole twentieth century before them. Anything was possible.

Jeffrey J. Mariotte visited us many years ago while he was touring in support of one of his many Buffy novels. Since then he has gone on to publish many excellent novels and comics of his own. If you are in San Diego, stop into his store, Mysterious Galaxy (www.mystgalaxy.com), another storied SF shop.

(janey in amber)
Jeffrey J. Mariotte

Sometimes her mother's house seemed like alien territory. After Dad's death, Mother had redecorated the place, almost top to bottom. The room that had been Janey's was called the sewing room now, although Mother had never done much sewing and rarely seemed to use it for anything. She kept a day bed there, which Janey and Jack slept in when they visited. At night, with the lights off, the room whispered to her, reminding her of half-forgotten memories, but when the sun streamed through white lace curtains in the morning it was an unknown land full of sights and odd floral scents that evoked strangers' lives.

What hadn't changed were the three maple trees in the backyard. Maybe they had grown a little taller, but it was hard to tell, because as a child they had always seemed so towering anyway. This time of year, afternoon sun angled between the houses down the street and lit the crimson leaves on fire. Those that had already fallen pooled around slender trunks like children hesitant to leave their parents' comforting sides. Janey kicked through them, dry and crackling underfoot, making her think of the cast-off skins of serpents.

"You like this place, don't you?" Jack asked.

"Yes." Janey answered without hesitation. She sniffed the autumn air, which carried hints of wood smoke and dark spices and enough of a chill to start her nose running. She touched its tip. "Out here, I mean. In the yard, it's . . . the most like it was. Inside . . . I can hardly find Dad in there at all. Or me."

"Fortunately," Jack said, draping a strong arm over her shoulders, "I can always find you, inside or out."

"That is a good thing."

"I think so."

Janey burrowed against his chest for a minute. His other arm wrapped around her, cutting the cold, like rolled blankets against her shoulders and back. "We should go in," she said, wishing she didn't mean it. She would give anything to stay here, in Jack's arms, captured in the dying rays of the sun. Like an insect trapped in amber, she could remain that way forever, watching the eons pass from within a golden cage.

"I'm sure she's fine," Jack said. "She's probably asleep."

"Probably. But I think we should look in."

Jack kissed her forehead. He hadn't shaved that day, and his chin rasped against her flesh. "Whatever you say, darling."

And Janey thought, idyllic, that's the perfect word for what this is. Idyllic.

Mother's room smelled bitter, like piss from one of her rare accidents mixed with some tart liquid medicine she had spilled, all of it confined in stale air. She didn't like having the window open, not this time of year. She was always cold and kept a space heater going, in spite of the central heating that kept the house at seventy-four degrees. Janey worried about her starting a fire somehow, but the space heater seemed safe enough. If it was knocked over it shut off automatically, and you could put your hand right on it without getting burned.

Janey pushed open the door a few inches and looked inside. The warmth slapped her face. Mother was sitting up in bed, eyes open, and she turned her head toward the door as slowly as if she'd had to force it through unseen tar. The hairbrush that always sat on her dresser was on the floor.

"It's Janey."

"I know that," Mother snapped, as she almost always did these days. She couldn't seem to bring herself to speak in a pleasant tone. Either it was an angry-sounding bark or a phlegmy complaint, with very occasionally a screeched dismissal.

"Okay, I just wanted to make sure." Janey didn't like to think about Alzheimer's, but there probably weren't hugely significant differences between one type of dementia and another. Her mother's mind was slipping away, and at this age Janey suspected it wasn't coming back.

She pushed the door open more. Her mother had lost weight since Dad's death, four years before. Lots of it. The skin on her face was pale and tight against her bones, like it might split at any moment and her skull would erupt from beneath it. Mother's mouth sagged open and a tiny wedge of pink tongue flicked out, then away again. "Is there anything I can get you?" Janey asked. She picked up the hairbrush and put it back where it belonged.

"No." Mother looked at the water glass on her nightstand. She liked having water handy, but the glass was three-quarters full. "No."

"Do you want me to read to you?"

"No."

"Jack was reading this article, this doctor, he said—"

"Please don't start with that," Mother said. She touched her hair; short and wispy, she had given up on it after her seventy-fourth birthday and taken to wearing wigs whenever she left the house. As if just remembering it was there, her fingers brushed her hearing aid.

"Start with what?"

"You know."

"I don't."

Mother made a huffing noise, and saliva dribbled down onto her chin. Janey hurried to her side, picked up the folded cloth napkin from the night-stand, and started to dab at Mother's chin. Her clawed fingers snatched it away. "I can clean myself."

"I know, Mother. I just wanted to help."

"If you want to help, then cut out the nonsense."

She seemed lucid at moments like these, but that was illusion, Janey knew. It was temporary lucidity at best, as shot through with holes as a soda can used for target practice. "I don't know what you mean."

Mother turned her head away and threw the napkin onto the bed. "Honestly," she said.

"What?"

"I'm tired." She closed her eyes. "Wake me when dinner's ready."

"Have you talked to Mother today?" Janey asked.

"She doesn't like me."

Dinner was over, the dishes washed and put away. Janey had built a fire, and she sat with her feet up on the sofa reading a hardcover best-seller from the 1980s she had found on the bookshelves flanking the living room fireplace. Jack was on the floor, his back against the sofa, where she could reach out and tousle his hair from time to time. His masculine musk wafted to her on the fire's warm breath.

"That isn't true," she said, putting her finger on her page and closing the book.

"Sure it is. She never has."

"Jack . . ."

"Remember when we were here, when your father died? She wouldn't speak to me the whole time."

"She was a wreck then. She barely spoke to anyone. She wasn't eating or sleeping, either."

"She's made it very clear, Janey."

"I think you're exaggerating. And anyway, I don't care, I love you, and that should count for something. Whether it does or not is her problem."

Janey protested, but she couldn't deny the truth in Jack's words. Her father had died suddenly, choking on a bite of bagel at breakfast one morning. A flailing arm had knocked his orange juice glass on the floor, shattering it. While dialing 911, Mother had tried to pick up the shards and had sliced open her right index finger, a wound that she said bled like a son-of-a-bitch and required two stitches to close. She told Janey the mixture of blood and juice had looked just like a particularly vivid sunset.

She had come right away, arriving late that night, and stayed for two weeks. During that entire time, she couldn't remember a single conversation between Mother and Jack. Maybe he was right after all.

"Thanks, honey," Jack said. "I appreciate that."

He turned back to the fire. She looked at the back of his head for a moment, his hair thick and sandy blond, brushing the collar of his red sweater. In the four years since, they had made periodic trips down from the city to keep tabs on Mother, who refused to move from her house. She didn't mind spending money redecorating, but she didn't want to leave her small-town home. Then her mind had started to drift, she rarely slept through the night, and she stopped eating right. Janey had hired a nurse to check in on her a few times a week, but found herself having to make the trip more and more often. Jack always came along, which made it easier on her.

Five days ago Mother had what she called a "dizzy spell." The nurse had let herself in and found her on the living room floor, soiled and still. The nurse had feared the worst until she touched Mother to take her pulse, and Mother had swatted at her hand and called her Sue.

Sue was Mother's younger sister, who had died at seventeen, more than sixty years before.

The nurse had telephoned, and Janey had rushed down.

Mother had been confused when they arrived, referring to the nurse as Sue or Helen, a woman who had lived down the street for years, and utterly ignoring Jack. Jack had insisted that part, at least, was intentional.

Janey didn't know how long they would stay this time. She didn't feel like she could go back to the city with Mother in this condition, clearly unable to fend for herself. Janey couldn't afford to pay for full-time nursing care, and so far Mother had refused to entertain the notion of moving into a senior facility. If she could make the obstinate woman pack up and go to the city, it would be so much easier. Janey's job was there, her life. Jack liked it here, but Janey didn't know how she would make a living in such a small town.

She opened her book again, found her place. No sense dwelling on it nonstop. A decision would be made. Maybe she would make it, and maybe circumstances would dictate it. But it would have to come in its own time, or she would just have to knock Mother out and drag her from the house.

She resumed reading, her free hand stroking Jack's broad shoulders.

Janey woke up alone the next morning. The bed was cool beside her, but still smelled of Jack. She slipped into a robe, tugged on heavy wool socks. Mother was sound asleep in her own room, a softly undulating lump under her blankets. A chair in her room had been overturned sometime during the night, so Janey righted it and then left, closing the door behind her.

She made breakfast, took a quick shower, put on a black sweatshirt, soft jeans and sneakers. Mother was still asleep, so she called her office, in the corporate headquarters of a sportswear company, to see if anything demanded her attention. There had been crises, she was told, but manageable ones. "You just worry about your mother," her supervisor said. "We'll take care of things here."

"Thanks, Barb. Jack and I will—"

"Who?"

"Jack," Janey said. "You know, my husb—"

"Look, Janey," Barb said. "I have to go. Take it easy, and don't worry about us."

Before Janey could respond, she heard a click and a dial tone.

She and Jack had never actually married. They felt married, that was the important thing. She called him her husband. She spent every night in his arms, never tired of gazing into his blue eyes, felt able to tell him every secret and know he would understand. Had anyone ever been more married, whether some church or government agency had validated their union? She couldn't see how.

She hadn't told many people about the minor deception. She must have told Barb at some point, though, and now Barb was sensitive about it.

When she turned around, Jack was leaning against the sink, his arms folded over his chest. "Everything okay, sweetheart?"

"Oh, I suppose. It's just . . . sometimes Barb is a little sensitive, you know?"

"Not everyone's as level-headed as you."

A slight flush warmed Janey's cheeks. "I try."

He crossed the kitchen to her, enveloped her in his arms. "You succeed," he said hoarsely. His lips found hers.

"Are you making tea?"

Janey spun around, startled by Mother's voice and not expecting her to be up and about, much less in the kitchen. Janey's hand went to her throat. Her pulse fluttered like a hummingbird's wings. "You startled me, Mother."

"I didn't mean to. You usually make tea in the mornings, so I wondered—"

"You should be in bed. I can bring it to you."

"I'm perfectly capable of walking around my own house and sitting upright at a table, Jane." Mother's robe was gray with yellow trim, a matching fabric belt snugging it in at the waist. Beneath it and at the cuffs, a faded rose nightgown peeked out.

"Sit then." Janey waved toward the mahogany dining table. Something else she had bought since Dad's death—for all of Janey's life they had used an old steel table with a spotted yellow plastic surface. That kind of plastic had a name, but she couldn't think of it now. Her heart had barely begun to slow. "I'll get the water boiling. Jack and I were just—"

Mother interrupted her as she sat in her usual chair. "Please, Janey, don't start that up again."

"What?"

"That Jack nonsense, of course."

"What on Earth do you mean?"

"I hope to hell you know what I mean."

"I don't have the slightest idea."

"You're not serious."

"I am, Mother. Whatever you're talking about, you need to—"

"He doesn't exist, Jane." Mother was snapping again. Flecks of saliva glistened on the dark wood of the table.

"Maybe you should go back to bed after all, Mother."

"Don't, Janey."

"But—"

"It's bad enough that I can't trust my own mind half the time. Don't try to make me think it's worse than it is."

"Mother, he was right here in this room!"

"And where is he now?"

Janey glanced over her right shoulder. He had been there a minute ago, leaning against the sink, then holding her in a loving embrace. "I don't keep track of him every instant. Maybe he went outside. Or to take a shower. What's the difference where he is right now?"

"I think you need to come outside with me."

"You shouldn't go outside, Mother, it's cold out."

"I'm hardly an invalid. I can walk around my own damn yard."

Janey started running water into a kettle. "Can't it wait until I make the tea?"

"I don't believe so, no." Mother started toward the back door.

Conflicting urges bumped up against each other. Should she drop the kettle, spilling water all over the floor and perhaps distracting Mother? But why? Whatever idea had cropped up in her addled mind would pass quickly, maybe by the time they got out the door and down the four concrete stairs to the yard. She wanted to shout out to Jack, to put all this to rest by summoning him back into the kitchen.

But Mother yanked the door open. Cold air shouldered into the room. Janey stuffed her hands into the pockets of her jeans and followed Mother out the door and down the stairs. The morning was frigid, more like winter than fall, a taste of what the next few months would bring.

Dry leaves whispered in a sudden breeze. Mother led the way to the back fence, passing between two of the maples. Janey hunched her shoulders against a chill more pronounced than the cold morning could account for. By the fence (wood slats, the reddish-brown paint peeling like early summer sunburned skin) her mother stopped, one thin arm pressed against a slat for balance while she scuffed away leaves and dead grass with her slippered left foot.

"What are we doing out here?" Janey asked. "It's so cold."

"I'm going to show you something," Mother said. Her mother had never minded the cold, Janey recalled, in her younger days. It was only recently that she had begun to complain and insisted on blasting the heat inside. Having cleared a space at her feet, Mother lowered to an awkward crouch and started pawing at the earth. Janey moved closer, peering over her mother's shoulder. Bit by bit, a flat slab of stone was revealed, bone-white beneath hard crumbled dirt and yellowed grass and those big red and brown leaves.

"What is that?"

"You don't remember it?"

"I haven't the slightest idea."

"It's Jack."

Janey tried to pay close attention, sure that she would have to report this entire incident to Mother's doctor. But she felt suddenly dizzy. The wind swirled leaves around them, chittering urgent warnings that wouldn't be silenced. She put both hands against the cool wood of the fence. Goose bumps mottled the flesh of her forearms. "Don't be ridiculous! Can we please go inside now?"

"Not until you look at this." Mother stood up. The stone was fully revealed now, eight or nine inches square, with uneven sides, mostly white but with gray and black streaks she hadn't noticed at first.

"I see it. It's a rock. So?"

"It's a gravestone."

"No it isn't."

"Well, not a real one. I can't believe you've forgotten."

"Forgotten what?" Janey touched the stone. It felt like a block of ice. She caught a whiff of Jack's musk, heard a sudden intake of his breath, as if something had startled him. But when she looked, he was nowhere in sight. The dizziness wouldn't leave her alone. "Is there . . . something buried under there? A bird or something?" Trying to force thoughts of Jack from her mind, she tried to remember any dead pets, but her parents had not been big on bringing animals into the house. She'd had some goldfish, but when those died, usually after only a few weeks, they went into the toilet or the kitchen trash.

"You put this here," Mother said. "You were nine. No, eight."

"What is it?"

"Not a bird." Mother rose. She was a head shorter than Janey, more so now that age had bowed her back, but they shared many of the same features: the prominent nose, the thin upper lip. "You said it was the grave of someone named Jack."

"Bullshit." Janey had always tried not to swear around her mother, who rarely swore herself. The word slipped out, and she didn't care. "You're saying I had some sort of invisible friend? I don't remember anything of the kind."

"Worse than that. You were a . . . strange girl, Jane. Especially after we moved here, left all your old friends behind. You had a hard time making new ones."

"So, what, I made up someone named Jack? Is that what you're saying? Why is he buried?"

Mother shook her head and balanced herself by gripping Janey's left arm. "Because he's dead."

"I don't . . . what do you mean?"

"You weren't satisfied with an imaginary friend. Worried your father and I half to death. You had to have an imaginary ghost."

"That's crazy."

"Let's go inside, Janey."

"Okay." Janey was shivering, her teeth clicking together. She led the way back and held the kitchen door for her mother.

The tea hadn't made itself. When her icy hands would cooperate again, Janey turned on the stove and put some Earl Grey bags in a pot. They were quiet while it steeped, then sat down together at the table. Janey laced her fingers around a purple mug and let the sides warm her hands.

"So what you're telling me is that I made up a dead person."

"A ghost," Mother said. "You made up a ghost. You called him Jack. We thought it was . . . well, very odd. But we were trying to be understanding parents. We were told in those days not to discourage imaginary friends. We didn't know if the same rule applied to imaginary ghosts, but we couldn't see why not. And you were so lonely after we moved here, always so sad."

"And his name was Jack." She realized she was asking her mother to repeat herself, but she couldn't help it. An ice cave had opened up inside her chest, where her heart used to be.

"That's what you told us. You wrote it on the rock in crayon, in big black letters. I'm sure it wore off ages ago."

"And you remember all this?"

"You'd be surprised at the things a mother remembers about her only child."

"I suppose." She didn't think her mother remembered what she had for dinner last night, but she remembered childhood nonsense from thirty years ago.

"You talked about him all the time. Jack did this. Jack and I did that. It was . . . it was eerie, really. As if you really believed in him. Like you could see him and talk to him, and he would talk back."

"I guess that's what kids do."

"I think most kids are happy to have live friends, whether they're imaginary or real. I never heard of anyone with a dead friend."

"A ghost."

"That's what you said. He could walk through walls. Sometimes he was invisible, sometimes not. You had made up a whole story about how he died. I don't remember all the details, but it was very dramatic."

Janey worked her head in a circle. She had been tense for too long, her neck and shoulders were beginning to ache. She heard cracking sounds. "And you never saw him?"

"Of course not."

"Was he my age?"

"A year older, I think. He had light hair and blue eyes. You said he was very handsome."

"Jack the invisible ghost was handsome."

"Not always invisible. Not to you."

Janey sipped from her mug. The steam tickled her nose. "And so, what . . . you think I married Jack because he reminds me of my imaginary ghost?"

Mother fixed her with sorrowful eyes. "Janey, there is no Jack. You're not married."

"Stop it, Mother. Just . . . that isn't nice."

"Think, Jane! Have you ever seen any of your own wedding pictures? Is there a wedding dress in your closet, or an invitation pressed in a book somewhere?"

"That doesn't mean anything. We were never legally—"

"Do you do things as a couple, with other couples?"

"We're busy people. Life is . . . it's complicated."

"Bring him in here, then. Let me see him."

Janey raised her head to call him, but his name stuck in her throat. "I . . . I can't . . ." Her voice sounded strangled, and she coughed, spilling tea on the table.

She walked through the quiet morning, along tree-shaded roads, her father's old leather barn-coat buttoned over her. She swam in it, but it cut the day's chill.

Four blocks from her mother's house was the main drag through town. Janey stopped on the corner and stared down the street. Signs ran together in her vision like trees in a forest, each of them screaming out for individual attention but getting lost in the thicket. Car lots, dry cleaners, liquor stores, supermarkets, bars, discount stores. There were families staying in motels, on their way to or from some other destination. There were salespeople having lunch or pie in a coffee shop's vinyl booths, thinking about what went wrong at the last call or how well the next would go. Lives were being lived all around, lives that would never touch hers. She felt she was watching them from behind thick glass, able to press her palms against it but not to pass through.

She hadn't been able to stay in the house. The things her mother had told her had been too upsetting. She had gone into the bathroom (the one she had used as a child, not in those days a guest bathroom stocked with useless decorative towels and little soaps and shampoos picked up at motels over the years) and wept until her eyes were red and puffy and her nose raw.

She couldn't decide if it was true or not.

The stone was there, but that didn't mean anything. Her first instinct might have been right. Maybe they had buried a goldfish or a parakeet there. Maybe it had been named Jack. Her mother's mind was confused, slipping through time and space like they were a frozen lake and she a kid in slick-soled shoes.

But her mother never slept through the night. She said things were knocked over around the house, and the sounds woke her up. Just this morning Janey had struggled to pick up a wooden chair—could Mother have upset something that big without knowing it?

Who else, though? If Jack was a ghost, would he be able to tip such a heavy object? Most likely Mother had run into it, getting up to pee during the night, and hadn't been able to lift it. By morning she had forgotten all about it.

The whole idea was preposterous. Jack would get a good laugh out of it.

She could hardly wait to tell him, to watch his face break into that glorious smile, to see the corner of his eyes crease and dimples carve his cheeks.

She took a last look at the street, watching the passing cars disappear into the distance bound for who knows where, and started back toward home.

"Mother says you're a ghost. And not even a real one, but a figment of my imagination."

"She's right,"

"Excuse me?"

"Your mother's right."

She had found him in the living room. The book she had been reading the night before was on the coffee table with a bookmark sticking out of it. Jack was in his usual spot on the floor, knees bent, back against the sofa. He wasn't reading, though. He never seemed to read, but he was always there when she did.

Here at Mother's house, anyway.

Something had been itching at her, and she realized now that she couldn't picture him at her place in the city. She never talked about him with co-workers there. She felt, somehow, that he was always around, close by, but did she only feel that when she was here? She couldn't be sure. That dizzy sensation she'd had earlier came back, and she sank onto the sofa. "I don't know what you mean."

"I'm just agreeing with your mother, darling," he said. Those blue eyes burned into her. "You made me up."

"What are you saying?"

"Touch me."

Janey laughed. "Don't be stupid," she said.

He held a muscular arm out to her. "Do it."

She reached for him, closed her hand on his arm, expecting to feel the corded strength she knew so well.

But her fingers came together. She blinked and he was gone, blinked again and there he was. He held her hand and smiled. She felt that, his flesh warm against hers, his fingers slightly callused (but where did the calluses come from? What sort of work did he do? She was unable to summon any memory of that, or of him spending time at any pursuits other than being available for her—and then only in this house).

"How am I supposed to respond to this?" she asked. "You're saying I created you, you wouldn't exist without me."

"That's right. I'd have no reason to."

"I don't understand."

"There's nothing to understand, dearest. The heat of your imagination brought me into this world. You dreamed me at night and pretended me every day, and here I am. All we have to do now is be together. That's all I've ever wanted. It's so lonely when you're away."

"So you're here even when I'm not?"

"I can't leave this place. That's why I have to keep drawing you back here . . . because you live so far away, and you visit so seldom."

"Drawing me back how?" Janey asked. Already a sick suspicion had started to twist her stomach. Her mother's story about Dad's death, choking on a chunk of bagel. "My father . . ."

"I can't lie to you, sweet. He was stronger than you might think. I had to pinch his nose closed and keep his mouth shut. It wasn't easy, but you stayed for weeks that time, and I was in heaven."

"What about Mother? Did you do anything to her?"

"I can't cause dementia," Jack said. "I can mess with her sleep, which doesn't help. I can see that she has a hard time eating. Maybe I interfered with her breathing a time or two. But only because I wanted you to visit more often."

Janey's chest tightened, her breath coming in ragged puffs. Being with Jack felt comfortable. Right. But he frightened her, too. She couldn't reconcile the battling emotions. He caressed her forearm, his touch soothing. "Now we can be together all the time," he said. "There's nothing to get in the way."

"But . . . I live in the city. I have my job, my home . . ."

"You don't need to work, dear."

"What do you mean?"

"Your mother had insurance, savings. You can sell the place in the city from here."

"I don't . . . Jack, what are you telling me?"

"Look out back," he said as casually as he might say, "It's raining, go see."

Janey rushed to the kitchen, her heart trying to break free of her chest. The back door was ajar. A few leaves had blown in and skittered across the linoleum tiles. Janey pushed through the block of cold air and stopped just inside the door.

Her mother's feet were on the second step, her head on the concrete pad at the bottom of the stairs. A pool of blood encircled it, as if the concrete were an iced-over pond and the impact had broken the surface. One hearing aid had come out and floated in the blood like a tiny boat.

She was utterly still. Even from the top step Janey could see that all life had fled her body.

"Call 911," Jack whispered at her shoulder. "They'll take her away, and we'll be alone at last."

"What makes you think I'll stay with you?" Janey asked.

His grip on her arm was tight, each finger clasping hard enough to hurt. She couldn't see him, but she breathed in his unique male scent, so familiar and calming. "You'll stay," Jack said with absolute certainty. "You'll stay with me."

Janey looked at her mother, and she leaned back into Jack, invisible Jack, ghost Jack, and as he wrapped his arms around her she knew that she would indeed stay, because at long last, she had come home.

I take this opportunity of adding ...
... of the desirability (whilst establish...
... additional classification) of insisting ...
... the formation of a District ...
... ge of a competent ...

(vedran)
Jonathan Carroll

He's no filet mignon; he's not even *steak*. He's chuck roast, maybe. London Broil at best."

This is how it began for Edmonds. It was the first thing he'd heard that morning after he sat down in the blue chair and looking out the window, asked himself what the hell am I doing here? But he knew the answer to that question: it was either get on the bus, or go home and kill himself. The choice was that stark and simple.

The big yellow and white bus sat parked at the curb, motor running, gray exhaust fumes puffing out its pipes. The driver leaned against the side of the bus by the open door, smoking a cigarette and incuriously watching the crowd. A large group of old people stood on the sidewalk nearby waiting to board.

Earlier while walking down the street toward them, Edmonds smiled for the first time that morning when he noticed how dressed up all those oldies were. The women had high frozen hairdos like spun glass that clearly indicated they'd just been to the hairdresser. Most of the men wore brand new shoes with no creases or scuffs on them, dark suits or perfectly pressed sports jackets, and all of them appeared to be wearing neckties despite the fact it was only six o'clock in the morning and their days of going to an office were long past.

Someone from the neighborhood had told Edmonds that once a month a bus parked at this spot, loaded up, and then rumbled off for a day's outing arranged by the town or a local senior citizen's club. It took these pensioners to neighboring towns with museums or historical sights worth visiting. Sometimes they motored into the nearby national park, had a hike around, lunch, and then returned to this drop off spot with some sun on their cheeks, tired legs, and the good feeling of knowing that their cameras were full of new pictures and the day had meant something.

Approaching this crowd now, Edmonds was hit by thick waves of warring perfumes. He could imagine every woman there spritzing on her favorite fragrance as she prepared to leave her house earlier this morning. Did the single women put on more perfume, hoping to catch the attention of the available bachelors who would be on the bus? Or was it the married gals who drenched themselves with scents so strong that they almost physically stopped Edmonds when he was ten feet away? Were there many single people in this group? If so, were there more men or women? When you are 65/70/75 . . . are you still looking for a life partner or just a nice companion for the day?

The sight of all those dapper old-timers eager to be off on their day's jaunt, wearing their wide neckties and thick-as-lead perfumes, combined with the thought of actually *having* a partner on a trip when you were 75 years old almost cut Edmonds in half with grief and longing for his lost beloved wife. The impulse to go home and just do it, end it, was ongoing and very powerful. End this unrelenting suffering and just go to sleep forever. He had a friend who was a cop. This guy said when done correctly, hanging yourself was the best and most painless way to go. After a few too many beers one night, he even demonstrated how to do it; not noticing that William Edmonds was paying very, very close attention.

Edmonds would be alone when he was 75, he was certain of it; if he even lived *that* long. There was the very real chance he would contract some monstrous disease before then that, like his poor wife, would painfully devour him from the insides before killing him.

Passing the door of the bus now, he suddenly veered hard left and climbed on. The driver saw this but said nothing. Why did Edmonds do it? Who knows? Self-preservation, or just *why-the-hell not*? Maybe a blissful unexpected moment of sudden lunacy? Who knows?

He was the first passenger to enter the vehicle that morning. Walking down the narrow aisle he chose an empty seat, plopped down into it and turned to look out the window. The cold stale air in there smelled of cigarette smoke and some kind of tangy industrial something—cleaner? Or the synthetic cloth on the seats?

People began to appear at the front of the bus. Some of them glanced at him as they passed; others eased themselves slowly and carefully into seats. Many of them softly grunted or puffed while doing it, their hands and arms shaking as they gripped seat backs or armrests, performing the twists and turns that were necessary to make in order to land their stiff bodies in the proper place.

Edmonds too had reached an age where he found it harder to get into and out of chairs, cars, bathtubs, and other places where his body needed to bend at unnatural angles in order to fit. He often groaned unconsciously now when he sat down—either from gratitude or weariness. Vivid signs that he was getting older and the wear and tear of time was beginning to show itself in earnest on his body.

"He's no filet mignon; he's not even *steak*. He's chuck roast, maybe. London Broil at best."

A portly woman was walking down the aisle, her man right behind talking loudly to her back. When she reached the two empty seats directly in front of Edmonds she glanced at him, moved sideways into the row and sat down by the window. Her husband followed and took the other seat. You could tell by the fluid way both of them moved that they were very used to this seating arrangement.

"I don't know why you think so highly of him."

"Ssh, not so loud. The whole bus can hear you."

Her husband half-turned, glared at Edmonds as if he were to blame for something, and then turned back. "Okay, all right." He lowered his voice a tad. "But really, tell me what it is about him that you like so much."

The woman took her time answering. "I like how dignified he is. I admire the way he hides his pain. It's very . . . noble. Many people who lose their partners want you to know how hard it is for them being alone and what they're going through every day. They want your pity. But not Ken; you know how bad he's hurting and what a loss it was for him. You can't be that close to someone all those years and *not* suffer when they die. But he never shows it; never burdens you with his pain."

Edmonds frowned. Who were they talking about? *It all sounded pretty damned familiar.*

The husband started to mumble something but she cut him off with an abrupt, "Ssh—he's coming. He just got on."

Edmonds looked up and saw a nondescript old man moving slowly down the aisle towards them. On reaching the couple, he stopped and smiled. "Good morning, you two. Are you ready for a little walking?"

"Good morning, Ken. Yes, we're ready to go."

Ken smiled and moved on.

A few minutes later Edmonds turned and looked for the old man. He was sitting alone reading a newspaper on the long bench seat at the very back of the bus. Edmonds stood up, walked to the end of the aisle and sat down next to him.

"Do you mind?"

"Not at all; it'll be nice to have some company on this ride. I'm Ken Alford." He extended his right hand.

"William Edmonds." Both men gave a good strong shake.

"Is it Bill or William?"

"Bill, William—it doesn't matter."

"Okay Bill. Would you like some breakfast?" Out of his coat pockets Ken pulled a cheese Danish wrapped in glistening plastic and a small red and white carton of chocolate milk. Edmonds gestured thanks but no thanks. Ken nodded, opened the milk and took a swig. Carefully capping it again he put it back into his pocket. With his teeth he tore open the plastic around the pastry and took a big bite. You could tell he really liked what he was eating because he kept closing his eyes and making mmh-*mmh*! sounds deep in his throat.

Edmonds liked that. Ken looked and sounded like one of those people on a TV commercial loving some new breakfast food or chocolate bar that was being promoted.

"This is the first time I've seen you on here, Bill."

"Yes, it's my first trip."

"Well, some of them are good and some are stupid, but there's always a part that's worth it."

A few moments later the front door hissed shut and the bus pulled away from the curb.

"I lost my wife last Christmas and that's when I started going on them. She didn't like to travel much, not even day trips, so we stayed pretty close to home. Then when she got sick . . ." Ken's voice remained steady and unemotional.

In contrast, Edmonds couldn't talk about his dead wife without tearing up or his voice catching in his throat.

"Are you married, Bill?"

Edmonds looked at his hands. "My wife died too. Recently."

"Ahh, that's tough. I'm sorry to hear it." But Ken didn't sound sorry at all—if anything he sounded sort of . . . buoyant. "Hold on—I want to show you something." Stuffing the rest of the pastry into his mouth, he brushed off his hands and reached into another pocket. This time he brought out a very sleek, quite beautiful folding knife. "Look at this—it's my Vedran Corluka." He held it out for the other man to take, but Edmonds only stared at him.

"Why do you call it that? Vedran Corluka is a professional soccer player."

Ken nodded and snapped his fingers. "Right! You're a soccer fan too. Excellent. Yes, he plays for the Croatian national team. But I call it that for a reason. This was the last Christmas present my wife gave me. I like pocketknives; I have a collection. But this one—well, you can see how 'specially nice it is. Victoria had it custom-made for me by a guy in Montana. I liked it a lot when I got it, but only after she died did I really start paying attention to it."

"Paying attention? What do you mean?"

"I went a little crazy after my wife died, Bill. We were married thirty-seven years and most of them were damned good. Did you have a good marriage?" Edmonds nodded.

"Then you know what I mean. Vedran Corluka was her favorite player. She didn't know beans about soccer, but she liked his name. She liked to say it. Whenever I was watching a game on TV, she always came in and asked if *Vedran Corluka* was playing.

"So that's why I gave this knife his name. It was her last present and he was her favorite player. I always carry it now. When I get really down, I just grip it tight in my pocket and that usually makes me feel a little better. It makes some of the sadness go away."

"That's a nice story. Can I see it?" Edmonds took the knife and examined it closely. It really was a beautiful object, but he was distracted because of what Ken was saying now.

"We don't pay enough attention to things. We know that, but we still don't do it. Only after something's over, or someone's dead, or it's lost, or it's too late do we realize we've been speed reading life or people and missing the details.

"After my Victoria died, I decided to go over everything I could—the things we owned, the memories I had of her, the memories other people had of her . . . stuff like that. But this time I gave it every bit of my attention. You know, like *re-viewed* it 100 percent like never before. It made such a difference!

"I can't be with my wife any longer because she's gone. But I can *know* her better than before—when she was alive. Whenever I pay really close attention to the details, then I learn more about her all the time. I discover things I never knew or even thought about. It puts the woman in a whole new light—like in a way I'm just meeting her for the first time.

"Sure it's a substitute for the real thing but it's all I've got left of her, Bill. It's the best I can do." Ken took the knife out of Edmonds' hands and said, "A couple of months ago I wrote to the knife maker and asked if he had kept my wife's letter ordering this. He returned it to me and I have it framed above my desk at home.

"See how beautifully the blade is carved? It's got perfect balance too. That kind of work has to be done by hand. All the best things in life are handmade, Bill: knife blades, bread, clothes, loving someone . . ."

When Edmonds got home that afternoon he sat down on the couch in the living room while still in his coat and looked around at the place. Where was his Vedran? What could he carry in his pocket and always feel his wife's presence through it?

What was the last present she had given *him* before she died? And what was the last one he had given her? Ashamed, he could not remember either gift. But was that really important? If you live together with someone for six thousand days so much is shared—does it matter if you can't remember every little thing?

With this in mind, Edmonds walked around their apartment. When he saw something unfamiliar—a book, a porcelain figure, a knickknack—he picked it up and tried not to put it down again until he could recall where the object came from, who had bought or given it, the circumstances, and why it came to become part of their lives.

There were many things—the wooden nutcracker from the New York flea market, the ball made of hematite her sister had given them, and the elephant carved out of amber that he'd brought his wife from Poland. Had she liked it? Distraught, he couldn't remember. It was kind of a kitschy thing but nice too. He stared at the small tawny animal while trying to remember the details, any details about the day he had given it to her or what she'd said about it. But he could not remember even one thing and it was mortifying.

There were so many blanks; his memory of their life together was full of black holes. He reviled himself for having forgotten so much about his wife and their time together. How could that be? How could he have been so careless? How could he have let so many evocative particulars slip through the cracks? Memories of a good life shared were the only real treasure time permitted you to keep.

And what a personal insult to her! He lived in an apartment furnished with belongings that had decorated and enhanced their days. But now he couldn't remember where too many of them came from or why they were even there.

Humbled and appalled, Edmonds moved around his home the next days like a tourist visiting a famous museum for the first time, only his guidebook was his flawed memories. Whenever he drew a blank looking at something, he studied the various objects until either their significance emerged, or he realized his recollection of them was dead forever. He moved those 'dead' items to one corner of the living room and tried to avoid looking at them because every time he did, he despaired. He planned to move them all into a closet and not think about them until he had sorted through what he *did* know.

When a week had passed, a whole week, he called Ken Alford and asked one question. The two men had had a nice day on the bus hanging around together and talking about their lives. At the end of it they had exchanged telephone numbers. Now after Alford answered the phone, Edmonds identified himself and got right to the point. "Ken, what if I can't find my Vedran? What if there's not one single thing I can hold onto and feel better because I know she's in it?"

"Oh it's there, Bill. Somewhere in your apartment, or your life, or your head, it's there. You just haven't found it yet." The old man's voice sounded amused and confident.

Edmonds lowered his head to his chest and pressed the receiver tightly to his ear. "But just the opposite's been happening, Ken: the more I look for it, the more I discover that I don't remember. I don't remember *so much* . . . it's terrible. It feels like whole chunks of my brain have been cut out. In my own home, things I neither recognize nor remember surround me. But they were all part of our life together!" Edmonds heard his voice at the end of the sentence and it sounded scared. He *was* scared.

Alford was silent a while but finally said, "Maybe the first half of life is meant for living, and the second half is for remembering—or trying to. When you consider it that way, both of us were wrong to waste time missing our wives after they died. Because mourning does no good: it only makes you feel helpless and lost.

"What we should do instead is try to remember and then savor whatever details we're able to dredge up from our past. *That's* possible and each time you do it, you feel good because it brings something more of them back to you; like you're rebuilding them from scratch." Ken suddenly laughed. "It's a little bit like you're making your own Frankenstein version of your wife out of what you remember about her." He chuckled again and then went on. "I'm being facetious but you know what I mean. It's one of the reasons why I always keep the knife in my pocket—touching it reminds me to stop regretting and keep trying to remember."

While listening to the other man speak, Edmonds held the amber elephant and turned it over and over in his hand. He wanted it to speak to him too. He wanted it to recount exactly what happened the day he gave it to his wife. What had she said? What was she was wearing? As Ken Alford talked, Edmonds closed his fingers around the elephant and silently mouthed the words "Tell me."

Danielle Ackley-McPhail is a talented editor and writer. Fans will recognize her kick-ass character Kat Alexander from an earlier story, "Carbon Copy" in the anthology Space Pirates *(Flying Pen Press).*

(the devil you don't)
Danielle Ackley-McPhail

W*elcome to debriefing hell.*
Kat thought it would just be herself and the members of the rescue team hashing over the details for Sarge, and perhaps the XO of their unit, 142nd Infantry.

Apparently, she still had one foot in hell.

From those involved, only she, Scotch, and Sergeant Daire were present. They stood before the resident top brass of Military Command. It felt more like an interrogation than a debriefing.

"Private Alexander, please relate your account of the events that took place on the Groom facility."

Kat took one measured step forward from where she stood at parade rest beside her sergeant and Scotch. Stopping ramrod straight, she saluted. At a gesture from the board she resumed parade rest. "Yes, sir. At 2200 I disembarked from the shuttle transport for reassignment to the Groom Experimental Complex. I delivered my orders to Station Commander Trask and was assigned quarters. At 2345 I was called to duty by Lt. Commander Connor."

"You were assigned duty less than two hours on station?" The question came from a stern-faced captain on the end, his stylus tapping a steady tattoo on the datascreen set into the table in front of him.

"Yes, sir. The normal shift crew had mistakenly been given leave, and the crewman I was covering had reported to sick bay."

"Continue."

Kat recounted how she had found things in disarray, with the shift understaffed and deployment schedules misaligned. The one woman on the board, a major, frowned as Kat admitted to deploying the *Rommel* out of sequence, despite the fact that her actions were all that had kept the flagship out of the pirates' hands.

Kat felt her jaw tighten. What did they want? It wasn't as if they'd disclosed the facts to her before using her to infiltrate the situation. The inquisition continued with her accounting how the *Alexi* had gone missing and the station commander had been unresponsive to her priority hails. She detailed her actions, from the unsanctioned High Alert to deploying the auxiliary black box. When she reached her encounter with what she'd presumed was Commander Trask, many members of the board shifted forward, interest bright in their eyes.

"What first betrayed the fact that the individual you faced was not the commander?"

"When I called up the schematic of the station and ran a scan, his presence on the station did not register. When he arrived on the command deck, the scan was still active, yet there was no mark of his presence on the display, indicating he was missing his identchip."

"You did not consider this might have been a system malfunction similar to the disruption in the duty assignments or the deployment schedules?"

"That was my first assessment, sir. However, his actions over the course of the encounter raised several doubts in my mind."

"And how did you respond to these doubts?"

What was this shit? For going on two hours now they'd been debriefed. Her foot throbbed in a steady beat—her face kept time with it until she wanted to scream at the board for being heartless, suspicious bastards—and her patience had disappeared an hour and a half ago. As the questioning went on and the ache of her injuries ramped up, she was less interested in answering than she was in getting out.

"I sought confirmation of my suspicions, checking the system for file access and using the auxiliary command deck to initiate remote observation of Commander Trask."

"So," Colonel Corbin, the ranking officer on the board, said, "you opted to investigate the command officer, rather than report your suspicions, is that correct?" The censure was overt in his voice.

Kat fought the impulse to snarl, keeping her own tone neutral through extreme effort. "A scan of the computer systems seemed to substantiate my concerns; my remote observation of Trask further supported my assessment that he was attempting to steal the schematics for the *Rommel*. With no way to determine who among the crew might be involved in the piracy, I judged it expedient to safeguard the system data before taking any further action."

More than one member of the review board frowned as her neutrality slipped at mention of Trask's name, as well as at the notable absence of his rank. The rest of the expressions betrayed nothing at her admission of independent initiative and the use of her military-funded training as a computer specialist for the unsanctioned observation of a superior. She was certain that they disapproved. Why, she couldn't say. Hadn't she accomplished what they'd intended?

Some glimmer of her thoughts must have slipped past her guard because every brow before her drew down in a scowl.

A familiar vibration went through Kat's jaw. "Lose the attitude, Alexander," Sarge murmured over his bonejack in a tone as sharp and cold as ice-coated razorblades.

Kat drew herself up to attention despite the fact they'd been given leave to stand at rest. Without a word, the others followed suit. They remained that way for another half hour as the board continued to grill her; the questions shifting more to what she could tell them of the function and performance of the composite, than the actual sequence of events that had exposed and subsequently destroyed the imposter.

By the time the colonel issued his curt "dismissed" Kat's fingers itched for her gauss rifle.

"With all due respect, Sarge," Kat said in a tight voice, her eyes locked on the back of her sergeant's head, "what the hell was that about?"

He didn't answer. He didn't stop or even turn. He didn't tear her a new one like she actually deserved. For that she counted herself lucky. Stretching her stride despite the agony of her foot, she followed him down the hall and back toward the docking zone and the systems check he'd ordered earlier. Beside her, Scotch easily kept pace, a gleefully amused look on his face as he glanced from her to Sarge, clearly waiting for something to give. Before Kat could catch up they were hailed by the crewman on duty.

The man's expression was determined, but not for long. "Sir . . ."

The look Sarge gave him cut the private off, the man's throat bobbing as he swallowed whatever he'd been about to say.

"We're here to check out a systems malfunction on our troop transport," Sarge said. "Keep your men out of our way so we can get the job done and get down to the business of some R&R."

The poor crewman seemed startled as he jerked an automatic salute. The only thing about him with any starch left was his ship suit. Newbie.

Sarge didn't hang around for anything more before he turned sharply and continued on to the berth where they'd tethered. Scotch and Kat were no more than a step behind him. Kat felt micro tremors course down her back. Stress. Fatigue. She'd already been on edge *before* spending hours under the lights. What she needed now was rest, but barring that, some action would do. Something told her to get ready for the latter. Tivo, the unit tech, or Campbell, their pilot, always took care of vetting the shuttle after any mission. On rare occasion, she'd even done it herself, but never the sergeant.

As they neared the shuttle, Kat automatically scanned the docking bay, making a mental note of the cameras and other security measures. She wasn't expecting trouble, but it never hurt to know what safeguards were in place. They were all pretty basic, but she did note something odd: one of the alarms was going off, polluting the air with a high-pitched squeal. There was a clear absence of any hangar personnel in the immediate vicinity, though she could see crewmen at work across the bay. Impressive, that. She didn't know what the alarm was, but she wished she'd had it ninety minutes ago; it could clearly empty a room.

"How come they haven't done anything about that?" she wondered aloud, looking around to see where the screech was coming from. "What is it, anyway?"

Scotch laughed and Sarge shot her a predatory grin; neither one said a word, though, as they did a visual scan of the bay. The laughter cut off as if it'd never been and the familiar gleam of a combat operative entered Scotch's gaze.

"All clear, Sarge."

The sergeant punched a code into the hatch key pad.

With a curse Kat locked her hands over her ears, the sudden movement throwing her off balance. Instant nausea gripped her.

"What the *fuck*!"

Similar cries echoed from across the cavernous bay as the hatch swung open. The unmuffled sound coming from inside was like an assault. Kat swayed as her equilibrium was shot to hell and only Scotch's arm bracing her kept her from landing on the deck. Sarge disappeared inside and the sound cut off abruptly. Was this the malfunction Tivo recorded?

"Inside," Sarge called from the belly of the craft. "Now."

Kat found herself back on the bench she'd vacated only hours before. Her ears still buzzed and all the pains were even worse. She groaned as Sarge handed Scotch the field medkit. Within seconds he stripped off both her left boot and sock, and was extracting a pressure bandage from one of the pack's external pouches. None too gently he slapped a transdermal patch on her ankle, snapped the seal on the bandage to activate the chemical coolant, then encased her foot in the bandage. Scotch then loosened her boot sufficiently to put it back in place. Lastly, he rubbed a bit of anti-inflammatory cream on the swelling around her eye.

She was busy clenching her teeth and fighting not to scream when it registered that Sarge was talking to her.

"You ever pull a fool stunt like that again and I'll have you out of my unit so fast the ink won't have time to dry before you're gone."

"Yes, Sarge." Her error wasn't in being injured, but in not disclosing the fact that she was; in combat that could get a teammate killed, or blow an op. She should have known better. She *did* know better. She'd just let recent events get her head twisted around. Scotch patted her good leg approvingly before pushing to his feet and stowing the medkit back in its place.

Sarge gave a sharp nod and turned to a storage locker. As he swung the hatch open, Kat gasped and found herself beside him before she'd realized she'd moved. Though she'd never personally set eyes on the unit, she knew what she was looking at: an auxiliary black box. The Groom's ABB, according to the etching on the pure black unit. *Thank you, Sakmyster!* she sent the thought winging in the direction of the GEC and the former comrade who had trusted her judgment enough to flaunt pseudo-Trask's orders. The rescue team must have intercepted it when they'd come to get her.

She could feel the shit-eating grin spread across her face as she looked up and met the eyes of her commander and her teammate. Their expressions matched her own.

"We've got him!"

With eager hands she reached for the unit only to have Sarge step in her way.

"*That* was them not trusting you."

Kat blinked. Gave her head a shake. Opened her mouth to ask what the heck he was going on about. Then it registered that he was answering her earlier question and her jaw clenched shut.

"*That* was them trying to determine if you had a grudge . . . or a conflict of interest. . . ."

She remained silent, breathing deep and getting her temper in hand.

"Well, soldier," he said, "do you?"

A few more deep breaths. *Really* deep. She focused hard on not buckling beneath Sarge's continued stare. "I guess that depends, sir."

"On?"

"If they are on our side or the pirates'."

He gave a slow nod and stepped aside.

With care she drew the battered microsatellite—or microsat—from the locker. "Did we do that?" she asked, running her hand over burn scoring and a hefty dent down the left side.

"They take that kind of stuff out of our budget when we don't play nice," Scotch said from the back of the transport. "Must have been our pirate, though how he knew it was there and why he didn't just haul it in and dump it somewhere else, I couldn't tell ya."

Kat grunted and continued to examine the unit. It was important to make sure she didn't wipe the core trying to access the information they were after. The external access was all but obliterated. She would have to crack the case. "Hey, Scotch. Grab my kit, will you?"

The tools landed on the bench beside her. Carefully she turned the unit over to access the bottom. The tech team that had designed this particular ABB model allowed for methods of quick and dirty access that would not endanger the internal circuits. Taking out her microtorch, she cut away the base along designated markings that were her safety zone. With the final burn she switched off the torch and set it aside to lift the battered housing away. As she suspected, the primary ports were useless, but there were several more inside for cases such as this. Again she wondered what had caused so much damage; even as far back as the late 1990s black boxes were known for being near indestructible and the technology had only improved. This unit was top of the line, evidenced by the fact that the receivers were still operational despite the abuse to the shell. And yet someone had clearly tried their best to turn it to ash.

Powering up her tablet computer—a specialist's unit, with more bells and whistles than a hero's parade—Kat networked the systems and did a hard burn of the data. Her field computer was made for such things, and yet the transfer was taking forever. There was an impressive amount of data on that ABB.

"Almost done?" Sarge looked on edge. "We have only so long before they wonder what we're doing in here."

"Sorry, Sarge; there's a lot more than I expected."

Scotch sprawled across the opposite benches. "We could always muss up Kittie's clothes a bit and let them think what they want."

If she weren't crazy-busy Kat would have made him pay for that one. Of course, she cheered herself with the thought that there was always later.

Finally, the dump was done. Not soon enough, though; from the front of the transport the comm squawked.

She stole a moment anyway to scan the data, searching for Trask's last coordinates before powering down. The comm squawked again and Sarge cursed, giving Kat a look. Quicker than spit she disconnected her machine. He took it from her and stowed it in the locker he'd taken the microsat out of earlier. She watched him a moment, then turned her attention to the gutted ABB in front of her. She had no clue what to do with it. As she was trying to figure that out, a hand came into her field of view. In it was a timed charge. Armed.

"Take it," Sarge said. "Slip it among the circuits and weld the housing back together. We'll launch it from the rocket shaft. If they ever find any of it they won't recognize it from any other bit of debris."

Kat did as she was ordered. When she was done, Scotch slapped a separator charge on one end for propulsion and jettisoned the evidence.

The comm squawked again and Sarge moved to respond.

"Sergeant Daire; go ahead."

There was a pause, then a crackle. "Sergeant, deck crew reports rocket fire from your vessel; explain."

Everyone tensed even further. They all recognized the voice. It was Colonel Corbin.

"Sorry, sir," Sarge said, his voice calm and completely reasonable. "My tech noticed some computer anomalies at docking. My specialist was attempting to correct the matter when a system glitch fired off the launch tube."

"A technician will be down immediately to check it out."

"Thank you, sir. That will not be necessary." Sarge didn't even flinch. "The issue has been resolved. My specialist is finishing her report now, complete with diagnostics."

Kat swore she could hear the officer's teeth grinding in frustration, but if so, his voice didn't betray it. "Very well, Sergeant. Have a copy sent to my office."

"Yes, sir. You'll have it in five minutes."

The comm went dead.

"Well?" Sarge turned to Kat expectantly. "That gives you four minutes to fake something convincing; start with that incident docking with the *McKay* a month ago, it's close enough."

Kat moved to the shuttle's computer banks. Her fingers pelted the keys like a driving rain, already halfway to the McKay file. She tweaked here, copied there, pulled diagnostics from the last overhaul and doctored the digital time stamp; with seconds to spare Kat had a brand-new report with nary an electronic footprint out of place. Behind her, Scotch let out a long whistle. Sarge just turned and headed for the back of the transport. "Send it," he called over his shoulder as he stowed the gear and secured the locker, rekeying his code so that all was as it had been.

"Sarge," Kat called to him.

He stopped and looked over his shoulder, but didn't say a thing.

"We *did* get him."

Sarge responded with one of his patented nods before he looked away, inspecting the interior of the shuttle to make sure nothing had been overlooked that might betray them. When he was finished, he waited by the open hatch for the two of them to join him. Just beyond his shoulder Kat could see several dock personnel had moved strategically closer to the shuttle. She started to tongue her bonejack off standby, preparing to use the subdermal comm to warn the sergeant. Before she could do so she caught the seemingly random movement of his hand.

There was nothing random about it; he'd just ordered her down using one of their field combat gestures. Yeah, something was up, but as long as Sarge was already aware, she would stand down and wait for his cue.

Sergeant Daire issued the next order aloud. "Corporal Daniels, the team's timing was a bit off on the last op; schedule a live-fire exercise for 0700."

"Yes, sir," Scotch said, and headed off across the docking bay to inform the unit and log the exercise with official channels.

Kat experienced a surge of adrenaline that flushed the fatigue from her system. Sarge's words said one thing, his hands another. They were going wheels-up in the morning, to use one of Scotch's favorite antique phrases. Alpha squad was being deployed, not the entire unit. And at 0400, not 0700.

Curious. She had to wonder why Sarge was distrustful of the crew . . . and the command staff.

She took a step forward and winced, forgetting to be careful with her wrapped ankle. She held her breath and caught the sergeant's eye, just waiting for him to tell her she was grounded. They stood with their gazes locked for a long, silent moment before Sarge gave a subtle nod. "Go rest up, Alexander. You have an exercise to run in the morning."

Kat's breath escaped on a grin. "Yes, sir!" Her salute made him growl, but it was balanced by the understanding in his gaze. He turned and headed off, leaving her to make her way to her bunk with some dignity.

"Quit dawdling, Kittie, and get your tail in here."

"Oh stow it, Rotgut." Kat snarled at Scotch as she slipped past him and moved into the belly of the shuttle. Everyone else was there already, except Sarge and Campbell. Joining her squad, she passed the load compartment, which was crammed with gear, including what looked to be a full complement of pulse cannons. Someone had been busy. Without a word, she settled into her spot on the bench and in short order reassembled her gauss rifle, checking and rechecking each connection before running a quick systems diagnostic. She hated breaking it down to begin with (a soldier wanted a gun if cornered, not a club) but carrying the weapon through the corridors would have drawn attention.

Everything was in working order.

She sat back, gripping the rifle, telling herself to relax and rest up. Of course, the more time that passed waiting for Sarge to come through the hatch, the more Kat got a bad feeling. She gave up on resting. Instead she gave her gear a thorough inspection, making sure everything was accounted for and stowed within reach. The whole time she tried to shrug off her fear, with marginal success.

The others sat back, reasonably relaxed and bullshitting, but she was ramrod straight on her bench, gauss across her knees and her eyes locked on the back of the shuttle, hardly aware that her rifle tapped against the bulkhead.

"Stow your weapon, Alexander," Sarge said when he finally came through the hatch. Campbell entered the shuttle behind him as Kat complied. The pilot locked down the hatch and the airlock before moving to join Sarge at the front of the shuttle. Their expressions were hard and focused as they settled in at the drive console and flew through the start-up sequence. The comm squawked and Sarge shot a look and a gesture back toward the waiting team. All eyes were focused on him and none missed the message. Quiet. ID-Dark.

Kat let out a sharp breath, which earned her a hard scowl. She lowered her head in acknowledgement and worked to regulate her breathing even as she pressed her tongue against the roof of her mouth. Theirs was a special ops unit. Official channels would deny it, but they could deactivate their identchips. Those in the back did so, as ordered.

"Shuttle 62-Delta; identify yourself, pilot."

"Corporal Anthony Campbell speaking."

"Identchip scan confirmed. One passenger registered; identify."

"Sergeant Kevin Daire present and reporting." Sarge's voice was cool, with just a normal shade of impatience.

"Acknowledged and confirmed. Are you prepared for launch, Corporal Campbell?"

"That is an affirmative, Control. The shuttle *Teufel* is ready for launch."

Launch command made no comment on the given name of their craft, merely continuing with protocol: "Please confirm the purpose and duration of your flight."

Sarge placed a hand on Campbell's shoulder, silencing him. "Sergeant Daire speaking; Corporal Campbell and I are embarking on a test flight to confirm systems are fully operational prior to scheduled live-fire exercise. Flight duration; 2.5 standard hours."

"Thank you, Sergeant, you are cleared for launch."

Kat and the rest of the squad strapped in before the docking collar released and the tether disengaged. Until the thrusters took them out of range of the *Rommel,* their drive engines would remain off-line, leaving them without gravity. It was going to be a while. The squad settled in for the wait. Handhelds came out, conversations continued, eyes closed, and peace—or at least quiet—reigned, until Sarge cleared his throat, that is. Everything but the shuttle stopped as the sergeant turned his chair about to face his men.

"We have a situation."

The last eyes opened and the men and women of 142nd Infantry—or Daire's Devils, as they were known—sat straight at attention.

"The details of our assignment," and here his gaze settled on Kat as he gave a brief nod of concession before continuing, "have not previously been disclosed to you.

"There is a reason we were assigned to the *Rommel*: It is suspected that the ranks in this quadrant have been infiltrated at all levels and key personnel have been subverted or replaced by composites. Apparently, they have targeted the vessel. Several attempts have already been made, including the recent events at the Groom facility."

Kat gritted her teeth, certain she was on the receiving end of covert glances from the entire squad.

Sarge then went on as if he hadn't stopped. "We, gentlemen, are Military Command's countermeasure. As such, we report directly to General Drovak and no other. Needless to say, this is a covert assignment; the *Rommel* command staff has not been informed. Our standing orders are first: to observe the crew, reporting on potentially seditious acts. Beta squad has drawn this duty. Our second objective: to actively pursue and halt pirate activity in this quadrant. That is where you come in. . . . Thanks to Private Alexander, we have a fresh lead on one of the subversives. As a result, this is a fact-finding/intercept mission. The intel we secure could be the break we need to neutralize this particular threat."

With that he unbuckled his harness and floated up to the nearest tether bar. He hauled himself hand over hand to the other end of the transport. At the storage locker, he used the leverage of his handhold to muscle his legs down to where he could slide his feet into the bootdocks. Kat watched as Sarge released the lock. He opened the compartment and withdrew her kit. Slinging the strap securely over his shoulder, he disengaged from the docks and hauled himself back toward the drive console.

"You ready for some satisfaction, Alexander?"

She accepted her kit when he stopped in front of her, but she didn't really need it. There was no doubt they were returning to the GEC, or the surrounding sectors, anyway. The data was there on her computer, but Kat had already memorized the last known coordinates of Trask's vessel. She rattled them off from memory, including the frequency at which he'd been transmitting.

"Impressive," Sarge replied in a dead-flat tone. Clearly, he was anything but impressed. "Now power that thing up to verify, and then determine what other useful data we've retrieved." He returned to the con without waiting for a response.

Yeah, so showing off wasn't the best idea. Kat deployed the tablet computer and sat back with it firmly in her grip. Start-up flashed by before she could blink. Opening the microsat data file, Kat quick-scanned what she'd downloaded.

"Oh shit!"

Heads turned at her outburst.

"Report, Private."

"Coordinates confirmed, sir." Even to her own ears, her voice sounded stunned as she rattled off the information she'd provided earlier. *I did it,* she thought. *I friggin' did it! Trask and his goons weren't quick enough!* A crow of laughter escaped her.

"And?" Sarge's voice was edged with impatience.

"Sarge," she managed in a normal voice, looking up to meet his stern gaze. "We are in possession of the collective data from the research facility. . . . All of it." An understandable thread of real satisfaction crept in by the time she was done. Before her last encounter with Trask, she had attempted to initiate a Full Alert, which would have dumped the station's research databases to the secure black box while wiping the primary servers, thus removing the prize from the reach of the pirates. Trask's people had crashed the system before she could tell whether she'd succeeded. Well, here was proof they'd failed to thwart her.

"Good to know, Alexander." Sarge's tone was still less than patient. "How about seeing if there's any intel on there of immediate use?"

She cringed and turned her gaze back to the file. "There are a number of other drive signatures recorded, sir. It's a long shot, but they might be useful in identifying and tracking the pirates." She didn't hold out much hope for that, but a soldier learned to use any tool that came to hand.

"Safe perimeter reached," Campbell cut in. "Setting course and engaging drive."

It wasn't as if they expected anything to still be there. No, they were heading to the coordinates to pick up the trail of Trask's vessel. Originally she'd taken it for an asteroid—as the pirates had intended—back when she'd still been on the command deck of the Groom facility. The ABB hadn't been fooled; it had picked up traces of the drive signature, the unique particle trail left by the ship's engines. They should be able to use that to track him. Of course, they had a ways to go, with not very much in between. That didn't dissuade Kat from linking the signal from the external cameras so it ran the feed on her screen. She'd always hated not seeing where she was going, whether it was a dirt road in a car, or across the galaxy in a shuttle.

There wasn't anything to see for the longest time. Under drive, all the cameras caught was the bright blue glow of passing space punctuated by random pulses caused by the proximity of something of sufficient mass to minutely affect the electrogravitic drive envelope. There wasn't a whole heck of a lot out there to worry about, and if they did come across something, there were proximity alerts in place to give them plenty of warning. Kat settled back and let the light patterns mesmerize her. She wasn't asleep, but it was the next best thing to it; her muscles took advantage of the distraction, relaxing until she was actually slouched against the bulkhead, eyes still fixed on her computer. She was barely aware of hearing the engines modulate for deceleration as they came out of drive—until the light patterns deepened and strobed wildly.

"Watch out!" An alert on the drive console went off moments after her shout.

"Campbell, evasive maneuvers!" Sarge snapped out the order as he helped man the controls. "Clear trajectory, two degrees port."

They barely missed the burnt-out hulk. Eyes still riveted, Kat hit record on her system, catching every frame as the external cameras tracked the wreckage they'd nearly plowed into. There would have been no coming back from that. It wasn't huge, but according to the data scrolling across the bottom of her screen, it was dense. The images were beyond disturbing.

It drifted there like a recently fissured geode. The exterior was nothing but a rock; the exposed interior was a compact craft smaller than one of the escape pods, the standard kind that had earned the epitaph "The Can" for good reason. What Kat saw on her screen was barely bigger than a sleeptank. The camera panned some more as they passed the obstacle.

Kat gasped and her grip on her computer white-knuckled. From over her shoulder she heard a chorus of "Damn!"s and not a few gulps before Sarge's voice cut through it all.

"Enough!" he barked. "Break it up."

She bit back a more vehement "Damn" of her own. She knew what they were looking at, and she felt cheated. "I was wrong; someone else got him."

"Private Alexander . . . disconnect that system link."

Crap.

"Sorry, sir."

Her breath was short and shallow as she broke the connection, unable to look away from the final image recorded: two thirds of an environmental suit still strapped into a conchair.

"Shake it off, soldier, and close that file." Sarge's voice was a faint echo floating overhead.

"I was wrong . . ." she murmured again, her finger jabbing the power down button.

"Maybe . . . we'll have to see," Sarge said. He then turned toward the rest of the squad. "Scotch, Brockmann . . . suit up for retrieval. I want anything you can find that may tell us something, including the remains, stat.

"Stow your gear and snap to, Alexander. We have a refit to execute." Kat looked back to the rear of the transport; Scotch and Brockmann were climbing into top-end versions of the standard MMU, streamlined and built for combat or recon. At their feet was tethered a neat package of standard retrieval gear, right down to a cryo-bodybag that was similar in principle to the coolant bandage strapped around her damaged ankle. She glanced at the rest of the squad as they maneuvered expertly in freefall, hauling gear from the load compartment, deploying combat armament, and fitting out the shuttle with pulse canons and thermal rockets not usually found on a transport. Tivo already had the cover off the two-stage weapons port, on the starward side—shuttles might not have a call to be armed but, in the Alliance, any vessel was capable of being retrofitted to meet combat needs. Kat watched as the tech slid in a cannon auto-mount, jacked it into the system, and replaced the tension cap, maintaining the shuttle's environmental integrity. There was a brief jolt and a mechanical *whir* as the external seal retracted on reconnect.

"The starward cannons are online and ready, Sarge," Tivo said. Dalton, the unit's deceptively feminine weapons specialist, reported similarly for port and aft cannons.

"Campbell, activate weapons control," Sarge said. "We may not see trouble, but all of you will damn well expect it, am I understood?"

"Yessir!" the squad responded collectively as they completed the refit.

Kat was still harnessed in, tablet in hand. "Sarge, put me on the retrieval squad."

He glanced down and gave her a hard stare. She couldn't blame him; she was the newest member of the unit and didn't even have all her clearances yet. "You are not yet rated for zero-g combat."

"All due respect, sir," Kat said, "they aren't rated for invasive data retrieval." She held up her computer. "It's the only way we have a chance of retrieving anything more than physical intel."

Sarge didn't look convinced. "Sure this isn't personal." It was one of those not-questions.

She went for bald-faced honesty. "Does it matter, sir? Because I could lie . . ."

That drew a quirk of the sergeant's upper lip, if not an actual smile. Just then Scotch drifted up from behind. "It's good, Sarge, let her come . . . we could use a mule to haul the gear."

Kat restrained herself from giving her teammate a sour look . . . or a non-regulation salute; his comment might have been flippant, but his expression was solid, steady, and serious. Both she and Scotch waited in patient silence for Sarge's ruling. Okay, not so patient, at least for Kat, but she was sure she *appeared* to be patient, and that was the important bit.

"Double-time it, Alexander," Sarge said by way of approval, "before our drive-wake propels the derelict out of range. We don't have fuel to waste coming about."

He hadn't closed his mouth on the last word and already Kat had her harness disengaged, her rifle retrieved, and was propelling herself toward the equipment lockers and her EVA suit, tablet still in hand and her gauss drifting behind her from its strap. She lost a few moments temporarily securing both, but still, she suspected she broke several suit-up records. Maybe she imagined it, or maybe Sarge really was chuckling behind her; hard to say, as she was already lowering her helmet over her head. Taking her microtorch out of her kit, she attached it to the utility mount on the back of her left gauntlet, then withdrew her tablet once more, slipping its safety tether over her right wrist and ratcheting it tight before activating the auditory command function on the unit. She could operate it in gauntlets, but why borrow the headache? Finished. She activated her bonejack and, with a press of her tongue against her upper jaw, switched it to squad frequency before positioning herself by the airlock.

"Ready for deployment, sir."

Sarge was already back in the drive compartment; only Scotch and Brockmann stood there watching her, 20mm recoilless rifles slung over their shoulders and amusement clear in their expressions despite the obstruction of their helmets. She could almost read their thoughts: *Newbie*.

So be it, she just didn't want Sarge changing his mind. Brockmann propelled herself past them to the airlock, her movements deft and efficient despite the zero-g atmosphere. Scotch stopped in front of Kat and held out a tether. She reflexively accepted it, not even thinking what it was hooked to.

Looking down, she sighed.

"I wasn't joking about the gear, private." Scotch's words buzzed along her jaw. In his other hand he had a pulse pistol. "Stow your weapon. Sarge is right; you aren't cleared for zero-g combat." He handed her the pistol, which she slid into an external thigh pocket. "This is personal protection only, should it come down to an encounter, do not initiate engagement; duck and cover or haul ass back to the transport with what we came for. Brockmann and I will take care of the offensive while you secure the intel." Then he grinned. "You do realize this is all academic, right? Not like there's anything out there for anyone to hide behind."

That took the sting out of the rest of what he'd said.

Their assignment was covert, which meant if it came down to it the higher ups would claim no knowledge of it, rather than raise the suspicions of the subversives. End result: if things went bad, in all likelihood, Alpha Squad would write off their careers. Of course, just in case they weren't hung out to dry over this, violating regs in a conflict situation could ground her, or even ensure Kat never rated for zero-g combat. Not much of a future in special ops after that.

Yeah, with that perspective, she was fine playing mule.

"Get your asses out there and get this done," Sarge snapped over their squad frequency, "before some overeager command crew at Groom mistakes us for more pirates."

This was by no means her first EVA. Nerves twitched anyway as Kat hauled the recovery kit. Not the easiest thing; it kind of resembled one of those shower kits with all the individual, zipped compartments that unroll flat so you can access everything or bundle it up compact for storage . . . only monster-sized. Bulky as sin and a pain in the ass to maneuver (clearly the designers did not consider the dimensions of the various airlocks it would have to go through), but better than losing a hundred thousand dollars worth of tools to the vacuum of space.

When she finally managed to get out of the shuttle, she had her first eyes-on view of the rock-ship. The rest of the retrieval team was already halfway there, putting the shattered mass into perspective: Compared to the vessel she'd just left, it was like a toy. The inside had to have had just barely enough room for Trask to move around, with some storage for necessities. She could not conceive that it was ever meant for manned space travel.

Her suspicions were confirmed as Scotch and Brockmann reached the derelict ahead of her. "Damn!" Scotch's response was drawn out and stunned. "Sarge," he called out over the band, "this man was *not* here willingly."

Kat came up behind him and grudgingly had to concur. It pissed her off, leaving her conflicted in her hatred. Whether the corpse strapped to the conchair was Trask or someone else remained to be seen, but whoever it was, he was a victim, not a collaborator. A closer look inside the pod revealed two things: the body was restrained, not secured, and the vessel had been welded shut.

"Get to work on that system, Kittie," Scotch said as Brockmann grabbed the retrieval gear from Kat and scrambled over the jagged lip. The woman lost no time in transferring the remains to the cryobag and scouring the inside of the compartment for anything that would aid them in their pursuit. Kat didn't know what disturbed her more: the ruthlessness of the pirates, or the detached manner in which her squad mate went about her task.

It's not easy sweating in space. Kat managed, though.

"Come on!" Scotch snarled, drawing her out of her thoughts. "You have a job to do, so do it. I'm not too comfortable with our asses hanging out here."

There was no convenient jack-in port this time. Not because the pirates were being tricky, but because of their ruthlessness. Her search for the primary systems didn't turn up much. Literally. No navigation system. No drive computer. Nothing but life support and communications. This was no ship; it was a coffin. Drop 'em and leave 'em was the catch phrase here. Katrion's stomach turned violently. Even if the real Trask was a willing participant, he didn't deserve this end. No one did. Which kind of robbed her of her focus: It was easier to get a handle on things with a face to hate. Trask had been a known quantity; now the enemy was unidentified, which gave them the edge. That really pissed her off.

She forced her mind off of that and back to the task at hand. This was going to be trickier than anticipated. Without any kind of port for infiltration it would take too long to manually hack in; her O_2 would deplete well before she was done, assuming external forces didn't interfere long before then. She powered up the microtorch she'd attached to her gauntlet, physically extracted what computer systems there were, and slid them into her kit. Crawling out from where she'd completed the extraction, Kat bumped into the conchair. She flinched and turned, in her mind still seeing the partial remains; reality interjected, though. At eye level she could now see the bottom edge of the conchair arm. The foam padding was shredded. Not clawed or torn, but little bits picked out quite purposefully. Katrion thought she could make out a name: Gorman . . . Corlain? It was hard to be sure; after all, the letters were anything but uniform. Powering up her microtorch once more she sliced through the padding where it was unblemished and ran the laser along the bottom until she could pull the strip away and stow it in her kit with the computer cores. There wasn't much left, which meant it was time to go. She turned to push off.

"Hey, Scotch . . ." The rest of her words drifted into space as the section of galaxy past his shoulder came into view. "Ah, hell! Company on your six."

Scotch cursed and Kat faintly heard him mutter about vipers in the nest. That was when it clicked that someone on the inside had to have given them away. Was it someone on the *Rommel?* Or one of their own men? Kat mirrored Scotch's curse. But now was not the time to dwell on betrayal; there were pirates to kill.

The rest of the retrieval squad carefully fired their jets for a controlled turn, both of them bringing to bear recoilless rifles, though what good they thought the weapons would be against an attacking frigate, Kat couldn't imagine. Of course, how pathetic did that make her when she looked down to spy her pulse pistol in her grip? Remembering her orders, she shoved it back into the pocket she'd drawn it from and secured her gear. With a blast of her thrusters she was flying for the *Teufel's* airlock before Sarge's command to retreat came over the band.

Sound doesn't travel in space. No atmosphere, nothing for it to bounce off of. It was a false cliché, though, that no one could hear you scream. There's plenty enough atmosphere in a helmet, and lots of enclosed surfaces that made the sound seem to go on forever. When one of the team bought it, Kat's head nearly exploded with the sound traveling along her bonejack. She didn't have time to spin around before the side of the *Teufel* was briefly lit up with the colors of hell until it looked like it was made of flame. The blast came from behind her; the pirates took out the derelict. Kat knew this because the explosion was enough to send her tumbling end over end, catching brief glimpses of the fierce, quickly exhausted blaze as unused air tanks in the derelict ruptured in the blast. Silhouetted by the flames was the large, limp form of one of her squad mates.

It was like being hit with a board. Kat told herself it was Brockmann, after all, the cryobag still floated nearby, but the fear that she was wrong damn near crippled her. She fired her jets to counteract her uncontrolled spin. Forgetting such things as orders and intel and pirate ships with pulse cannons, she went flying toward the wreckage.

"Back to that shuttle, Private!" The voice was familiar, if not the tone. "Now!"

She didn't sob. She wouldn't sob. Soldiers didn't, you know. (Yeah. Another lie.)

"Where you at, you sonofabitch?" A western twang crept into her voice as she snipped at Scotch. Her temper had always carried echoes of her PawPaw, though this time it was heavy with relief.

"On your 4 o'clock, get your tail to the shuttle; we have to get out of here."

"Brock . . ."

"Get going," Scotch said. "I've got her, and the sorry piece of shit we came out here for."

Katrion wanted to argue, only her training—and her relief—kicked in.

It took one jet to spin her, and both to send her on her way. The left jet gave a little sputter and an early warning light blinked on in the rim of her visor. Her powerpack was running low. Shouldn't be an issue; she was less than twenty yards from the airlock. Of course, by the time she was facing the shuttle it was too late. The attacking vessel was spewing pirates with heavier armaments than anything she had. Several broke off in an attempt to deprive her and Scotch of their burdens, and likely their lives; the others took potshots at the *Teufel*, pinning the rest of Alpha Squad on board. The unmarked frigate came around firing warning shots that shook the shuttle. Their flight path was about to bring them in close, like they planned to grapple on to the hull. The *Teufel* was just able to keep them at bay using the thermal rockets. Katrion waited for the shuttle's engines to fire up in a strategic retreat that would take the rest of the squad away from the risk of capture. That would signal the end for the retrieval squad and the mission objective, but she couldn't believe Sarge would sacrifice the squad for just two men.

Daire's Devils weren't that easily intimidated, though: with a *whoosh* and a light cloud of venting atmosphere, the airlock opened. All she could see were Tivo, Dalton, and Kramer, the three best shots in the unit, in positions of cover around the open iris. Each of them had a short-order 50-cal. in their hands and a secondary weapon slung over their shoulders. They were methodically picking off any pirate within range. One of the unfriendlies was closing in on Kat's position, despite the fire team's cover. There were too many for her team to hit them all.

Kat was on her own. She deployed her pulse pistol and fired. Nothing happened and the pirate drew closer, his weapon trained on her head. Her breath quickened and acid burned her throat. *Not like this, damnit!*

From the direction of the *Teufel*, Kat spied a flash of weapons' fire as Dalton noticed her predicament. The pirate's body jerked with the impact, the round traveling straight through the environmental suit. Blood and atmosphere formed a cloud around the slowly twisting remains.

Better you, than me. Kat shuddered and returned the malfunctioning pistol to her pocket.

With the rest of the pirates occupied, Kat glanced toward Scotch. As her eyes settled on her teammate she wanted to call out, to warn him; there was a pirate closing in from behind. She could activate her comm against combat procedure, but even that wouldn't be in time.

No way in hell! With a grit of her teeth and barely a glance at her powerpack warning light, Kat fired her jets full thrust. Her pulse pistol was useless, but her gaze locked on the microtorch still affixed to her gauntlet. She had one chance. The enemy's attention was completely fixed on his target. He had no clue his buddies hadn't dealt with her. Minute adjustments of her body-posture shifted her trajectory until she was aimed straight at the pirate's head. She powered up the 'torch and gladly burned the last of her reserves.

Impact. A jolt and a pop, a brief swirling cloud as the pirate's suit vented atmosphere, and more of that screaming—this time from Kat—as the momentum sent her tumbling against the inertia of her victim's body, her arm locked in place, the gauntlet scorched and her wrist throbbing.

She screamed again as the wrist bent back against her weight as much as the gauntlet allowed, saved from a break by the suit's rigid structure and the fact that the 'torch tip finally cut itself free. She must have accidentally reactivated the comm because Scotch's voice rippled along her jaw, soothing after an initial curse of his own. "Damn, Kittie . . ." His arm locked around her waist and drew her down as he gave a burst of his jets to halt her spin. "Remind me to steer clear once you are rated for zero-g!" There was relief in his voice as well as a new level of respect.

She shared the relief, but the rest of what she felt was a confusing hodgepodge she was too uncomfortable to consider. All she could manage was a groan as she tried to use her own jets to back away. They sputtered and she noted the warning light had transitioned to red. She was tapped and trapped. Looking anywhere but at him, she noticed the rest of the Devils had come out to play, even now forcing the pirates back.

"Come on, Kittie, time to go home," Scotch murmured, tucking her tighter against him as he went full thrusters toward the *Teufel*.

"Wait!" She fought against him, though what she thought that would accomplish with her powerpack spent, she didn't know. "Brockmann . . . and the . . ."

Before she could protest further, one of their squad zipped past and headed back with the remains of their comrade, and their objective. She damn well hoped they'd garnered something of use. Even if this did put them one solid step closer to pinning the bastards down, it was scarcely worth the loss of a teammate. Kat seethed, more than ever wanting to get a bit of her own back against the pirates.

Now was not the time, though. A scan of the zone showed that everyone else had already fallen back to the shuttle. Kat gave up and settled in for the ride; Scotch was only looking out for her. That's what teammates did.

They were nearly there when a warning came across the comm. "To your 3 o'clock, stat!" Scotch dodged to the left, sending them spinning. The fire team must have missed one. The heat of the laser blast they'd barely evaded bubbled the surface of Kat's visor while her curses blistered the inside. Apparently the pirates were still in the game. Her stomach spun as Scotch corrected and slammed them past the airlock iris, right into the internal hatch. "Go! Go! Go!" he barked as the airlock closed, practically on the tips of their boots.

As the chamber filled with atmosphere they shed their helmets, but remained suited. They propelled themselves through the hatch and to the open bench by the drive compartment. Kat and Scotch settled side by side.

"Strap in!" Sarge bellowed. "Dalton, take the con and get those cannons firing."

The *Teufel* shuddered and warning alarms went off. From the sound of it, the pirates were firing chaff rounds off their hull. More useless intimidation. The pirates wanted something, or the *Teufel* would already be a cloud of vented gas and debris. The shuttle's pulse cannons whined and popped. More detonations just off their battered hull.

This game of tag was getting old.

"Campbell, ready the thermal rockets; Dalton, charge the pulse cannons and hold fire. Engage on my mark. Target their engines." Sarge issued the orders in a sharp, clipped tone. "I have the con." He brought the shuttle in hard and fast despite the continued fire from the pirate vessel. Kat could visualize his maneuvers, remembering the last position of the enemy ship. He brought the *Teufel* arcing along the pirates' starward side and pulled ahead, giving Campbell and Dalton a clear firing solution from all ports.

"Game over," Sarge growled. "All weapons, fire!"

They were too close. The resulting explosion as the frigate was destroyed shook the *Teufel* hard enough that those in back would have fallen to the deck if they hadn't been strapped in. Alerts went off as they took some collateral damage. *Gotcha!* Kat thought. The rest of the squad cheered as Campbell took over the helm and aimed them for the *Rommel*'s coordinates.

"Better get some rest, Kittie-Kat," Scotch murmured, pressing his hand to her cheek. She rested her head on his shoulder. Kat wasn't sure which startled her more, the fact that he'd touched her, or that she'd instinctively leaned against him afterwards. She was about to jerk upright in protest when he said, "We still have live-fire exercises once we get back."

"You mean . . . we're not for the brig once we dock?"

Scotch chuckled. "Shh. Don't even think it; Sarge has us covered. There's a surprise training op registered by those who cut our orders. It'll have come down channels by now."

Kat swallowed hard and looked up to meet his eye. "And Brockmann? What do we tell them about her?"

His eyes went solemn. "The truth. A pirate ambush. She'll not be the first soldier to fall during training. Now settle in and get some rest already. He's not gonna take it easy on any of us after this. There's too much at stake."

Despite everything that had just passed, she had no doubt Scotch was right. Dutifully, she attempted to shut off her thoughts and let herself relax. Still, the tension bubbled up and out of her like a Tourette's outburst.

"I wanted Trask!"

Scotch grunted and pressed his cheek against her head. She ignored the hint and went on.

"Now I have no clue who to kill, damnit!"

He chuckled and reached up, gently rubbing her ear and against the pressure point behind it. The returning tension drained out of her and the world started to dim.

"Better the devil you know . . ." was the last thing she heard him murmur in agreement before she drifted off.

Walt is an up-and-coming game designer who has been writing for Green Ronin and Cubicle 7. This is the first of what I hope will be many more published Black Family stories.

(the dungeon out of time)
Walter Ciechanowski

A small part of the Pine Barrens burned to the ground just after midnight on August 13, 1984. As one of over a thousand small forest fires in New Jersey that year, this particular one went largely unnoticed; a line in the newspaper. I was one of the few that truly understood its significance.

Now, almost a year later, the dark events surrounding that blaze still bring a chill to my spine as I prepare to do what I must to finally purge the darkness that I'm certain still stains my soul. Letting out a long breath, I close my eyes and concentrate on the hours preceding that horrific night.

It began on a Saturday afternoon, the first day of the second Chandler family summer vacation of 1984. I was sitting in the backseat of the Buick with my sister Janet while my parents sat in the front. My father was driving down Route 72, a country road that seemed to connect the Jersey Shore to the rest of civilization. We were going to have "a week of sun and fun" as my dad was fond of saying.

I *really* did not want to be there.

It wasn't because of the blazing sun or the fact that our car lacked air-conditioning. It wasn't because I was wedged to one side of the back seat due to the amount of luggage stuffed between me and my sister. It wasn't even because of my father's futile attempts to get half-decent reception of some old song he recognized on the radio.

No, my reason for not wanting to endure this painful family vacation had nothing to do with any circumstances beyond one: it kept me from playing *Dangerous Dungeons* with my friends for an entire week.

I know it sounds silly, but *Dangerous Dungeons* was more than just a game to me. It opened up new worlds of adventure that were far more interesting than the life of John Chandler. His life was boring and predictable; school, homework, television, sleep. Rinse and repeat. In *Dangerous Dungeons*, I could be a mighty warrior, a fiery warlock, or anything else I could imagine. I even had the power to create entire worlds, each far more interesting than this one.

I was creating a world just then, feverishly jotting notes in my spiral-bound notebook. I'd been curious about adapting *Dangerous Dungeons* to the superhero genre, and I was using this ride to do just that. I even had my Walkman on so that I could drown out my family's conversations as well as the ancient music that my father tuned in for a few seconds at a time.

In spite of my objections to being on this vacation, I was content for the moment. I'd already figured out the basics of creating a superhero and I was now working on converting the magic system to emulate superpowers. I smiled as I imagined my friends' reactions to how effortlessly elegant my solution was. Unfortunately, my giddiness was short-lived. Janet punched me in the arm. I howled in pain.

"Punch buggy!" She pointed out the open window toward a canary Volkswagen Beetle. I glared at her and prepared to hit her back. She shrieked.

"John! Janet! No fighting!" Mom gave us a hard glare that was more menacing than her warning. I suspected that she was more concerned about the potentially fragile goods packed between us rather than whether we might hurt each other.

"I never agreed to play," I said, coming off less as an injured innocent and more as a whining brat. I could see my father's eyes roll in the rear-view mirror.

"Yes, you did." Janet sounded like a little sister, even though she had a year and a half on me. "You nodded when I asked you at the last circle."

I sighed. I'd had my Walkman on ever since we left Philadelphia. I barely remembered passing through the many traffic circles along the way, much less Janet asking me to play some silly game with her. Jarred from my concentration, I decided to look around a bit before returning to my game design.

We were surrounded by the Pinelands on both sides of Route 72. I could see the contentment in my family's faces as they took it in. To them, this stretch of forest was a cathartic experience, a washing away of the stresses of their normal lives. The seagulls flying through the air, along with the road itself, promised them a relaxing vacation.

But that is not what I felt or saw. Already confined to a small section of the car, I felt even more claustrophobic and isolated within the foreboding pines. If something bad were to happen, there seemed to be no help for miles. In a sense, I felt much like a typical *Dangerous Dungeons* adventurer except that, in real life, I lacked his survival skills. No, far from being comforting, this isolated stretch of highway only made me nervous.

Keeping my eyes riveted to the passing forest beside me, I began to craft a *Dangerous Dungeons* scenario. I could see an unfortunate soul, about the same age as me, although taller and a bit faster, rushing through the trees away from some unseen danger. It would not save him, though, and he knew it. I imagined the unearthly howls of the vicious creatures chasing him, like a huntsman's dogs flushing out his prey.

The flushing was especially apt, as the young man bolted out of the tree line and raced toward our car. It was all in my mind, but at the moment, that boy was more real to me than the seagulls and the sun. In fact, my mind had edited them out. It was now pouring rain in the dead of night. The poor soul was clad in a drenched Members Only jacket and jeans as he waved his hands furiously for my dad to stop. For some reason I felt I knew this boy, even though he was only a character painted in my head.

And then the dogs burst from the trees behind him. They were horrid reptilian creatures, large and hairless, with glowing, green eyes and foaming, too-large maws. The boy didn't stand a chance as two of the savage beasts leapt upon him from behind. One dog ripped out his throat and the boy's blood sprayed across our windshield. A third dog didn't bother with the easy kill, turning its attention instead towards me. I recoiled in horror as the beast howled and leapt through the window of the car.

From my family's viewpoint, of course, I'd just squealed and jumped for no apparent reason. My sister found it hilarious.

"See a dragon?" Janet chuckled. "Maybe we should call Reverend Bobby."

I glared at her. The *Dangerous Denizens* supplement described twelve different devil lords. As far as many gamers were concerned, Reverend Robert Fitzpatrick should be the thirteenth. For almost two years he'd crusaded against the "evils" of *Dangerous Dungeons* and put former role-players on his television program *Good Neighbors* to speak out against its cultish influence. He encouraged "people of faith" to conduct book burnings, purchasing as many *Dangerous Dungeons* books as they could to fuel their "spiritual bonfires."

My father caught an episode of Reverend Bobby's show once while flicking through the channels. It happened to be one in which Reverend Bobby was interviewing a couple whose son supposedly committed suicide due to the influence of *Dangerous Dungeons*. He mocked me for weeks, periodically looking through my closet to make sure I didn't have any "warlock cloaks" or dead chickens hanging inside.

Unfortunately, the harassment didn't end with my father. Bullies were always looking for reasons to inflict themselves on others, and Reverend Bobby gave them a perfect excuse. I'd been beaten quite a few times in order to "drive Satan out of me" and left on the ground next to my broken pencils and torn papers. It wasn't long before my non-role-playing friends began to shun me and I could forget about dating "normal" girls.

Still, I'd persevered. I wasn't going to let anyone stop me from doing what I enjoyed. *Dangerous Dungeons* was a very important part of my life, perhaps *the* most important part. It wasn't my fault that no one understood that. I replaced my headphones and decided that it was time to do something more constructive.

I settled back into my seat and returned to my superhero notes, but it was difficult to concentrate. I could brush off Janet, but for some reason I just couldn't shake the feeling that somewhere in the pine trees someone — or some*thing* — was watching me.

While our family vacation was supposedly an escape from our everyday lives, it was not, as our mother constantly reminded us, an escape from God. While our suitcases were packed with casual summer clothes and beach wear, we all had at least one church outfit packed as well. Our first full day on Long Beach Island was Sunday, so the first thing on the Chandler agenda was to go to church.

I didn't particularly like going to church. The fantasy worlds I lived in were more real to me than the one that the reverends preached about. I found it particularly difficult to sit through the sermon. While even I had to admit that Reverend Luke was a great speaker, his warnings about the rat race kept reminding me of that boy I imagined running through the woods the day before. It wasn't long before I'd tuned out the sermon altogether, imagining myself running through those woods in search of safety. I shivered again when I recalled those dogs with the glowing eyes.

The day was blazing hot, and I was especially uncomfortable considering that I had rarely ventured outside since our June vacation. We had a late breakfast at a small restaurant across the street from the church, during which I pleaded with my parents not to make me go to the beach with them. It was an old argument that my parents chalked up to my lack of self-esteem.

I guess they had a point. Prior to my introduction to *Dangerous Dungeons* two years ago, I was slim and enjoyed outdoor sports. Now, however, I was a bit overweight from long afternoons and evenings spent sitting around a gaming table. That point was driven home during the first Chandler vacation in June. I went to the beach after church, stripped off my shirt, and promptly fried as the sunlight hit my milk-white skin for the first time. I endured sun-poisoning for the rest of the trip.

The silver lining of that experience was that my parents didn't object too strongly this time. We went back to our rented house and, while the rest of my family got ready for the beach, I tugged on shorts and a tee and headed to my favorite shore destination: the Toy Box.

The Toy Box was a small red building that sat on the main boulevard only a few blocks from where we were staying. It had been open since we first started coming to the island and I vaguely recalled stopping in there once or twice as a child. It wasn't until August of last year that I felt compelled to venture inside. I was so glad I did! Much to my surprise, it turned out that the Toy Box had a good selection of *Dangerous Dungeons* and other related products.

I could feel my excitement building as I walked toward the store. For me, the Toy Box was an oasis in the desert; the only place where I truly felt comfortable amongst the lean bronze throngs of people on the island. If I had my way, I'd be here every day of vacation, but I knew that I'd be lucky to step through the threshold of my personal Mecca one or two more times before we headed back to Philadelphia.

Small bells attached to the door announced my presence as I stepped inside. My nostrils were immediately assaulted by the acrid scent of cigar smoke coming from the checkout counter. Sal, a beefy old man wearing a checkered shirt and suspenders, sat quietly on a stool, puffing away at a thick cigar as he mulled over a newspaper crossword puzzle while holding a short pencil between his pudgy fingers. It was the first time I'd seen Sal since June. He paused from his puzzle just long enough to give me a brief "hello." I was going to ask him how his summer had been so far, but I was a bit unnerved by the strange look in his eyes behind the small reading glasses perched on the bridge of his nose. I don't know why it bothered me, but I settled for an acknowledging nod and walked past the counter.

I was certain that Sal was still staring at me as I headed towards the gaming shelf at the back. I also heard his stubby fingertips dialing a telephone number. Was he calling someone about me? I shook my head; I was probably just being paranoid. I thought about that boy running through the Pine Barrens again. I now imagined him here, casually examining the latest *Dangerous Dungeons* book, unaware that the dogs were silently stalking him. I interpreted Sal's whispered, gravelly voice as he spoke into the telephone as an order to strike, and the boy was running once more as the dogs burst through the shelves of toys, models, and games to get to him.

I dismissed those thoughts when something caught my eye on the role-playing shelf. I eagerly grabbed the game box, my excitement growing as I saw spandex-clad characters attacking each other with various powers. *Four Color Adventures* was boldly emblazoned on the cover. I almost shouted for joy as I realized that I could spend the rest of my vacation creating superheroes rather than designing a game for them.

"It's a pretty good game, John," a voice said from behind me. "It uses a universal mechanic."

I recognized the voice. He was one of Sal's employees and the resident expert on role-playing games. He wasn't much older than me, although he was taller and almost rail-thin. He had a mop of brown hair that partially hid a pencil tucked above one ear. We'd had several good conversations about games over the past two years.

"Hi, Marc." I laughed. "Good to see you again."

Marc tapped the box that I held. "*Four Color Adventures* is put out by the same people that designed *Dangerous Dungeons*, but this was developed by their British division in London."

"British?" My heart sank. I'd read a couple of British comics and was disappointed; I guess I just didn't get their sense of humor.

"They write excellent stuff," Marc said, obviously picking up on my nervousness. "You should read some of their *Dangerous Dungeons* adventures. They're light years better than the regular ones."

"Really?" Relying on my allowance, birthdays, and Christmas for new material, I only owned a handful of adventures.

"Definitely." Marc pointed to the shelf. "Take a look; I think there's a few of them wedged between the *Dangerous Dungeons Players Guides* and the *Dungeon Crafters Handbooks*."

I glanced up to see a few shrink-wrapped adventure books, and reached up and pulled one free. As I did so, a small piece of paper fluttered to the ground. It looked like a comic strip. I groaned as I realized what it was.

"I bet that's a 'Fact Tract.'" I said, picking it up.

I hated Sean Carter almost as much as Reverend Bobby. Mr. Carter and his devotees invaded book and hobby stores like missionaries, sticking his comic strips into role-playing game books to remind you of their "occult influences" as you browsed the games. No one was quite sure who Sean Carter was except that he, like Reverend Bobby, was on a crusade against my favorite hobby.

"Yeah, they're pretty funny." Marc chuckled. "The evangelist looks like Matt Houston."

The *Matt Houston* television theme played in my head as I glanced at the comic in my hand. It depicted a young girl who plays a role-playing game called *Dark Dangers* and soon joins a witch coven. She almost gives her soul to Satan, but a pleasant young man with a healthy head of hair and a mustache—he actually did look a bit like Lee Horsley, the actor who played Matt Houston—has a conversation with her. She reaffirms her commitment to Jesus Christ during a book burning in the final frame.

"He does look like Matt Houston," I agreed.

Marc glanced over at Sal. The old man's back was to us. Marc dropped his voice a bit.

"John, I told you that I played with Dave Garrison, right?"

I knew he was teasing me. During our conversations over the last two vacations, Marc had spoken of his games with Dave quite often. As the creator of *Dangerous Dungeons,* Dave Garrison was a role-playing legend and Marc was the only person I knew who'd played with him. I'd listened with a mixture of fascination and envy. My favorite story, of course, was the "Steve and the Dread Portcullis" story, a humorous account of a role-player thinking that a portcullis was some type of creature barring his way into a keep. While Marc wasn't at that session, he'd heard from Dave that it was true.

"Of course," I said, deciding to bite. "He's your Dungeon Crafter, isn't he?"

Marc nodded. "Dave's hosting a game tonight and there'll be an empty chair at the table. Want to join us?"

Did I! I tried not to leap in the air. Every time Marc told me about his game sessions with Dave I'd hoped for an invite, but he had never offered one until now. There was no way that I'd pass up this opportunity. "You don't have to ask *me* twice!"

"Good." Marc smiled, although it faded fast when he saw Sal stirring in his seat. "I get off at seven. Why don't you meet me here at seven-thirty and we'll ride to the game together?"

"Sounds good," I said, although I wasn't sure if I could sell it to my parents. They thought I played enough games at home. "What time does the game end?"

Marc chuckled as he pretended to look busy reorganizing a shelf. "We usually stop around midnight, although sometimes it can run over if we're in the middle of a combat or something."

"Awesome," I said. "I'll have to make sure it's okay with my parents, though. If I'm not here by seven-thirty, don't wait for me."

"Hope you can make it," Marc said as he returned to his work.

I could hardly contain my excitement as I walked to the front of the store and put *Four Color Adventures* on the counter. Sal sighed as he put down the crossword puzzle he'd been working on and rang it up on his ancient cash register.

"Fifteen ninety-five."

I paid him and was about to leave when Sal reached under the counter and pulled out what looked like a velvet dice bag.

"Here."

Puzzled, I opened the bag. Inside was a set of six polyhedral dice. No, scratch that, there were seven. Unlike most of the dice sets I had, this one included a second ten-sided die that had "tens" marked on it. I pulled the twenty-sider out of the bag. The die was heavier than I was used to and was carved out of green stone, with red numbers printed on each face.

"These are really nice! Thank you," I said. "But why?"

Sal shrugged. "It's a special edition, made out of green soapstone. I had ten sets to give away this month as part of a promotion."

Ah, so *that's* why Sal was acting so suspicious when I entered. He was counting sales for the free dice. I was thrilled that I was one of the lucky ones. I'm sure the dice weren't worth much, but I felt like I'd just won the lottery.

"Why me?" I asked.

Sal studied me carefully. "You look like the kind of kid that will use these soon, and the manufacturer is interested in feedback. I figure you'll have some for me before you head back home, right?" He shot a glance back at Marc.

"Definitely," I said, carefully putting the die back into the bag.

"Then enjoy." Sal paused as if he had more to say, but then he just bit his lip and returned to his crossword puzzle. I wasn't about to press him; I couldn't wait to get out of there.

"Thanks again!" I said as I dropped my bag of dice into the paper bag that held my newly purchased game and practically floated out of the Toy Box. Only a few minutes ago I was wondering how I would convince my parents to let me play tonight. With these new dice, I had my answer.

Tonight would be glorious. I was sure of it.

It was 7:25 when I returned to the Toy Box, wearing a backpack that held the most important things in the world to me: my *Dangerous Dungeons* books, a notebook, my fancy new dice bag, my old dice, some character sheets, graph paper, and pencils. I also wore a windbreaker over my tee shirt and shorts, as there was a chance of rain. I didn't see Marc anywhere, and decided to wait by the entrance of the store.

Even though I was early, I was already impatient. Why wasn't Marc here? I imagined the dogs again, although this time they were stalking *me*. One hid behind the cars parked in the middle of the street, watching me. It crept ever closer, disappearing every time I'd look. It crept up behind me and I could feel its hot breath breathing down my neck . . . I spun around to vanquish it with an imaginary Demon Slayer sword . . .

. . . and stared Marc right in the face. I jumped.

"You ready?" he asked.

"You bet!" I said, feeling pretty embarrassed.

"Okay, then. Let's go."

I followed him to an old forest green Chevy pick-up truck parked across the street, ironically where I'd conjured the dog. I tossed my heavy bag into the bed and climbed into the passenger seat as Marc entered the other side.

"So where are we going?" I asked.

"The mainland," Marc said as he backed the truck out. "Dave's house is in Woodland, just outside of Chatsworth."

Those names meant nothing to me. "Is it far?"

"About twenty minutes away," Marc said. "It's just off of Route 72."

We spent the rest of the drive talking about *Dangerous Dungeons*. Since I needed a character to play, I asked Marc what professions were available. I'd been considering playing a knight or ninja, but Marc informed me that what the group really needed was a forester, as they were currently trekking through a wooded wilderness and the player that usually played the forester was the empty chair tonight.

After we'd established what I'd be playing, Marc began telling me about the events of the game so far. I listened intently as we passed over the Causeway and up Route 72, past the numerous gas stations and restaurants that greeted the summer traffic with signs and flags heralding the latest specials.

My gaze rolled lazily over them all until I spotted the old Causeway Diner. My father had mentioned that it had been around when he was a kid and it was obvious. The façade, covered in stainless steel panels and neon, looked like it belonged in the fifties. Still, it wasn't the diner that was distracting me; it was an older man standing in front of it.

He was dressed in a long raincoat and wearing John Lennon glasses. He looked almost ethereal against the contrasting stainless steel and dark, clouded sky. I imagined him to be the Angel of Death, if the Angel of Death drank coffee. He sipped from a Styrofoam cup as his eyes seemed to follow us as we passed the diner. I shuddered, returning my full attention to Marc's stories.

It was getting dark and a few droplets of rain hit the windshield as Marc turned onto a dirt road. We were heading straight into the Pine Barrens. I began to feel a bit nervous; I recalled the boy I'd conjured the night before running through these very woods. I cracked a joke to calm down.

"Couldn't Dave afford a place on a paved street?"

Marc laughed. "He likes the outdoors. Don't worry, we're almost there."

But I worried. I was certain that I saw *things*—shadows, moving branches, glowing green eyes—in the trees as we drove past. It wasn't difficult to imagine one of my characters in the same situation. We were two against an increasingly dark and hostile world.

We drove a few more minutes over the winding road until we came across a cabin sitting next to a swamp. There was no number or mailbox. Parked in front were a Jeep and a Ford truck. Marc pulled up next to the Jeep and stopped. I pulled my hood over my head to protect me from the drizzle as I stepped out of the truck.

I glanced around. The cabin was isolated; besides the dirt road, there was another unpaved road covered in beige stones, the kind that substituted for lawns in shore yards. This road followed the power lines towards what I presumed was civilization. I felt a chill as I turned towards the swamp to my left. A large tree stood a few yards into the murky water. Its knotted mass of bare branches looked ominously like tendrils in the dimming light. I had most of the statistics worked out for a monster based on it as I stepped onto the porch.

Marc was about to knock when I heard the sound of tires grinding over gravel. A Harley Davison soon appeared on the rocks. The rider wore a black helmet with a visor covering his face, boots, blue jeans, and a faded *Return of the Jedi* tee shirt. Long hair poked out from beneath the helmet, and when the driver stopped and took it off he had a mustache and beard to match his hair. He looked to be at least a decade older than me.

"Hey, Steve," Marc said. "You're usually the first one here. Running late?"

"Nah," Steve said as he dismounted and grabbed a brown bag from his driver-side pannier. "I was here half an hour ago. Luckily, I discovered that Dave was running low on Cheetos before it was too late. Who's with you?"

"Our latest victim—John Chandler."

I tried not to giggle as I shook his hand, wondering if this was the same Steve from the Dread Portcullis story. I must not have succeeded, because Steve and Marc exchanged knowing glances at each other before guiding me into the cabin. The door creaked loudly as Steve pulled it open.

While small, the inside of the cabin was a role-player's dream. The front and largest room had a large circular oak table surrounded with chairs at its center. A couch and a couple of chairs lined the walls. Something seemed a bit off with the angles of the walls, as if their edges weren't perfectly perpendicular with each other and the ceiling. Normally something like that would distract me, but I figured that this was an old house and probably not professionally built. It shouldn't surprise me that the angles weren't perfect.

The walls were adorned with maps and character sketches, all of which were likely part of Dave's world. I marveled at the intricately detailed world map, which was about the size of four posters. Portions of it were blank; I presumed that they were unexplored regions. I felt my excitement building; perhaps I'd help fill them in.

I was so absorbed in the map that I barely noticed the other three men in the room. Like Steve, all appeared to be in their thirties or even forties. Carl, a stout, balding man a good foot shorter than me, gripped my hand with a surprisingly strong handshake. Ken, with his feathered blonde hair, seemed the youngest of the group next to Marc, wore a hooded green Eagles sweatshirt.

Of course, the man I most wanted to meet was Dave Garrison. He was already sitting at the oak table with his six-panel Dungeon Crafter's Screen set up so that none of us could see his notes or dice rolls. While I owned a published screen, Dave's looked custom-made. The side facing the rest of the group was pure black and each panel contained a different large yellow rune.

Having never met Dave, I'd pictured him as a fifty-something giant of a man with a bushy beard—something akin to Gandalf or Merlin. In reality, Dave was a bit more human. He had short, black, wavy hair with a matching goatee. His angular face conveyed a youthfulness that belied his true age, although I guessed he was around 40. He wore a small pair of reading glasses. When he stood to shake my hand, I noticed that he was actually slightly shorter than me.

Dave followed the handshake with a short interview on my *Dangerous Dungeons* experience. He then went over the house rules and sat down with me to create my forester character. After several dice rolls and a rather generous granting of supernatural items, I was sent to the other end of the table.

It was just after nine, raining, and already dark as we began. One of Dave's house rules was that he liked to play by candlelight, so we were each given a taper in a candle-holder and Steve passed around his lighter to light them. Dave had several candles positioned around his screen; I noticed that he had one candle for each crease, which meant that he had one for each of us in addition to the one in front of him.

I marveled at how quickly Dave could set a scene, incorporating the sounds of the rain outside as well as music from carefully prepared cassette tapes that he played on a boombox. As the forester, I was essentially the party leader, which made me feel somewhat uncomfortable with a group of strangers. Our characters were trekking through a dark forest in the midst of a growing storm. I couldn't help but feel that the scenario seemed familiar.

Still, Dave kept the descriptions coming and when he announced our first combat encounter—a fierce ogre—a flash of lightning illuminated the dead tree in the swamp outside. I swear it had moved closer! The rest of the group shouted combat orders as they prepared to throw the dice.

While it wasn't unusual for people to play with their dice during the game, there was something peculiar about the way this group did. Each player had set his dice in strange patterns on the table and each pattern, while different, seemed to share symmetry with the patterns set by the others. Every so often one or more players would change their dice pattern after a series of dice rolls.

Our characters were heading towards an abandoned hilltop keep. The tension grew as we fought our way through numerous dangers and the storm outside seemed to grow with it. As Dave described us battering down the keep's door, the whipping winds pounded against the cabin. I glanced outside. *The tree looked even closer!*

I'd now lost my train of thought; Dave had to prompt me back into the game. Feeling foolish for being frightened I covered it by announcing that my character was racing inside the keep, having not heard Dave say that the ancient skeletons on the floor had just stood up wielding rusty weapons. It was a stupid move, one that I'd heckle a player for back at home. I felt ashamed that I allowed some spooky shadows to cut my participation in the game short. Thankfully, Carl came to my rescue by having his elf wizard, Larc, throw an earth bolt spell that shattered most of the skeletons before they could skewer my character to bits.

I tried to keep my mind in the game after that. Exploring the keep was quite enjoyable and I'd have some great stories to tell my friends at home about working our way through treacherous traps and fighting unpublished monsters from Gary's imagination. As we finally fought our way to the Dark Temple of Khonshu on the top floor, I glanced at my watch and felt disappointed. It was 11:55. My evening with the greatest Dungeon Crafter I'd ever played under was about to end. Still, we pressed on. Marc said that we'd play out the final fight even if we ran out of time and I was certain that a great battle awaited us. I was wrong.

Our characters stepped into the temple to see that it was open to the sky although no rain entered. A twenty-foot marble statue of the lunar falcon-headed god held his hands upwards, where the full moon had just turned blood red. I noticed that the players rearranged their dice one final time and Marc's warrior, Kram, pushed my forester into the center of the room. My character now stood at the center of a chiseled mosaic circle in the floor. Dave had me make a saving roll and, after I failed, announced that I could not move. I glanced at my watch; it was midnight.

Dave said something that I didn't understand. The others chorused the same unintelligible words. My blood went cold. *My God!* I thought, *they're chanting!* I tried to flee, but I was frozen in place. The rest of the group looked at me as they continued chanting. Lightning struck again. *The dark tree was right in front of the window!*

I tried to scream but no words would come out. I glanced at my watch again. It was 11:58. Time was moving backwards? I could feel a cold sweat pouring down my face as Dave finally said something in English.

"I call to thee, the Crawling Chaos! We have prepared the ritual sacrifice! We call upon you to release the Hounds!"

As I watched in horror, a swirling black mist appeared above the table and formed itself into the shape of a man, about the size of a Ken doll. It stared at Dave first, who bowed to it. The miniature man looked to its right and left, receiving bows from each of the other players. Finally, it turned to face me. I recognized its face.

It was Matt Houston!

"You're dead, John." Marc cackled wickedly in a way I'd never heard him laugh before. "But don't worry, before this hour out of time is over, you'll never have existed at all."

Shaking, I found my voice and demanded to know what he meant. They all just laughed at me. I suddenly remembered a name, Andrew Marcel. *My God! Andrew was the boy running in the woods! He was my friend, and until that moment I did not remember him!*

"H-how?" I said.

"The Great Old One needs sacrifices in order to rise," Dave said in the same tone he used when describing the game encounters. "*Dangerous Dungeons* provides the key. You think on a different level now, John, and the Great Old One has touched you. Its Hounds will consume your very being while 'fixing' history to ensure that you aren't missed."

"That's what happened to Andrew!" I said, recalling more about him. "He introduced me to *Dangerous Dungeons!*" I looked at Marc. "And the Toy Box!"

"Andrew was a bit smarter than you, I'm afraid." Carl grinned. "He had the sense to run before we could complete the binding ritual. The Hounds still got him, of course."

I looked at the table in a new light; the candles, the runes, the symmetry of candles and dice, the changing of dice patterns. This was no ordinary *Dangerous Dungeons* game; it was a ritual! I fell for it hook, line and sinker because my head was in a fantasy world. Now I was about to be excised from reality. It was a shockingly cruel irony.

I noticed Steve and Ken look at the poster map on the wall. The corner of the walls and ceiling that the map was set against was shimmering. The shimmer expanded, revealing a pair of sickly green eyes. *The Hounds were coming for me!*

I don't know why, but I snatched my dice up. As I did so, my feet could move again! I sprang from my chair—the others howled in surprise—and fled out into the rain and darkness, screaming the whole way. As I passed the dead tree, its gnarly branches whipped at me like tendrils. Somehow, I managed to escape being snatched. Hearing harsh, unearthly barks and the pounding of paws against the porch boards and the stones behind me, I bolted down the dirt road that brought me here.

I heard a sloshing sound and looked back to see the tree moving! Its trunk ended in three stubby legs with small roots growing from them. It lurched towards me even as three dogs closed the distance between us. I swallowed hard, knowing I was doomed. *Why didn't I listen? Why didn't I throw away my* Dangerous Dungeons *stuff before it was too late? My God, first Andrew, now me!*

That was when I heard another person chanting in front of me, catching me off guard. I stumbled and fell. I looked up to see that man from the diner, wearing a trilby and reading from an old book. I was about to run from him as well when he stopped chanting and smiled down at me.

"Keep hold of those dice," he said.

The dogs snarled behind me as the old man resumed reading from the book. I instinctively turned and held up my arms to my face as the Hounds reached me, but to my surprise they stopped short and barked at me instead, green foamy saliva dripping from their mouths. Behind them, Dave's group and the lurching tree approached.

The old man slowly stepped in front of me as he continued to chant while reading the book. Thunder crashed as the winds and rain grew torrential. I squeezed my eyes shut, listening to the Hounds yelping as the lightning struck around us. I opened my eyes as I heard screams of terror and pain back near the cabin. The tree was on fire, and it swept up Dave and the other gamers in its tendrils as it flailed about like a wounded, dying animal before crashing back into the swamp. There was no sign of the Hounds.

"Come," the old man said as he closed the book and helped me to my feet. "Don't look back; it's better for you that way."

A few minutes later we were sitting in the Causeway Diner. The old man had ordered tea for himself and a coffee for me, although I wasn't thirsty. I sat curled up in the booth, holding myself as I shook.

"You can relax now," he said. "It's over." He glanced outside.

Two fire engines raced down Route 72 towards Dave's house.

"Who?" I said, my voice stilted. "I. . . . How. . . . What?"

"Calm down," he said before sipping his tea. "You're quite safe. I doubt your friends will harm anyone again. Have some coffee. Please."

I slowly unclenched my fingers from my arms and took the cup in both hands to sip my coffee. I had to admit, it tasted good. I opened my mouth to say something, but the old man shook his head.

"Drink. We have all night for questions. I'll save you the trouble and begin with the obvious; *Dangerous Dungeons* is a conduit for a cult eager to unleash a terrible force upon this world."

"The game . . . is dangerous?"

"No more so than any tool," he said. "Those men intended to destroy you as they did your friend."

"You remember Andrew?" I looked up at the clock. It was 12:10. An hour had passed that no one else remembered.

"Yes. It was because of him that I began investigating Mr. Garrison. Andrew Marcel disappeared from this world last summer."

"But I couldn't remember him! And Dave said he was erased from history! How do you remember him?"

"I'll show you." The old man took a pencil from his shirt pocket. He wrote Andrew's name on a napkin and promptly erased it. "See?" he said, pointing at the napkin. "When you erase something it usually still leaves marks; impressions of what was there. If you've studied such occult practices as much as I have, you learn to read the marks, even when they've been supposedly erased.

"You've felt those impressions as well. Andrew was a part of your life; your mind had to fill in the gaps with new information. Still, Andrew left an impression on you that could never completely be erased. *Déjà vu*, if you will."

"That's why I kept imagining him," I said, pretending to understand the preposterous. "So who are you?"

"Dr. Adrian Black," he said. "Currently a professor at Temple University. My family has studied occult practices for a long time. This," he patted the old book that now sat on the table, "is a copy of the *Al Azif*, painstakingly copied by my ancestor, Esteban o Preto, in Lisbon in 1062. Thankfully, it contained the counter-ritual necessary to end Mr. Garrison's madness."

"How did you know that I would be next?" I asked.

"I didn't." Dr. Black shrugged. "I kept an eye out for the signs of occult activity and I knew that Mr. Garrison and, more importantly, Marc Molina, were recruiting victims. 'Sean Carter' is a myth created by the Crawling Chaos; the Fact Tracts were created as a form of reverse-psychology, strengthening the appeal of *Dangerous Dungeons*. Sometimes if you want someone to do something, the best way is to tell them not to do it."

"So Reverend Bobby is in on it too?" I asked.

"No. He's sincere. He honestly believes that *Dangerous Dungeons* is a tool of Satan to tempt people away from God. He's devout, but no fool. Without proof, he wouldn't believe in living trees, alien dogs, or games that wipe you from existence, and he's not about to go traipsing through the woods with someone like me to prove it. He'd more likely believe that I was trying to set him up for bad press.

"Unfortunately, he's unwittingly a more powerful recruiter than the Crawling Chaos itself. *Dangerous Dungeons* sales have risen exponentially since he began his crusade against it. For every book he burns, he inspires many more to buy the game and play it."

"So the game *is* evil," I said.

"No," the old man said pointedly. "It's just that the cult now has a larger pool to draw from. It makes them a bit more difficult to stop, that's all."

I looked out the window towards the smoke rising in the distance. That cult had trapped me easily. I resolved not to let that happen again. Still, there was one question I had left to ask my benefactor. I held up my dice bag.

"What about these?"

Dr. Black sipped his tea. "As I said, I didn't know who was next, nor was I confident that I'd get there in time. As it was, you would have been killed without protection. I created these to give to likely victims."

He took the dice bag from my hand and dumped the contents on the table. Picking up the 12-sided die, he turned it so that I could see that, in place of the "12," there was an odd symbol imprinted on the face, a single line with five shorter ones branching off it.

"This is a potent magical symbol against summoned creatures," he said. "It broke the enchantment holding you to your chair and it stopped the Hounds from touching you. It doesn't work for long, but it bought you the time you needed."

"Any particular reason that you chose the 12-sided die?" I asked.

"If Mr. Garrison or any of the others saw that symbol, they'd know that they were being watched. I needed to ensure that they wouldn't see it." The old man chuckled. "And as every player of *Dangerous Dungeons* knows, you never use the 12-sided die."

I opened my eyes as I returned to the present. That long night was over and I was finally able to confront it with my eyes open and my strength restored. I stepped up to the curtain, holding my Bible to my chest, as I prepared for my introduction. Dr. Black warned me that this wouldn't work, that Reverend Bobby wouldn't take everything at face value, but I had to do *something*. Maybe someone would listen before they ended up like poor Andrew.

"Ladies and gentlemen," Reverend Bobby said, smiling for the camera and the studio audience, "we have a special guest on *Good Neighbors* today. I'm pleased to introduce John Chandler, who survived a harrowing experience while playing *Dangerous Dungeons*, Lucifer's game. . . ."

(the wonderous boundless thought)
CJ Henderson

It was, all in all, a very hot day.

The Weather Control Board was trying something radical. They were always doing things like that when there was a big shake-up in management. With their new corphead sworn in two weeks earlier, it was almost a certainty the dink would want to show everyone that he was his own man, capable of setting policy, making decisions.

For the last three days of July, 2112, the temperature had gone steadily skyward. Instead of the several generations' worth of tradition which placed as acceptable the range 66° to 78°, the new guy was calling for a radical return to ancient standards. The day before had been an uncomfortable 82°, and the current day was threatening to reach 84°.

Still, it was not so bad. Such trivial politics affected those rare, out-of-doors spaces only. Indeed, Benny and Albert had moved the group sex for that day out to the balcony and found those hours with Marci and Frank and Janet to be pleasant enough. The added effort from labored breathing, and the resulting sweat—actual sweat—that had been different.

Interesting.

"Oh, I just love you, Frank." Benny said the words with all the politeness society demanded. To be honest, Benny felt so wonderfully relaxed, so drained of all tension, that he found his brain actually desiring to play with Frank's idea. Focusing himself on Frank long enough to clear space for this new notion within his brain while its electronics shifted his current workload from one section of his mind to another, he followed up his required words with a question, curiosity jangling him in a part of his brain rarely called upon to do much of anything.

"Make a presentation?" he asked. "Relate to me, citizen. What's this drama you've discovered, anyway?"

Frank and Benny were opposites, within the narrow band of physical perfection nourished by their environment. Frank was solid and muscled, as the machines exercised his structure to fulfill its natural potential. Benny was well-toned, but taller and much lankier. Albert was the everyman model, somewhere in between them. Marci and Janet were equally beautiful specimens. In this Eden, beauty was the standard—which did not keep them from appreciating it. Albert, of them all, was the most focused on the physical interactions, a true gourmand. His endless fascination with excitation and achievement of orgasm constantly refueled their play.

Frank closed his eyes; it always made transmission easier. He was still downloading several old television series into files in the back of his brain—how clever they had been in olden times, despite their limitations—as well as trying to finish listening to two operas and six songs by different groups he enjoyed. To have to share-link, connect along the mechanical route grown into his head, up the satellite feed, and then into the minds of several others, while doing so many other things always made Frank a bit nauseated. Thus, he shut his eyes. What Frank wanted the others to hear echoed along one channel of their minds while he transmitted his own commentary on it which they absorbed along another. Benny's absorption rate was quite higher, moved faster, for he was actually interested, focusing precious current-time attention on his friend's discovery.

Janet and Marci and Albert were following along, to greater or lesser degrees. Of course, they found themselves saving bits and pieces of it for later. It simply did not do, one had to agree, to get caught up in some front-lobe fascination while some delicate, potentially risky, physical maneuver was executed. Sex, boundless, endless, meaningless sex was supposed to be fun. Not an invitation to the emergency room.

Slowly, though, Frank's discovery began to capture the attention of the others, even Albert, who was carefully adding entry number 4,352 to his database of sexual fluid taste comparisons. As the various groupings reached satisfying climaxes, all were aware of an unfinished process, an unmet need. After several hours, especially after the heat reached an unbearable 85°, the group found themselves lounging inside like the rest of the sane people. Waiting for the kitchen robots to serve whichever meal came next, they found themselves getting back to Frank's big idea.

"So, could you just condense that all for me?"

Everyone smiled at Albert. Their minds whirling with multiple fascinations, all of them continually downloading from the various museum data banks, historical archives and commercial and entertainment sites, and all the rest, they all focused their remaining attention on Frank as he real-time explained his current preoccupation to them all, especially carnal Al.

"Well, I suppose one would have to start with comparison. We all live in a fabulous age—correct?"

Naturally, everyone agreed. It had taken terrible things, wars and famines and pestilences which had reduced the population to a whit of its former self, but at last the race had reached a point where it had bundles of technology and very few people to support. Of course, the Earth had seen its inhabitants reach this state more than once. But this time no Dark Ages had ensued. No, this time mankind had shoved forward and stopped slaughtering itself just long enough to spawn a paradise pleasant enough to suit everyone.

"Ginkles, Frank—how could things be better?"

"Better orgasms," laughed Janet.

Marci giggled, nodding her head in agreement. Benny flashed them both a wicked smile. Frank agreeably nodded, but signified his desire to continue. Whispering and nudging each other into seriousness, the friends assured him he could proceed.

"We have everything we want, correct?"

Again there was a wave of jocularity, but in the end, a consensus was reached that the current age was one of marvels and unlimited access to everything that had ever been imagined in all the long history of mankind. People lived as long as they desired. Everyone had work they could be proud of, some toiling as greatly as eight, nine hours every week. Foods from around the world were obtainable at a moment's notice. Robots did all minor chores, and most major ones. One could eat endlessly and never gain weight, or not eat at all. One could visit the moon, picnic in high orbit, study the bottom of the oceans, climb the highest mountains, go surfing in the morning and sky diving at night—all without leaving their homes, all without leaving their favorite sex partners.

Anything could be downloaded directly into one's brain. The entirety of that wonderful organ had been mapped, charted and mastered, so that now it controlled the body the way its owner wished it to be controlled. It was a perfect, utterly delicious world, one with all the learning, sleeping, sex, eating, or anything else one could want at their fingertips twenty-four hours out of every day.

"Well, that's what this idea is all about. Focus all—I stumbled across this in the oddest place. I was thumbing through the philosophy warrens . . ."

Marci and Albert went amazingly cold. Boredom settled across Janet's brow as well, although she was always too much a team-player to give offense to any. Benny was still game, and even the daunting tedium of trying to understand the rantings of those jolly headknockers of ancient times would not put him off that afternoon. Maintaining Benny's attention and having Janet's generosity, Frank dared to continue.

"Forget who said it, that's as inconsequential as yesterday's breakfast. But what he said was . . . this." Frank's face took on such an excited look that even Albert began to wonder what lay in the unconscious files he had yet to review.

"It seems that this age, this level of wonders, of plenty and satisfaction—all of it—has been reached before by man. There was an Earth, previous to ours. Somewhere else in the galaxy. And on it, people could do whatever they wished, whenever, just like us. But there were some of them who . . . how to say it, what's the word . . . they were, were . . . bored! Yes, that's it—men and women who got bored!"

Frank's face glowed with excitement. Waving his hand in front of him as if it were an instrument of instruction, he said, "Yes, they simply reached a point where they had been amused and fed and fucked to where it simply didn't matter to them anymore, where nothing the entire world could provide could make them happy any longer."

Janet frowned. Her eyes narrowing to slits, she raised her own hand to capture the attention of the room. Frank instantly acknowledged her right to speak, delighting in his position of, what could he call it—moderator? Teacher—oh, he liked that thought a great deal. He smiled in her direction.

"I don't understand," she said. "Sense, please? How can one not be delighted when they're lacking for nothing? You have to be happy when there's nothing missing to make you unhappy. Don't you?"

"That's just it; that's just it," Frank said. "There is one thing you don't have when you have everything."

"Nothing," ventured Benny, his voice a frightened question.

"Yes!" Frank's eyes gleamed as if reflecting the light of a directly viewed sun. Actually raising his voice, he startled the others as he nearly shouted, "Yes! When you have nothing, you then possess the challenge of getting everything!"

The paradox frightened all within the room for an instant—even Frank. Marci instinctively huddled closer to Albert, her hands fidgeting with flesh she had explored so thoroughly it was hard to remember that it was not in some way her own. Her eyes, however, stayed linked with Frank's, as did those of all the others.

Glorying in his circle of attention, Frank told them: "It seems that once this former Earth, previous Earth, whatever, reached its pinnacle—much as we have—that somehow, some of its inhabitants grew dissatisfied. They wanted—"

"More?"

"No, less. Much less. They wanted a new world to conquer. They didn't want to simply relive history, they wanted to make some of their own."

"But what could they do?" Janet's eyes still narrowed, she asked her question with a curiosity which could have emptied the world of felines.

"Start a war? Go off conquering? How could it be allowed? The safeguards, the preventors—"

"No, no, don't worry," Frank whispered, his calm sending assurance through the others. "They weren't brutes, genetic throwbacks of some sort. They were like us, marvelously, exactly like us."

"Except that they were bored."

"Well, yes, there was that. And that's what made the difference. No, they took a ship to another world. One of the starspanners—"

"You mean like in the museum?"

"Yes, one of those." Frank puffed with pride. They were getting it. They were really getting it. The static level in his head was so slight, he knew that all of the others had turned away from their monitors, had mentally shut off their information-gathering circuits in favor of listening to his amazing story.

"They took a starspanner and they hunted for another world. Another Earth. But one in its dawning days. Before civilization. Before people, really."

"You mean . . ." Marci hesitated. The idea was so big, it forced her to actually use her own mind. She felt a twinge as that section of her brain awoke. Her automatic systems falling over each other to get out of the way of actual conscious control, she stammered, "They, they went looking . . . for a world with, with what? Dinosaurs running about or something?"

"Close. They came here at the time of the neanderthals. They were the missing link that everyone used to search for. It was found, and after much research, it was uncovered through backward engineering of DNA memories—these, these wondrous men and women, these pioneers, these marvelous explorers, they did it. They pushed out into the black; they found our Earth here; they determined it was close enough to their planet of origin that it would support them, and they simply came down and started living."

"They weren't . . . alive . . . ?" Benny was officially confused.

"They were alive, you nimrod," laughed Albert. "He means they were taking control of their lives, living or dying by their wits, the strength of their arms—right?"

"Exactly," Frank confirmed. "They came down and mated with the primitives and started a brand new world, our world, this world, on its way to all we have now."

The group remained quiet. Stunned. Even Frank, now that he had heard the idea out loud, was cowed by the immensity of it. Slowly the five began to discuss the all-encompassing notion. Suggesting scenarios, wondering about possibilities, they turned the revolutionary bit of information into a powerful and quite moving discussion which replaced their next meal and sleep period. It was not, of course, powerful enough to stop their cravings for bodily enjoyment. They rambled on about their ideas, in between the countless mild explosions of pacifying pleasure. Finally, however, one of them asked of Frank the question all of them had began to wonder.

"So, were you, I mean . . ."

The query was put forth cautiously. It was, like their entire discussion, a thing of such magnitude that it had to be shaped and caressed into life just so, coaxed into perfection.

"Frank . . . really—were you thinking, ah, were you asking us, to . . . to be like those explorers? I mean . . . did you want to do the same thing? Start a new world? Our world?"

Frank blinked. He had been startled—knocked backward by the force of a handful of words. His brain, however, always ready to serve, focused on what had happened. He had disseminated a new idea, and others had listened. He had spoken, and left others inspired. He had learned, and passed on learning. Without machines. Without approval.

Him.

Glorious Frank.

"Yes," said another of the pack, wondering what it would be like to have to survive. To be mother, father, and god of a new civilization, it was so sweeping, so titanic, so . . . "Is that what you were thinking, Frank?"

Time passed, second by second, sweeping eon by sweeping eon, the totally overwhelming superlativity of what he had said now being reflected back to him in an even greater idea. Was he, he asked himself, was he proposing that they go to the museum, take a starspanner, and go to the stars? Was he actually that bold, that daring, that bored with being done for, that energized by the thought, the wonderous, boundless thought of doing for himself, that he was indeed proposing such a thing?

Janet's hand wrapped around Frank's leg. The idea of such outlandishness, such scintillating bravery, stirred something deep within her that she had never felt before. Suddenly, she found the back of her mind considering the idea of actually applying for breedership privileges. She found herself thinking of going out in the daylight, flouting the sunlight, following another, a man, her man, anywhere he might go.

Her body moving with the practiced, serpentine limberness for which she was famed, Janet slipped alongside him and sucked his erection into her caressing mouth. She wanted him inside her, needed him, desired contact with his flesh as she had no other man.

"Ahhhh, ahhhh . . ."

Frank was honestly surprised at his inability to answer the question. It

was almost, he thought, as if he were enjoying Janet's enthusiastic ministrations so deeply that he could not switch on his other brain functions.
He wondered, could that be a part of it? Did the independence those who
established the humanity he and all alive were heir to so electrify them
that they felt actual . . . dare he think the lost word. . . .

"Ecstasy?"

"Huh?"

"What'd you relate, Frank?"

Wheezing, his mind exploding, Frank felt a terrifying dissolving sensation,
as if the orgasm building between himself and Janet threatened his very
existence. Flailing at the edge of this unknown abyss, Frank called upon
all the restraint he could find within himself, croaking out: "Well, no . . .
not really."

Janet's head sagged in sudden disappointment as Frank's member went
as limp as an arm fractured in fifteen places. As Janet's frenzy diminished
and the others found their automatic circuits beginning to reconnect, he
told the gathering: "I guess it hadn't occurred to me because it's been done
so many times."

"So many times," Albert said. "What do you mean?"

"Oh, that group that settled our Earth, they weren't the first ones to do
that kind of thing."

"Really?"

"Oh, yes. The data collected showed that this is at least the fifty-third
Earth to be colonized by such restless types."

The idea struck them all gently. How amusing. So many planets turned
into paradise—so many worlds made perfect and ideal and whole, by those
who resented the idea of perfection.

Finding themselves falling behind in their private data collections,
knowing they would soon be drooping in the daily charts, looking foolish to the others who shared their world of inactive dreamers, the group's
brains took over and began reconnecting them to that which mattered.

Instantly the great database, the marvelous placator, began to feed
them all they needed to stay focused on themselves to the exclusion of
everything else. Her mind filling with facts which would never mean anything to her beyond their individual existence and the certainty that she
had them correctly categorized within her mind, Janet slid herself over
Frank's muscular body. Pushing him down gently as she limberly straddled
and consumed his once again erect penis, she purred as he responded to
her magnificently subtle movements.

His head back in the pillows, staring up at her, Frank shoved aside the
notations filling his mind long enough to ask, "Geekers, if I had, you know,

wanted to go start another Earth, I mean . . . would you have wanted to go?
I mean, with me?"

Janet wondered at his question. Moving up and down the length of him,
enjoying the moment, as she had been trained to enjoy all moments, as
had he, as had they all, there in the bosom of their loving machines, she
pictured herself for a moment on the surface of some other planet, some
Earth-like world, dressed in animal skins, planting crops, fighting creatures for survival, giving birth indiscriminately, dying—

"Oh, I just love you, Frank," she said, emptily.

To which he nodded, just as emptily, in return.

Catherynne M. Valente and S.J. Tucker blew into the store on their Palimpsest *tour with their entourage of whirling corsets, joy, and laughter. I only regret we didn't have room for the fire spinning! Cat's story ends our collection on a beautifully wistful note.*

(proverbs of hell)
Catherynne M. Valente

We have generally agreed amongst ourselves that there are three trees in Hell. One is a juniper, one is a fir, and one is a maple. We do not know how they sinned in life in order to deserve punishment here. The commandments of trees are theirs to keep. Under each tree is a house; around each house is a garden. In each garden are various root vegetables, peas, pumpkins, and a pair of mated crows who call out to each other the lonely hours. Despite much searching we have never found anyone to be at work in the other gardens, though we keep our own faithfully. My brothers and I toil in the house beside the juniper, and we strive in a sad Reversal of Adam's work. We struggle to remember: the name of that black bird, of that orange fruit, of those three trees, our own names.

I have heard it said that hell is the absence of God. I cannot say I feel His absence here more keenly than I did in life. I never heard His voice sound like golden ice tumbling into the cup of my ear when I was a man. Why should I hear it here, in the grey dust, with the crows staring blankly from their perch on the pea-stakes?

— The Confessions of Orry of Pandemonium

At Vespers, the Imp comes. I do not know if Vespers produces the Imp, if it is her natural hour, like a fish compelled to leap at dawn, or whether the Imp produces Vespers, dragging the blue minutes behind her through the dust. Either relationship seems logical enough. The Imp, after her way, is unhelpful in determining causality. We have named her Noster, for ours she is, and ever shall be. Her knuckles come scraping on the gate of wire and bone each evening. The crows nibble at her, pulling a strip or two of flesh from her cheek, her shoulder. She allows it; I have come to understand that this is an affectionate gesture between them. She, after all, feeds them. They see her coming and their throats water. They hop down from the fence posts and offer up a slice of gourd or a turnip in tribute, in tithe.

The Imp has always come. She will always come.

When she knocks at my cell I cannot contain my excitement—why should she knock? Do I have the power to deny her entrance? Yet she knocks, and it is a gentle thing, not a pounding, not a shattering. Perhaps it is because I thrill to her and do not turn away her soft, three-knuckled rapping that I shall never leave this place. She settles down upon me, her ropy hair like leather straps slapping against my face, her thin, muddy limbs shivering. Her eyes do not burn, but in them are long staircases without end, turning and turning in blackness.

She moves against me and I groan—sometimes I try not to, but the sound escapes me before I can remember my morality. She stares at me, pulling me down the staircases of her gaze, her breath hot and smoky and resinous, and at the moment when I, if I were a man, would enter her and shudder my way towards the semblance of God, she puts her fingers to my belly and tears me open with a twisting, awful clutching, and I weep in shame, and there is warmth and wetness between us, and I spill out into her hands, bloody and quiet. She takes my liver. It will grow back by morning. I heard another tale like that, when I lived. They forgot to mention the tenderness of the eagle, the eagerness of Prometheus hanging on the rock.

"Do you know what a demon is?" she whisper-hisses, her cheeks hollow and human, the wetness of me soaking her, reddening her lips, her small breasts. She enters my house brown, and leaves it red. I reach up and brush her hair from her face. Her teeth are long, and she inclines her chin just a little, so little that one who knows her less well might miss it, into my palm.

"When a gravid woman dies, she passes through the iron gates with her child still sleeping inside her. She comes to Pandemonium heavy and wan, and when she kneels on the black bed to give birth, her child is a true citizen, truer than she can ever be. Its first act of torture complete, it will rise from the red wreckage of its mother; it will go to school as children have always done, write its hermetic sums in chalk on a green board, love a certain teacher, bandy arcane seals with its compatriots. It will grow up, and one day it will be told by a weeping golden statue to go to a dry and dusty place where two crows stand black watch over a patch of peas and pumpkins, and tear a monk's heart from his body, because once, just once, he lost faith."

When she pulls away from me, the blood is terribly dark, and there are stains of me on her throat. She goes to my brothers now, and I cannot bear it, that they should have her and I should not.

I remember the iron gate of which she speaks. It is rusted and low, its posts twisted up into weird rosettes. It creaks, and swings in the wind, battering against the long fence at the end of all things.

The nature of Pandemonium is as follows: the sky is perpetually moonless, showing an aortal spray of stars, though on the broad earth high noon reigns, and midsummer. We walk in sunlight and wavering gray grasses, yet the ceiling of this place is forever black and star-slashed. I know none of the constellations. Once we made our attempts at renaming these warped polygons—but it is so hard to remember where we left them. That was the Liver of God, there in the West, I think. There is a road, for carriages and horses that never come. Black roosters wander and squawk, snapping at bluebottles with bony beaks. There is an old windmill; there is a stone well. We have a horse; her hipbones slice through her hide, and her eyes are clung with yellowish milk and flies. She eats coals, and will not let us ride. We call her Astoreth, and like an old and ornery cat, have come to love her.

There are sudden storms of rain and wind, coming quickly and passing slow. We have come to understand, over the years, that this is the sound of angels falling.
—The Confessions of Orry of Pandemonium

I remember a rope of rosevines burning in autumn, my eyes stung by the sweet-acrid smoke, curling like petals falling up towards a dying sun.

It is this memory, long disconnected from whatever once rode with it—love or sorrow or loss or lust—that clings to me like paper blown against my leg, as I scrape in the pea-flowers tangled around our gate of bones, though I dwell now in a wasteland without roses, or ropes, or autumns, or suns. That is the nature of things in this place. Each time Noster climbs onto my lap and takes to herself my heart, my liver, my blood, more memories peel from me, onion-infinite. I remember once that I copied a Latin tale of a thunder god who lay with Memory for nine days, and conceived nine daughters, all alike in beauty and grace, who grew to govern all art and song—but how must it have been for the lightning-master, to stumble from Memory's body, drained of nine children, and so much more, for Memory is vicious and never takes less than everything.

One day I will not recall that story either. But today I do, as I gather black-stemmed mushrooms from the dark-houses we built for Astoreth when she lowed and complained that the tornado of the fall of Radueriel plucked too mightily at her mane. My arms brim with the florid, scalloped fungi that grow here, crenellated and creased as old maps.

I am not sure I ever knew why I am here. None of us remember that— that which should be first in any confession! I was guilty of this sin, at that time, and therefore the cosmos is a balanced place and full of sense. The Imp says I lost faith—some days she says I lost faith. Some days she says I was greedy and fat, some days that I tried to bribe the Pope into apostasy, some days that I was a bourgeois trickster who made my business fooling the workers into mute oblivion. Once she told me a long tale of a friar who got his nuns with children and buried the little bodies in churchyards. I listened politely, as to a folktale I had never heard before. It made no answering ring in the bell of my soul, nothing that cried: I have done this thing, that was me, my soul knows that weight!

I am ashamed that I know I was once a monk by habit only—I dwell with men I call brothers, I make beer and pray and know what vespers means, I write my Confessions. I know that these are the proper behaviors of holy men. I have forgotten when I started to do these things, when they had meaning for me. Yet I think, I think I understand that when a man walks the same halls for all the days of his life, measures out the same yeast, repeats the same prayers from the same books, writes his secret self in a book of vellum, then in death he merely continues on, walking and measuring and praying, like an echo.

I wish I could remember how I died. It seems like a useful thing to know.

There is a storm coming. The doors bang on their hinges, creaking and crying. Astoreth is upset, snapping at the crows with her rotted jaws. The process of the fall of the angels is ongoing—I suppose it seems silly now that when we were men we thought everyone took sides, strapped on armbands, joined battle, and that was the end of it. One choice, made once. But what war was ever waged so? Through the slats of the sky we can sometimes glimpse the cities of heaven, the way you may glimpse deer in a wheat-field when lighting illuminates the grain, briefly as a blink. There is a resistance there, and small revolts, for the race of angels wear their will on their sleeves. They continue to fall, ever so occasionally, and around their tumbling bodies comes thunder and whirlwinds, blasted air, electricity. We are like hounds now—we can sense the dropping of the barometers on the sea of glass.

It is my turn to minister. In my satchel go mushrooms and pumpkin rinds and a flask of our ashen beer. I wait in my cell for Vespers. I cannot go without performing my penance. I cannot go without tasting her on my lips. Her knocking comes like dawn.

"Do you know what a demon is?" She clenches me between her bony knees, her leathery face keen and dear against mine. The shape of her lips is perfect, a beatific sneer. She closes her eyes and strains against me, her arms thin and strong. She rides me, I can feel myself a beast beneath her, her servant, her chattel. I hear a little slushing sound as her tail makes shapes in the dust. I tell myself she is not like this with the others. That her fingers in my ventricles are more tender, that the taste of my blood is sweetest. Her eyes wheel fire.

"We were all of us angels, once. You can still smell it on us. The seal of heaven on our foreheads, the kiss of God. It smells like silver boiling. The first of us would not bow down to Adam. Then they would not work as menial laborers, wrestling and staying hands and spouting iambic prophecy. Then some few of us said 'Adam is dead and gone. Can not our friends return, and our lovers, our brothers and sisters?'" Noster clears her throat gently, as if recalling a painful thing. "And some of us cried out in the dark, saying 'We wish to feel your love, O Lord, and we do not, for your face is turned to Earth. Will you not test us as you have tested men, make us to suffer in your Name, ask of us terrible deaths, so that we may warm ourselves at the fire of your Heart?' And thus we learned, all of us, that to ask a question of the Lord Highest is to be cast out of Heaven—it matters little what the question is. We forgot to submit; we asked at all."

Her hooked hands grip my cheeks and there is so much blood between us.

There is a town some miles off. No matter where an angel falls, one must always pass it—it lays always between us and where we must go. The streets are dust; the roofs are stone. There are houses with broken windows and doors, a market with withered carrots and an onion or two, and a heavy quiet on the ground. The street is stony; the water tower a baleful moon. Once, I came here when I was new, and the pain of my heart being sliced from my chest was fresh and intense. There had been a flood. I asked of a clerk with hollow eyes like beams of singular light if I might sleep a night in the dark inn he kept.

"What sin brought your bones to my roof?" he said softly.

"I do not know, brother."

The clerk sagged. "I do not know either. Do you think, someday, I will meet someone who does? Will they be tired? Will I have a bed for them, will they be hungry? Will I have enough of succor left to ease them?"

His eyes lowered, their light extinguished, and his eyelids tumbled down like drawn curtains, past his cheeks and his chin, thudding softly on his weathered table.

—The Confessions of Orry of Pandemonium

I enter the town and the stars wheel above the low rooftops. My shadow precedes me, and there is a yellow light on all I see, stormlight, the prescient light that knows a tale of rain. I bring our black mushrooms and thin beer with its head of ash, our melons and our anemic peas, to the market. One of the crows hops curiously behind me, snapping his beak. No one stands grocer at the bleak, wind-emptied stands. I leave my fungus, my drink, all my artfully rotten things. They will be here when another walks through, just as, now, for me, there are small, hard apples, sour and green—and paper, impossibly precious. My heart quickens to see a ream of vellum riffled by the stale breeze. I press my hand against it and she is there, without warning—they move like that, not with the pop or flash of what we once suspected was the stuff of black magic, but with shrugging simplicity, the way you suddenly realize your mother has been cooking in the stone kitchen for a quarter hour while you read tales of dancing skeletons. She is no magician—you simply did not notice.

It is like that. She is there, my demon, my Noster, her brown hand on mine.

"You are pleased," she says, a growling and a grinding in her voice.

I cannot speak. I am dizzy—my blood expects to be spilled out at the sight of her. It can hardly bear to be kept inside me.

"You are going to see the angel," she says, laying her head on her shoulder. Her hair smells ripe and richly foul, matted and twisted.

She is not touching me and I cannot bear it. I can almost remember when I dreaded her hands in me, but it is so dim, so distant. I reach out and take her hand like a winter branch, pressing it to my chest. The claws pierce the skin lightly; blood trickles. She bends her head to it and suckles the wound. Looking up through hanging ropes of hair she whispers:

"Do you know what a demon is? We were humans, just like you. We don't like it any more than you do, coming to a wretched farm at the same time every day to rip out the viscera of souls we have no quarrel with. It makes us sick in the beginning, the blood and the fat and the stink of it, how hot blood is, how thick. Some of us cry, our first time, with red on our thighs. I cried. It's a miserable business, as awful as being ripped open, to do the ripping. It's a punishment, like anything else. And we don't remember why we should be punished either. If I think hard, I can remember what the sun looked like, that is all. And I am so sorry, that what I am hurts you so. Take the paper, call it a bandage. Call it penance."

"I will write beautiful things on it," I whisper, "a confession greater than Augustine's."

The river that flows through the prairies is dark and full of stars—it reflects the sky, not the sunless light that coaxes mean things to grow. Its current is quick, its fish colossal, gross. Their fins are ragged sails, dripping, rising, disappearing. I would like to tell a rollicking tale of how my brothers and I caught one, feasted upon it, found it sweet, tasting of all the dead fish we remember passing our living lips. But they are knowing and keen and turn away from hooks.

It is not a river of forgetfulness, or a border between life and death. I seem to recall tales of a ferryman, and coins, of a black passage and souls wailing on either side, of a river of fire and one of ice. It was all so pretty, the things we wrote of this place. No, it is just our river, endless, dark, deep. There is a bridge

to the north, nearest the hills. It smells like mud and salt.
— *The Confessions of Orry of Pandemonium*

Noster walks with me. She does not want to miss our appointment. In me I can see a satisfaction — she will miss her ministrations with the others. It is I she follows.

The rain comes, when it comes, in a wall of sound and warm wetness, drenching us, churning the road to a river. We watch everything go dark and silver, the wind whipping grasses into our calves. Noster does not seem to mind; her slices mend. So do mine. In the wash of it, the filth and blood comes clean from her hair, her face. Tracks of mud run down her cheeks as though she weeps earth. She looks almost human, almost like me. She could be my sister. Her hair is dark, her eyes a kind of green, her skin weather-beaten but skin, nonetheless. I do not look at her hands, or her tail, or her hooves like a pig's, but simply watch her girl's face, so terribly a girl's face, her teeth tightly held within gentle lips.

We stop by one of the empty farms, where identical crows guard identical pumpkin-flowers, and she pushes me down below the fir tree and climbs into my lap. I grip her for the first time around the waist, wrap her in my arms, pull her down to me, where my body waits for her, sharp with recognition. She groans and turns her head from side to side, slapping me with rain. She raises her hands and opens me, searching, probing for the heart at the heart of me, and finding it, shudders, cuts, arches her back as though in a memory of wings. My blood splashes the fenceposts. I am empty. I will come heartless before the angel, as I should.

"Do you know what a demon is?" she whispers.

"Will it be true this time?" I ask, looking into her eyes, falling down their staircases, falling up into black.

"Of course not."

"Tell me."

"When Adam first spoke, his first word summoned a demon. So too his second, and his third. Every new word summons one of us out of the depths. There are mud flats full of glassy eggs where we lie, waiting, for human mouths to twist around some new thing. Words bring us, words banish us. Language teaches you to lie, to become cruel, to wheedle, to cajole. With each sentence you command a phalanx, a century of demons, clothed in verbs, feasted upon nouns. We are everything you say."

"What word are you?" I ask. I do not expect an answer.

"Elohim," she says. I cannot tell if she is smiling. I touch the inside of her wiry arm.

"I believe you," I say.

What lies over the hills that gird this valley? None of us can say. Some days I think I will set out walking and see their backsides, some days I even pack a small bag, I tell my brothers I am going, I kiss Astoreth though she snorts derision. Once or twice I have even opened the gate. But if I go, Noster could not find me in the lands beyond Pandemonium. The crows laugh at me, and they are right to caw. I am rueful.

In my dreams I cross the snowy peaks and see spread out before me another valley, like this one, its twin. I see the juniper, the fir, the maple. I see the crows, the town. I see Astoreth worry an apple. I see the grass move. The trees repeat, the horse, the birds, forever.

— The Confessions of Orry of Pandemonium

The blast radius is enormous, flattening grass for miles around the angel, who lies on the earth, crumpled, hugging its knees to its chest. We watch it, Noster and I. We are dispassionate. The angel is bronze, its three faces planed, angular, streaked with mud and the ordure of heaven. It oozes rust from a dozen wounds. Its wings are a snarl of bronze knives; they flap feebly, huge, vicious. It has no feet—they are deformed, unformed, tiny stumps like a baby's. Out of three mouths it sobs quietly. It cannot get up.

"Do you know what an angel is?" Noster says softly. "It is a limb of God, and God is a worm. Cut in half, it does not die, but grows new godhead from its injury. It is only a pity God Himself does not know His nature. But we do. All of us. We know."

"I believe you," I say.

"Why did you come after it?" She shakes her head.

"Who else will nurse it?"

Together, Noster and I climb down into the pit of the angel's landing. The earth is brittle, irradiated. It crumbles like old bones beneath our toes. The bronze angel whimpers, shivers—it is mute, shattered. It has one breast, one testicle—both are stamped upon, ruined. On either side of it we lay down: Noster curls into its arms with muscles like razors, I lean my face on its broad, cold back, my arm draping its waist, groping for Noster, clasping her hand around the angel, a closed circuit of limbs.

The rain howls down upon us, the wind bellowing hollow and sere. The starry sky spins and arches, the grass whistling, stiff, unyielding. The hills, far off, gleam dully. We begin to kiss the angel, in silence, in the secrecy of night, until he calms, and weeps only but once in a little while. We lay there, rough trinity, waiting for the storm to pass.

THE LEGACY OF... BETWEEN BOOKS

BY: STEVE RESSEL

CLAYMONT, DE - 1979

Lawrence M. Schoen holds a Ph.D. in cognitive psychology, spent ten years as a college professor, and currently works as the director of research and chief compliance officer for a series of mental health and addiction treatment facilities in Philadelphia. He's also one of the world's foremost authorities on the Klingon language. In 2007, he was a finalist for the John W. Campbell Award for Best New Writer. In addition to his work as a SF author, he operates Paper Golem, a speculative fiction small press. His wife tolerates most of his eccentricities, but refuses to learn to speak Klingon.

Lawrence C. Connolly's novel *Veins* was a Black Quill and Eric Hoffer Award finalist for 2008. In 2009, he released *Veins: The Soundtrack* and *Visions*, a collection of his sf and fantasy stories from the top genre magazines. His stories have been reprinted in a variety of best-of and retrospective anthologies, such as *Year's Best Horror*, *Best of Borderlands*, and *Best of the Magazine of Fantasy and Science Fiction*. His latest stories are available in *Cemetery Dance* 59, *F&SF* Aug/Sept 09, and *Darkness on the Edge: Tales Inspired by the Songs of Bruce Springsteen*. His forthcoming novel *Vipers* is due in 2010.

Maria V. Snyder switched careers from meteorologist to novelist when she began writing the New York Times best-selling Study Series (*Poison Study*, *Magic Study* and *Fire Study*) about a young woman who becomes a poison taster. Born and raised in Philadelphia, Pennsylvania, Maria dreamed of chasing tornados, but lacked the skills to forecast their location. Writing, however, lets Maria control the weather. Her new Glass Series (*Storm Glass* and *Sea Glass*) combines two things Maria loves, the weather and glass. Readers are invited to read more of Maria's short stories on her website at www.MariaVSnyder.com.

Gregory Frost is a writer of fantasy, science fiction, and thrillers, and a finalist for every major award in sf and fantasy. His latest work is the duology *Shadowbridge* and *Lord Tophet*, voted one of the best fantasy novels of the year by the American Library Association. It received a starred review from Booklist and Publishers Weekly. His previous novel was the historical thriller, *Fitcher's Brides*, a finalist for both the World Fantasy and International Horror Guild Awards for Best Novel. Publishers Weekly called his collection, *Attack of the Jazz Giants and Other Stories*, "one of the best fantasy collections of the year." He directs the fiction workshop at Swarthmore College in Swarthmore, PA.

Patrick Thomas is the author of over a hundred short stories and eighteen books, including *Fairy with a Gun*, eight books in the popular fantasy humor series *Murphy's Lore* and the *Mystic Investigators* series as well as the upcoming *Dead to Rites*. He has co-edited two anthologies including the forthcoming *New Blood*. Patrick writes the syndicated satirical advice column "Dear Cthulhu" which has been collected in *Dear Cthulhu: Have a Dark Day* and *Dear Cthulhu: Good Advice for Bad People*. Ten of his books are part of the props department at *CSI*, two of which are on Greg's desk in the Bullpen. Drop by his web site at www.patthomas.net.

John Passarella is the Bram Stoker Award-winning author of *Wither*, *Wither's Rain*, *Wither's Legacy*, *Kindred Spirit* and *Shimmer*. Columbia Pictures purchased the feature film rights to the co-authored *Wither* in a prepublication, preemptive bid. John also wrote the media tie-in novels *Buffy the Vampire Slayer: Ghoul Trouble*, *Angel: Avatar* and *Angel: Monolith*. A member of the Authors Guild, the Horror Writers Association, the Science Fiction and Fantasy Writers of America and the Garden State Horror Writers, John resides in Logan Township, New Jersey with his wife and three children.

Visit John Passarella's self-maintained official Website at http://www.passarella.com.

Mike McPhail is the award-winning author and anthologist of the military science fiction series *Defending The Future*, published by Dark Quest Books. He is a member of the Military Writers Society of America (MWSA), and the creator of the Alliance Archives (All'Arc) series and its related Martial Role-Playing Game (MRPG), a manual-based, percentile system, that realistically portrays the consequences of warfare.

He attended the Academy of Aeronautics in New York, as well as enlisted in the Air National Guard. His military career and lifelong dream to join NASA was ended by illness, so he chose to put his hard-earned technical skills and imagination to use as a graphic artist, writer/editor and game designer.

Jonathan McGoran is the author of the forensic crime thrillers *Body Trace*, *Blood Poison* and *Freezer Burn*, all as D. H. Dublin. Writing as Jonathan McGoran, his short fiction has been podcast on www.variantfrequencies.com and crimewav.com and his satire has appeared in *Philadelphia CityPaper*. He is a member of the Mystery Writers Association and the International Thriller Writers, and a founding member of the Liars Club. When not writing under his own name or as D. H. Dublin, McGoran is communications director at Weavers Way Co-op in Philadelphia.

Jonathan Maberry is a multiple Bram Stoker Award-winning author, magazine feature writer, playwright, content creator and writing teacher/lecturer. His novels include *Ghost Road Blues* (winner of the Stoker Award for Best First Novel in 2006), *Dead Man's Song* (2007), *Bad Moon Rising* (2008), and *Patient Zero* (St Martins Press 2009). Upcoming novels include *The Wolfman* (2010, Tor/Universal Pictures), *The Dragon Factory* (2010) and *The King of Plagues* (2011).

Henry Long is an artist. His art is communicated through painting, drawing, writing, poetry and photography. He was born in 1962, and raised in the small coal mining town of Ashley, Pennsylvania. He has had over 300 art exhibitions, including a recent show of over 400 works in Berlin, Germany. He has published 11 chapbooks of poetry and has done hundreds of poetry readings for over 30 years. He believes the Universe believes in him. He and his wife Emma, also an artist, celebrate the Human Condition. They are happy.

For more information visit www.henrylong.com or www.myspace.com/henrylong or www.facebook.com.

Jeffrey J. Mariotte is the author of supernatural thrillers *Missing White Girl, River Runs Red,* and *Cold Black Hearts,* in addition to (as Jeff Mariotte) many other books and even more comic books. He lives on the Flying M Ranch in southeastern Arizona. As a co-owner of specialty bookstore Mysterious Galaxy, he has a soft spot in his cold black heart for independent booksellers (and their customers).

Jonathan Carroll is the author of 15 novels and one short story collection. He lives in Vienna and can usually be found at www.jonathancarroll.com.

Danielle Ackley-McPhail, award-winning author and editor, has worked both sides of the publishing industry for nearly fifteen years. Her works include the urban fantasies, *Yesterday's Dreams, Tomorrow's Memories,* and the novella, *The Halfling's Court: A Bad-Ass Faerie Tale,* the *Bad-Ass Faeries* anthology series, and *No Longer Dreams*—all of which she co-edited—and contributions to numerous anthologies and collections, including *Dark Furies, Breach the Hull, So It Begins, Space Pirates* and the upcoming *Barbarians at the Jumpgate* and *New Blood.* Danielle lives somewhere in New Jersey with husband and fellow writer, Mike McPhail, mother-in-law Teresa, and three extremely spoiled cats. To learn more about her work, visit www.sidhenadaire.com.

Walter Ciechanowski discovered roleplaying games at an early age, when he accidentally purchased the Dungeons & Dragons Basic Set. Trying to make sense of it all sparked a life-long love of roleplaying games and introduced him to the works of J.R.R. Tolkein and H.P. Lovecraft. It is also what led to him stepping into Between Books for the first time. Over the past several years Walt has been writing for numerous RPG publishers, including Adamant Entertainment, Green Ronin, Mongoose Publishing, and Paradigm Concepts. Walt lives in Springfield, Pennsylvania with his wife, Helena and his children, Leianna and Stephen.

CJ Henderson is the creator of both the Teddy London supernatural detective series and the Piers Knight occult investigator series. Author of over 70 books and/or novels, hundreds of short stories and comics and thousands of non-fiction pieces, he is one of the most revered, witty and urbane genre writers of our time (if he does say so himself). For the chance to comment on his story in this volume, to read more of his work, or to browse in the obligatory store every website feels it must have these days, please feel free to drop in on him at http://www.cjhenderson.com.

Catherynne M. Valente was born in the Pacific Northwest in 1979, and is the author of *Palimpsest* and the Orphan's Tales series, as well as *The Labyrinth*, *Yume no Hon: The Book of Dreams*, *The Grass-Cutting Sword*, and five books of poetry. She is the winner of the Tiptree Award, the Mythopoeic Award, the Rhysling Award, and the Million Writers Award. She has been nominated nine times for the Pushcart Prize, shortlisted for the Spectrum Award, and was a World Fantasy Award finalist in 2007. She currently lives on an island off the coast of Maine with her partner and two dogs.

Steve Ressel was the director/producer of Nickelodeon's *Invader Zim*. He worked in television animation, directing on *Rugrats*, *The Wild Thornberrys*, *Aaahh!!! Real Monsters*, *Santo Bugito*, *Duckman*, *Rocket Power*, *God, the Devil and Bob*, *Jumanji*, and others. His work has won him numerous awards, and he has been nominated for multiple Emmys in his career. Currently he is finishing inking on his 300 page comic book/graphic novel *The Lost Boys* (www.thelostcomic.com), editing/illustrating his animation production textbook, and writing screenplays. Greg Schauer pointed out the Joe Kubert School to Steve in 1986 and set him on his path to comics, illustration, and animation. Now look at him.

Joe del Tufo is a photographer and one of the founders of Mobius New Media. He can be found online at www.joedeltufo.com.

Marcella Harte™ has been an illustrator since the wizened age of eight and has continued to take great relish in her profession ever since. She attended The University of the Arts in Philadelphia, PA and is a member of both The Graphic Artists' Guild as well as The Society of Children's Book Writers and Illustrators. She presently lives in Bear, DE with her loving husband and ever-growing stacks of books and artwork. She invites everyone to look her up on www.harteillustrations.com.

Nathaniel G. Sawyers, a professional tattoo artist and illustrator from east Tennessee, would like to take this opportunity to dedicate his work for "Beneath Between" and "Janey in Amber" to his father, Billy Sawyers, who has shown him the definition of the word hero.

Mickey Freed lives in the idyllic town of Renaissanceville (a.k.a. Claymont, DE) with his wife, Ellen and standard poodle, Scully FreshBones Anasazi. By day, Mickey is an engineer working with various incarnations of mass spectrometers. On the down low, he's been doing fine art photography for the past 7 years and has had works exhibited at the Delaware Art Museum, the DCCA, and the University City Arts League in Philadelphia. Photography done during 2009 has been almost entirely devoted to infrared black and white.

Allen Koszowski has been published in the sf/horror/fantasy genres since 1973. He has won the World Fantasy Best Artist Award and other awards as well as having been the artist guest of honor at the World Horror Convention, The World Fantasy Convention, The Necronomicon (in Providence), the Albacon, the Killercon, and others. Some of his publishers include Midnight House, Cemetery Dance, Deadletter Press, Centipede Press, Subterranean Press, Midnight Marquee, Whispers Press, Weirdbook Press, and many more. He has published more than 4,000 pieces of art. Currently he also edits, illustrates, and publishes his own magazine; *INHUMAN*. He is married and has two children. He is a decorated Vietnam Vet and former US Marine.

Blair Webb's (www.cafepress.com/ghostmanbook1) love for comics and his determination are what have brought about *Ghostman*, which started out in 1998 as a mini comic he sold to friends for $1. Blair's greatest influence was his grandfather, Joseph J. Sheeran. His other influences include Eileen, his wife, and Logan and Abriana, his children.

Don Bethman is hiding somewhere in Wilmington, Delaware. From who, or what, it remains unclear. He created the comic mini-series "Paper Cinema," starring Eli Wallach, which received the Xeric Award, and continues to do graphic design work to this day.

Brian Thomas graduated from Kent State University. Armed with a portfolio, a talent for sculpting and a kick ass mullet, Brian entered world of design. Brian was a designer for Mattel/Tyco toys, animation director for MaraStar Communications and is now the owner of Epiphany Arts LLC. Brian spends his free time as an independent filmmaker and medieval reenactor.

Mike Oreszczyn has a BFA in Visual Communication Design with postgraduate work in web design. Since the 1990s he has occupied himself with everything from graphic and web design, being head of advertising for a national distributor, stone carving, stained glass, to designing maps for his favorite games. He has been to 41 of the 50 states, but resides in Wilmington, Delaware.

Ric Frane utilizes a multitude of media to create strong sexy images in fantasy, horror, and related genre. He has done illustrations for numerous publications around the world. Baron Von Reign is Ric's Steampunk alter ego. Using mixed media and twisted humor, he creates images of gothic and dark fantasy.

Nora Schaefer is a freelance illustrator working and living in Philadelphia, Pennsylvania. She works with a variety of materials including collage, watercolor and ink. Inspired by dance, literature and film, her work is often narrative and whimsical. She received her BFA in Illustration from the University of the Arts in 2009.

Burt Hopkins was raised by wild teachers in the suburbs. With no dogs, cats, spouse, or fractional children, he chased his dreams of being an animator only to descend into the underworld in order to pay rent. When his day job allows, he draws and writes. Twitter Feed: Hop_The_Younger

Joseph Gangemi was born in Delaware in 1970, and graduated from Swarthmore College. His published works include the novel, *Inamorata* (Viking, 2004). He wrote the screenplay (with Steven Katz) for the 2007 Sony Pictures release *Wind Chill*. He lives outside Philadelphia with his wife and daughter.

W. H. Horner is Publisher and Editor-in-Chief of Fantasist Enterprises, an independent publishing house specializing in fantasy and horror short fiction anthologies, novels, art, and music. He holds a BA in English and a MA in Writing Popular Fiction. William is also the founder and director of the First Writes, a writing group that meets in Wilmington, Delaware. For more information about William and his freelance editorial services, please visit www.whhorner.com, and to learn more about his projects with Fantasist Enterprises, please go to www.fantasistent.com.

Jeanne B. Benzel is a teen librarian at a public library. She has been a bookseller, worked in magazine and newspaper publishing, and spent three years with the independent publisher Innisfree Press.

Greg Schauer has been the proprietor of Between Books since its inception oh so many years ago. He has done his best to promote literacy, debate and the arts in his community. He has played around with being a writer, an artist, an editor and a concert promoter. Someday he will decide what he wants to be when he grows up.

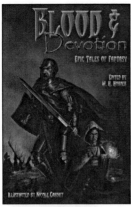

Brave warriors and devotees to the gods follow the paths their faiths have put before them, and when religious fervor meets skill of arms and magic, kings will fall, armies will collide, and men and women will perish for their beliefs.

Blood & Devotion contains nine short stories and novellas of epic fantasy, accompanied with art by Nicole Cardiff.

Trade Paperback • 270 Pages (Estimated)
9 Stories • 12 Illustrations • $16.00
ISBN 13: 978-0-9713608-8-4 • ISBN 10: 0-9713608-8-X

www.FEBooks.net

Twenty classic and two all new stories in one visionary collection!

For three decades, Lawrence C. Connolly has defied category, writing across genre to create stories where dreams are reality, the future is now, and a lone madman may be the sanest person in the room.

Presented here with all new introductions that discuss the origins of the stories and featuring a retrospective essay about the road to publication and beyond, *Visions: Fantasy & SF* is a must for lovers of dark fantasy, science fiction, and heroic adventure.

PRAISE FOR THE STORIES
GREAT HEART RISING: ". . . gritty believability."—*Tangent Online*
DAUGHTERS OF PRIME: ". . . a tantalizing enigma."—*Locus*
FLASHBACK: ". . . a great psychological tale of deception."—*DreadCentral.com*
PRIME TIME!: "Clever stuff."—*The Fix*

Trade Paperback • 268 Pages (Estimated)
22 Stories • Lightly Illustrated • $16.00
ISBN 13: 978-1-934571-01-9 • ISBN 10: 1-934571-01-6

Fantastical Visions IV

Edited by
W. H. Horner

Illustrated by
Stephanie Pui-Mun Law

The Fantastical Visions series features selections of stories that explore the sub-genres of fantasy.

Young men and women struggle to find their places in worlds harsh and beautiful. Lives are changed as people grapple with relationships and the consequences of their decisions. Greed and cunning are sometimes punished, and sometimes rewarded. Sometimes it is better to give than to receive, and sometimes a gift can be a curse.

Eighteen works of modern myth explore the many facets of the human condition, taking the reader on an emotional journey through fantastic landscapes.

Trade Paperback • 308 Pages
18 Stories • 27 Illustrations •$17.00
ISBN 13: 978-0-9713608-7-7
ISBN 10: 0-9713608-7-1

Featuring the art of Stephanie Pui-Mun Law

Fleeing from what should have been a perfect crime, four crooks in a black Mustang race into the Pennsylvania highlands. On the backseat, a briefcase full of cash. On their tail, a tattooed madman who wants them dead.

The driver calls himself Axle. A local boy, he knows the landscape, the coal-hauling roads and steep trails that lead to the perfect hideout: the crater of an abandoned mine. But Axle fears the crater. Terrible things happened there. Things that he has spent years trying to forget.

Enter Kwetis, the nightflyer, a specter from Axle's ancestral past. Part memory, part nightmare, Kwetis has planned a heist of his own. And soon Axle, his partners in crime, and their pursuer will learn that their arrival at the mine was foretold long ago . . . and that each of them is a piece of a plan devised by the spirits of the Earth.

A finalist for the 2009 Eric Hoffer Award.

Nominated for the 2009 Black Quill Award for Best Small-Press Chill.

Appeared on the Preliminary Ballot for the 2008 Bram Stoker Award for Superior Achievement in a First Novel.

Trade Paperback • 260 Pages • 8 Illustrations • $15.00
ISBN 13: 978-1-934571-00-2 • ISBN 10: 1-934571-00-8

www.VeinsTheNovel.com | www.FantasistEnt.com

Fasten your seatbelts and prepare to take your reading experience to a whole new level. With *Veins: The Soundtrack*, author and musician Lawrence C. Connolly provides a series of instrumental soundscapes inspired by themes and scenes from his critically acclaimed supernatural thriller *Veins*. Performing with his band, Connolly delivers a mix of trance, rock, and ambient compositions designed to complement the novel.

The CD also includes two music and spoken-word bonus tracks, each showcasing a complete story from *Visions*, "Aberrations" and "Echoes."

Packaged with Star E. Olson's distinctive cover art and including a synopsis and full production credits, *Veins: The Soundtrack* is a must for every dark fantasy reader.

Read the book. Hear the soundtrack. Enter a world where fantasy lives.

6 Tracks & 2 Bonus Tracks • Total Run Time: 38:13 • $10.00
UPC: 700261267371 • ID#: FE-934571-00-2

Polish your cutlass and prepare your spells for what awaits on a journey across leagues of unimaginable adventure. Ride the waves to mystery and magic.

Featuring 28 stories of mermaids, pirates, and magic beyond your wildest dreams, including tales by Danielle Ackley-McPhail and Patrick Thomas, and an introduction by Lawrence C. Connolly, *Sails & Sorcery* is beautifully illustrated by Julie Dillon.

Trade Paperback • 456 Pages
28 Stories • 42 Illustrations • $23.00
ISBN 13: 978-0-9713608-9-1 • ISBN 10: 0-9713608-9-8

www.FEBooks.net

Magic surrounds us. The Enlightenment did not kill it with science, nor did the Industrial Revolution extinguish it with mechanation. Elves may feel cramped in the big city, but they get by. The wild lands disappear, but werewolves still find time to hunt, though with care.

Explore 26 worlds of mystery, wonder, danger, and horror in *Modern Magic*. You may find them to be not unlike the world in which you live.

Trade Paperback • 280 Pages
26 Stories • 35 Illustrations • $17.00
ISBN 13: 978-0-9713608-4-6 • ISBN 10: 0-9713608-4-7

Breinigsville, PA USA
03 November 2009
226973BV00002B/1/P